The Blood
And
The Barley

The Strathavon Saga

Angela MacRae Shanks

ANGELA MACRAE SHANKS

This book first published in 2018 by Braeatha Books.

ISBN 978-1-9999624-1-8

Cover Design by Morven MacEwan
MikeDotta / Shutterstock.com
Mark Pitt Images / Shutterstock.com

John Barleycorn was a hero bold,
Of noble enterprise;
For if you do but taste his blood,
'Twill make your courage rise.

'Twill make a man forget his woe;
'Twill heighten all his joy;
'Twill make the widow's heart to sing,
Tho' the tear were in her eye.

Then let us toast John barleycorn,
Each man a glass in hand;
And may his great posterity
Ne'er fail in old Scotland!

From *John Barleycorn: A Ballad* by Robert Burns.

A Note of Thanks

To Andy Ellis, who read it first and kept me on the right path. I am eternally grateful, Andy, for your encouragement, your generosity, and most especially your patience! Without you, this book would simply not exist. You are a man generous in both time and knowledge.

CHAPTER ONE

Strathavon, a Glen in the
North-Eastern Highlands,
May 1780.

MORVEN MACRAE STOPPED to rest on a spur of weathered granite jutting from the hillside. The higher she climbed, the thinner the soil became until at last the hill exposed its backbone in an eruption of rock that broke through the surface. The climb had forced her lungs to work hard, only her breathing was mostly ragged for another reason. And although she was warm with a fine sheen of sweat on the back of her neck and a clamminess in her palms, Morven trembled. She clenched her teeth, trying to control the quivering, for it was not the chill of day's end that caused it. The trembling stemmed from within. Drawing an unsteady breath, she released it slowly through pursed lips. Oft-times that brought a sense of inner peace.

Feeling a trace easier, Morven let her gaze sweep out over the familiar glen below and away to the dark bulk of mountains in the distance and felt her resolve hardened. Clouds were amassed there in ominous banks, a shimmer of movement there too, and as she began to climb again, she sniffed at the damp air. It was heavy with the scent of earth, with a pungent zing, and her innards coiled a little tighter – a storm was coming.

The breeze sharpened and stung her cheeks, for any warmth had ebbed away with the daylight and moor and mountain stood grey now. On an eve such as this, unearthly folk did roam abroad and 'twas wise to be wary, to be ever on guard against them. Glancing around, she loosened the thick woollen shawl, her arisaid, that she wore around her waist and tugged it up to protect her shoulders. Its warmth might quell the shivering that insinuated a faint-heart, for although she knew herself to be thrawn, Morven was no lily-liver.

She'd taken the steeper, westerly route up Carn Liath and the voice of the river Avon – the A'an in the Gaelic tongue of her folk – was weaker here, little more than a whisper. Once more she paused to cast about, searching for the stone she knew had stood on the hillside since long syne. It was near, she could feel it, and paused to catch her breath by a twisted juniper tree, its gnarled roots distorted, burrowing sideways into the hill. Instinctively curious, Morven bent to determine the reason for the tree's contortions, and there was the stone, half hidden in the undergrowth.

'Thanks be!' she gasped.

Kneeling, she pushed aside the lower boughs digging into the earth with her fingers until she'd exposed the entire stone. It was studded with lichens, silvery and yellow, yet the strange symbols cut into its surface were still clearly discernible. The sight brought a wondrous sensation welling through her innards, and she let it pulse over her with a little shudder as she ran her fingers over the marks and closed her eyes, trying to visualise those who had made them and grasp their meaning. They were Christians, the age-auld cross haloed at the joining of arms and stem, the wheel of life Rowena called it, was a potent sign of their faith although the other symbols, knotted and intricate, were alien to her.

Withdrawing the wooden crucifix that hung from her neck, she pressed a kiss upon it, then laid it at the foot of the shrine. To which ancient saint the stone was dedicated, Morven had no notion, but she prayed nonetheless, directly to God, first in her native Gaelic, then more guardedly though with equal earnest in English, the tongue of her foreign king and government.

> *'Dear Lord, God of our fathers. The night*
> *will be observed ancient and heathenish ways.*
> *Yet we, yer flock, never stray from our faith.*
> *Lighten our darkness, Lord, and banish the death*
> *of winter from our land that we may*
> *receive the fruits of the earth in their season.'*

She swallowed, her tongue dry, feeling a vague sense of hypocrisy. As always her faith sat uneasily with her. It vied with her innate belief in the supernatural, in the Gaelic otherworlds, with her natural wariness of the faeryfolk said to inhabit the *sitheans* or faeryhills plentiful in the glen. She often wondered how other folk reconciled these beliefs – what Father Ranald called superstitions – with an unwavering faith in God and, more particularly, Church. Lacing her fingers together, she frowned and went on,

'Forgive me my foolishness, Lord, my weakness,
that I may be delivered from doubt. Fer I
believe in the Holy Ghost, the Holy Catholic Church,
the communion o' saints, the resurrection of the
body, and the life everlasting. Amen.'

She retrieved the crucifix and, pressing her cold lips to it once more, returned it to its position around her neck. 'Forgive me,' she whispered, then continued her climb.

By the time the ground levelled out near the crown of Carn Liath, and even the most tenacious trees had given way to little but stunted heather and rock, the blood was thrumming in her head, and a powerful sense of foreboding churned her belly. The light was dwindling rapidly, and she had to strain her eyes until they watered, but sure enough, trails of shrouded figures were emerging now, faceless in the half-light. They made their way from many hillside paths and converged near a circle of tinder and brushwood prepared the previous day. From the centre of that ring, a slab of dark granite reared. It had once risen ten feet in height, so it was told, though it stood at maybe a little under six now and was canted at a precarious angle, tilted through the years by the muckle winds that skirled and clawed up the glen.

Morven took a moment to steady herself, listening to the furtive murmur of voices. As befitted the significance of the ritual to be enacted, the voices were tense and conspiratorial. Beltane night. She shuddered at the name, recalling all she'd heard of such a night. What went on upon the hilltop she knew of only from the tattle-tongues of the glen, from nudged whispers and dark knowing looks, and from what she'd managed to glean from Rowena.

It involved a *Beathach* – a beast. Many said it was a man made to look like a red deer stag. But for all that was said, rightly or wrongly, it was the most important observance of the year, for if it went well their harvest would be plentiful, the black cattle would thrive, and their other activity, the whisky smuggling, would be profitable and go unchallenged. Yet should it go badly, the *daoine sìth*, the faeryfolk that lived underground in the *sitheans* might take offence, might turn against her folk, and then all could be lost. There was even risk in the ritual itself, that much had been plain from her father's reaction when she'd suggested that she could represent their family, the MacRaes of Delnabreck, should he and her brother Alec not make it home in time.

'God's blood!' he'd flared. 'Beltane's sinful. Nae daughter o' mine will play any part!' Scandalised by the notion, he'd fixed her with a black look.

'But you go every year,' she'd said in return. 'Does that nae make *you* sinful, then?' She was close to the bone now and knew it well, for her da could be quick to anger, but 'twas all so unjust.

His face darkened. 'What I do may be sinful, but I do it fer the good o' kin and croft, no matter how ungrateful. Under this roof, Malcolm MacRae answers to God and God alone.' He rubbed a hand through his wispy beard. 'Ye're too young, anyhow.'

'Eighteen, Da. Old enough to work the still, to tend the beasts, and do all the skivvying but nae old enough to take yer place at Beltane, nor ever will be I'll wager.' It hurt to know he thought so little of her, that he considered her a mere lass, in some way deficient compared with her brother Alec.

'Aye, ye work hard.' He acknowledged it with a curt nod and glanced at her mother. 'Lord knows, if I could lighten yer burden I would, but with yer mam nae yet back to her full strength there's naught to be done.' He frowned and exhaled forcibly through his nose. 'Ye're too young fer Beltane though. Christ, ye might even be…' He shuddered and stabbed viciously at the clumps of peat on the fire.

'Rowena has faith in me.' No sooner were the words out than Morven regretted them. Her father's face stiffened, and the temperature in the room dropped.

'Rowena Forbes is no more mistress in this house than you are. Ye'd do well to mind that. Now away, I'll hear no more of Beltane.'

But that was not the end of the matter. When the eve of Beltane came close, Alec and her da were still away to the south seeing to the sale of illicit whisky, some twenty ankers in all, and Morven agonised over Beltane, and the consequences should not one of her kinfolk play a part in it.

Racked with uncertainty, she'd turned to Rowena, the person whose judgment she trusted above all others. Rowena was her neighbour and confidant, wise and insightful, she was Morven's guide in all things. The widow had regarded her young friend with solemn eyes.

'I'd sooner it not fall to you, Morven,' she admitted. 'But if neither Alec nor yer da can be there, or if … if yer da should deem his attendance unnecessary, then I fear 'tis you must go. Keep covered up though, dinna catch the *Beathach's* eye, and hang well back from harm's way.'

She blinked then, as if seeing the girl before her in a new light, one she'd perhaps been reluctant to acknowledge. 'There are dangers mind, though there are sometimes pleasures too. Ye're a grown woman Morven, 'tis nae fer me to judge.' She smiled distractedly. 'But I'm thinking the risks from nae going are greatest. Ye must mind and make peace wi' yer maker first though, aye?'

With her father gone, it had been easy to slip away, although Morven imagined her absence would not have gone unnoticed for long. She took a quick breath. Rowena's warning still echoed in her ears, and she pulled her arisaid up to cover her head, tucking in all giveaway wisps of her chestnut hair and partly concealing her face. These were heathenish rites, and although she'd likely recognise every one of tonight's participants, she'd no wish to draw attention to herself.

With her head suitably shrouded, Morven strained her eyes in the half-light, perceiving the gathering had grown now; many shadowy figures having silently manifested from the gloaming. She slipped amongst them. Most of her neighbours were still recognisable: the McHardys, Hal's tuneless whistle unmistakable as he brushed by her shoulder, and Donald Gordon of Craigduthel croft, his old blue bonnet blackened and reeking of peat smoke from his habit of wearing it whilst sat at the firestone. Most were male and had tried to conceal their faces, although here and there an uncovered head stood out brazenly from the rest. Recognising these cottars and herdsmen, simple folk she'd known all her life, the tension at her core eased a fraction.

Taking her guide from the assembled crowd, Morven kept on the move, following the ebb and press of people, striving to keep her face covered but all the while searching for the woman who inspired her, for her dear friend Rowena Forbes. Not finding her, Morven's search grew more urgent. Unconsciously she quickened her pace, her senses heightening. A clamminess built at the back of her neck, and as she filtered the growing darkness, it felt as though her eyes overfilled their sockets. Where was she? She blinked and rolled her head to break the tension. All would be well once she found Rowena.

But after much fruitless milling and mingling, and with her jaw beginning to ache, her temples too, she'd still not found her. Perplexed, Morven drew to a halt, recognising Rowena's daughter standing at the edge of the crowd with her long pale hair uncovered and fluttering in the breeze. Breathing hard, Morven stood to watch her.

Talking with familiar ease to a man in belted plaid, Sarah was forced to stretch her lithe young body upward, and he to bend his down that she might reach his ear, for the man was easily half Sarah's height again. Yet who was he? No Strathavon man reached such a height. He glanced in Morven's direction and then, curiosity plainly aroused, turned fully toward her, studying what she imagined could be seen of her face with distinct interest. She jerked her gaze away. *Where was Rowena?* And why was Sarah here? In the vanishing light, Sarah appeared paler and more strikingly lovely than Morven remembered, and she carried herself with assurance, but ... why was she even here? Sarah was scarce sixteen.

Bewildered, Morven began to move again, her unease mounting. There came a strange sound now, she held her breath to listen. 'Twas coming from the crowd; a buzzing like the drone of bees. A pulse began to beat in her throat, a strange excitement tightening her chest. The buzzing grew louder, then the gathering parted to reveal the Beltane *Beathach*.

She fell back from its path instinctively, the suck of her breath loud in her ears, and heard the same sound echo around her. It walked upright like a man, yet not a man, its haunches did undulate like those of beasts. The head was outlandish, thick-necked and crowned with antlers, grisly against the dying light in the sky. Unable to take her eyes from it, she glimpsed a bearded chin beneath the muzzle, and a flash of pale throat before it turned and uttered a bellowing roar.

The breeze sharpened, and needles of fear pricked her temples. Those around her were just as fearful. Expressions were furtive, gazes cast down, eager to avoid a meeting with those of the creature.

Materialising at her shoulder, Sarah hissed into Morven's ear. ''Twill be me chosen the night. Can ye nae feel it? *I'll* be the May Virgin.'

With a sharp word of warning, Morven reached for the girl's hand, but the *Beathach* had heard something. It halted, head tilted toward them, listening. Within the empty sockets, Morven sensed keen eyes focused upon them.

To her right, a flicker of flames lit the darkness, and the reek of wood-smoke filled the air. The Beltane ring was kindled. The wheeze of pipes inflating followed, and then the tentative skirl of the bagpipes and the beat of a drum. Some preparation, a fine powder of sorts, was flung on the flames and they sparked green and blue, flaring high, heady with the whiff of brimstone and some underlying substance.

A subtle music then began to take shape. It roused the glenfolk, instinctively prompting them to move. Within moments they were dancing. They danced with the sure-footed grace of those born to the hills, feet weaving among the heather, skipping deftly over tussock, rock, and rise. The playing quickened, inciting them further, giddy and breathless, then gathered pace again.

Morven felt it too. She was seized with vigour, and a thrilling sensation arose in her innards, coursing through her limbs and setting her feet dancing. The crowd moved as a chaotic mass now, Morven carried with them, and then as if by some collective but unspoken accord, the turmoil ordered itself. Hand sought hand and clasped fast. With backs to the ceremonial ring, the gathering began to circle it. Slowly at first, then faster and faster until the dark shape of the *Beathach* lurched by.

Sarah's hand slipped from Morven's grip, and she spun away, lashing Morven with tendrils of her hair. Morven tightened her grasp on the other hand she held and twisted to see who it was attached to. It was the giant she'd seen earlier. She tried to shake him off, but he hung on regardless.

The playing doubled in pace, became wild and reckless, inciting the dancers to an unseemly dash. The *Beathach* moved alongside them, undulating and stiff-headed, grasping at the dancers as they flitted by. The shadows closed in on Morven, tilting and lurching, while the beat of drum grew ever louder, and the blur of faces fell away in the darkness. That darkness now seemed to have texture, to be made of shifting shades of grey. The very air had substance to it that coalesced and then dissolved, only to form again like curds from the whey. The night sky appeared packed with pinpricks of light swirling in an ocean of ink and that ocean was changing again, like sand beneath her feet, melting and moulding and twisting into eddies, then speeding away to look like distant stars in the heavens.

A strange sickness overtook her, and from what seemed a great distance, she heard voices singing in the Gaelic tongue. They called for the earth to be fertile. To ripen and bear fruit. Rising together, they urged the natural energies to grow potent, to be virile and impregnate the land. Pungent fumes billowed in her face, and she staggered to a halt.

The images became carnal. Impressions of rutting stags, cattle mounting, and cot-lads openly straddling young girls swam in her head. Disorientated, she lost her grip on the stranger's hand and would have fallen had not strong arms held her up. She faltered, giddy and a little nauseous, and swayed in relief against the cottar who prevented her fall.

Yet something wasn't right. Rising above the stupefying fumes another pungent but familiar odour assaulted Morven's senses. Poached in Glenavon Forest and carried home for her and her mother to butcher, the stench of deer carcass overpowered her. She cried out in alarm. A swift and crushing pressure bore down on her ribcage, then the ground lurched away beneath her feet as realisation struck. The *Beathach* had her in its grasp.

It was useless to struggle yet she did so anyway. Never had she felt so helpless. A drum-beat struck once more and fell silent, the hammer of her heart loud in its place. Flames flared briefly, then the stone slab took shape before her. There was silence now but for the crack and ripple of fire.

Fingers dug ruthlessly beneath her ribs, and she gasped, writhing to free herself. Twisting her body, she saw the assembly stood still now, watching the spectacle from behind the fiery ring, their faces lit by its glow. She drew a desperate breath, trying to calm herself. Whatever was to come would likely be over in moments, yet her heart pounded so fiercely, her chest ached with it.

The creature swung her down onto the slab of granite and made a great show of pawing at the heather and braying like a wild stag. Beneath her, she felt stone, cold and unyielding, and made a scramble to remain upright and gain mastery of herself. The creature's head swayed close. There was no face, merely a velvety muzzle, but when it snorted, Morven was engulfed in a cloud of whisky vapour. Her fear died. This was no beast, only a man playing one. She'd known that, but the recognition he'd required copious amounts of whisky before he could carry it off, calmed her. She almost laughed. The fog in her head began to clear, and she remembered why she'd come. A fair reap was needed, and calves for the droving markets, else there'd be no paying the rentals come Martinmas and no feeding the bairns come winter. She'd not wished for it, but she had been chosen and must play her part.

Looking again at the watching crofters, Morven saw many avert their gaze, although others did seem transfixed. Sarah stood amongst them, watching intently, a look of resentment on her face. Abruptly she turned and was gone.

The crowd began to stamp their feet, crying out, goading the *Beathach* to plough and plant the waiting earth. She swallowed. Plainly that was the part she must play. The creature began to circle her, moving in, snorting and pawing, then, sensing she was no longer afraid, grunted, 'Best mak' a good show o' it, then.'

She gasped as it straddled her, pushing her down, a heavy weight on her chest and abdomen, and again the stench of whisky and deer carcass was unimaginably foul. She closed her eyes, held her breath, and the remorseless pounding began. Pinioned against the stone slab, the jar of bone was excruciating, and the creature wheezed a fine spray of stale liquor over her face. Yet she endured the wild sham mating with as much dignity as she could muster, bearing the deed in tight-lipped silence. Then, to the thunderous approval of the onlookers, he faked the climax and, leaving her splayed in a heap, danced away deftly and leapt the flaming barrier with all the agility of a young hind.

Morven struggled to her feet. Her skirts billowed, and she fought them down, a rise in the strength of the wind hampering her efforts. A blast of hot air hit her full in the face, and she reeled away, shielding her eyes with her hands. A gasp went up from the crowd. Within the ceremonial ring, the wind whipped and swirled, and Morven stared in horror.

The burning ring now rose in a wall of flames. Wherever she looked, there was nothing but fire. Another squall struck her with the fury of a banshee, spinning her around and knocking her down. She gasped, for the flames now leapt even higher, snapping and roaring. Dear God, how would she escape them?

There were shouts of alarm from those on the other side, and someone began to shriek. Desperate to find a way out, Morven ran to and fro, not knowing where to turn, flames licking at her heels. The wool of her arisaid began to burn, and she flung it from her, then snatched the smouldering pile up again pressing it to her mouth and nose. Her lungs began to ache and she coughed and wheezed until her eyes and nose streamed, and she could no longer see where to run. The wind battered her again, almost blowing her onto the flames, and she stumbled to the ground. Beneath her, the heather curled alight. Flailing at it, she shrieked and pulled herself onto the stone slab, clutching at the cross hanging at her throat.

From the far side of the flaming barrier, she could hear frenzied shouting. Yet her heart told her nothing would be done. The ritual, the ring itself, was too sacred. An age-auld magic had been conjured, and no-one would interfere, for that could bring down unspeakable ills on the glen and its folk. No-one would risk that. Retching now, she remembered a chilling tale she'd overheard yet only half understood as a child. A tale of another lass and another Beltane night. A lass no-one spoke openly of, whose grave on a hillside folk still tended, but who'd done something that terrible she could never be buried in the consecrated ground of the chapelyard.

'Pity Lord! Have pity!'

To her left, amid shouts and screams, the blazing barrier exploded in a hail of flaming missiles. A swathed figure ignited briefly, rolled to the ground, then barreled toward her. Not understanding, she cowered in fright, the hair on her nape standing on end.

''Tis alright,' said a strange voice. 'I'll not let harm come to ye.' She looked up into the face of the stranger, tight now with concern.

He lifted her and carried her through a brief blister of intense heat, then out into the stormy night, laying her down in the darkness some distance from the blaze. Exhausted and unable to fully comprehend her escape, she lay still, wheezing and sucking in gulps of clean air, listening to the growing clamour around her.

Above the sough and whine of wind, there were angry voices. They rose in alarm and confusion, some folk trying to beat out the now burning heather while others tried to stop them.

'The Beltane ring!' shrieked one old man. 'Disaster! 'Tis disaster foretold.'

No-one asked if she lived and no-one came close enough to find out. She looked up to see the stranger, now a solitary figure, still thrashing heroically at the flaming heath.

'Who is it brings ruin upon us?'

'Thon stranger. Does anyone ken who he is?'

The change in the mood was unmistakable as all now recognised the significance of the man's actions. Morven felt the ugliness grow and struggled to her feet as a pack of angry cottars advanced on him.

'Wait!' she cried. 'He'll nae ken. 'Tis a stranger he is, he'll nae understand what he's done.' She felt the hostility transfer to herself as stricken expressions now hardened and were directed at her. 'He did save me. I'm thankful. He meant nae harm.'

The crowd made a menacing sound.

'The lass speaks true! What are we, savages?' Donald Gordon's voice was shrill, the old cottar from Craigduthel now the focus of every stare. 'Naeone has even tended her. 'Tis shamed of ourselves we should be, and thankful 'tis nae her smouldering body we're collecting.'

A grudging murmur of acknowledgement followed this, then all turned to watch the stranger pick his way over the smouldering remains of the Beltane ring. He'd removed the protective covering from his head, and his dark hair was laced at his nape, revealing a face both surprisingly young and ardent. Locating Morven on her feet at the margin of the gathering, his strained expression darkened at the sight of her taut, soot-smeared face.

Stumbling toward him, she extended her hand. 'Sir, these folk believe ye've wronged them. But I give ye thanks fer my life.' She gripped his hand. 'I'm Morven MacRae. I'd be honoured to learn your name.'

Necks craned collectively to hear it.

'James Innes of Tomachcraggen.' He swept her a bow. 'Jamie, I prefer.'

There was a combined intake of breath and Morven was momentarily at a loss: Tomachcraggen was Rowena's croft.

'Tomachcraggen is held by the widow Forbes,' said a blunt voice. 'So who in blazes are you?' The question was from Alexander Grant of Achnareave but was poised on every lip.

'Her nephew. Son of her brother James. I was born in this glen but have bid in Inverness until two days ago. My family are all dead, but for Rowena and my cousins, and they've need of me.' The young man raised his chin a fraction, a gesture not lost on the crowd.

Morven felt a tingle of excitement. The name James Innes … it meant something, but what? Her eyes widened, her breath caught in her throat. This young Highlander, and she could see now that the giant was no more than three or four years her senior, was from the family who'd taken her orphaned mother in near forty years ago. He was Rowena's brother's son. But that meant, as Rowena and her own mam were brought up together, that he was also the son of her own mother's brother – or at least, her mam thought of him as a brother.

The gathering digested this information in stony silence.

'Aye,' muttered Jeems, a crony of her father. 'I mind his kin. They were put from Druimbeag when my lads were but nippers.'

Morven was aware of a tensing of muscle in the young man beside her. He nodded, a flicker of anger crossing his face.

'Aye, 'tis true enough. Reivers took our cattle, and my father was paupered. Unable to pay his rent, the factor had us evicted.' He swallowed, a shadow crossing his face. 'I have no memory of it, I was only a babe. My father took my mother and me to Inverness to find work.' His jaw tightened a fraction, but he kept his voice level. 'He died eight days ago, my mother and sisters too. The morbid throat did take them.'

Morven blanched; little wonder Rowena wasna among the gathering, she'd be crushed by this news.

There was silence, then Elspeth MacPherson, the miller's wife, cleared her throat. 'Yer folk, Jamie, they were well thought on. In the glen, I mean.'

'Aye,' Hal McHardy chipped in. 'I mind them too.'

'Mebbe so,' grunted Achnareave. 'And I'm sorry fer yer loss and all, but what ye've done here …' he shook his head, unable to put the scale of the ruination into words. 'God help us, I say, fer 'tis paupers we'll be, or bones fer the filling o' pauper's graves.' He shook his head. 'You be marking my words.'

Jamie looked blankly at him, then turned to Morven with a questioning lift of his brows.

'He means,' she said, 'that the rite, the ring itself, is age-auld and sacred. An enchantment it is, a pact wi' the faeryfolk that we might be spared the hardship and suffering that is life in these high glens.' She swallowed over her parched tongue. 'Here where the auld ways are still followed we live by them and survive.'

'The ring mustna be touched. It must burn the night through. Only, ye've beaten out its flames, scattered its bones ower the hillside.' Achnareave lifted his hand to the litter of smouldering brushwood in a futile little gesture and stared hard at Jamie.

Jamie returned the look with open bewilderment. 'I wasn't to know of yer superstitions, sir. But I couldna let the lass burn. Ye'd not have wished that, would ye, faery charms or not?'

'She'd have come to nae real harm,' Achnareave spluttered. 'But ye've laid waste to this place. Ye're an outsider. Misinformed.' Pointing a quivering finger, he brought his face, working furiously, to within inches of the younger man's chest, his voice lowering in judgement. 'The instrument of our undoing. That's what ye are.'

There was a murmur of agreement from the crowd, and Morven felt her anger rise, tempered a little by confusion.

'Faith, she'd have burned alive!' cried Craigduthel.

'And how would we live wi' ourselves then?' blurted Elspeth.

'And who,' Craigduthel demanded, rounding angrily on Achnareave, 'would be the one to explain it all to her da?' He nodded grimly, glaring around at the others as each took turn to slide their attention down to their feet. 'Aye, Delnabreck. Who'd be barefaced enough to tell him we'd left his only daughter to burn?'

Jamie blinked and shook himself, plainly mystified by the complexities of glen life, and leaned in toward Morven. 'I meant nae harm. I hope ye see that. But if I've done ill in some way, I pray ye can forgive me.' He turned to examine the faces in the crowd.

'I ken that.' She shivered, struck by another blast of wind, not knowing what to say. Had he saved her life? In her heart, she knew he had. And so his treatment now seemed unjust. Mightily so. And yet … yet she should not have come here. A humiliation it was, one that near cost her life. Only, Beltane was necessary, Rowena had said so. What, then, did all this portend?

She looked more closely at the young man beside her. He was Rowena's kinsman, she could see her likeness in him, and seeing it, a stubborn desire to protect him stirred within her. She swallowed, ready to speak up on his behalf when an arrogant but familiar voice rose above the others, high-handed and imperious.

'Damn it all, sir, Achnareave is right! You've no business here tampering with what you neither know nor understand. It comes as no surprise to learn you're a kinsman of the Forbes woman. Damnable mischief-makers, the pair of you!'

Morven gaped as William McGillivray, staunch Presbyterian, factor to their laird the Duke of Gordon, and local Justice of the Peace, pushed his way through the crowd flinging aside his homespun guise.

What she'd expected of the hilltop ceremony, she little knew. But the factor's presence she'd not foreseen, and it astounded her. Was it incurable curiosity that brought the factor up Carn Liath on a black Beltane night? Or an infernal wish to oversee? To make certain no pacts were forged here that might threaten the interests of his Grace the Duke? No crimes committed against king or government. Or was it, perhaps, a wish to gather evidence of sins or darker deeds? There was no way of knowing, yet, whatever it had been, his presence struck consternation throughout the gathering and brought home to all the threat of eviction. A fate all held in dread.

Jamie's face darkened, the tightening of a muscle along his jawline unmistakably marking his anger.

'I'll have ye know, sir, my aunt is decent and kindly. No offensive words will I allow said of her.' His voice came low but laden with such focused intent that the air near crackled with his anger. He held the factor's gaze, unblinking. 'God will witness my truth, but I swear no finer kinswoman could a man wish fer.' Turning, he swept his gaze over the gathering, and then, with a look of open challenge, brought it back to rest on McGillivray's slack-jowled face.

There was an immense presence about the towering young Highlander, a courteous yet rigid quality that allowed no crudeness or abuse of those precious to him. Several of the hill-folk agreed, despite the factor's standing with their laird. 'A healer,' someone called.

McGillivray guffawed. 'I've heard it said, sir, she's a priestess of the black arts. And a stinking Papist,' he muttered under his breath.

With a gasp of rage, Morven blundered forward to defend her friend, but within her limbs, a mighty trembling had arisen. She felt giddy and weak. The blood drained swiftly from her head, her vision swam, then everything shrank away to blackness. She knew she'd dropped to the ground, could feel the roughness of heather against her cheek, the ridge of a stone jutting into her hipbone, but rising was beyond her. For a lingering moment, she could still hear voices.

'The MacRae lass!'

''Twill be the shock.'

'Is she just here herself, then?'

'Aye, Delnabreck's away wi' a consignment.'

'Who'll be getting her hame?'

The silence stretched for barely a heartbeat before a male voice spoke up, soft yet self-possessed.

'I will. It'll be my honour to see the lass home.'

Instinctively she knew the voice, unknown to her before that night, belonged to Jamie Innes.

CHAPTER TWO

MORVEN CAME ROUND to find herself being carried through the darkness, her head cradled in warm linen. A fold of plaid was wrapped around her, tucked carefully in place beneath her shoulders, and an overpowering odour of burning arose from it. Her head snapped up and she sucked in a mouthful of frigid air.

''Tis alright,' said a low voice. 'Ye're safe with me.'

A brief image of demonic flames and blistering heat arose before her, and she let out a half-sob before the memory dissolved in the night. The hold on her tightened, and the voice murmured something reassuring, something the wind caught and whipped away. All she could see of her rescuer was a vague shape, but his voice was calm and held a note of certainty, and the steady jolt of his strides lulled her into a place of peace. She slumped back, a little embarrassed by her childish liking for the refuge he provided.

'Morven,' he said tentatively. 'D'ye know who I am?'

'Aye,' she said at once. 'Ye're Jamie Innes. Rowena's kinsman.'

'Thank the Lord, I was thinking the smoke had harmed ye, ye lay that still. Are ye hurt, d'ye think?' They came to a halt in the darkness, and she felt his scrutiny.

'No, I dinna think so … maybe my throat. Can ye let me down?'

He set her down at once, and a chill stole into the places his warmth had reached and enfolded. The wind was even stronger now, and she stumbled as a cross-blast battered against them. He steadied her with a hand beneath her elbow, and she murmured her thanks through chattering teeth as a bout of shivering took hold.

'Ye've had a shock,' he told her. 'A powerful one. A drop whisky might ease the shivering, but I've naught but water.' She felt the weight of a hide flask being pushed into her hands. 'D'ye think we could sit a moment? 'Twould be useful, fer I've little notion where we are, nor where we should be headed.'

They sat in silence on what felt like a tree root, awkwardness creeping over them. The wind was a constant baying at their backs now, the cold feel of rain carried on it.

'I think,' he said, 'your swoon was just yer mind's way of taking ye someplace else, someplace safe, that ye might rest and recover.'

It was generous of him to say so, and she felt the tension in her body ease a little. Slowly, like an injured animal, she conducted a careful assessment of herself. Her tongue felt parched and dry, her throat too, her eyes smarted, and a grimy coating of soot covered her face and neck. She took a mouthful of the water and let it roll around her mouth, then swallowed it down. It made her cough, but it helped, though brought attention to a painful lump that seemed to be lodged in her throat. She drank some more, and at length, her shivering abated a little. Jamie sat patiently, allowing her the time she needed.

'I owe ye my life,' she managed at last. 'You've no kinship with me and yet …' she twisted toward him but could see little in the darkness.

'I've seen enough death these last days,' came his reply. 'I'd no wish to stand idle witness to another. Not one I could prevent.'

'You risked yer own life though. Fer mine.'

'Och, I did only what any man would do.'

In the darkness, she pressed her lips together, and the silence fell thick between them. Intuitively she sensed the direction of his thoughts, felt his confusion.

'Only,' he said at last, 'I believe none would have. Saved ye, I mean. I believe they'd have left ye to burn.'

'No-one meant to harm me.'

'No. But no-one meant to help ye either.' He shifted restlessly at her side. 'It seems to me, those folk were more anxious over their superstitions, over a rickle o' kindling than with yer safety.'

She swallowed, considering his words. 'It must seem that way, I see that, truly I do. But 'tis best nae to judge the glenfolk too sorely. They didna rightly know what to do, and it all did happened that quick.'

'But surely, the right thing to do was clear?'

'To you, aye,' she said slowly. 'And maybe to me as well.' Only, was it so clear? He'd saved her life but in doing that, he'd destroyed the Beltane ring. What calamity might that bring? She swallowed. ''Twas nae so clear to those others, though.'

'How so?'

She sighed. How best to explain it all to someone not brought up to the hardships of the glen? Not moulded by the beliefs and fears she was shaped by?

'There are … are forces set loose on Beltane night,' she ventured at last. 'As I'm sure ye ken.' A shiver coursed up her spine at her unguarded words on such a night and she swallowed. 'Supernatural beings are abroad that folk are anxious nae to offend. 'Tis a faeryhill, Carn Liath, and the rite itself an enchantment. One we seek to weave each year in the hopes of a decent harvest and mebbe less trouble from the gaugers.' The skin of her scalp began to prickle and a sensation of being watched crept over her. 'Twas unwise to put such sentiments into words, especially on the slope of the very faeryhill itself and on the cusp of an uncanny storm, but it couldna be helped.

There was silence for a moment, but for the whine and rush of the wind among the trees, then he gasped, 'So ye've done this afore?'

'No, never have I attended such a rite, nor did I ken what to expect. Only, I'm thinking no Stratha'an man, no cottar or herdsman would dare interfere wi' the Beltane ring fer fear of the ills that might summon.'

'Even to save a life?'

'Aye, I think even fer that. Though I may be wrong to say so. In truth, they didna know what to do. And in the moment, fer 'twas decided in a moment was it not, they were sorely torn. In two minds whether to save me or save their livelihoods, and so mebbe ensure their hold upon the land, at least fer a time.'

'Their livelihoods? I dinna understand?'

'No, I'm forgetting.' How could he understand when he'd been taken from the glen as a swaddler? 'Forgive me.'

'There's naught to forgive,' he replied, puzzled.

She took a deep breath and a tightness knotted in her chest. 'I shouldna have been there, my da forbade it. Only I went against him. I feared harm would come to my kinfolk if no-one from Delnabreck took part.' She tugged at her arisaid, wrapping it closely around her. 'And I thought of the winter past when the snows came wi'out mercy driven on a pitiless wind. The excisemen, they did stalk us through the snow demanding siller, then seized our whisky fer the Crown. The Crown,' she made a scornful sound in her throat. 'Fer themselves, most like. I thought on that, and on the sorrow; thirteen bairns died of hunger, and the beasts froze in the byres. So the reason I went was the same reason all those others did, and 'twas the same reason they didna rush to save me.'

'Forgive me. I still don't understand.'

'I was afraid our harvests might fail. Afraid of another deadly winter, afraid o' the gaugers, but most of all afraid we'd not be able to pay our rent.' She stood abruptly and sensed him respectfully do the same. 'Fear of eviction,' she said with a quiver in her voice. 'Is the darkest fear we all carry in our hearts. Fer land, *this* land, land that was our fathers', is more precious to us than life itself.' She steadied herself with a hand on a nearby sapling, thankful for the darkness that concealed the agitation in her heart, and that likely her face betrayed.

She sensed him lean instinctively toward her.

'The Beltane rite is age-auld.' She forced a calmness to her voice. 'Though its origin is lost now to myth and legend. Rowena believes 'tis as auld as Carn Liath itself and nae to honour it is to beget trouble.' She swallowed, trying to clear the lump still lodged in her throat. 'To open the door to disaster.'

There was silence for a moment, then he said, 'I think I do understand.' A sudden squall lashed at their backs, and he helped her back down to the relative shelter of the tree root. 'My father had that fear. He spoke of it only once, but I mind it still. He said … he said the sorrow of his eviction would stay with him always, and I believe it did.'

'Then I'm heart-sorry, Jamie. D'ye see now why I canna condemn them?'

'I think so.' He exhaled softly. 'Only, I believe ye must have a great heart, Morven, to forgive such a thing, and wi' such grace.'

She tensed, feeling uncomfortable at his words and perhaps that she'd revealed too much of herself, for wariness was woven into her very fabric, though she didna much care fer it. 'I went against my da,' she said softly. 'And so what happened I did bring upon myself.'

'Nay,' he said firmly. ''Twas a chance of nature, the rising o' this storm. Though were I yer father, I'd not have let ye go either, nae to be shamed in thon vulgar display.'

Remembering that, Morven hunched down into herself, her humiliation a wretched grubby thing that clenched her belly. 'Twas something she'd like to forget.

'I didna mean to reproach ye. And anyhow,' his voice sank. ''Tis me they blame.'

That much was true, for with the wrecking of the Beltane ring desperate days had been foretold and Jamie's part in it, regardless of his motives, would be long remembered.

He made a rueful sound. 'You heard that old herdsman, I'm the instrument of yer undoing.'

She winced, hating Achnareave's harsh words, yet understanding them too.

'Ye must think us a godless and superstitious breed Jamie, and maybe we are, but we're what our lives have made us. Our lives and our fathers' lives afore. What ye did took courage,' she said gruffly. 'I see that, and I give ye my thanks. Give them time, and they'll see it too.' But thinking of what he'd done, Morven couldn't help feeling a twinge of bitterness. She was now beholden to him and being the woman she was, the feeling was far from welcome.

'I hope so.' He fell silent, and she sensed him fidget beside her. 'What of thon other man?' he said at last. 'The one that spoke offensively of my aunt? He's nae like the others, nae one o' the glenfolk?'

'That was the factor, William McGillivray, though why he was there I dinna ken, 'tis a mystery, and a troubling one at that.'

'He called my aunt a priestess of the black arts. What was it, d'ye suppose, he meant by that?'

She drew a long breath, then released it through her nose while she thought hard how to answer. 'I've heard tell McGillivray's a bigot and a fool, fer he listens ower-much to McBeath, the head of His Majesty's excise in these parts. And McBeath,' she snorted, 'he's naught but a maggot. But McGillivray's the laird's man, Jamie, the Duke's eyes in the glen and the law, fer he's the local magistrate and 'tis best nae to rile him.'

'A magistrate?' Jamie made an incredulous sound in his throat.

'Aye, though 'tis said he serves his own pocket better than any bench.'

'But I'd not thought to finding a magistrate at the Beltane fire. Mixing wi' herdsmen and wearing their garb.'

'Nor I,' Morven admitted. 'No good will come o' it. He'll be away tattling tales to his Grace, telling how we're all damn heathen savages!' She bit her lip; likely Jamie was thinking that too. But she still hadn't answered his question, and her heart gave a bitter twist. How to explain what she scarcely understood herself? Yet she must explain it somehow, for she owed him that much.

The wind was whipping around them, fingers of ice finding their way beneath her arisaid, the rain coming in earnest. She shivered, and he bent at once to attend her, pulling the woven wool up to cover her head and tucking it under her chin. There was little shelter on the hillside, but it was clear Jamie had no intention of moving until she'd given him an answer.

'What he said of Rowena,' she managed at last. 'I dinna rightly understand it myself. Only … Rowena's nae like other women. She has gifts that do single her out, that mark her as different. The sight fer one thing and wisdom of the plants and their potions. She kens how to work charms, and she sees things others dinna. But I believe her greatest gift is her healing. She helps folk in their troubles. It canna be a sin, I'm certain, but …' She faltered, almost afraid to go on. 'But some folk call her ungodly and … and name her a *witch.*'

In the end, she stumbled over the word, the wind seeming to whip it from her lips and in the silence that followed she wondered if Jamie had heard her. She took a quick breath. 'Most folk hold her dear, as I do, but there are others that miscall her, folk like McGillivray with closed minds and so-called pious ways. McBeath though, he's the worst of them. 'Tis he invents tales of her witchery, and the factor listens to it all and believes.' She swallowed, her jaw sore from bracing herself against another bout of shivering, her heart sore too. The words felt like a betrayal, yet the factor's accusations needed some explaining. 'I believe McGillivray turned on ye tonight Jamie, simply ower who ye are.'

'As I'm Rowena's kinsman?'

'And being so puts ye under the same suspicion. To McGillivray, at least.'

He gave no answer, and the silence closed in again, Morven conscious he was battling his outrage and confusion, his anger only held in check by an innate sense of good manners. And he *was* angry, for she could feel the rage in him and quailed a little at its ferocity. What must he be thinking? Returned to the glen of his birth to find his kinswoman accused of witchery, his own selfless act turned upon and used to damn him too.

The rain turned to hail, a stinging squall, the rattling hiss of it echoing around them, although the banks of cloud had lifted a little and Morven could now see the gleam of his sark beside her in the darkness, the darker shape of his head bent and held in his hands.

'Forgive me,' she whispered. 'It wasna my place to say those things, only I thought ye should ken. The spite though, 'tis my belief that comes from McBeath. We call him the Black Gauger, fer his soul's as black as the excise garb he wears. As fer the factor, Da says he's no more than a pompous windbag swollen wi' the hot air McBeath feeds him.'

Jamie gave a short laugh.

'Only McGillivray has sway ower the laird, so we must mind and not give him cause to remove us. He's a respectable Kirk elder, a member of the Presbytery, and so has say ower our lives. Power to try cases – petty things that rile him. He and the Black Gauger are of the same faith, though the gauger does seek to profit from this connection fer his own advantage. Yet we're fortunate here, truly we are, for His Grace has sympathy with the Roman faith.' She sighed.

'Tis likely the only reason every last one o' us has not been removed already.'

'Lord,' Jamie gasped. 'What manner of place is this?'

Morven shook her head, at a loss for a moment, then a surge of stubborn pride swarmed around her heart. ''Tis our home,' she said fiercely. 'This Highland glen. It's in my blood and yours, and I'm proud to call it hame.'

'I meant nae disrespect.' He lifted his head and stared at her.

'I know. And I meant none in return. I meant only our laird hasna seen fit to follow the lead of so many others and dispossess us all merely fer following the auld faith. The Jacobite faith.'

A glimmer of moonlight had slipped between the banks of cloud and she could see a little more of his face now, cast in light and shadow, staring intently at her.

'My aunt Rowena,' he said slowly. 'She's judged sorely, then?'

Morven smiled, love for the woman spreading a warmth around her heart. 'There's scarce a soul in the glen that's not felt the tenderness of Rowena's hand and known the value of it,' she said softly. 'She's set bones, calmed fevers, and healed more wounds than I can count. She's even cured madness.'

'How does that make her a witch?'

''Tis a word that slips a mite too easily off the tongue if ye wish my opinion. Rowena does nothing but live her life in harmony wi' the wild places, the forests and the hills, the spirits and the magic. 'Tis the way of her. She's blessed wi' the gift of stillness and so can listen to the melody of the heavens, seeing things others miss. She teaches that this earth, this land that we all have the care of, can provide the cure fer every ailment ever suffered if we would but open our eyes to see it.' A familiar sense of wonder excited her heart at the thought, and she struggled to keep her voice level. She'd no wish to shock Jamie, only to make him understand.

''Tis those like the factor that live a lie,' she went on. 'Shut in their mighty houses wi' their fancy things about them – their book-learning and their grand notions. 'Tis they deny the laws of nature, thinking instead to shun it all and cry it wicked!' She was breathing hard now, trembling inside. 'But I ken who I'd sooner follow. I'm Rowena's student. Her apprentice and she's teaching me all that she knows.' Her voice cracked a little over the admission, and she breathed in, calming herself. 'So, if 'tis a witch ye're thinking her, well, ye may as well be thinking me one too.'

He was staring intently at her, and even in the bitter cold, she felt herself flush. What must he be thinking now? That the smoke had addled her wits? But she was unrepentant; what Rowena knew she knew, no matter the means of it, and what she did for others she did so without questioning the rights or wrongs, for what explanation did the easing of suffering need?

'You misunderstand me,' Jamie said in a tight voice. 'I believe nothing ill of my aunt. She's been a true kinswoman, given me a home, a family again, and I'm more indebted than I can say. She and my cousins are now my responsibility, and, God willing, I intend to keep them safe.'

He was still staring at her, unsmiling, and she saw the tightness in his jaw, the smoulder in his dark eyes and felt oddly affected by it. He blinked suddenly as if banishing some sorrow and she remembered what he'd said; that he'd lost his entire family. She shivered. He rose abruptly and slipped a hand under her elbow, helping her to her feet.

'I've kept ye out on this foul night long enough. Can you walk, d'ye think?'

***

It was difficult negotiating the descent in the darkness without a moon to light their way. After its brief appearance, the moon slunk back behind a dense layer of cloud leaving them in near blackness. Morven stumbled, made clumsy by the chill in her limbs, although beneath her arisaid she was dry, the tightly woven wool having saved her from the worst of the rain and hail. She glanced sidelong at the dark shape of her companion, squelching through the sod and the heather.

'Forgive me, d'ye wish my arm?' Misreading her glance, he extended his hand. 'Cold can stiffen muscles.'

'Thank ye,' she replied. 'But I can manage.'

In truth, she knew the slopes of Carn Liath well, far better than Jamie, who'd been following a winding deer trail she realised, down the steepest slope of the hill where the descent was strewn with treacherous scree. She chose to take them north, straining her ears in the darkness for the sound of the river, stopping often to confirm her bearings and to leave the reek of burnt heather behind. Jamie seemed content to follow her lead, trusting her ability to steer them clear of perilous burn-cut gullies, avoiding the worst of the whins as they descended, and taking the easiest path through the dense lower forest. Even so, they were forced to hold onto each other as they negotiated the steepest part, which was cobbled with slippery moss-covered stones, and she felt uncomfortable at the feel of his firm muscles beneath her fingers.

Her earlier climb felt like a lifetime ago now. Sarah's odd behaviour came to mind, and she turned to ask him about it, though plainly he was thinking of her too.

'I should be searching fer my cousin,' he said. 'Young Sarah. Rowena only let her come because she'd be with me. Only I lost sight of her in the crowd, and then with the flames and all, I'm shamed to say she slipped my mind.'

'She can be a mite headstrong.' Morven smiled, thinking of some of the mischief Sarah had got up to in her short life. 'But she kens these hills as well as any. Likely she's hame already.'

'I pray ye're right,' he muttered, and she silently prayed it too.

By the time the dark outline of Delnabreck crofthouse came into sight, low and squat on the haughland of the Avon, the sound of the river sliding over its stony bed was loud in their ears, and the piping cries of oystercatchers gave shrill warning of their approach. Most of the Beltane participants would be home now and likely discussing the events, particularly Jamie's part in the proceedings, over a stiff dram, a bough of rowan fixed over the door to ward off evil.

'That's Delnabreck by the river there,' she told him. 'Tomachcraggen's two miles further on, though there's a decent enough track to follow.'

'I'll see ye safe inside, Morven.' He led her across the infield rigs where the shadows of black cattle raised their horned heads to them, jaws stilled in surprise.

Inside, Grace MacRae sat alone at the fireside. Her face was tinged grey while her eyes and the tip of her nose were reddened and raw-looking. On seeing her daughter, she struggled to rise from her chair.

'Thank the Lord.' She crossed herself. 'I've been that worried –' She cut her outburst short and stared in astonishment at the young giant who ducked through the doorway behind Morven and stood, towering and uncertain, in the dark room.

The sudden warmth of the crofthouse brought a shiver to Morven's flesh and her eyes watered, guilt at her mother's stricken appearance pricking her conscience and quickening her tongue. 'This is Jamie Innes,' she blurted. 'Kinsman to Rowena. He's her nephew from Inverness – her brother's lad.'

Grace stared at Jamie as though she beheld a ghost. Her eyes widened, and a little puff of breath escaped from her lips, then she sat down hard, a hand raised to her throat.

'An honour, Mistress MacRae.' He swept her a bow, his sodden plaid dripping onto the flagstone floor.

Grace made wheezing sounds, struggling to find her voice, while her reddened eyes wrinkled and watered in delight. 'Dearest lad,' she managed. 'I'd ken ye anywhere. You've the Innes eyes, yer father's eyes.' She blinked and shook her head as if to verify he was real, that she'd not conjured his image from staring over-long into the fire. Remembering her manners, she dragged her gaze from his face and stood to greet him. 'I'm that glad to meet ye, Jamie.' Clutching at his wrists, she turned to Morven. 'We didna know … that is, Rowena didna mention ye were coming.'

'No. I came two days ago and brought ill news. Rowena's not left the cot-house since.' He swallowed, regarding Grace tenderly. 'You knew my father well, I think?'

She nodded with an eager smile. 'Like a brother.' Her smile widened, her eyes misting at the memory. 'We were all brought up together ye see; yer da, Rowena, and me. Though I was a foundling of course, yet he never treated me as anything but a sister.' She drew Jamie toward the fire, nudged him toward her husband's blackened rough-hewn chair. 'Such a decent man, though you'll not be needing me to tell ye that. I've nae seen him in years, not since he left the glen, though he's never far from my thoughts. I'm certain I'll ken him whenever I see him.' Her eyes shone. 'He's with ye, aye?'

Jamie's hesitation lasted a fraction too long. 'I fear not,' he said at last. 'There was sickness came to Inverness. The morbid throat.' He swallowed again, and Grace's eyes fastened in horror on his lips, waiting for the terrible words to come. 'He was one of the first to fall. Later my mother too was struck, she who nursed him, and then my sisters also sickened and died. My father was the last to lose the struggle, though I fear 'twas a broken heart, finally, that brought his end.'

'Then they're all gone?' Grace breathed in sharply and sank back into her chair.

He nodded.

At her mother's stricken expression, Morven's heart squeezed. She knelt at her feet and wound her arms around the frail body, pressing her cheek against her mother's chest, breathing in the aroma of fresh-baked bannocks her mother always wore. 'I'm heart-sorry,' she whispered.

After a moment, she opened her eyes and glanced up at Jamie. He was still standing behind her father's chair, his face drawn and contrite. 'Please,' she indicated the seat. 'Sit, and I will bring ye whisky.'

'Is Mam a'right, Morven?' A small voice spoke out from behind a curtain in the corner.

'Aye, Rory, she's fine.' She forced a normal tone. 'Is Donald sleeping?'

'Like the dead.'

Kissing her mother's limp hands, she rose and pulled back the woollen drape that concealed the interior of the panelled box-bed where her young brothers slept. Inside, Rory lay on his side, his copper head pressed against the smaller darker head of his sleeping brother, six-year-old Donald. Donald's round untroubled face was turned up serenely. Rory, at thirteen, was hot-tempered and single-minded like his father and spent much of his day attempting to shake off the unwanted attentions of young Donald. Yet at night he always held him close, his arms enclosing and protective, while his face nuzzled the side of his brother's neck.

She tucked them in, stroking Donald's smoothly rounded cheek, and kissed Rory on the top of his head. Aware that Jamie was now standing beside her, gazing at the boys, she glanced up into his face. He met her gaze levelly, a tightness to his own, then glanced away.

'Come, seat yourself.' She guided him back to the fireside.

He accepted the offered dram and flicked his gaze around the room. The cot-house was humble, yet Morven had never considered it to be pitiably so. Her home was no different from the others scattered throughout the glen. Yet following the sweep of his gaze, she realised it might seem a poor hovel when compared with the fine townhouses of Inverness. The old stones of the hearth and the rafters above were crusted and polished black with peat smoke while blackened cooking pots and girdles hung from rusting chains suspended over the fire, a sliver of fir-wood thrust between the links to thwart wily faeryfolk that might steal down the chimney. In the shadows, a crude dresser displayed an array of turned bowls while an assortment of chairs, unmistakably made from large slices of tree trunk, faced the fire. The only other lighting in the room, other than from the fire itself, came from two fir-candles held in iron clips poking from cracks in the drystone wall. Beneath one a door led into a further room where her parents slept while her own bed, heaped with blankets, lay beneath the other.

Jamie appeared to notice nothing amiss. 'It pains me to be the bringer of such news,' he said gruffly.

'When?' Grace croaked. 'When did this happen?'

'Eight days past.'

'And ye'd not the sickness yourself, Jamie?'

His face darkened, and he set his drink down on the floor. 'I was untouched. Spared by the Lord in His infinite wisdom.'

Morven glanced at her mother. Almost imperceptibly, Grace shook her head; in the presence of such bitter grief 'twas best to say nothing, she seemed to say. After a moment, Jamie retrieved his whisky.

'We're deeply sorry fer yer loss,' Grace ventured. 'Ye must treat us as kin, Jamie.'

Witnessing the strength of will her mother employed in keeping her own grief from showing, Morven's heart constricted. For her mam wouldna be wishing to torment their already grieving guest by exposing how raw was her own pain.

'I'm grateful to ye fer seeing Morven home,' Grace continued. 'She shouldna have gone to the Beltane fire, but Morven's a mind unto herself.'

'A privilege.' A ghost of a smile flitted across his face. 'And 'tis a pleasure to speak with another who knew my father well. To know he was well thought of.'

'He was loved … Rowena and I …'

'I know. Rowena has told me. And has taken the news hard. What wi' losing Duncan last year.' He shook his head. 'She's struggling to cope – wi' the croft, wi' her heartache, with all of it. I hope to ease her burden any and every way I can.'

'She's fortunate to have ye, Jamie.'

He shrugged. 'I'm the fortunate one. She's given me a family again. She's all the kin I have left now. She and her bairns. 'Tis sorry I am I never knew Duncan. I've heard such a lot about him. Though little of … of what became o' him. He was killed in a skirmish wi' excisemen, I believe?'

Grace nodded. 'Shot defending his whisky. Trying to smuggle it south to the Lowland towns where he'd have sold it fer a tidy profit. A profit that's needed fer the paying of rental on his land. On Tomachcraggen. He was alone that day,' she said softly. 'So we'll never know what truly happened. We can only imagine a little.'

Morven glanced at her mother. She'd never heard her voice concerns over Duncan's death before. Her mother's worries were commonly for more mundane matters, domestic cares, yet shared grief had plainly loosened her tongue.

Jamie looked from one woman to the other, his interest sharpened. 'There is some doubt over the events?' he said. 'Some question regarding the true nature of his death?'

'I didna say that,' Grace said quickly. 'I dinna ken, is the truth o' it. I only know Rowena does believe so. And she's rarely wrong.'

He sat back, a little frown creasing his brows, and examined his dram for moment, considering, before downing it and regarding the empty vessel with some respect. 'So, it's true,' he said. 'What my father always told me. Ye do make the finest whisky here.'

'That we do,' Morven confirmed.

He handed her the empty vessel and rose with some reluctance. 'Forgive me, but I must take my leave. I thank ye fer your kind words, Mistress MacRae.'

'Please, call me Grace.'

He inclined his head.

'We'll be seeing ye at the shielings, then?' she asked. 'Malcolm will be moving the beasts to the hills whenever he gets hame.'

'Shielings?'

'He's a town lad,' Morven reminded her. 'He'll nae ken what shielings are.'

He shook his head, and Grace explained.

'Summer pastures in the high hills. Every holding has rights to shieling land where the cattle are taken fer fattening. That way we can sow our crops wi'out hindrance from straying beasts. Each year we've a ceilidh upon the hilltop, and all are welcomed. Alec can play the pipes fit to make yer heart break and Morven,' she turned to her daughter, 'can sing like one o' the Lord's angels.'

'Away!' Morven shook her head.

'I believe I'd like to hear that,' he said with a shy smile.

***

Outside, Morven stalled him with a hand on his forearm and thanked him for not mentioning the events of the Beltane fire to her mother. 'She doesna keep well,' she confided. 'And would only fret ower what's happened. 'Tis done and I'm still living, thanks to you. No good would come from telling her. My Da will hear o' it and may tell her, but I'm thinking even he'll not dare.'

'I understand. She'll nae hear of it from me.'

She thanked him again and watched his dark outline until it merged with the night, then returned to her mother.

Grace had picked up her spindle and was spinning wool, the distaff tucked in the crook of her arm. Her cheeks were wet with tears. Morven knelt by her side.

'I'm heart-sorry,' she whispered.

She knelt there for some time, quiet, watching her mother do battle with her grief. Hardship had blurred her mother's features, and the pain of loss was marked deeply on her face, yet still, her gentle nature was plain to see. Morven recognised the high forehead and delicate heart-shaped face as features she'd inherited herself, although her own determined mouth and wary eyes, quick to anger but easily hurt, were undoubtedly from her father. Inheriting his single-mindedness had given her a restless nature that meant she could never be like her mother, no matter how hard she wished it.

At length, she said, 'I didna ken Rowena's brother once held the tenure of Druimbeag. Such a beautiful place, and to lay empty so long. Ye've not mentioned it afore.'

Grace dried her face with a corner of her shawl. ''Twas long syne and folk have mostly forgotten. I'll never forget, but 'twas a strange business.'

'Strange? How so?'

'He was a handsome man and folk took notice o' him, especially the lassies. But 'twas puzzling only *his* beasts were driven off that night and none o' the others in the glen touched.'

'What are ye saying, Mam?'

'Only what folk were thinking at the time. Jamie's father was an honourable man, a born leader, but there are always some that canna abide seeing others do well.'

'Ye think it wasna reivers took his cattle?'

'I canna say. But wi' no cattle to sell, he couldna meet his rental and the factor had him evicted. He was a proud young man and didna wait fer the factor and his men.' Her face darkened at the memory. 'He took his wife and bairn and loaded their things onto his cart, and then he pulled it himself all the way to Inverness.' Fresh tears brimmed in her eyes. 'Folk came out to see them off, they were that well thought on. I wasna much older than you are now. He thanked them all fer their kind words and then ...' She swallowed, and Morven was unsure whether to ask her more or leave her with her thoughts, when she continued.

'I didna learn he and Rowena werena my real brother and sister till later, nae till I was twenty and about to wed. But he'd kent all along. He kept the secret, hoping to shield me till I was auld enough to understand.'

The fir-candle on the far wall guttered and spat, then flared momentarily, throwing Grace's face into long shadow and exposing a brief glimpse of her younger, open-hearted and vulnerable self. Love for her filled Morven's heart, along with a desperate desire to always keep her safe.

'I thought I'd see him again someday,' Grace whispered. 'I've prayed fer him often enough. He was such a decent young man.' She sat back in her chair, her face pale as bone. ''Twas a shock to learn he was dead, and seeing his lad so like him.'

Morven thought of Jamie's father, tried to picture him in her mind. Did the first James Innes have the same powerful presence as the second? Likely he did. The thought of his son helping Rowena manage Tomachcraggen was reassuring. She'd seen the struggle Jamie spoke of, had felt Rowena's growing anxiety over the rental due at Martinmas. Would all be well now?

'Jamie will be a godsend to Rowena,' she said slowly. 'He'll likely take ower the whisky-smuggling. After all, 'tis *uisge-beatha* that pays the rentals in this glen nae black cattle, and we all know it.' For a year now, she'd fretted for Rowena. Now, at last, she saw her friend's deliverance. Jamie's coming might secure Rowena's hold on Tomachcraggen, might ensure the rental was met in full this year and hence deny the factor grounds to remove her. For the factor held no great love for Rowena, that much had been made clear tonight.

Yet something else now bothered Morven, something of long-standing. Though she'd never heard her mam voice doubts over Duncan's death before, she'd long sensed Rowena was far from satisfied with the accounts given of the incident. And Rowena *was* rarely wrong.

'Jamie's father tried to stay away from the smuggling,' said Grace. 'He thought it best to keep on the right side o' the law. Believed he could manage wi' just the cattle and a few sheep, though he helped his own father with the whisky.' She sighed. 'If he'd smuggled like the rest he might still be living in the glen now, but he'd his pride, and I loved him fer that. I miss him,' she whispered. 'I miss him till it makes me sore.'

CHAPTER THREE

IT WAS ANOTHER TWO days before Morven's father and brother returned. Their trip had been successful, and the whisky had fetched a reasonable price in Perth where a local distiller had bought up the entire consignment for resale under his own label. Yet her father was not overly pleased.

'Two pound,' he grumbled. 'Two miserable pound, that's all thon rogue paid us fer each ten-gallon anker, yet I ken fine he means to re-barrel the lot in his own casks and sell it in Edinburgh at ten, mebbe even eleven pound a cask.'

'Still, Da,' Alec soothed. ''Twas a fair price fer country whisky and would've seen us bonny if it hadna been fer the pony.'

'Aye, poor bugger.' Malcolm shook his head. 'I'll need to replace him.'

'What happened?' asked Morven. She'd seen the convoy's return from the riverbank where she was tramping blankets and realised at once a garron was missing. It was Firth, the black gelding, a willing wee pony. The loss of a garron signified trouble of some order.

'We were fortunate.' Alec accepted the bowl of barley-broth his mother passed to him.

'Fortunate!' Malcolm snorted. 'Is that what ye call it?'

'If we'd run into gaugers, Da, we'd have lost more than the pony.'

'But what happened?' Morven repeated.

'Had to shoot him.' Malcolm kept his gaze on his broth and spooned doggedly.

'Aye, snapped his foreleg stumbling down a hillock wi' the heavy ankers on his back.' Alec sighed. 'We were making good time as well, following the drover's route that snakes through Glenshee, keeping to the haughland o' the Shee Water where it's fine and flat when we came on tinkers. A great band o' them. And damned if they didna tell us gaugers were riding the route wi' redcoats from Corgarff.'

'Redcoats!' Grace's eyes widened.

'Did ye see them, Da?' Rory could barely contain his excitement.

'Ye should've taken the claymore.' His eyes darted to the far wall where an oak kist contained a huge two-edged broadsword.

'No, lad.' Malcolm ruffled Rory's copper hair with a giant hand. 'I didna need yer Granda's sword.' He chuckled gruffly at the youngster's keenness to do battle. 'We led the garrons up into the foothills o' the Cairngorms, tried to find cover amongst the forests and the braes. Only the lead pony slid doon a steep-sided bank, dragging the others down wi' him. Each crashed into the other in a skelter o' rocks and rumbling kegs, and in the tangle, the poor beast was crushed.' He rubbed a weary hand over the grizzled hair at the back of his neck. 'Came doon hard, and his leg snapped under him like kindling.'

He slanted a look at Rory and young Donald. Both wore the same broad adoring expression and blinked in unison, transfixed by their father's heroically unkempt appearance. 'I'd nae choice but shoot him.'

'We thought the shot might draw them onto us,' Alec said. 'And hid in a copse the full day. At nightfall, we loaded the ankers onto the other garrons and crept away. With the others laden so heavy, we could only manage a slow pace but made it to Perth safe enough.' He sat back and sought out Morven with his eyes, quirking her a regretful little smile. Firth was her favourite.

'We'd no way of knowing if the tinkers were speaking the truth or playing tricks.' Malcolm scowled into his bowl. 'There's nae been redcoats stationed at Corgarff in ower a year.'

'Ye did right,' said Grace. 'Ye ken what happened to Duncan.'

'Wheesht, woman! There's nae need to speak o' that.' He thrust his empty bowl at her. 'I missed Beltane, but it couldna be helped. If we'd had the ten ponies –'

He stopped short and eyed Morven suspiciously. Grace had given her away, her gaze darting to her daughter's face at the mention of Beltane, then sliding guiltily to the floor.

'What's this?' He glared at Morven's reddening face. 'I forbade it. Did ye go against me, lass?' He stood suddenly, eyes blazing.

There was no point in denying it. 'I did, aye.'

'God's blood!' He turned and slammed his fist into the meal kist beside her.

She flinched but stood her ground. She'd done it for the sake of Delnabreck and all who lived there and would damn well stand and defend herself. Yet if Alec, or even Rory, had gone against him as she had, the fist her father was now nursing might well have met soft young flesh instead of solid ash. Swallowing, she squared her jaw.

'Someone had to go Da, and there was only me.'

'*Only you*?' He choked on his rage. 'Ye stubborn wee devil. Ye might've been –' He glanced down at the youngest of his sons who gazed up adoringly, then cleared his throat. 'Well, ye ken yerself.'

'She meant well, Da.' Alec came to her defence as always. 'She just didna think of the dangers. 'Twas a bold act though, d'ye not think?'

'I do not. 'Twas foolhardy.'

'But she did it to protect the croft.'

'And ye imagine I dinna ken that?' Malcolm snorted irritably. 'Only the ritual's nae always a show, oft-times the lass is ravished!'

'What's ravished?' asked Donald.

'And there's danger from the fire, never heed the ungodliness of the act.' Grunting in exasperation, he ignored the boy.

'It *was* a show,' Morven blurted. 'At least,' she added hastily, 'I'm fairly certain it was.' She hadn't known about the ravishing and swiftly decided now was not the time to reveal she had been the Beltane virgin.

'Now now, dinna be so hard on her.' Grace ladled more broth into her husband's bowl and tried to nudge him back down into his seat. She flicked Morven an apologetic look. 'She came to no harm, didn't she? And did it wi' the best o' intentions. Anyhow,' her eyes clouded. 'I've something, and someone, to tell ye about.'

'But I forbade it.' Malcolm poured himself a sizeable dram from a keg near the hearth and, still glaring at Morven, proceeded to drain it in one gulp. 'Why must she aye disobey me?'

Morven felt her hackles rise. 'Oh, aye,' she blurted. 'Had Alec done it, ye'd have patted him on the back. But since 'twas yer contrary daughter carried out the deed, then clearly, a mortal sin has been committed!' Her innards knotted in frustration. 'Why is it everything *I* do has to be stopped? Everything *I* want must be a sin? D'ye hate me that much?'

There was a moment of stunned silence during which a rash of livid colour surged into her father's face and worm-like veins popped out on the sides of his neck. Even his ears turned the colour of fresh salmon.

'Why, ye ungrateful wretch! I'll thrash yer hide.' He fumbled with the belt on his plaid, then, realising his kilt would drop to the floor if he unfastened it, cast around for something to thrash her with.

'Da, Da, she didna mean it,' cried Alec. 'Did ye, Morven? She just feels … stifled atimes.' He pushed her roughly behind him, shielding her from their father's wrath.

'No, Da,' she conceded. 'I ken ye dinna hate me. Ye just … just seem to thwart everything I do.' She let her breath out but held his glare, a glint of challenge still lingering in her eyes. 'I'll take a thrashing if 'twill make ye feel better.'

Malcolm's jaw tightened a fraction, then his shoulders slumped and he sighed, weariness dragging at his features. He sat back down. 'I wish to keep ye safe,' he muttered, 'is that so wrong? But I dinna wish to thrash ye.' He flicked his hand at her. 'Away with ye, I need to wash, and doubtless, Alec does as well. Give us peace.'

Grace lifted the big boiling pot onto the crook. Looking up under her lashes, she shifted her gaze pointedly to the door.

With a resigned nod, Morven turned and fled.

She was still bitter as she squeezed water from the blankets and hung them from a rope stretched between the cot-house and the byre. Her da always made her feel that way, worthless somehow, yet foolhardy whenever she tried to prove her worth. He refused to see how much she'd already learned from Rowena and set little store by the skills and insight the widow possessed. Morven sighed. 'Twas easy to love her sweet-natured mother but her father, though he commanded her utmost respect, was a sight more difficult to love. She hung the last blanket and dried her hands on her arisaid. Yet she did love him. And knowing it, she unclenched her teeth and smothered her resentment.

Turning her back on the cot-house, she clambered onto the infield dyke and sat on the cold stone. There was not a breath of wind to cool her cheeks, the deergrass and bog cotton up on the peat banks barely stirred. It was one of those rare May mornings when the scent of pine and heather rose thick and languid on the air, when time had a hushed unhurried quality as though it had passed clean by the glen without a backward glance. Weak sunlight filtered through a layer of gossamer cloud, bringing a haze of green to the birkwoods straggling up Seely's Hillock and promising some warmth for later in the day. 'Twas a perfect day for gathering herbs.

With her mind set, she slipped from the dyke and fetched a heather basket and hide gloves from the byre, then set off for the river. It was many months since she'd picked herbs on the far side of the Avon yet something about the sunlight glinting on the young leaves of Druim forest caught her eye and drew her there.

She climbed down over the grassy lip and onto the Avon's broad stony floodplain, picking her way over the polished boulders and stones. Oyster-catchers had laid eggs on the shingle and the sight of their comic strutting and indignant pik-pik cries at her approach brought a smile to her face. She skirted the vulnerable eggs and stood cautiously at the water's edge. The Avon was a swift peaty river, its amber waters foaming over its stony bed like good ale. Pools of swirling water formed eddies near the centre where salmon and brown trout lay. Yet its depth was deceptive, its speed perilous, and it was many a sober fisherman told tales of waterhorses and kelpies frolicking in its dark waters. 'Twas wise to be ever watchful and wary.

The boatman, Robbie Grant, greeted her warmly and guided her into the boat with an appraising eye that lingered over-long on her briefly exposed ankles. His conversation was innocent, but his eyes held a knowing conspiratorial gleam. Morven couldn't recall seeing him at the Beltane fire but sensed he knew all about it.

'Ye'll be returning later, will ye?' He hauled on a rope threaded through iron rings on either side of the boat.

'Aye, I've herbs and nettles to collect.'

'Up at Druimbeag?' He gave her a toothless grin.

'Aye ... most likely.' It hadn't been her conscious decision to go to Druimbeag, but now that he spoke the name she knew that was indeed where she was heading. Over the last few days, it had been none too easy to shake thoughts of Jamie from her head. There was something intense about him that intrigued her. And an air of melancholy. She wished to see again the place where he'd been born, and where his equally extraordinary father had played out his last days in Strathavon.

Over the years, she'd been to Druimbeag many times. Among the plants of great value that grew there, a rare white willow could be found. Rowena had spoken of it, had told her magical plants often take hold in the places where folk once lived and turned the soil. Perhaps the people's toil enriched the land, yet Morven believed it was something more profound.

Robbie slid the boat onto the shingle bank. 'Here ye are, Miss MacRae.' He lifted his bonnet to her with a sly grin.

Climbing out, she instinctively held the folds of her gown as close to her body as possible. Did every tongue in the glen wag to the same tune? Likely so. Then 'twas only a matter of time before her father learned the full details of her ordeal on Carn Liath. It hardly took the gift o' far-sight to foresee his reaction. He'd not always tended toward a foul temper, but this last year he'd shown little else. She'd even thought of asking Rowena for a tincture to ease his dark moods, though in some odd way Rowena seemed to be at the root of them.

Leaving the river behind, she climbed the low ridge, the *druim* that gave the place its name, up to the dilapidated building that was the crofthouse. It was a beautiful place. A thicket of young pine saplings now grew where once proud rigs of barley and oats had held sway, and the scent of pine resin filled the air. Beneath her feet, tender bracken fronds unfurled from a litter of autumn leaves left untouched but for the foraging of deer. Following the sound of water, she discovered a dark burn carving its way through the rock, bearded with trailing fronds of weed, and it seemed as though for centuries its peaceful burbling had gone unheard. Beyond the crofthouse stood a much older forest dark with pine and larch. Unchecked, it had nurtured rich groves of hazel and gean, elder and the spindly-silver trunks of birch.

The cot-house itself was a sorry sight. The heather thatch had mainly gone, and the timber uprights and cross-pieces were visible through the missing roof. An old crow's nest now sat there. The door had swollen and splintered and what remained of it hung askew while the gaping windows stared out blankly. Yet at the near corner of the building grew a protective rowan, the tree Rowena was named for, placed there for protection, for the deep magic found only in rowan-wood. 'Twas a telling sign. It spoke to her of the beliefs held dear by the folk of Druimbeag.

She hesitated before entering the cot-house. It seemed disrespectful, and Morven shied away, attracted by the sight of sweet woodruff growing by the crumbling byre. Gathering some, she discovered feverwort, comfrey, and meadowsweet. With a gasp of delight, she identified a tiny patch of red clover beginning to uncurl and knelt to pinch off a few sprigs. 'Twas an important herb for her mother's complaint, though a rarity in all but the most sheltered spots. Rowena's store of dried herbs laid down the previous year had begun to dwindle, and it was important to replace them.

She worked with quiet concentration, plucking and picking and digging up roots with her small dirk. The burbling of the burn and the cooing of wood pigeons soothed her senses while the sun warmed the chill in her fingers and the last trace of tension from the encounter with her father seeped gently away.

She didn't recognise the sound at first. The low murmur seemed to belong to the forest, but when it came again, she froze, prickles of alarm firing at her temples. 'Twas a human sound. She twisted her head to listen, and the hair rose on the back of her neck. It came again. She was certain it came from within the ruined cot-house.

Faeryfolk were said to take over old human homes, 'twas common knowledge. Intrigued by the human race, they were known to carry off new-born babes and replace them with changelings.

Every fibre of her body told her to flee, yet something held her back. Rowena called them the *Daoine Sìth*, men of peace. Slowly, she crept closer to the house.

The murmuring came again, louder and more distinct. It was a male voice, low yet not rough. She edged closer to an empty window, then caught her breath – 'twas praying! She craned forward to peek through the missing window but her dirk, which she still held in her hand, scraped along the stonework with a loud rasp.

There was a sudden scuff of earth, then a voice called out. 'Who's there? Show yerself!'

Gasping, she darted back from the window. The voice was oddly familiar. There was no time to hide. The rickety door was forced roughly open, and she found herself staring up into the stern face of Jamie Innes, her heart crammed in her throat.

His eyes were darker than she remembered, black almost, and close-set with thick dark brows that arched down over his eyes. He didn't smile but blinked in bewilderment at her, something clutched in his hand.

'Forgive me,' she stammered. 'I … I didna ken ye were here. Ye scared me.'

He let his breath out, and the strain visible on his face relaxed a fraction. 'Nor I you. I didna know *anyone* came here.' He frowned. 'What is it ye're doing?'

'Gathering herbs.' She swallowed and lifted the basket of greenery for him to see, feeling not unlike a mischievous child caught poaching on the laird's land.

'Ye gather herbs here?'

'Aye, 'tis a good place. Rowena says the best herbs aye grow in soil that folk have tilled in the past. This is such a place.'

He nodded, assessing, then leaned back against the rotting doorframe, head cocked appraisingly. 'I'd not thought to seeing ye again so soon,' he said softly.

'No. I've nae been here since last summer. I … I dinna ken what 'twas brought me here today.'

Whatever it had been, she silently wished it had taken her elsewhere, anywhere else, that she might be delivered from the uncomfortable scrutiny he was now putting her to. Her cheeks began to flame, and she glared at the ground. 'I've disturbed ye.' She turned to go. 'I'll be letting ye back to yer business.'

'I was praying.' He opened his hand to show her the crucifix and rosary beads he held. 'Fer the souls of my kinfolk. I've no graves to pray at, nae here, they were buried in the chapelyard at Inverness. I thought …' He swallowed, focusing on something beyond her shoulder, and she saw again the lines of pain drawn sharply on his face. 'I thought I'd feel closer to them here, where once they were blithe.'

A shiver ran up her spine, and she said softly, 'I heard ye praying. Only I thought 'twas …' she shook her head, feeling foolish. 'I thought 'twas *na daoine sìth*, the men o' peace, up to some manner o' devilry inside the house.'

'And ye were ready to confront them?' The corner of his mouth gave a slight twitch, although there was a note of something like respect in his voice. 'That was real bold of ye.'

'I'm nae altogether certain what I planned to do.'

He slipped the sacred things away into his sporran and peered into her basket. 'Can I be helping ye with that? The herbs and suchlike, they look much the same to me. Rowena has them hung all over the crofthouse, but if you point out the ones ye want I could dig them up fer ye.'

'Thank you, but I have what I need from here. Nettles are sprouting by the infield dyke though. We could cut the tips fer soup.'

'You eat nettles?'

'Aye. We all do. Rowena says ye must eat something green every day. Nettles are good fer the blood.'

'Do they not sting yer mouth?'

'No,' she laughed. 'Nae once ye've boiled them. Do they nae eat nettles in Inverness, then?'

'I dinna think so. We had kail.'

Morven snorted. 'Da says kail's fer soft Lowlanders.'

He flinched. 'I was born here. In this cottage.'

'Forgive me.' She cursed her thoughtless tongue. 'I didna mean anything by that. Ye can help me if ye like.'

The drystone dykes of stone enclosures were still evident around the croft and had been skilfully made. Along the length of each embankment, they found swathes of nettles sheltering, their bright green shoots furred with stinging hairs. Morven put on the gloves and sliced off the tips with her dirk. The gloves were too small for Jamie, who perched on the dyke with the basket watching her with interest.

Conscious of his continued study of her, she felt compelled to fill the awkward silence between them. 'My da and brother got home this forenoon,' she told him. 'Only Da's nae best pleased with me fer going to the Beltane fire.'

'You told him what happened?'

'No. Mam let slip I went in his stead, and he was that riled I judged it best to say no more.' She sighed, dropping the nettle shoots into the basket. 'He'll hear what happened soon enough I'm thinking, whether it's me tells him or not.'

'And will be angered?'

She rolled her eyes. 'I'll wager he'll thrash me till I've not an inch of flesh to sit down on that's nae black-and-blue and then tell me it hurt him to do it.' She laughed mirthlessly at the prospect.

Jamie looked aghast. 'Ye mean he'll strike you?'

'Aye, most like.' She looked curiously at him. 'Have ye never been thrashed, then?'

'Well, aye. But my father would never strike a woman.'

'Mine might,' she said bitterly. Though the change in her father, his new black moods, had much to do with Rowena's decision to pass on her knowledge to his daughter, though why that should be when he'd welcomed her teachings at first, she couldn't fathom.

'I could speak with him, if ye like. Tell him what happened.'

She cocked a scornful eyebrow at him. 'You being a man, ye mean? You do a better job?'

'No, I meant only … I might manage to deflect his anger.'

'Right noble of ye! But I'll thank ye nae to interfere, I've no need of yer assistance.'

Then, feeling a little mean, she added, 'Da's turned real crabbit lately. With Rowena especially, but with me and most other folk too.' The change in her father had bothered her for some time, had shamed her in truth, though she'd never spoken of it. Not to Rowena, not even to her mother. 'Much of it's ower my learning from Rowena. I'm nae minded to stop, though.' She looked directly at him, challenging him to oppose her. ''Tis Tomachcraggen I'm going to now wi' these herbs. We could keep company if ye're agreeable?'

The corner of his mouth twitched again. 'That'd be verra agreeable.'

***

Robbie Grant could barely keep the smirk from his face as they climbed into the boat together. It dawned on her that he must have taken Jamie over the river earlier, and knew full well Jamie was at Druimbeag when he'd asked her if she was headed there. She groaned inwardly. Was she forever to be linked with Jamie in folk's minds? Never allowed to forget the humiliation of the Beltane fire?

Jamie paid the man little heed but gazed up to the hills of Cromdale and away to the distant shoulders of Ben Avon, still snow-capped, with a wondrous look on his face. Satisfied the tables were now turned, Morven took the opportunity to do some studying of her own.

Jamie's was a face of contrasts, she judged. The boyish lines and downy shadow on his chin betrayed the fact that he could be no more than twenty-one or two, yet he wore the poise and possession of someone far greater in years. The strong jaw and dark eyes, deep and closely set, half-hidden by arched brows, added to the air of intensity he conveyed, and she could see that for all his youth he was serious and thoughtful. There was a dignity to the way he carried himself, a vein of good breeding that seemed to run through him, lending him confidence and influencing his manners. His size was quite shocking up close. He towered above almost everyone she'd ever known, yet for all his size there was a grace to his movements, an essence of flowing energy and lean muscle that was wholly central to him.

At the riverside, Jamie angled his body to block the boatman's prying gaze as she climbed out of the boat and gave the disgruntled man some snuff from his sporran in payment. As they made toward Cnoc Daimh, the wooded rise that concealed Tomachcraggen crofthouse, she looked back over her shoulder and saw the boatman standing on the riverbank staring after them.

The crofthouse at Tomachcraggen sat in a hollow, the heather of its roof and its old weathered stones almost indistinguishable from the ageless hills that encircled it. The cultivated land, what there was of it, was set out in traditional rigs and dreels and throughout the long winter months had been gnawed to the quick by Rowena's cattle. Looking down on it from the rise, the pattern of human toil was clear to see – a poor scrape of land wrested from the whins and the heather.

They found Rowena in the sheepcote. On seeing them, she set her milking cog to one side and flushed with pleasure. 'So, ye've met my nephew?' She took Morven into her embrace.

'At Druimbeag,' Morven replied, then whispered, 'I was that heart-sorry to hear …'

Rowena pressed her a little closer and drew a long breath. There was no need to say more. Comfort was given and touchingly received without need of words. Morven felt her friend draw another steadying breath, then they parted.

'And at Beltane,' she added. Had Jamie told his kinswoman of her ordeal? She thought not and was glad. Since hearing his sad news, Morven had kept away from Tomachcraggen, had allowed Rowena time to mourn her brother in peace. Looking at her now, she perceived new shadows beneath the older woman's eyes, although her expression was as enigmatic as ever.

Inside the cot-house, Rowena examined the contents of Morven's basket, exclaiming at the discovery of precious red clover. As always, her home was a delight – a rich collection of vibrant colours and aromas. Bright vials and flasks, oils, powders, and potions caught the eye while sheaves of dried roots and herbage hung from the crossbeams. The resultant aroma was one Morven had loved since childhood. Mingled with peat smoke from the fire, it lay thick and fragrant on the air.

'Are my cousins not here?' Jamie flicked his gaze around the room.

'There's a dominie in the glen today, a schoolmaster,' explained Rowena. 'Teaching on the haughland of the Lochy Burn. I've sent them along to learn their lessons.' She gestured for them both to sit down. 'William was keen to go, but Sarah ...' She smiled ruefully. 'Sarah wasna for it at all.'

'She may need to read someday,' Jamie told her earnestly.

'Aye, mebbe. Did ye ken?' She turned to Morven, 'that young Jamie here can both read and write?'

Morven looked at him in astonishment, and he grinned back a little awkwardly.

'I've something I must tell ye, though.' Rowena pulled a chair up close. 'I'd a wee visit this forenoon from Isobel McBeath.' She turned to Jamie to explain. 'She's wife to Hugh McBeath, the resident exciseman at Balintoul. She warned that redcoats are riding wi' excisemen, orders from the king she said, to rid the Highlands of the scourge o' whisky smuggling. They're patrolling the high passes.' She held Morven's gaze uneasily. 'We must pray yer father and young Alec get through safe.'

'Oh, they did,' Morven replied. 'They got hame just after dawn.'

'And all went well?'

Morven nodded, repeating what her father had told her.

A muscle in Rowena's jaw twitched, and she nodded thoughtfully, then reached for ale and drinking cups. 'A celebration, then?'

'Forgive me,' said Jamie, frowning. 'But why would this woman give away so much when her own husband is a gauger?'

Rowena nodded, pouring out the ale. 'Isobel is one o' the glenfolk, ye see, and her kin were all smugglers afore her. Though she's marrit to that toad and I believe she must love him, her loyalties are sorely torn. Oft-times she warns the glen women of gaugers working in the area, and in return, they give her the friendship she sorely lacks and wee gifts o' fish, cheese, wool, and that.' She nodded at the question forming on Jamie's lips. 'Of course, McBeath knows nothing o' this and 'twould do no-one any good to tell him.'

'I see.'

'But she came here today, owing to being heavy wi' child again and desperate fer a healthy bairn. She hoped I could help her.'

'Isobel has had eight pregnancies,' Morven confided. 'But no bairns – they've all been miscarried or stillborn.'

'Dear Lord!'

'Aye,' said Rowena. ''Tis a shadow of herself she is. I've given her a tincture to strengthen her blood, but I fear fer her life this time.'

'She'd have taken the greatest of care, though?' Morven said. 'Nae to be seen?'

'I'm certain she was discreet … heedful to go unnoticed.'

Jamie's interest was aroused now; he fixed Morven with a sharp look. 'This McBeath, he's the man you spoke of, the Black Gauger, the exciseman the factor pays so much heed to?'

She nodded.

'Then he'd not wish his wife to consult wi' my aunt?'

'Well, no, as I said, he speaks ill of Rowena, though he's known fer his rabid preaching. He blames her I think, fer the infants that died, believes she's laid a curse upon him.'

'A curse?'

'To die childless.'

'But that's ridiculous!'

Again, Morven nodded. She could see signs of alarm on Jamie's face now and felt the first stirrings of it herself.

'That being so,' he said slowly. 'Should anything ill happen to this child, mightn't he then believe my aunt had caused it?'

Morven frowned. 'If he was to learn of her visit here, then aye, he'd likely be suspicious. And … and there can be little more hope of this bairn's survival than the others.'

Grim-faced, Jamie turned to his aunt.

Rowena had kept quiet during her kinsman's journey to this conclusion, although her breathing had quickened a fraction and her lips had thinned to a fine line.

'He'll nae hear of it, nae from Isobel.' The lines of her face hardened. 'But I'll not turn the poor soul away, no matter who she's marrit to. Let him think what he will – I'll not abandon her.'

'But, Rowena,' Jamie pressed. 'I fear he'll do more than just *think* poison, he'll whisper it too, and into the ear of the factor – thon bigot McGillivray.'

Rowena struggled to meet her young kinsman's gaze. Swallowing, she stood and crossed to the window.

'A plague on his poisonous tongue,' she muttered. 'But I've no wish to speak o' that man.'

CHAPTER FOUR

THE CRASHING OF THE cot-house door against the old stone wall jolted Morven from a shallow sleep. It was late, the darkness thick as ink, the fire smothered to a glow, yet her father carried no light. It seemed he blew in on a draught of pure whisky vapour, the potency of the drink he'd consumed, coupled with the sheer volume of it, protection against the cold dark night. Grunting, he reeled by her bed and pitched inelegantly into a chair, the timber groaning under his sudden weight.

Morven watched him from the refuge of her blankets and caught the stale reek of the Craggan Inn upon him. He fumbled for more whisky and then gagged a little as the rawness of the spirit scorched the back of his throat. He knew. She sensed he was now thoroughly acquainted with every shameful detail of her ordeal on Carn Liath and the thought made her quail. Fortified by ale and whisky, there'd have been any number of cottars at the inn only too willing to recount it all. Yet watching him stare sightlessly into the hearth, there were no signs of anger, no explosion brewing, nae even a curse or bunched fist. Perhaps she now meant so little to him that he deemed her unworthy of his rage, yet that notion was somehow worse. Miserable, she curled herself into a ball beneath the blankets. The anger would come she sensed, and when it did, there'd be hell to pay.

At length, he rose with a mutter and made his tortuous way to the far side of the room, to the doorway and the tiny bedchamber he shared with her mother. In the darkness, Morven listened for the sound of their low voices. Would he tell her mother what he'd learned? Speak of the leaping flames, or, more shameful still, the consequences of her escape from them? But no, instead he roused her mother for another purpose, the need plainly upon him to indulge the baser appetites of his flesh.

She buried her head beneath the blankets, pressed her fists to her ears, but nothing could smother the sounds of his pleasure. In the end, she fell to reciting the words of the Lord's Prayer, over and over, in a bid to drown out his grunts and the wild creak of timber.

***

Come morning, they flitted to the shieling.

Morven walked beside the cattle with her brothers, watching the beasts sway on their hardy legs. The beasts were in a sorry state, months of hunger had so reduced them they could barely walk and the MacRaes were forced to match their slow pace. Despite the cattle's thick coats, the hollow of flank and sharp outline of bone protruding at haunch and shoulder was plain to see. Yet still, they lowed joyfully, perhaps catching a sense of the occasion.

Despite herself, Morven's spirits rose. The spring flit to the shieling heralded the end of the long dark days of winter, and all around her new life was emerging as the glen roused itself from winter's grip, re-clothing the bones of the land. The hilltop *ceilidh* was a celebration of the land's rebirth, an excuse to be carefree.

It was only a two-mile journey on foot or by pony, but with the cattle and laden cart, the MacRaes were forced to wend a wide detour around the shoulder of Carn Odhar, avoiding the steep gorge where the Lochy Burn carved a gully through the hillside on its way to join the Avon.

At length, Malcolm helped Grace from the cart's board seat. 'I'll be leaving ye to put the place in order.' He nodded at the pile of goods Alec was heaping in the heather. 'If there's to be a feast, ye'll be needing something fer the pot. Alec!' He called his son to heel with a curt twitch of his head.

The bothy, no more than a simple stone hut, sat on a plateau of moorland a hundred feet or so below the granite crown of Carn Odhar. Hidden from the glen below, it afforded them a grand vantage point, a view of the mist-shrouded hills of Cromdale and, further west, the dark grandeur of the distant Monadhliath Mountains, the higher tors lost in cloud.

Morven disentangled a stool from the pile Alec had abandoned and set it down for her mother. In truth, there was little needed doing, the bothy was but a humble shelter and needed no more than a quick sweep-out. She sent the boys for water and kindling and soon had the place put to rights. Straightening, she eyed her mother's pale countenance.

'I could make the bannocks fer ye,' she suggested. 'Ye look fair worn-out.'

'Aye,' Grace conceded. 'I am. Ye'll mind and mark them the way Rowena likes, fer the offering, aye?'

'I will.'

The seasons of the year – sowing, ripening, and harvest reap – were each celebrated and, as was Strathavon tradition, offerings were made on the hillside to ensure a prosperous year. The bannocks used were a deal larger than the daily kind and were marked with a cross on one side of the oat dough before being baked on a hot girdle.

'Rowena will be away gathering greenery fer the offering.' Grace began the slippery business of cleaning trout for the feast. 'She'll nae be here till later, wi' young Jamie and the bairns.'

'I doubt Sarah would thank ye fer calling her a bairn,' Morven observed. 'She's sixteen now, remember.'

'Aye, I know. But she's still a bairn in my mind.' Grace stopped what she was doing, and her face took on a distant, wistful look. 'I remember the day she was born, Rowena was that proud. She was the sweetest child, an angel I thought, wi' silken silver hair and eyes like a summer sky.' She swallowed and looked down at her hands, bloodied and shiny with fish scales. 'Losing her da has brought many a cloud to that blithe sky.'

'For Rowena, too.'

'Aye, fer them all. Only Sarah tries most especially hard to hide her hurt, is what I think.'

'D'ye think she minds her mam teaching me the healing? I mean, d'ye suppose she's hurt by it?' Morven had often wondered about this, had sensed she might feel so in Sarah's place.

Grace considered for a moment. 'I dinna believe Sarah has a notion to be a healer. Nor do I believe she has the disposition fer it. Ye're different, you and her. Besides, she still has that selfish streak all bairns are born with.' Grace chuckled. 'And can be a peacock at times, though dinna go saying I said that!'

'So, wouldna be the best choice?'

'Rowena chose you fer a reason.' Grace filleted a fish with a deft stroke. 'She does naught wi'out careful thought. Duncan's no longer here to keep a firm rein on his daughter, God rest his soul, and though Rowena sees many things and I love her dearly, when it comes to Sarah she doesna aye see what's beneath her own nose.'

Morven had known Sarah all her life, and there was no doubting she could be a braggart. But she was also charmingly naïve, and the combining of this charm with a degree of swaggering boldness always made Morven smile. When they'd been younger and more carefree, they'd shared secrets together, dreaming of romantic Jacobites who'd sweep them up and defend their honour with sword and dagger. Remembering that, a wistful glow dispelled her doubts.

By midday, hill-folk had begun to drift up Carn Odhar from all directions, word of a *ceilidh* spreading quicker than that of an excise raid. The MacPhersons of Lochy Mill were first to arrive; Alastair, a cautious and serious man, with his wife Elspeth, a ruddy-cheeked woman carrying a brace of grouse. John Chisholm, the cooper, arrived next, along with his wife and eldest lad, also John, and then Donald Gordon and his family from Craigduthel croft. When her da and Alec returned with a dozen or more hare skewered on a birchwood switch, the McHardy clan had made their appearance, every one of them it seemed, and all in all it was a fair-sized gathering that settled itself on the hillside.

Alec and the boys cut armloads of whin and kindled a fire on a patch of bare ground. Once the first flare of flames had quietened, folk gathered around to toast their fingers, feeding the blaze and watching a pale trail of smoke curl skyward. Not one to be forgetting the proprieties of a Highland welcome, Malcolm rolled out a keg of whisky and doled it out to all and sundry.

Come early afternoon, when Rowena appeared with Jamie, Sarah and young William, Malcolm's face was far from the only one flushed with the intoxication of that welcome. The sound of bluff laughter rang out over the hills, and the aroma of country whisky, bannocks, and fresh hare roasting on a spit had stirred the conversation to a rowdy pitch. The welcome extended to Jamie, however, was more cautious.

Alexander Grant of Achnareave, the old herdsman who accused Jamie on Carn Liath, hadn't thought to grace their *ceilidh* with his presence, though plainly the superstitious sentiments he'd voiced that night were alive and well among some of the others gathered.

'Innes, is it?' scowled John Chisholm, not bothering to rise from his recumbent position. 'I've heard tell of ye.'

'My nephew,' answered Rowena with a tight smile. 'From Inverness.'

'Yer brother's lad?'

'Aye. The lad was born at Druimbeag.'

'Was he now?' He sat up with renewed interest.

Although there were signs of wariness evident in many a face, above all it was a keen sense of curiosity Morven detected in her neighbours. James Innes was plainly a name well-known and well-respected hereabouts. Yet from the furious whispering and furtive exchanges she intercepted, Jamie's character was clearly a matter for debate. As she helped serve whisky to her neighbours, she couldn't help overhear snatches of conversation. It seemed being the son of James Innes didn't necessarily mean he was anything like his father. He'd wrecked the Beltane ring after all, without a second thought. Strangers were oft-times treated with suspicion, yet Morven couldn't help feeling one who'd saved her life deserved a sight better treatment.

Jamie maintained a well-mannered grace regardless of the ill-concealed speculation and hostility around him.

'Come away to the fire and take a dram,' said Grace, clearly mystified at his reception.

'Thank ye.' He inclined his head to her, but his eyes sought Morven out, engaging her more deeply, and she felt a twinge of conscience at the hurt she saw there.

'I'll be fetching ye a drop barley-bree,' she murmured and hastened away to get it. On her return, she found young Dugald McHardy, an inquisitive wee lad of around five years, standing in front of Jamie, staring in fascination at his patterned brogues. Such fine footwear was rarely seen in the glen. Squatting, the lad reached out a hand to touch.

'Dugald!' scolded his mother. 'Come away from there. What did I tell ye?'

Dugald's blue eyes widened.

'Dugald!' And he was gone. Scooped up and hastily bundled away. The boy's mother, Eilidh McHardy, could be heard chastising him severely in Gaelic.

Jamie took the vessel Morven thrust at him and sat down heavily. 'I'd not thought on them setting so firm against me.'

''Tis aye their way wi' strangers,' she admitted. Then troubled by the regret in his voice, added, 'Never heed it, they'll come around once they get to ken ye better.'

He nodded and turned away, bestowing a tight smile on Sarah, who'd come to sit beside him in the heather. Sarah touched her drinking cup to his and leaned to whisper something into his shoulder, a gesture Morven found touchingly intimate. She turned away to find Rowena.

The widow was standing by the bothy, a heather basket filled with leaf and branch at her feet. This formed part of the rite of offering. Morven joined her, and between them they emptied the basket, strewing boughs of birch and rowan around the fireside and adorning them with sprays of ling and cowberry and the delicate leaflets of twinflower; a rarity of ancient pinewoods. Lastly, Rowena drew a hollowed stone from the basket and whispered a few words over it before placing it in readiness by the fire. 'Mebbe you could gather up the bairns,' she said, 'and then I'll make a start.'

When she returned with the troop of reluctant children, Morven was brought to an abrupt halt by the sight of her father standing over Jamie. They were talking in an earnest but grave manner, Jamie seated and looking up. Jamie's back was toward her, but she had a perfect view of her father's face. His jaw was clenched, and there was such a look of wretched resentment in his expression that her heart gave a lurch. He placed a hand on Jamie's shoulder, then with a curt word stalked away, his shoulders hunched about his ears. She shepherded the children to Rowena, then hurried to Jamie's side, dropping into the heather.

'What did my da say?' she whispered.

He looked at her in surprise. 'He thanked me.'

'Thanked ye?'

'Fer saving ye from the flames.'

Speechless, Morven sat back. Trawling the gathering with her gaze, she found her father with Donald Gordon, yet he was very much on his own. There was an air of bleakness about him, undefined yet as solid as a gable-end. He hawked and spat into the heather and Morven's insight was gone; her da looked as he always looked, surly and aloof. She turned back to ask Jamie more, but he silenced her with a swift movement of his hand; Rowena was preparing to speak.

Widowed in her thirty-seventh year, Rowena Forbes was a woman in the mid-stream of her life, yet there were few signs on her of the passing of the years, little evidence of the grief she'd borne, or the rigours of a life eked out on a parcel of impoverished upland moor. Nor had the years dulled the fairness of her face. 'Twas said by some that the bloom on her was uncanny, even devil-sent, yet to Morven, her friend shone as vital as a pearl among pebbles.

Smiling, the dark-eyed widow clapped her hands for silence. 'Come away and welcome all.' Her eyes swept above the heads of the gathering to light, for a lingering moment, on her nephew an inch or two above the rest. There was a flush on her cheeks, and beneath the white three-cornered kertch she wore, her eyes shone bright with perception.

'I dinna pretend to speak wi' our Creator,' she began. 'That's fer Father Ranald, and I'm certain he does it well. Yet I hold, as do ye all, that we give up the age-auld customs of our folk at our own loss. This land is nae ours by right of deed or paper, yet by our blood and bones, we are the nurture of it. In our names, dug on ageing chapel-stones, we're charged to hold it safe. In honour of our fathers, links, each one o' us, in a chain that winds back into the mists of auld.'

She had the attention of every man, woman, and child. Not a hair stirred. Glancing sidelong at Jamie, Morven recognised the spell upon him. Rowena had long held the power to enthral and, watching her weave her spell, Morven shivered, feeling the casting of its threads.

'Nowhere in deed or title is found our claim to these high glens,' she continued. ''Tis in the holding o' this land in our hearts that we do claim that right. In the turning o' the sod, in the ache of muscle when a long day's reap is done. And in the knowing of each rise and hollow, each tree that shapes the forests of our hame. 'Tis only then, when honour and respect are given, when the land is imprinted on our verra souls, that we may be provided fer.'

She picked up a bannock from the pile Morven had made earlier and broke it in two. 'If we keep alive the customs that served our fathers well, then they'll serve us as well.' She whispered a few words over the offering, then looked up, her eyes seeming to engage with every soul gathered. A tremor ran up Morven's spine.

'Accept thee our offering, o fox,' she said in a voice that carried clearly to all, 'and spare us our lambs.' She tossed one half of the bannock over her left shoulder and into the fire, where it sizzled and caught alight. 'Accept thee our offering, o eagle.'

At length, when she'd made offerings to each of their adversaries, including carrion crow and exciseman, which she plainly viewed in the same light, she smiled and turned to Morven. Morven handed her a staved wooden vessel filled with fresh milk, then glanced around, aware of eyes lancing into the side of her head. Sarah blinked and looked back at her mother, leaving Morven with an odd cold feeling.

'Ever we must bid *na daoine sìth* to bear us no ill,' Rowena said in a voice rich with the lilt of the Gael. 'If we live in harmony wi' the folk o' the *sìtheans*, then these hills will sustain us all.' Bending, she poured some milk into the hollowed stone. 'Accept thee our offering, guidfolk, and spare us our milch cows.' She piled more bannocks by the milky offering, careful to place them cross-side down and cause no offence. Suddenly her back stiffened, and her head came snapping up. Alarm flared in her eyes. Morven heard it too, the muffled thud of hooves ringing on the heather of the glen below.

Alec was first on his feet and darted to the rocky shelf, flinging himself down and crawling, lizard-like, to the edge. He gestured frantically for silence. The gathering sat motionless; a herd of deer in the archer's sights, breath stilled in their throats. Rowena dropped soundlessly to the ground, and Morven became aware of the crackling of the flames beside her and the tell-tale smoke that spread in a plume above her head. There came a pressure on her forearm, and she looked up into Jamie's bewildered face.

'What is it?' he mouthed.

'Excise, mebbe dragoons.'

'But what is it we've done?'

'The whisky.' She nodded at the keg still sat by the bothy door.

One of the ponies, perhaps sensitive to the tension in the air, whinnied suddenly, a great piercing gust, followed by the others in answer and a volley of what seemed like earth-shattering sounds rent the air. There came shouts from below, followed by the unmistakable sound of horses being spurred up the hill at a furious pace.

Alec came sprinting through the heather. 'The Black Gauger! Wi' two others.'

'Redcoats?' Malcolm was on his feet now amidst a sea of confusion.

'No, cottars from Balintoul.'

'Help me get the keg inside the bothy!'

Craigduthel helped Alec and her father roll the whisky inside, but there was neither time nor opportunity to hide it. Three mounted men charged their midst, scattering bairns and beasts before them. There were shrieks of terror as mothers scrambled to snatch bairns out from beneath the thunder of iron-shod hooves, while the leader, a powerfully built man with thick whiskers and clad in a black lum hat and tailed black coat shouted for them all to keep still. Morven found herself wrenched from behind, dragged backwards and thrust behind a sizeable rock.

'Forgive me.' Jamie was breathing hard beside her.

Together they craned their necks, scouring the fray for their kinfolk.

'That's McBeath,' she hissed. 'Thon strapping great bull of a man wi' the pistol.'

McBeath had drawn his mount to a halt by her father and now brandished his pistol in Malcolm's face. Malcolm stood his ground, feet planted wide in the heather, ruddy face dark with rage.

'Well, well, Delnabreck. Having a wee celebration, were ye?' The exciseman leaned from the saddle and used the barrel of his pistol, pressed beneath Malcolm's chin, to tilt the crofter's head back.

Malcolm gave no answer, but at the touch of cold metal his nostrils flared wide, and he fixed the exciseman with a murderous stare.

'These are *your* pastures, are they no?' Deliberately, the exciseman fingered the sword that lay against his left leg.

''Tis common land.'

'Used by you? To pasture *your* beasts?'

Malcolm's jaw tightened. ''Tis so.'

The gauger's grin widened but failed to reach his eyes. He swivelled his head and scanned the rag-tag gathering, then sat back and gestured to the hirelings with his pistol. 'Search the bothy.'

They leapt to it at once, dismounting and ransacking the neatly ordered hut. Within moments they rolled out the keg, and the exciseman's lips parted in triumph.

'Whatever have we here?' He slid from the saddle and picked up a discarded drinking vessel, bringing it to his nose. His grin widened. 'Unless my nose deceives me, and it rarely does, a drop illicit whisky. Seize it!' he ordered, gesturing to the keg. 'And you,' he turned back to Malcolm, making little attempt to contain his elation. 'Are under arrest.'

The reddening of her father's face was all that betrayed his fury, yet Morven felt his rage as keenly as did every man, woman, and child there gathered. 'God, Da,' she breathed. At her side, Jamie reached and gripped her shoulder.

A length of rough-twisted hemp was produced, and the sharper faced of the two hirelings advanced on her father with it.

'Let him be!' Alec leapt forward to prevent his father being taken. The hirelings were upon him in a heartbeat, cursing and grappling to pinion his arms. One of them dealt Alec a chopping blow with his pistol, catching him across the shoulders, and Malcolm bellowed his rage.

McBeath squinted scornfully at Alec. 'Well, well, if it's no the MacRae whelp. At the family business, too, eh? Take him as well.' And he jerked his head in Alec's direction.

'The keg's nae theirs,' said a gruff voice.

Morven twisted her head to see. It was Donald Gordon of Craigduthel, his aged face a little greyer than usual.

'The whusky's mine,' he said in a flat but authoritative voice. He rolled his shoulders in a dismissive shrug. 'I brocht a drap along fer the *ceilidh*. Delnabreck there doesna do the whusky any mair.'

At Malcolm's scowling look, he lapsed into Gaelic. 'Never heed, man, let the black divil think it mine, that way he'll nae touch ye. I've paid him his price, and nae doubt he'll be after more o' that.'

'Yours?' McBeath turned on Craigduthel, squinting suspiciously at the weathered face beneath the black-crusted bonnet. Belonging to the rolling green hills of the Borders, the exciseman had no knowledge of the Highland tongue and considered it primitive in the extreme. 'Is that so?' He flicked his attention back to Malcolm and lifted one brow, waiting.

'Aye,' Malcolm muttered at last. He returned the exciseman's stare. ''Tis Craigduthel's keg, nae mine.'

A nerve twitched beneath one of the gauger's eyes. There was an abnormality there – Morven remembered Rowena calling it a squint – and he blinked, breaking his stare. He shifted his gaze back to Craigduthel. 'Well, Donald.' He tossed the drinking cup aside. 'That's different. I'll no be seizing *your* keg.' He laughed lightly, although it was evident he still carried himself like a primed pistol. 'Leave things be!' And he pounded Donald soundly on the back.

'Why isn't he taking it?' said Jamie.

'Craigduthel pays him. To let his whisky through wi'out trouble.'

'A bribe, ye mean?'

'Some say fifteen shillings an anker. The Black Gauger's as rotten as a pile o' dung. Da would never pay him; he'd sooner run him through.'

Jamie made an odd sound in his throat.

Some spittle had flown from the exciseman's mouth, and he wiped it away with his sleeve. His expression had soured, and he grimaced at the white-faced folk, perhaps drawing some compensatory satisfaction from their fear. Grace was ashen-faced and held William by the hand, while wee Donald was pressed into her skirts. There was no sign of Sarah, but Morven's heart near missed a beat when she saw Rowena.

The exciseman's gaze fell on her at the same moment, and he started, staring at her. Thinking the exciseman distracted, Rowena had scrambled to the fireside and was hastily salvaging what she could of the trampled offering. McBeath mounted and nudged his horse toward her, his gaze fastened upon her face. As he drew closer, he looked down at the hollowed stone; it still held its milky offering and beside it sat the pile of offered bannocks.

'Witchery!'

Rowena straightened and regarded the black-clad figure with disdain. 'Nae witchery.' She picked up a bannock, turning it over to reveal the cross marked plainly on one side. 'We're all Christians here.'

'Papists,' he sneered, glaring around the gathering. 'I see what's astir here.' His eyes flicked back to Rowena, and he shifted his mount a little closer, his nostrils widening as though he meant to breathe her in. 'Ungodly work. Blasphemy. False idols.'

Rowena looked up with raised brows. 'Ye see all that, do ye?' She looked directly into his eyes, one of which roved wildly. 'Then mebbe ye need to tame that unfettered eye.'

With a hiss, he drew his sword. The blade whirred in the air; before Rowena could blink, its point was pressed against her throat. Jamie started forward, and Morven gripped his shoulder.

'He'll nae harm her,' she said quickly. 'Nae wi' all these watching.'

Rowena's face was calm, her dark eyes inscrutable, and against the girth of the exciseman's sword, her neck appeared as slim and graceful as a swan. With admirable dispassion, she raised her hand and gripped the cold steel of the blade, then pushed it deliberately away.

'We honour the land of our fathers,' she stated. 'In the same manner our fathers did, and their fathers afore them.' Turning her back on the mounted figure, she continued to replace her birch and rowan boughs.

'I'll lay odds McGillivray knows naught of this,' snapped McBeath. 'I believe,' he narrowed his eyes and spoke to the back of her head, ''tis time I acquainted the factor with the heathen goings-on here.' He said no more but left Rowena to imagine the rest. Flicking the reins, he turned his mount's head and with a creak of leather was gone, leaving his hirelings to scramble after him.

'Are ye harmed, aunt?' Jamie's voice was hoarse with shock.

'I'm fine.' She brushed his concern away with an airy smile.

Jamie stared after the men, little more than dark blemishes now against the tapestry of the land. 'So, that … I can scarce call him a man, that wretch is the one ye call the Black Gauger? 'Tis he should be in fear o' the law fer drawing his sword against an unarmed woman.'

'Aye,' said Alec. 'But that'll never happen.'

Morven shivered, chilled by the malice of the man, and searched for her father. He was sitting atop the offending whisky keg, his livid colour receding, and was pumping Donald Gordon by the hand.

'But fer you, Craigduthel,' he told the old crofter. 'I'd be on my way to the gaol. Ye'll take a dram with me? Alec! Whisky fer oor friend here!'

Grace sobbed softly to herself, and her eyes followed Malcolm as a puppy would its master. Yet Morven knew she'd make no show of him in front of their neighbours.

With the tension gone, the hill-folk soon rallied themselves and, aware they could now make merry without fear, set to the festivities with fresh vigour. Morven found a cup pushed into her hands.

''Twill steady yer nerves,' Jamie told her. And she found, sipping at the liquor, that it kindled a soft glow inside her.

Alec inflated his pipes, and, winking at Hal McHardy, struck up a lively tune. As if waking from a dream, folk tapped their feet in time while others rose to dance. Hal, shaking his head in feigned reluctance, joined them on his fiddle and in no time the gathering rollicked to the foot-stamping sound of reel and jig.

'Would ye … wish to dance with me, d'ye think?' Jamie was at her shoulder.

She smiled reluctantly, but before she could say aye or nae, he'd pulled her up and, throwing her a reckless grin, was burling her through the heather at an enthusiastic pace. For all his size, he was an accomplished dancer, surprisingly lithe and highly attentive to her. She sensed every eye upon them and felt herself flush. It was more than curiosity that drew so many stares. His sheer presence was hard to ignore. Yet glancing around, it seemed every head was bent to its neighbour, every gaze furtively focused on them. The heat of his hands on her waist seemed to radiate to her cheeks. 'Twas uncomfortably hot. A disturbing memory of leaping flames returned, and she pushed him sharply away.

'Are ye alright?' He tried to take up her hands again to recommence the dance, but she clasped them behind her back.

'I'm … a little hot.'

He faltered, his gaze searching, full of self-reproach. 'Forgive me. I should've been more careful of ye. Would water help?'

She nodded, looking around for Rowena, or her mother, or any reasonable means of escape. She'd no wish to insult Jamie, but the whispering was an embarrassment. It brought back memories she'd dearly like to forget. Glen tongues did love to wag, but that they now wagged about Jamie and her was clear. And beyond humiliating.

When he returned with the water, she feigned exhaustion and begged him dance with someone else that she might recover. A flicker of regret crossed his face, and she felt a pang of contrition, only a pang though; the urge to distance herself from him was overwhelming. Yet it did seem a betrayal too. She was beholden to him, though that knowledge was far from welcome.

She sat down with her mother to watch the others revel. The release of tension acted as a tonic to the humble crofting folk, and they stamped and clapped and kidded up their heels.

'Did ye not enjoy yer dance wi' Jamie?' her mother asked.

'Aye, I liked it fine. Only,' she frowned, 'I wasna so keen on the onlookers.'

Grace looked a little mystified, and Morven sought to distract her, pointing out the swarm of young admirers jostling to partner Sarah. Even as a wee bairn, Sarah had shown a blustering confidence that far outstripped her humble roots. Yet, looking at her now, pale hair flying loose about her waist, it was clear she'd grown in loveliness and audacity both, and used them now in equal measure.

At length, they stopped to feast on roast grouse, hare, and trout wrapped whole in dock leaves. Ale flowed freely, food abundant too, and the chafe of hunger was stilled for a while. When the last bone had been picked clean, Alec lifted his pipes and began a pibroch, the classical pipe music of the Highlands. With skill, he pulled together the recurring threads of the melody, playing with his heart, the emotion of the music reflected in his face. The gathering was stirred and roused, then moved to melancholy. Watching Jamie's face, Morven saw his breathing quicken, swept along by the intensity of her brother's playing.

As the drone of pipes faded plaintively away, folk stamped their feet for more. Alec beckoned to her and, knowing what was to come, she rose eagerly to join him. Her voice was strong, with the lyrical cadence of the Gael, and singing with Alec was always a tonic. When she sat down, she felt Jamie's gaze upon her again and despite herself, her own, too, was drawn inexorably to him. She could not have explained the feeling his expression, full of his emotions, raised in her, for she didn't understand it herself.

At the urging of the crowd, all much flushed with whisky, Alec reverted to reels and jigs, and she felt a pressure on her elbow. 'Would ye do me the honour again?'

Regretfully, she shook her head.

Hard pressed to resist it, Alec handed his pipes to Craigduthel, who could squeeze out a tolerable tune, and seizing Sarah by the hand danced her round and round the bothy. She grasped him about the waist and in a lusty press of kilts and skirts rode out the tune amid ribald whistles and shouts. At last, flushed crimson and abashed, Alec let her go and returned, reluctantly, to his piping while she swept him a mocking bow.

By the time the shadows had lengthened on the hill, and the sun dipped below the Cromdales, folk had settled themselves into wee groups. Rowena sat with the MacRaes and gently pressed Morven's arm.

'I've something I would ask ye,' she said.

'What's that?'

''Tis a lot to ask.' She took a long breath. 'I'd not ask it if there was another way.'

'What is it?'

'Will ye teach Jamie the whisky-making? Take him to yer bothy and let him watch how 'tis done?' Rowena swallowed at the enormity of what she asked. By necessity, the still was hidden away in the hills; a place known of by only a trusted few.

Morven drew a startled breath, glancing instinctively at her father. ''Tisna fer me to say.' Though she generally worked the pot-still through the sowing and reaping months, 'twas her father laid down the law in the matter of whisky.

Rowena nodded, turning dubiously to Malcolm. 'I ken ye'll nae wish to take the risk Malcolm, and I canna blame ye fer that, 'tis a great thing I ask. I'd not ask it if Duncan were here, but with our own pot-still discovered. Destroyed,' she corrected. 'I canna think what else to do.'

Jamie squeezed her shoulder. 'I wish to help my kinswoman manage the croft,' he told an incredulous Malcolm. 'But she tells me it's whisky-making that pays the rental, nae cattle, and I ken little of the distiller's art.'

'Aye, that I can believe.'

'Only, if we'd whisky to sell,' Rowena pressed him. 'There'd nae be the same danger of being put out by McGillivray, whether the man cares fer me or not.'

'Are things so bad, then?' Grace put in.

'I canna see how I'm to find the rental come Martinmas, already I'm behind. 'Tis my beasts will go to his Grace this time, and without them I'm finished.' She turned back to Malcolm, snaring him with her eyes. 'The lad knows well the need fer secrecy, should ye give it, ye have my word he'll not betray yer trust. And … and once he's familiar wi' the way 'tis done, he'll set up his own bothy.' She looked a little darkly at his louring face. 'Will ye help us?'

Malcolm made a strangled sound and turned away, fixing the hills of Cromdale with his stare.

'Sir?' Jamie prompted.

Her da had always hated being put upon, yet Morven sensed he'd once have agreed to this readily enough, and with a deal more grace. 'Da!' she pleaded.

He turned back to Jamie and nodded once to him. 'Ye may watch the lass and learn. And I'll thank ye to repeat my business to no man!'

'I'm indebted to you, sir.' Jamie moved to clasp the crofter's hand, but Malcolm was already on his feet and hoisting the keg atop his shoulder.

'No more than I am to you,' he muttered, and stalked off across the heather.

'Bless ye,' Rowena whispered after him. Her eyes were guarded and watchful.

Jamie quirked a smile at Morven, perhaps embarrassed he'd made no mention of this earlier in the day.

'What are ye all gawping at each other fer?' demanded Sarah, appearing suddenly at Jamie's shoulder. She looked hot and rattled and tugged on his arm. 'Have ye an aversion to dancing wi' yer own cousin, then?' she blurted.

'No, no. Not at all!' And with a startled smile, he allowed her to lead him away.

CHAPTER FIVE

SINCE CHILDHOOD, MORVEN had heard tales of whisky-making in the high glens. *Uisge-beatha*, the water of life, had been distilled in Strathavon since the days when Saint Columba first trod the Highland passes, bringing with him the word of God. Some claimed the tradition was older still. Yet Parliament and King George cared little for Highland traditions. The Highlands stood for rebellion, a proud outlandish race holding British rule in contempt. In the years since the last Jacobite rising, government reprisals had been many and harsh. Lands were forfeit, clan chiefs were turned into landlords, and a wave of enforced evictions spread throughout the Highlands. Even the Gaelic language and the playing of the pipes had been proscribed.

For the crofters of Strathavon, it was the aggressive taxing of their whisky, the currency of the glen, that bit the hardest. Highland whisky was more than fierce liquor, it embodied the battered pride of their race, and they were damned if they'd pay the Crown for the privilege of distilling it. And as southern palates had now acquired a taste for the fiery liquor, the glenfolk were more than eager to provide it.

For long now, the smugglers of the glen had bought their barley from McGillivray, though the practice rankled bitterly with every one of them. His prices were high, twice those charged in the market town of Elgin, though his grain was no better and made no finer whisky. But there were reasons enough. Those that bought from McGillivray enjoyed his protection to a degree. They were still forced to carry on their illicit trade in secret, and just as many had their whisky seized, but when they landed up before him, and invariably they did, William McGillivray the magistrate doled out fines of merciful leniency. To those, that is, that sourced their barley wisely. The fact that such a system served to perpetuate the scourge of whisky smuggling, as well as fatten McGillivray's pocket, went wholly unremarked by the authorities of the land.

In Strathavon, the crofters marked it well. They cursed his thieving ways and grumbled over his prices, yet still, they paid. Even Malcolm MacRae, sour and crabbit though folk said he was, coughed up for malt that granted him a measure of protection from the gaol. Yet as Morven trudged the rutted cart track through the Shenval Pass to Lochy Mill that forenoon, Rowena revealed her young kinsman would sooner buy in Elgin.

'Elgin?' Morven's eyes widened. ''Tis a three-day ride!'

Grimly, the widow nodded.

'But … did ye nae press on him the risks of that? If he's caught and comes up afore McGillivray…' There was little need to say more, both women were aware of the route the factor's wrath could take.

'He's a man o' principles, though,' sighed Rowena. 'Like his father.' She sat down on the heather bank at the side of the track and massaged her brow. 'I urged the lad to buy from McGillivray, but he wished no truck with the man. Called him a contemptible rogue and a bigot. Said he'd heard all about the factor, how the man believes me a priestess o' the black arts. He'd no wish to waste what little money his father left him in fattening the pocket of such a man.'

Morven paled, she'd not meant him to act so rashly. 'I meant only to warn him,' she said. 'Nae to get on the wrong side o' the factor.'

Rowena smiled a little crookedly. 'The lad's a keen sense o' justice, ye see. His da was the same. Jamie thought it a dishonour to his father to throw away the wee bit siller his da left him on the likes of McGillivray.'

'I can see that, but still –'

'I know.' Rowena rose and, hooking her basket over her left arm, offered Morven her right. 'We must pray the malt makes fine whisky, is what we must do. And above all, pray the lad's nae caught.' Tightening her grip on Morven's arm, she set them on the track again, both women sunk in their thoughts. 'He's had tragedy enough,' she said softly.

The lonely hills seemed to frown down on Morven, their brows stern and accusing. A bitter wind buffeted her ears, and she hunched herself against it. At last, as they broke from the high pass, the MacPherson's mill on the Lochy Burn came in sight where their patient awaited them.

'Rowena!' Morven clutched at her companion's arm. The conical Hill of Achmore was visible in the distance, a pall of black smoke wrapped like a winding sheet about its summit.

'The Balintoul signal.' Rowena's breath whistled in her throat as she thought hard. 'We'd best keep on and warn them at the mill.

Likely Alastair has barley he's malting and the gaugers'll be upon him afore he kens what's what.'

Morven blinked the wind-pricked tears from her eyes. Sympathisers in Balintoul had raised the hilltop fires in warning of an imminent raid by excisemen. Gathering up her skirts, she hurried after Rowena.

The buildings of the mill, low turf-thatched steadings, enclosed a dirt yard where flecks of grain and chaff swirled. The largest building, with its mill wheel, housed the grinding stone while the smallest, with its reeking chimney, was home to the MacPhersons and their sons. Alastair MacPherson was clearing weed from the millrace and seemed relieved to see them. He threw down his rake and beat vigorously at his breeks, raising a cloud of dust.

'There was nae need fer such haste,' he observed, noting their breathless and dishevelled state. 'Elspeth's abed, but nae rappin' upon the Pearly Gates just yet, I'm thinking.'

Rowena cut through the proprieties. 'Ye'll have malt here, Alastair?'

'I … er …' He blinked at her. 'I wouldna like to say.'

'It's nae my business if ye have,' she assured him. 'But the warning fires are blazing atop Achmore, and I'm thinking the gaugers'll make the mill their first call.'

The miller spun on his heels and sprinted to the kiln. 'Ye saw the signal yerself?' he shouted over his shoulder.

'Wi' our own eyes. Is there aught we can do to help?'

He stopped for a moment, the muscles of his face working. 'My lads are out at the sowing.' He shook his head. 'I'll have to manage wi'out them. If I bag the malt, will ye help me hide it?'

Morven nodded. 'Only make haste!'

Above the kiln, the drying floor was spread thickly with swollen grains, their thread-like shoots beginning to wither in the warmth from a peat fire. The musty aroma of malt was potent and overwhelming; any excise officer would recognise it instantly. They grabbed shovels and brooms and began scooping it into sacks.

It was sweltering work. Within moments, Morven was flushed and sweating, the muscles of her arms beginning to burn and dust catching at the back of her throat. Alastair thrust his head out of the tiny loft window, then hastily drew it in again and redoubled his efforts. No-one spoke. The rattle of rough-drawn breath was the only sound above the rhythmic *shoomf* of the shovels.

At last, grim-faced, Alastair tied the last sack.

'Where can we hide it?' Morven wheezed.

'I canna think.' The miller peered out of the window again. 'Once they get a whiff o' this, they'll turn the whole place ower.'

Panting, Rowena leant on her shovel. 'Elspeth's abed, did ye say?' She wiped the sweat from her brow with a corner of her plaid. 'I might just ken a place, but first I must speak with her.' She hurried away, leaving Morven and the miller to heave the heavy malt sacks onto the man's handcart.

When Rowena returned, her face was set in a calm but determined expression. 'If it's McBeath that comes,' she told them, 'we might be in luck.'

'The Black Gauger! Where's the luck in that?'

Rowena nodded darkly at the miller. 'I've no great love fer the man either.'

'No, I ken ye've not.'

'Only, we both know how eager he is to sniff out whisky and the malt of its making, yet I doubt he'd be willing to risk his own neck to secure it.'

'How'd ye mean?'

'Wait an' see,' she said with a tight smile. 'Stow the malt under Elspeth's bed and leave the rest to me.'

Alastair gawped at her. '*Under her bed?*'

'Ye'll be thinking it madness, but if ye'll but trust me.'

He made an odd sound and turned to Morven.

Morven had no notion what Rowena planned to do but instinctively recognised the miller must do as she directed. 'Rowena would never harm Elspeth,' she assured him.

'I ken, but –'

'Then, please. Do as she bids.'

Barely had the last sack been concealed when Morven heard the ring of hooves on the packed earth of the yard. She ran to the door. There were two gaugers; she recognised McBeath at once, and his companion was the duller faced of his two hirelings. They were accompanied by a patrol of six Black Watch dragoons, resplendent in Government Tartan, crimson coats, and wide shoulder belts. Each was armed with musket and sword.

'No-one move!' bellowed McBeath. The slight hint of a smirk lingering at the corners of his mouth betrayed how much he relished the task set him, not to mention the importance he believed it ascribed him. Company horses shied nervously, snorting and prancing in the cramped yard. 'Search the mill and kiln. Look in every byre and festering hovel.' He turned a mite scornfully on the patrol officer. 'You do know what it is you're looking for?'

The officer gave him a withering look and gestured for his men to dismount and begin their search. Shifting the reins, he turned his horse's head and brought his mount alongside the exciseman's beast. The words of their exchange did not reach Morven, although the tone was plain enough – toes had been stepped on. Snorting, McBeath slid from the saddle and advanced on the kiln-house. Alastair loitered in the doorway.

'A guid morning to ye, gentlemen,' Alastair offered. He shot Morven a look, then reading her frantic eye signal, snatched his bonnet from his head. 'Can I be helping ye wi' anything?'

'I doubt it.' McBeath shoved him roughly out of his way.

The patrol officer seemed a deal more civil. Tucking his feathered hat under one arm, he nudged his mount forward and nodded deferentially to Alastair. 'Sergeant John Shiach of the 7th Black Watch.' He settled his hat on his crown again. 'Pray pardon the intrusion. There's no need to be alarmed, sir. If you could but tell me how many people you have here?'

The miller twisted his bonnet. 'Just myself, my wife, and two women friends who're tending her. She's sickly.'

'My sympathies. You don't, then, keep malt here for the illegal distillation of alcohol?'

'Lord, no!' A further indignant denial was forming on Alastair's lips when McBeath burst from the kiln-house behind him.

'There's malt here! I can smell it as plain as day. Doubtless, they were kilning it as we arrived. I want it found.' He glared at the sergeant, who stoically returned the look. 'Well, get to it, man! If need be, I'll have the place turned inside out!'

Morven's heart was hammering in her throat, but she maintained as calm an exterior as she could feign, standing guard beneath the lintel of the MacPhersons' home. Advancing on her, the gauger's eyes narrowed in distrust. 'Out of the way!' he snapped, shoving her roughly aside. Then, squinting, he turned back to look her up and down. 'I've seen you before.' His eyes raked her face. 'You don't belong at the mill.'

A flush burned at her throat, and under his scrutiny, she felt it move upward drying her tongue. 'I –'

'You forget yourself, Mr McBeath,' cut in the sergeant. 'My men are just that – *my men*. Here to assist in the arrest and detainment of lawbreakers. I see no such felons here. Any searching for contraband, any turning inside out, I believe is entirely *your* concern.' Regimental hooves clipped soundly on the pressed earth of the yard. Alongside them now, the sergeant nodded once to Morven, then cocked his head at the exciseman, brows raised in irritation.

'You're refusing me the service of your men?' McBeath exclaimed in disbelief.

'Not at all.' The officer's expression tightened, endeavouring to maintain a reasonable manner despite the trials of the situation; his men had just emerged from the mill, their splendid uniforms covered in a fine dusting of flour. 'Should you find any desperate criminals,' he assured McBeath, 'my men are at your disposal.' Ordering his men to follow suit, he spurred his horse to the rough dyke at the entrance to the yard and waited there while the detachment filed through. They regrouped in the heather around their superior to await further orders.

McBeath drew breath viciously up his nose. 'Pompous arse!' He kicked the door wide and stalked into the cottage, his assistant scuttling after him.

Morven threw Alastair a desperate look. Had they given Rowena enough time? Shaking his head, the miller followed her inside.

Rowena was working quietly at the hearth, her plaid wrapped like a mask over her mouth and nose. She looked up at the intrusion and raised her brows at the two men. Wrong-footed by her presence, McBeath stumbled over a three-legged stool, cursing it to damnation. He recovered quickly and turned on the miller.

'Well, well, Alastair, taken yourself a new wife, have ye? Or is it the bonny witch has turned to whoring now to meet her rental?'

Alastair reddened at the insinuation. 'Elspeth's poorly. The widow Forbes is here to tend her. Her and the lass.'

McBeath's eyes flicked to Morven, fixing her with a sceptical look. 'Are they now? Poorly, eh?' He turned back to Rowena, his gaze drawn greedily to her face, a hard glitter in his eyes.

'Elspeth has smallpox,' Rowena informed him. She directed her gaze to the door on the far wall behind which lay Elspeth's sickbed. The plaid had deadened her voice but did nothing to lessen the impact of her words.

'Smallpox!' The hireling backed to the door. 'Saints preserve us!'

'I'll do what I can fer her,' she continued. 'But I fear she's in God's hands.' Turning back to her preparations, she asked Morven to pass her a root from her basket.

''Tis a trick, Dougal. Can ye no see that?' McBeath threw his assistant a scornful look. 'Granted the widow Forbes is here, but d'ye no think we'd have heard if there was smallpox in the glen?'

'I dinna ken,' Dougal muttered.

McBeath's interest was drawn back to Rowena, and he took a step closer, his nostrils flaring as he breathed her in, a wolfish grin turning the corners of his mouth. She had pared the root Morven passed to her, revealing a grainy white substance, and now dropped it into the bubbling pot.

"Tis barely a half-hour since we got here,' she said wearily. 'And I'd nae even broken the news to Alastair, though he may be infected too. I suggest ye leave now afore it's too late.' She looked up slowly, the threat riding the air between them.

McBeath flicked his tongue out, assessing, his eyes still fastened on her face. 'Ye'll no mind if we take a wee lookie round first though, eh? After all, 'tis our own health we'll be risking.' His grin lingered, and he gestured with his head for Dougal to tackle the other room.

Dougal's eyes widened. 'I dinna ken,' he mumbled.

'Come, man!'

The hireling was trembling and glanced at each of them in turn, perhaps hoping a means of escape would materialize. Wiping his hands down the sides of his breeks, he edged forward, pushing the door with the toe of his boot. It swung open a foot or two. He took a quick breath, jerked his head through and then recoiled violently. 'Sweet Jesus!' The chairs at the heavy oak table clattered to the floor as he scrambled to make his escape.

The exciseman stared after him. Twitching in exasperation, he stalked to the door and threw it wide. It crashed against the wall and rebounded, almost closing again, but not before they all glimpsed Elspeth's face livid against the white linen pillow. It oozed with purple encrusted pustules.

'Dear Lord!' Alastair swayed on his feet.

Watching him, Morven felt a stab of conscience. The miller's dismay was plainly genuine and was all the more touching for being so. She glanced into the pot hanging over the fire. Not all the ingredients in the brew were known to her, although she recognised blaeberries by their vibrant colour. Elspeth's pustules, she surmised, oozing in a thin oat gruel. She caught Rowena's eye. Something flickered there, a wry acknowledgement perhaps, or maybe a warning. She glanced away.

McBeath seemed rooted to the spot. His face had turned a nasty grey, his grin now stretched to an indeterminate line, and a tick appeared under one eye.

Alastair pushed past the gauger, his bonnet wrung tight in his hand. 'Elspeth, my love.' He lapsed into Gaelic, the only language through which he could adequately express himself, and Rowena spoke softly to him in the same tongue. He turned and stared at her.

Morven's gaze was drawn to the strange drape that hung around the base of the bed and the peculiar sack-like lumps that bulged from it. She prayed the exciseman's gaze would not be similarly drawn. But there was no danger of that; he hurtled from the room, bellowing for his mount.

From the comparative safety of the saddle, he shouted to Rowena. 'If this be sorcery, witch-woman, ye'll reap a whirlwind!' He shuddered and spat some noxious substance onto the ground. His horse reared, knocking him back in the saddle, then careered from the yard scattering the patrol of dragoons with the exciseman clinging on at a drunken angle.

**

Alastair reached out tentatively and brought his thumb across his wife's cheek. A pustule smeared wetly and came away squashed onto his thumb. He gasped and looked over at Rowena.

'A deception!' He examined the pustule more closely. 'I thought it might be devilry, but 'tis nothing o' the kind.' He shook his head. 'A mere trick!'

Elspeth chuckled delightedly. 'And worked like a charm.' She sat up and twisted about. 'Ye ken, I believe I'm feeling better.'

Rowena nodded and began packing her things.

'Bless ye,' said Alastair, and reached to grip her hand.

CHAPTER SIX

'DOWN THERE?' JAMIE looked incredulous. 'There's never a whisky still down there! I see nothing but rocks and water.'

'Ye're nae meant to see it.' Morven was forced to raise her voice above the thunder of falling water, yet there was laughter in it. 'That's the idea. 'Tis hidden. Disguised.'

He peered down at the chasm cut by the Lochy Burn. Water hurtled through a series of spouts and falls before crashing in an ear-splitting din on the rocky ledges below. From the top where they stood, an icy mist rose and beaded in his hair. 'Are ye certain this is the place?'

'I'm certain.' Had she nae made the climb a hundred times or more? 'Twas easier than it looked. 'See that bank to yer left?' She pointed with her head. 'The one that rises in a wee ridge wi' bracken sprouting from it?'

He craned forward. 'I see it, aye.'

'That's the roof o' the bothy. The entrance faces the falls and a cave burrows into the hillside there. Perfect, aye?'

'Perfect,' he reluctantly agreed. 'But a treacherous climb fer a slight young lass like yerself. Is there nae a way up from below?'

At thirteen, she'd distilled her first dram in that very cave, though he wasn't to know it. 'Aye,' she said a mite stiffly. 'There's a way. But it's nae any easier and means making a two-mile circuit down the hill wi' the malt. I can manage the climb just fine, though.'

By the time they reached the bothy, she could tell by the glint of amused respect in his eyes that he understood her to be no faintheart. Several times, he attempted to help her down over sharp overhangs and slippery moss-slimed ledges, but each time she firmly rejected his help. She could manage the dripping walls blindfolded, in truth, revelled in the rare lushness of the gorge. Ferns and liverworts sprouted from every crevice and clinging to the steep banks gnarled rowan and alder bent their branches to the spray.

Only once did he succeed in helping her. She hitched up her

gown, tucked it into her arisaid, and prepared to leap the last few feet. A look of alarm flitted across his face, and instinctively he raised his arms to catch her. Unable to deflect her plunge, she leapt straight into them. Clasped tight in his hold, the thunder of falling water seemed to fade away, and something passed between them. They both felt it, for he didn't chide her for her rashness but released her directly and waited while she untied the sack of malt and hurled the rope up into an overhanging tree. 'I didna hurt ye?' he asked.

She shook her head, mightily embarrassed, and eyed him warily. A flicker of confusion crossed his face. Still keeping him in sight, she straightened her gown, attempting to smooth her ruffled dignity. He was here to help Rowena, and nothing mattered more than that. Spreading her hands wide, she croaked, 'This is our bothy.'

It was cool and dark inside and surprisingly dry. Puzzled, Jamie looked up to examine the roof. Plainly man-made, the branches of still-growing trees had been bent over and laced together, then covered with a layer of turf. In the wet conditions, bracken had taken root and now sprouted quite naturally from the roof. A perfectly ingenious camouflage. He looked at her in astonishment, and she nodded, pleased at his approval.

'Everything's stored in the cave,' she told him. 'I'll light a fire, and then ye'll be able to see better.'

Using the tinderbox and kindling her father stored in the cave, she raised a fire inside a hollowed cairn built for the purpose. Intrigued, Jamie stepped out onto the rocky ledge to watch the smoke blend imperceptibly with the spray from the falls. He shook his head. 'Ye've thought of everything.'

'I do believe so, though it wasna my doing, da fashioned this place fer the whisky-making when I was a nipper. It's never been discovered, but we're mindful of coming and going here, nae to bring notice to the place, if ye take my meaning.'

'I do.'

Inside the cave, she showed him the cauldron used for the mashing process, the fermentation cask and the tin still with its head and strangely coiled copper worm. An assortment of earthenware jars was piled in readiness and smelled strongly of whisky. As their eyes became accustomed to the dimness, she noticed Jamie's shone and he examined everything minutely, eager to get started. Together they carried the heavy cauldron through from the cave. Jamie's gaze fell on a pile of heather and blankets in a dark corner. 'Ye dinna sleep here?'

'Ye might if the distilling's at a critical stage and canna be left, but

I've never slept here.'

He appeared relieved to hear it.

They lifted the cauldron onto the fire, setting it atop the cairn made to hold it. There was an opening near the base of the vessel; Morven plugged it with heather and then sealed it with caulking. Building up the blaze beneath it with dry peats, they filled the cauldron with water, then sat back on piles of empty sacks to wait for the water to boil. While they waited, Morven opened the sack of malt and examined it. 'Twas fine malt; plump grains of barley soaked and allowed to germinate, then withered over a peat fire. She slanted a look at him, then slid the malt back into the sack.

'Is something wrong?'

'Nae wi' the malt, no.'

'What then?'

She sighed; was her unease so plainly marked? 'Ye shouldna have gone to Elgin fer it,' she said bluntly. ''Twas too risky. Ye should've bought it from McGillivray like the rest o' us.'

'Aye, Rowena warned me. It's just we have so little. I'd no wish to waste what we have on that grasping cheat. Nae when there's a chance to break free of him.'

'We'd all like to break free of him.' An image of McGillivray's arrogant face with its fleshy dewlaps forced its way into her head. 'But the risks are too great.'

He studied her curiously. 'Does my safety trouble you so much, then?'

'Nae just yours. Only, I hope it wasna *my* words made ye do it.'

'I see.' He let his gaze drop with a hint of disappointment. ''Twas a matter of honour to me. And self-respect.'

'Honour's an indulgence ye can scarce afford,' she pointed out. 'The risks are many, and you've others now to think on.'

He said nothing but stared into the cauldron, watching tiny bubbles begin to pearl on its side. His jaw tightened a fraction.

'It wasna my intention to judge ye.'

He looked up, and his eyes were hard and dark now with what she took for anger. 'My kin are all that's left me. Each one is dearer than my own life. I'd not put them at risk on an indulgence.'

'No, I see that.' He meant it, she could see it in his eyes; they changed, glittered like scales of mica. Not for the first time, she sensed 'twas a bold man would cross him.

Dropping his gaze back to the steaming cauldron between them, he made a little dismissive gesture with his head, endeavouring to soften the hard lines of his mouth.

'Forgive me,' she murmured. 'I see now ye love Rowena as much as I do.' A strange sensation arose in her belly at that knowledge; it made her feel light, like thistledown. 'You'd never knowingly endanger yer kinfolk.'

'I've seen what it is to be evicted. The loss of our home left my father bereft … shamed. He was only half a man after losing Druimbeag.'

The water was boiling now, she emptied the malt into it, then bent to stir it with a wooden spurtle. 'This needs to mash in the hot water now. Here, ye can stir it.' The steam had brought a flush to her cheeks that she was thankful for; it helped conceal the swell of emotion that rose in her heart at his words. Even now, she couldn't be sure he fully understood how malleable was McGillivray; as soft as clay in the hands of the exciseman. But his heart was true. Nothing ill would happen to Rowena, nae with such a kinsman by her side.

'Ye were lucky, though.' She did love to have the last word. 'Ye mightna be again.'

He seemed to accept what she said and sat back thoughtfully on the empty sacks. 'Ye're right, 'twas foolish. Perhaps I wished to prove a point.' He smiled, a little shamefaced. 'And I *was* lucky, for had I met gaugers, doubtless they'd have paid me a deal more heed than the redcoats did.'

'Ye came on redcoats, then? On the road from Elgin?'

He nodded. 'I travelled at night wi' the ponies, tried to keep out o' sight during the day.' He stirred the mash absently. 'I could hear them coming from way off; the thud of iron-shod hooves, the jingle o' fancy horse fittings, and as they neared, the clip of English tongues. I hid the malt in a clump of broom and made out I was that drunk, I'd passed out. They took a kick at me, tried to find out who I was, but when I did nothing but mutter and snore they rode away.'

'Christ, Jamie!'

He quirked her a lopsided grin, running his hands through his hair, pushing the damp locks back from his brow and fixed her with a steady, slightly remorseful look. 'If I've alarmed ye with my actions, I –'

'No matter. Had it been the Black Gauger, I doubt ye'd have been so lucky.'

'Then I pray I prove a more able smuggler than a judge of circumstance.'

She chuckled. 'Ye'll do just fine.'

Then, feeling she'd perhaps over chastened him, she added, 'I've never fathomed why we're bound by law to pay duty to the Crown on our own whisky. We make it ourselves from our own barley. 'Tis no different to making porridge from our oats. Even supposing we were able to pay, seems like brazen thievery to me.'

He looked directly at her, a light of affinity glowing in his eyes, eyes that didn't seem so dark now, then puffed his cheeks out with a lightning smile. 'I suppose, 'tis but another way fer southern rule to impose and interfere.'

She laughed, then confided, 'To outfox the gaugers, Jamie, ye must be wily. 'Tis worth the trouble though, fer in the ale-houses of Perth and Edinburgh they do pay a king's ransom fer Highland whisky, and ours, from the glen of the *A'an*, is most particularly sought.'

'Then I relish the opportunity to supply it.' After a moment, he canted his head at her. 'Why does he dislike my aunt so? McBeath, the Black Gauger?'

The question unsettled her. Rowena had never spoken of it, and she wondered if 'twas right for her to do so. She knew not the full details, but enough, she supposed, to satisfy Jamie's need to know more.

'I dinna ken the full story,' she confessed. 'But I'll tell ye what I do know.'

He sat forward, hands clasped beneath his chin, and stared into the cauldron. An air of stillness descended on him.

She drew a deep breath and cast her memory back to the tales her mother told of the glen before McBeath came and the changes he brought.

'He first came to Balintoul as a young man, afore I was born. The man he replaced was fair-minded, local to the glens. He knew Highland folk had been distilling whisky in these hills since long syne. Those caught could expect a hefty fine or gaol, their whisky seized, and their still-equipment destroyed. But he always allowed a decent time to pass afore he raided the same folk again, so they could make up their losses. That way each managed to scrape a fair living.'

She looked over at Jamie; the set of his shoulders revealed he was listening intently. 'Folk soon noticed McBeath was different – lazy and paid no heed to traditions. Instead of handing folk ower fer punishment, he demanded money. Wished an arrangement, a payment fer each anker he allowed through.'

'He was idle and thought to profit from being so?'

'And from the poverty and pride that keeps the smuggling alive.'

'There could be no complaining to the factor, I suppose?'

'Some tried, but McGillivray wished no involvement wi' the

whisky trade, no knowledge o' what's done with his barley once it leaves his barns. He's long been on familiar terms wi' McBeath and will hear nothing ill of him.' She sighed. 'Even now he still holds the man above reproach, is happy to let him court favour and send him word of the goings-on in the glen.'

'But if folk had all stood-fast against him? Refused to pay?'

'It mighta worked, I suppose. I think some thought it a fair-enough arrangement though, and went along.' She paused, choosing her words carefully. 'Your folk didna, though. And neither did mine.'

'And this is from where his dislike stems?'

'No, 'tis something deeper. He'd been here near a year when he waylaid yer granda and yer da on their way to the coast wi' a sizable consignment. He demanded passage money, but yer granda refused. What money he had was needed fer paying rent and feeding his family. Only, McBeath was fair taken wi' Rowena — even now I believe she's a great beauty — and said he'd not be bothering the Innes smugglers again if he could only have her fer his wife.'

Jamie's head snapped up. 'The gall of the man!'

'Yer da was enraged. The notion of selling his sister fer the right to smuggle unhindered, and to a gauger no less, fair raised his blood. He drew his dirk, demanded satisfaction fer the slight on his family. But yer granda was a canny man and said Rowena was free to choose her own match, only he'd be needing to ask her himself.'

'Did he truly believe she'd accept him? A young beauty bartered like a pouch o' snuff!'

''Tis my belief even now he considers himself a princely catch,' she said dryly.

'So, when Rowena turned him down —'

'He wasna best pleased.'

Jamie sat back, searching, she sensed, for some way to convey his disgust without scandalising her.

'When she married Duncan, he was enraged. Couldna conceive why she'd choose a common cottar when she could have a respectable officer o' the Crown. But they were devoted, as ye ken, and this riled him still further.'

'So, he's a spurned man, eaten wi' resentment?'

'I dinna pretend to understand the man, but 'tis my belief he still cradles this injury. Has nurtured it ower the years. 'Tis possible he loved Rowena once, or at least the notion of her as his wife, who can say, but what regard he once had has soured. 'Tis now a poison that eats away at him, fer he still wants her, I believe. But fears her too.'

'Fears her? He calls her a witch. A harsh word — a dangerous word – for a woman who merely followed her heart.'

Morven gave a little nod. 'Only he calls her a witch ower the bairns he's lost. He believes she's cursed him to die childless.'

'He actually believes she'd do such a thing, even supposing 'twere possible?'

She exhaled scornfully. 'He doesna understand Rowena, is all I can say. Though … since Duncan, I believe she struggles wi' herself a deal more, nae to blame the man, nae to hate, fer hatred has never been a part of her.'

'No, I see that. 'Tis plain his claims are born of wounded pride. Held wi'out a thread of truth!' He rose to his feet and cracked his head on a branch of the roof.

'Plain to us.' She curbed a smile at his fierce loyalty. 'But nae to all who listen to his ravings. If ye've finished braining yerself,' she added, 'ye can help drain off the worts.'

He held a small barrel in place for her while she loosened the plug at the base of the mash-tun and drained the sweet infusion through a heather filter, then refilled the caldron for her from the surging burn.

'We'll need to boil it up again,' she said. 'Each batch of malt will give two mashings and the spent malt, draff it's called, will feed Rowena's cattle ower the winter.' They sat down to wait for the brew to boil again. She could feel his eyes upon her.

'How many infants did ye say he'd lost?'

'Eight. So far.'

He blinked at the enormity. 'And she's not of a strong disposition, his wife, nae likely to bring a healthy babe into the world, this time or any other?'

'Wi' Rowena's help perhaps, but he'll not let her near his wife. Nor will he allow the poor woman a rest from the strains of childbearing, such is his desire fer a son. 'Tis … 'tis the way of some men, I believe.'

He looked curiously at her, and she dropped her gaze to the pungent cauldron that steamed and foamed between them. 'With each babe that died, he's become more suspicious, looking fer signs of witchery on the wee bodies. He was enraged when the last bairn died. 'Twas a little ower a year ago.'

Jamie groaned. 'And now his wife's to have another child. Or not, as is more likely the case.'

They sat in silence, listening to the muffled thunder of the falls and the malty brew gently boiling with softly erupting plups. When Jamie spoke again, there was an edge to his voice.

'This man, I feel fer the loss of his children, but he should seek solace from the Lord, not a perverse revenge on my kinswoman.'

'I believe, perhaps, he canna help himself.'

He stared hard at her, then blinked slowly and turned his head a fraction, staring out at the dark-stained walls of rock, sodden and weed-streaked. 'My father's dearest longing was to return here, to Stratha'an, to see his sisters again, and Duncan. He spoke of Duncan often, held him in the highest regard. He yearned to see Druimbeag one last time and would wish me to protect Rowena. I wish that too. I'm part of a family still, thanks only to her. All I wish now is to protect her and what's hers.'

At his words, powerful sensations swelled in Morven's heart, and she was lost for what to say, struggling to put the sensations into words. She merely nodded, staring at him.

He rose and came to kneel before her, taking up her hands. A tremor ran up her spine.

'I give ye my word, here and now.' He lifted her hands and folded them within the rough warmth of his own, locking eyes with her. 'I swear to protect my kinfolk. No more of my kin will be forced from this glen. I swear to you, I'll not allow it.'

Later, she could not recall how it happened. But in an instant, she was pressed against him, held tight as though she was more precious to him than the kin he spoke of, the thud of his heart loud in her ears. He bent his head and said something, an oath perhaps, and she arched her back and twisted herself free, glaring at him.

'Forgive me,' he stammered.

CHAPTER SEVEN

FOLLOWING JAMIE'S STARTLING behaviour, Morven was much preoccupied. She lay awake at night puzzling over it. His passion had taken her breath away, frightened her in truth, though hadna seemed unfitting, somehow. Only the manner he'd chosen to show it. She supposed the urge that prompted him had been born of the moment, a fleeting thing, aroused by his great desire to protect his kin. She swung the bundle of food up over her shoulder. He'd apologised for the liberty he'd taken, 'twas best to forget it, likely he'd done so already.

From the doorway, she looked back at her mother. 'I'll be away now. I told Jamie I'd meet him at the bothy, but he'll likely wait fer me at the top o' the gorge.'

'Fine, lass. I've something I would tell ye, though.' There was an odd catch in Grace's voice. 'Ye can spare me a minute, aye?'

She nodded, giving her mam an odd probing look. Something was changed about her, but she couldn't quite put her finger on it. Her face was as thin as ever, yet her eyes cradled a secret glow, and there was a strange air about her she couldn't place. 'What is it?' she asked cautiously. 'Has something happened?'

A rosy blush pooled at Grace's throat and spilled onto her cheeks. 'Aye, something's happened.' She broke into a smile. 'I'm to have another bairn.'

Morven stared at her. Her mother's last two pregnancies were marked by twin crosses in Strathavon chapelyard. Pitiful, unfinished infants. The pain and toil of bringing forth those tiny souls had near taken her life.

The smile faded from Grace's face, and lines of anguish replaced it. Her eyes pressed Morven to speak, to show some sign of having heard her news.

'God, Mam. 'Twill kill ye!'

A shadow of old grief clouded Grace's eyes, and she seemed to recede into herself, crushed by disappointment. 'I thought ye'd be that pleased. Another wee brother or maybe even a sister, God willing.'

'I am pleased ... just, 'twas a shock. But I'm fair delighted.' Morven attempted a smile, but her face refused to comply, mirroring instead her horror. This did explain a few things. But her mam wi' child again? She'd not even considered such a thing. Her mam was in her fortieth year; she'd thankfully assumed her childbearing years behind her.

'Are ye all right? I mean, do ye need me to stay? Do anything fer ye?' She ran her gaze down over the wasted body.

'No, no. Off ye go and meet Jamie.' Grace wore a wounded expression. She picked up the milking cog. 'Yer da says we'll have a lass fer certain this time. He says I'm stronger, sure to have a healthy bairn.'

Morven clenched her teeth. What manner of man would continue to press his seed on a woman too weak to bear his children? Could he nae keep his filthy urges to himself?

'He knows, then?' At her mother's questioning glance, she smoothed the cutting edge in her voice. 'What ... what about Alec and the boys?'

'I told Alec and yer da the other day when ye were at the bothy. Fair delighted yer da was, went to the Craggan to celebrate. I'll nae be telling the lads till later, ye ken what they're like. They'll be expecting it to arrive any minute. I wanted ye all to myself though, thought mebbe we could look out the cradle together.' Her voice dropped wistfully. 'I expect 'tis in the byre.'

Morven's mouth was dry as chaff, but she nodded and summoned as sincere an expression as she could muster. 'We'll do it when I get back. I promise.' She stared at her mother for a few more moments, then stepped out into the brisk morning air and crossed the heath at a half-run.

The urge to weep and weep and scream to the heavens of her father's senseless lack of self-restraint rose like a spate in her throat; it near choked her, and she cursed and damned him to hell. Every ghastly detail was forever etched in her memory. How could it be any less for him? Thirteen she'd been the first time, old enough to know her mother's life hung in the balance.

She'd stared at the door to her parent's bedchamber for hours, willing it to open and her mother to call her to her side. But it remained sealed hour after lingering hour, time dragging, the air in the cot-house grown tense and suffocating. Inside the tiny chamber, Rowena plied her skills and charms, allowing no-one entry lest they sap Grace's strength. At length, her nerves frayed, Morven scooped up wee Donald and blundered out to wait with Alec in the yard. Only a year her senior, Alec took her cold hands in his and tried to rub some warmth into them.

All day, her father worked the crop rigs, eight-year-old Rory close by his side. When darkness came with gory streaks of red staining the evening sky, he sat by the fire, a keg of whisky at his side, and drank himself into oblivion. Morven watched him and fought down her own panic. Every muscle in his body stood rigid, and he drank with quiet savagery.

The night stretched endlessly, until, at last, bowing to Rory's pleading, Rowena allowed them in to see their mother. Grace's hair was stuck limply to the blankets, and her breath whistled through lips clamped tight with pain. Unable to speak, her eyes pleaded for release while she writhed endlessly, biting her own hand to stifle her cries. Wordless, they filed out again. Morven's swollen heart filled her throat, and she wondered bleakly how Rowena could bear to watch such suffering. Closing the door behind her, Rowena addressed Malcolm with grim determination.

'If she lives, there can be no more bairns. D'ye understand me?'

His shoulders sagged, and he looked at her with the cold heat of self-hatred blazing in his eyes. 'Will she live?'

''Tis God will decide that, nae me, I can make ye no promise. The bairn willna draw breath, though.'

He nodded as if they'd struck some diabolical bargain and turned back to his drink. He seemed unmoved.

Rowena prepared a faery charm at the fireside and greased her hands with mutton fat. She closed the door grimly behind her. It could have been little more than a quarter hour that passed, yet it was the longest stretch of Morven's life. The sounds that came from behind the door chilled her blood, and, wringing her hands, she found them wet with tears that slipped unchecked down her cheeks. Dimly, she recognised Alec's voice praying through the torture of the screams.

At last, stony-faced, Rowena carried the bloody bundle away. The child was a girl, only half formed. They buried her in the chapelyard the next day. Over the following weeks, Father Ranald called often, preparing Grace for a likely meeting with her maker. Yet with Rowena's tireless ministrations, Grace slowly returned to them, weak and spiritless but alive. Despite Rowena's warning, she suffered an almost identical ordeal the following year, and another bundle of unformed MacRae flesh was buried in Strathavon chapelyard.

Morven slowed her pace. She could see Jamie waiting for her by the dark gash that was the Lochy Gorge and curbed her rate to a walk. Her breathing was ragged, and her hands shook. Her fury still simmered beneath the surface, a cold needle of dread fuelling it along with an image of her father's surly face.

'Ye shouldna wait fer me here,' she said curtly. 'If the gaugers see ye, they'll wonder what ye're about, and they'll soon sniff us out.' Her voice was stiff, and she could hear the coldness in it.

'Forgive me, I didna think.'

'No, but ye must if ye wish to outwit the Black Gauger as much as ye say ye do.'

He blinked. 'I thought to help ye with the climb.'

''Tis me that's here to help you,' she reminded him.

She was halfway down the rock-face, scrambling resolutely from ledge to slippery ledge, the bundle of food gripped in her teeth when his mystified reply reached her. 'I've never forgotten that, nae fer a minute.'

She winced and dropped onto the ledge at the opening to the bothy. She thought of his arms around her the last time he came here, that bold impulsive embrace. A man he was, like her father. He'd be taking what he wanted and to blazes with the rest.

He dropped down beside her in a fluid movement, and she spun around and ducked into the dark fume-filled bothy. The worts had been fermenting for three days. The aroma hit them immediately, its pungent notes intoxicatingly familiar.

'Phew, it's ripe in here. Smells more like a brewery.' He laughed lightly, untouched by her dark mood, although she could feel him studying her with a puzzled concentration. 'It's finished, is it?' He bent over the fermentation cask, examining the froth-topped wash with interest.

'Aye, but dinna breathe-in ower the cask. 'Twill knock ye on yer back.' Fermentation was a violent business, producing clouds of noxious vapour; she knew from experience exactly what it could do.

'It does all this by itself, then? Ye can just leave the cask fer a day or two to be getting on with it?'

His innocent questions prompted an involuntary scoffing sound to escape from her lips. Over the last three days, she'd kept a watchful eye on the process, returning to the bothy often to beat the foaming liquid with a birch-wood switch to prevent it from overflowing. Ignoring him, she said, ''Tis ready fer the still now. Let's be getting on with it.'

He made no movement, but she could feel him assessing her with an air of hurt confusion. 'Something's wrong. Ye're angry with me.'

She met his eyes at last, though no more than a glance. 'There's naught wrong'.

He reached out and gripped her by both wrists, the touch bringing her head snapping up. 'There's something. Ye must tell me.'

'Aye, there's something!' She wrenched her hands away, blazing him a look. 'Only it hasna a docken to do wi' you!'

She was conscious of him tensing. 'I shouldn't have done it. I thought mebbe ye felt the same, but,' he swallowed, ''twas unforgivable.'

His expression was so stricken and contrite, so very earnest, her anger began to evaporate. 'What are ye haivering about?'

'I shouldna have seized ye – embraced ye like that. I've thought o' little else, but 'twas wrong of me.'

She felt a sudden urge to laugh; a great gushing release of tension, yet the eyes that regarded her were heavy and wretched. 'Have ye naught else to occupy yer mind?' she quipped. Then, seeing him wince, added more lightly, 'I've thought of it too. Ye did take a mighty liberty.'

'I know. I caused offence, and rightly so, I can make no excuse fer my actions.'

'Offence? Nay.'

'There's no need to indulge me, I see it in yer face, ye've not the guile to hide it. Ye're still angry now.'

She pressed her eyes shut, suddenly weary. Despite what he said, her anger had left her, his mistaking of its source perhaps dousing the last of its embers and she shivered, a chill in her flesh. It was cold in the bothy, the walls running with the drip of stale steam. She felt the shock of her mother's news cut into her heart, prompting a fearsome trembling. Groping, she found an upturned anker to sit down on and clasped her hands in her lap to keep them steady.

'I'm nae angry wi' you. I spoke harshly …' She shook her head, feeling guilty. 'But it wasna you brought on my anger, 'twas another did that and … and some fearful tidings.' She gave a little shrug. ''Twas only an embrace atween us. I've forgotten it already.' That was hardly true, but it seemed the thing to say.

He stood with head bowed but brought it up a fraction as she spoke, studying her from beneath dark lashes. He'd clubbed back his hair, and the fine down on the nape of his neck was illuminated by the crisp light from the bothy opening. He seemed young and vulnerable, the air of authority he wore fallen away and the sensitive young man beneath exposed.

'I'm so verra cold,' she said, and a fit of shivering rocked her.

He shrugged off the woollen shortcoat he wore over his belted plaid and held it out to her. 'May I?'

She nodded and let him wrap the garment around her, then he rubbed her icy hands the way Alec had done all those years ago. His own were warm and work-roughened, but gentle in what they did. She felt a lump rise in her throat. Happed in his coat, she watched him kneel and set about building a fire. He kept quiet as he struck sparks from the flint and blew on the tinder-dry curls of lichen, but glanced up at her continually. His expression was grave and more than a little puzzled. When he was done, and the kindling crackled aglow, he worked peats and fir-cones into the pile to raise as much warmth from it as he could.

'Ye've had a shock, I think.' His gaze was steady on her face.

She nodded, feeling a helpless sob well in her throat. To her horror, it burst from her lips with a loud shudder and the tears gathering behind her eyes escaped to slide down her face.

He reached out tentatively and touched her cheek, catching a tear on his finger, and stared at it in wonder. Her face crumpled, then the sobs came in earnest, racking from deep in her belly, bunching and aching in her throat, only to burst forth in uncontrollable gasps and sobs.

'Lord, Morven!'

Without hesitation, he lifted her from the upturned anker and carried her to the fireside, settling her on some blankets as close to the warmth as possible. He placed the anker down beside her and sat on it himself.

'Warmer now?'

She nodded, not trusting her voice, as another sob wracked its way through her body.

'Nae yet, I think.' Leaning over, he placed his arm around her shoulders, pulling her close while she shivered and sobbed.

Her embarrassment seemed complete, yet somehow his tenderness prompted an even greater flood of tears. She tried to twist away, to hide her shame, but he held her tight, pressing her into the linen of his sark.

'Dinna fight it. I think no less of ye fer yer weeping.'

Unable to stop, she gave herself up to her despair. The sobs came hard, like when she was a child, and there was no stopping them, until, at last, there was nothing left, and she lay limp and spent against him.

'What must ye think of me?' She struggled to rise; her nose was running, and she'd left a damp patch on his sark.

He drew her back at once, a hand firm on her shoulder, and used a corner of his plaid to dry her face.

'Better now?' he asked, and she nodded, still shivering. 'Will ye let me warm ye?'

She had scarce a chance to consider the request before he lifted her onto his lap and drew his plaid around them both. She tensed at this further familiarity, but his body seemed to radiate warmth, a balm that soothed and relaxed the rigid lines of her own. Slowly her muscles loosened, and she wound her arms around his waist, soaking up the warmth of him, made almost drowsy with it. He smelled of things she'd never known it possible for a body to smell of. Grass and hay and gorse flowers, peat smoke and a musky salty tang that was his own, mingled with the familiar scent of Rowena's home. Sniffing, she breathed him in and felt somehow lighter than she'd any right to feel.

Trying to clear her throat, she made a small sound, and he stirred. Then she felt his lips on her cheek and the roughness of his chin as he bent his head and brought his mouth down on hers. His fingers were on the back of her neck, lifting her head, guiding her mouth that it might allow his to fit her own more easily. The shock was exquisite, and her breath caught in her throat. She responded instinctively, returning his kiss, allowing his touch, gentle as it was – almost reverent. Never had she felt more vulnerable, unguarded, yet somehow precious.

His breath left him in a rush, warm against her neck.

'I care fer ye, Morven. Did ye not guess?' He drew back a little, studying her face. 'I know ye dinna … that's all right.' He smiled crookedly. 'My da taught me always to be honest. I just wanted ye to ken.'

A welter of emotions assaulted her. Fear at what this meant, confusion at his tricking her, and a bitter shame at her own response. Was this another liberty? One she'd allowed this time? He'd saved her, and so she was beholden. Was this how he'd take his payment?

Yet staring at him, all she could think was that she felt safe, not misused, felt as though the world inside her was moving faster now, somehow leaving her conscious will behind and she was all melted and a-stir.

She swallowed, a painful lump filling her throat while her mouth was dry as an old quern stone, and speech was beyond her.

Taking her silence as a negative response, he blinked and took one of her hands. 'Enough about me. Can ye tell me what it is that troubles ye? It wasna me, I think?'

She shook her head.

'Something else, then?' He looked away, allowing her time to collect herself. 'If ye'd rather nae speak of it, I'll not press ye, of course, but I've long found it helps to talk.'

Her throat hurt, yet her body was another matter; she felt the blood singing in her veins. But how could she speak of her mam's condition with a man? With Jamie? The thought of such a conversation, 'twas unthinkable, unseemly, and brought a furious flaming to her cheeks. Father Ranald was the one she should confess the fear and darkness in her soul to, he was the Lord's instrument, had renounced the bonds of manhood. Yet in her heart, she knew 'twas Rowena she would unburden to.

There were certain herbs to be found and a preparation brewed from them that would bring away the child ripening in her mother's belly. The Father would call it a mortal sin she supposed, but she thought it no more so than what her father had done. Yet her mam would have none of it, and Rowena, however loath, would doubtless respect Grace's wishes. A strong urge to change the subject came over her.

'We should begin the distilling,' she croaked. ''Tis the most skilled part, so ye'll need to pay close heed.'

He gave in graciously, letting her go, but still watched her as though she were some treasured object that he'd broken.

It was plain the still was like nothing Jamie had seen before. His eyes widened as she drew back the hide covering that protected it and he stooped to peer at the outlandish contraption. It consisted of a sizeable tin pot, complete with elongated pear-shaped head, and with a great length of convoluted copper pipe protruding from its crown.

'The worm,' she said, holding up the copper coil. ''Tis the most valuable piece o' the still. When it wears out ye must replace it. Only there's a way to make the Excise pay fer it.'

'Why would they do that?'

More comfortable now that she was on familiar ground, Morven allowed a smile to lighten her face. 'Ye take the worn-out worm to the Resident Officer and, wearing yer most guileless countenance, tell him ye've discovered an illegal still. Take him to a place as far from yer own bothy as can be, where ye've scattered some malt about the smoorach of a fire. There's a handsome reward fer discovering an illicit still – five pounds forsooth. Aye,' she said, seeing his eyes widened. 'A tidy sum. Once ye have it, ye can pay a wee visit to the nearest coppersmith. Copper's dear, so ye'll not be left wi' much once ye've bought a new worm, but yer real reward will be knowing 'twas treasury money paid fer it and nae yer own hard-won siller.'

Jamie chuckled delightedly.

She was pleased to see him treat her father's pot-still with the greatest respect. Together they lifted the battered old pot onto the cairn at the fire. 'Twas a snug fit. On a bank of earth to one side, she positioned the cooling cask, then fitted the worm inside, the end protruding from a hole near the base. Once the hole was suitably sealed, she worked at luting the coil back into the head of the still while Jamie filled the still with the wash. Draining directly from the hills of Cromdale, the water of the Lochy burn was ice-cold; perfect for cooling and condensing. Together they used an assortment of wooden containers to fill the cask from the hurtling falls. Once the head was fitted back onto the body of the still, she sealed it in place.

'We'll need a fair few jars,' she said, searching through the selection in the cave. 'Nae everything that comes off is pure whisky. We only take the middle run o' spirit, the rest is run off separate, and we'll need to re-distil it.'

As the wash inside the still began to heat to near boiling point, the head started to rattle, and the worm emitted a soft hissing sound in the cold water. Jamie looked over at her, clearly fascinated, then gasped as condensed spirit began to run into the earthenware jar.

'The foreshots,' she said, dipping a finger into the jar. 'See how oily it is?' She pulled her father's tasting cup from the bundle she'd brought with her from home. 'Ye can taste it if ye want.' She filled the cup with the thick clear liquid.

Watching her face, he knew only to take the smallest of sips and screwed his face up at the taste. 'Lord, it's evil stuff!'

'Aye, 'twill burn in a cruisie lamp better even than fish oil, but we're nae finished with it yet.'

It was vital to judge the next part of the process correctly. As the oily foreshots continued to run off, she took constant samples testing its scent for impurities and observing how it clung to the sides of the cup. Finally, she tasted the spirit and looked over at Jamie, who appeared to be holding his breath.

'This is it.' She swiftly changed the jar for a ten-gallon anker. 'This is pure spirit. 'Tis still raw mind, and will need time to mature, to develop its own character.' She handed him a cupful. He whistled softly at the smooth texture, then gasped as the fire of the spirit burned the back of his throat.

'Devil's brew!' he gasped. 'Or maybe devil's fire is a more fitting name.'

'Mountain dew,' she said softly and sat back, satisfied with her work. ''Twill run off pure spirit fer the next half-hour or so, then the lower alcohol tailings will come through. We'll draw that off separate and mix it wi' the foreshots fer another distillation.'

He nodded, fascinated by the hissing and steaming beast and she knew he'd paid close heed to everything she said. Despite her turmoil, she sat at peace watching the steady run of whisky from the end of the worm and feeling the familiar lulling sensation induced by the vapours and the rhythmic hiss and rattle of the still. Her anger toward her father seemed more distant now, and Jamie's presence was oddly comforting. She opened the bundle of food and shared cheese, bannocks, and heather ale with him. Her own appetite was feeble, but the ale was a balm to her painful throat.

''Tis so beautiful here.' He looked through the steam and out toward the hills of Cromdale.

'Oft-times I fancy these bens and braes have tales to tell. Ours is a much-troubled land.'

'You speak like Rowena,' he said. 'She's been a strong influence in yer life?'

'Since ever I can mind.'

'Will ye tell me about it?' he coaxed.

Her first instinct was to shrink from this intrusive request. It felt too intimate; an unwanted probe into a cherished but private bond. Yet he'd not grown up with his kinswoman as she had done, perhaps 'twas only right to share her with him.

'My earliest memory is of her story-telling. Of dark winter nights cooried at the firestone listening to her tales of auld.' Her voice grew husky as the memories crowded back. She could hear again the rippling of the flames, the soft clacking of the spinning wheel, and Rowena's voice, fascinating and persuasive, weaving its spell.

''Twas the noble tales of Gaeldom I loved most in those days.' She'd close her eyes and the other listeners with their weathered faces and shining eyes would simply fade away. Then the mountains would whisper and call to her; they spoke of battles long forgotten, clashes and strife and endless struggles. Even then, no more than the wide-eyed sprout that she was, she knew Rowena would influence the course of her life, in truth had already done so, and she welcomed it. 'Later, she taught me the value of our Highland customs and something of our story.' And her father had added his own bitter memories. 'Such a sorry tale we have.' Her eyes clouded. 'My Granda died on Culloden moor wi' a great many of his clan.'

Jamie's eyes darkened. 'My father spoke of those days too.'

A deep sense of injustice had grown in her belly. Yet again, it was Rowena that taught her how to channel those feelings, and she'd seen that it was in the guarding of the collective memory that those gone before were truly honoured. Over time, a sense of unity with the past flourished and a greater understanding of herself. The grandeur of her home became a reassurance, a tangible reminder of who she was and where she belonged. Inhospitable to many, the land ensured her culture remained un-subdued, almost untouched by their foreign king and rule.

"'Tis in the keeping alive o' the auld customs,' she said, unconsciously quoting Rowena. 'That we do the greatest honour to our fathers.'

'And ye're still learning from her? Her apprentice. Learning to be a healer, of the spirit as well as the body, I think?'

'I am.'

Then, sensing he shared at least a measure of her fascination with his kinswoman, she relaxed her guard a little and revealed more. 'When Rowena was no more than a bairn,' she confided, 'she met an auld woman, a *cailleach* she took fer a tinker-woman, but who she soon learned was of the faeryfolk.' She glanced sidelong at Jamie, conscious he might question this, but there was no sign of mockery in his eyes. 'The *cailleach* taught Rowena the things that were once kent by all: which plants heal and which harm, how to gain favour wi' the men o' the *sìtheans,* and how to foretell things from signs around ye. She saw something in Rowena – something rare.'

'I think I know what she saw.'

Morven's breathing quickened. 'I feel it too, it does strike a fire in me!' she said, blushing. 'I was fifteen when Rowena saw it in me.' It was the most momentous day of her life, a turning point from which she measured the rest of her days. 'And every moment since I've given thanks fer it.'

He said nothing, though he watched her closely, and she understood from his silence that she'd somehow moved him. Emboldened, she went on. 'What she tells me most is to be aware, open to all possibilities, in this realm or any other, nae matter how far from accepted certainties it all might seem.' She frowned and glanced away, sensing she'd revealed too much.

'Seems like sound advice,' he said gruffly. 'Sometimes ye must trust yer instincts, I believe.'

Clearing her throat, she began testing the whisky for signs of the lower alcohol tailings coming through. The change was a subtle one and required careful monitoring.

'My mam's to have another bairn,' she said abruptly.

'Well, that's the grandest news!' Smiling, he half-shook his head. 'I'm delighted.'

'Aye,' she replied without enthusiasm.

As the middle run of spirit came to an end, she drew his attention to the change in the aroma and consistency of the liquid and was satisfied he could recognise the difference. He removed the anker and replaced it with an earthenware jar to collect the tailings. Looking at her, a little frown creased his brow. He said, 'Why do I feel it's nae such grand tidings?'

Her heart began to beat against her breastbone. Clenching her teeth to keep the tears away, she looked at him with venom in her eyes. ''Twill likely kill her! 'Tis why the tidings do a-fear me so!'

His eyes sprang wide. 'Kill her?'

'Aye, fer the last two stillbirths near did so. 'Tis only thanks to Rowena she still lives. Yet my father,' she shook her head, breathless with rage. 'He canna keep his urges to himself. Even knowing 'twill likely be the end of her, even then, he must still be taking his pleasure!'

'You mean, he knows the dangers of getting yer mother with child again? Yet still he ...'

'Aye, 'tis what I mean.' Now that she'd said it, she knew she should not have done so. Her da was still her da. And this was an intimate matter. A matter atween her mother and her father, and none other.

Jamie's expression hardened. 'The man would beat ye and force himself upon a sick woman, 'tis little wonder Rowena does suspect him of treachery!'

'Treachery?' She slanted him a look.

'Of being in league wi' McBeath. Party to Duncan's death.'

Her mouth dropped open. 'Rowena would never say such a thing! And ... and what do ye ken of my father to slur him so?'

He blinked and straightened, for he'd been leant toward her with an ardent look on his face, and gentled his voice, 'Forgive me, but 'tis what Rowena believes.'

He did not touch her, yet she felt as if he'd struck her a mortal blow. 'Yer a liar! A scoundrel and a liar fer saying such a thing!'

'I pray yer pardon if I've wounded ye, I know not the man. I only know my kinswoman's fears, though,' he swallowed, 'better had I kept them to myself.'

'Aye, better by far! Ye're only here, in this most secret place, in that my father did allow it. And he did that to be Christian, to help

Rowena. Is that the act o' someone treacherous?'

She took several ragged breaths to steady herself, glaring at his face, all earnest and sincere, damn him. Narrowing her eyes, she nailed him with a look of blatant hostility. 'I must show ye how to make whisky, and show ye I will, fer I've given Rowena my word. But I'll hear no more o' yer lies. My father is a decent man, and loved Duncan as a brother. I'll thank ye to mind it.'

'Morven! Are ye there, Morven?'

Beside her, Jamie flinched. Still glaring at him, she canted her head to listen, then turned and stepped out onto the dripping ledge, peering up through the spray. Alone at the top of the gorge, Donald looked small and forlorn.

'What is it, Donald?'

'Ye must come,' he shouted down to her. *'Rowena needs ye. Ye've to come at once.'*

She shrugged off his coat and thrust it at him. 'I must go.'

He nodded. 'I'll finish off here, and … and if ye trust me, I'll manage the second run through the still.'

'Trust ye!' She snorted.

As she made the climb up the rock-face, she could feel his gaze upon her and stopped to look down. The lines of his body were drawn and contrite but he smiled up at her and raised his hand in a gallant salute. Gritting her teeth, she turned back to her climb.

.

CHAPTER EIGHT

NEARING THE TOP OF the gorge, Morven could see Rowena's lad was also waiting. William was an agreeable lad, quiet and deep, and never happier than when the dominie was in the glen. He was fair, like his father, but had Rowena's dark and impenetrable eyes. He offered her his hand and she scrambled the last few feet, then stood, damp and breathless, eyeing the two boys.

'Beggin' yer pardon.' William regarded her gravely. ''Twas my mam sent me to fetch ye. Ye've to come with her to Balintoul, her and two women-folk, as quick as ye can.'

'D'ye know what the matter is, William?'

He frowned, unsmiling, though she knew his smiles were rare, even more so since his da died. 'It has something to do wi' the Black Gauger. Mister McBeath, I mean. Two women rode out from Balintoul, in a fair lather they were, but,' he shook his head, 'I dinna ken what 'twas ower. They're waiting fer ye at Tomachcraggen now.'

'Never heed.' She'd find out soon enough if she didn't know already.

The bay mare, Shore, was tethered to an alder, scratching her rump, twitching her tail at the midgies that feasted on her haunches. Plainly William had called at the shieling in his search for her, and her mother had given him the pony along with wee Donald as a guide. Such was her father's vigilance, even Rowena's lad was not privy to the whereabouts of their still. She cast a dubious eye over William's mount. Old Trauchle the beast was known as, a plodding flea-bitten old cuddie hardly built for speed; the beast was plainly spent already. Quicker to travel alone.

'William here will take ye home.' She lifted Donald up onto Trauchle's back, settling him foremost on the pony, bare legs dangling from beneath frayed kilt. He squinted down at her but said nothing. He'd long learned that being the youngest of the family meant he was excluded from what he imagined were life's adventures until he was judged old enough.

'You be taking care,' warned William, and she nodded and untied the mare. With a tight smile, she mounted and urged the pony into a canter, pressing the mare through thick heather and whin, then into a gallop as they made easier ground. The route was a winding one, and she'd to curb the mare's enthusiasm through the birks and juniper scrub, avoiding the many rocks and great schist outcrops that patterned the land.

By the time they picked their way down the ridge of Carn Meilich, the sun was well risen and the mist that lay in the lower reaches of the glen had begun to burn off in the warmth from a watery sun. Yet despite the day's gentle warmth, Morven shivered, glad when the low outline of Tomachcraggen came in sight.

Sarah was waiting by the sheepcote, cracking her knuckles. 'They've gone wi'out ye,' she cried. 'Couldna wait any longer. What took ye so long?'

Morven's heart sank. 'I came as quick as I could, but was busy at the still and none too easy fer William to find.'

Sarah nodded; she knew well the need for secrecy that surrounded illicit whisky-making.

'I'll need to get after them. How long've they been away?'

'A while,' Sarah hazarded. 'Ye ken it's McBeath's wife they've gone to?' There was an ominous note in her voice. ''Tis her time and it's nae to be an easy one by all accounts.'

'I thought as much.' There seemed little more to say; Morven wrested Shore from the scrape of herbage she'd found and urged the pony on again.

''Tis the grand house on the hill,' Sarah shouted after her. 'The one wi' all the lum pots.'

***

It was market day in Balintoul, the generally peaceful township a heaving mass of Highland cattle fussed over by anxious herdsmen and eyed in turn by shrewd buyers from the coastal lowlands. Morven looked on the scene with dismay. Suitably removed from the offensive odours of the marketplace and the general squalor of the rest of Balintoul, the exciseman's home stood on high ground at the far end of the settlement. She'd need to negotiate the milling beasts to reach it.

'A bonny bit silk fer a bonny lass?' A pockmarked man with livid drinker's nose clutched at her sleeve. Grinning, he fingered the rolls of gaudy French cloth he peddled from the back of a cart.

She shook her head. 'I need to get through.'

He shrugged and gestured at the herds of cattle blocking the road. Granted they were noisy, but she judged them to be largely docile. Gritting her teeth, she drove the garron on into the crush, her words of reassurance to the pony swallowed by the din. The stench of dung rose in her nostrils and flies followed the beasts in swarms. Shore threw her head, showing the whites of her eyes, and Morven slid from her back stroking her neck and murmuring softly to her, then elbowed her way through, tugging the nervous pony behind her. The cattle bellowed their indignation, but she pushed their horns away with her free hand, and they tossed their heads at her. Then she was free, dusty and a mite jostled, but unharmed nonetheless.

She knew the exciseman's house at once. Impressively large, it was the only two-storeyed dwelling in the settlement and stood out conspicuously from the other humble homes. Built of butter-yellow sandstone with a slate roof and crow-stepped gables, she counted eight chimneys rising from its roof. Testimony, if any was needed, to the wealth the exciseman had accumulated from the simple crofting folk of Strathavon.

Rowena's grey mare was tied to a post in the front courtyard along with another shaggy little garron; she tethered Shore alongside. The heavy oak door stood ajar. She knocked twice, then stepped quickly across the threshold, making her way down a dark hallway. Doors led off into further rooms, where amongst the lavish furnishings, she caught the gleam of well-buffed brass. Such finery was alien to her, and she felt her heart quicken in her throat. ''Tis only a house,' she muttered to herself, yet even so, it took an effort of will to still herself, to quell the raggedness of her breathing, and she stood a moment listening for the sounds of a woman in childbirth and for Rowena's familiar voice.

Small scuffling sounds came from the doorway at the end of the hall. She passed the curve of the stairway and made toward it. The door stood open; the room beyond seemed to be a large dingy kitchen. Swallowing, she poked her head around the door. A grey-haired woman stood with her back to the door and fretted aloud in Gaelic, opening cupboards and rifling anxiously through the contents. She seemed harmless enough. Morven cleared her throat. Whirling to face her, the woman's eyes flew open, and she made a startled sound in her throat.

'Forgive me. I'm looking fer Rowena Forbes.'

The woman steadied herself with a hand on a dresser-top and fanned her face furiously with the other. Her colouring was high, and she muttered, 'Merciful heaven,' under her breath. Then her face closed warily. 'Ye're Morven, are ye?'

'I came as quick as I could.'

The woman hesitated, then her face seemed to crumple. 'I doubt 'twoulda made a difference lass, however quick ye'd been. She's gone, poor soul, and God forgive me fer saying so, but I'm thinking 'tis a blessing.' She crossed herself and dabbed at her reddened eyes.

Morven's heart lurched. 'And the child?'

'The bairn as well. 'Twas dead in her belly these last days. Likely Isobel kent it, but couldna bring herself to face the knowing. There's a … a deal o' blood, mind. Mistress Forbes said 'twas the bleeding that finished her – it wouldna stop and her that weak. She's still up wi' Isobel now, making the poor soul as decent as can be expected. It wouldna do to go leaving her like that.' She shuddered. 'Looking as though some mischief had befallen her. Wouldna be wise, if ye take my meaning.'

She glanced down at the items she'd taken from the top shelf of the dresser: jars of preserve, pots of salt, flour, spices, and such. 'I was looking fer a tincture,' she said in explanation. 'A potion Mistress Forbes gave Isobel; one she'd nae be wishing the exciseman to find if ye understand me.'

'Where is Mr McBeath?'

The woman curled her lip. 'Bending his elbow at the Balintoul Inn, most like.' She turned to face Morven more squarely, and her chin rose a fraction. There was frankness in the faded grey eyes, a staunchness of character in the homely well-scrubbed face. 'Isobel hadna many friends, nae real ones, but I liked her in spite of her choice o' man.'

'Was it you came to the glen to find Rowena?' Morven asked.

'Wi' my sister, Jessie Chatton. I'm Ellen MacPherson.'

'Isobel was fortunate, I think, to have such friends.'

Ellen gave a shrug. 'She was a goodly soul … aye bringin' wee gifts, things fer our bairns. She loved bairns.' Her lip quivered. 'And her never to know the love o' her own littlins.'

Conscious of intruding on the woman's grief, Morven excused herself, then turned back to her. 'He doesna know, then?'

'Nae that she's dead, no, though he kent her pains were upon her. He'll need to be told, mind.'

Morven nodded bleakly.

The stairway curved delicately upwards, six doors leading off the expansive landing at the top. Instinctively Morven chose the first door, somehow reluctant to call out to Rowena in the hushed stillness of the house knowing Isobel lay dead somewhere close by.

The room was a dim sparsely furnished bedchamber, a stone fireplace at the far end. An iron bedstead filled the space at the window; Morven's eyes were drawn there. The bedclothes had been stripped – if indeed that's what they were. Soaked in blood, they'd been tied in a dripping bundle on the floor. A figure lay stretched out on the bed, still and pale as parchment. With a sickening jolt, she recognised the lax contours of Isobel's face. The woman had been dressed in fresh linens and lay on a clean sheet, although the scent of blood still swam in the air, metallic and offensive.

Rowena arose from the corner behind the door where she attended a small blackened object. She showed no surprise at Morven's silent arrival, but her eyes were full of pitying regret. 'I could do nothing,' she said bitterly. 'The child plainly died some days ago.' She laid the object on the bed. Morven recoiled; it was a tiny shrunken infant, its face dark with contused blood.

'Lord!' she gasped.

'She might've lived but fer the bleeding. 'Tis the scourge o' childbed, the bleeding. Oft-times there's nothing can be done. 'Twas as though every one o' her veins opened and wept fer this wee soul.' Rowena dipped a rag into a pail of water and began to dab at the blood and scum clogging the tiny nostrils and laying thick among the folds of lip and eyelid.

'Did she speak?' Morven whispered.

'Only to say what she wished Hugh to ken – that she was sorry.' Her voice hardened. 'She was too fine a body fer the likes of him.'

'I dinna doubt it. But Rowena, I'm thinking he'll be fearful riled now, will wish to lay blame fer this. And … and we both ken where he's laid it in the past.'

'Aye, he's cried me witch and child-killer. As if I'd cause this. As if any woman would.' Rowena put a hand out to touch the still figure on the bed, almost in apology.

Morven looked again at the pitiful form on the bed. Isobel Gow, she'd been before she wed the exciseman. A handsome young woman, plump and brown as a dunnock before the endless years of childbearing took their toll. The figure stretched out on the bedstead, thin and sunken-cheeked, bore no more than a passing resemblance to the blithe young woman she'd once been. With a shiver, Morven banished a sudden vision of her own mother similarly laid out.

'Ye did all ye could,' she croaked. 'But I'd not wish yer assistance to be misunderstood.' A small bronze charm was tied around Isobel's neck, a likeness of Brigid, the ancient guardian of childbirth, and a flask of a pale-yellow liquid stood by the bed. She picked it up and sniffed at it.

'Hawthorn flower and mustard seed,' said Rowena. 'An infusion we've spoken of afore. A remedy to bring the blood together, most especially after childbed when the bleeding's loath to diminish. But this,' she reached out and touched Isobel's hand, her voice aching and wretched. 'This was unstoppable.' Meeting Morven's gaze, she pushed a wayward coil of dark hair back under her kertch. 'I sent Jessie Chatton to fetch silvered water, but she's nae back yet.'

Silvered water, Morven had been dispatched to collect it on many occasions and had witnessed astonishing results from its use. She knew it to be water taken from a ford through which both the dead and the living had passed, one containing a silver coin. 'Twas generally drawn from the ford at Achnareave on the way to Strathavon chapelyard. The woman would be some time returning from there.

'Rowena,' she said, gripping the older woman's forearm. 'Ye shouldna linger here. I sense a … a danger in this place.' She'd felt it since entering the house, a malignancy hanging in the air, its charged presence crackling along her nerves, pressing her to get away. ''Twould be wise to be gone from here afore the exciseman returns, d'ye not think?'

'I've no wish to meet wi' the man either,' Rowena replied. 'But I've done nothing wrong, nothing that wasna my Christian duty. The man needs to be told, but 'tis only proper to wash and wrap the bairn afore we go to him, and to cover them both decent-like.'

'Quickly, then.' The desire to get away was almost unbearable, but dutifully Morven rolled her sleeves.

There was no more clean water, Rowena had used it all, and neither woman wished the delay of traipsing to the township well to fetch more or waiting while Ellen did so. They cleaned the infant as best they could with the foul pink-stained water, their hands and fingernails discoloured with it, and then searched for linen to use as a winding sheet. The wee body was still supple, though the tiny features had begun to collapse in.

'A boy,' Morven observed. ''Twas likely a son the gauger was wanting.'

Rowena made a scornful sound in her throat. 'He'd nae even the time o' day to give to his wife, never heed a child.' She sighed and moderated her tone. 'I believe he wished a son fer his own conceit, a symbol of his manhood, a feather in his bonnet to boast of to the factor.'

Morven tore off a strip of linen with her teeth and glanced sidelong at Rowena. The widow, normally so even and composed, appeared stricken by the fate of Isobel and her infant, saddened to the point where her fingers trembled as she worked.

'Isobel was already taken wi' her pains afore he even left fer the inn,' Rowena expanded. 'Yet still he left her here wi' only a maid. The girl ran off in fright and 'twas Ellen found Isobel here in childbed. She'd to pay the girl to come back and stay with her mistress while she and Jessie went fer help. The girl made flight again the moment we returned, such is her fear of her employer.'

Morven could well imagine that fear; the thought of dragging the Black Gauger from the Balintoul Inn to tell him that his wife and child were dead filled her with horror.

At last, Rowena laid the swaddled infant down by his mother's side. ''Tis sometimes possible to save the bairn's life ye ken, even after its mother's death,' she said softly. 'By quickly cutting it from the womb afore it dies too. I've done it successfully only once, but 'twas already too late fer this wee soul.'

Morven opened her mouth to voice her abhorrence at such a proposal, but the words froze on her tongue. A dark shape rose in shadow on the far wall. She spun around and her heart near burst from her chest. Hugh McBeath stood in the doorway – he filled it – dark in both garb and countenance. He nodded slowly, knowingly, looking from one woman to the other. The hair rose on her scalp.

Armed with sword and a pistol at each hip, up close he was bigger than she remembered. Unconsciously she measured the distance to the door and the small gap his bulk left in the doorway for them to escape by unscathed, and didn't rate their chances. His whiskered face twitched, fox-like, as he assessed them. Looking down, she saw that a flask swung from his right hand, a spherical brightly-coloured flask like those Rowena bartered from the tinkers. He glanced down at it, slowly rolled the liquid inside, then cocked his head back up at them.

Instinctively both women edged backwards, partly concealing the bed.

Again his mouth twitched, and he inhaled, nostrils flaring. Morven sensed an unaccountable surge of triumph in him, a perverse sense of excitement. He'd expected this, had deliberately left his stricken wife knowing full well Rowena would come.

He raised one eyebrow at Rowena, then stripped her down in a slow scornful examination. 'Well, well, Mistress Forbes, you must be acclaimed throughout these lands. You attended the most remarkable recovery from smallpox this side of the Highland line.' He grinned mirthlessly and advanced into the room. 'But I dinnae take kindly to being duped.'

Faced with such acute danger, Morven's senses were heightened, her thoughts achingly clear. He'd nae even looked at his wife, she scarcely seemed to matter to him, his entire attention was focused upon Rowena, a trembling eagerness in him.

'I tried to save her, only the bleeding …'

The twitching at his mouth ceased, and all trace of amusement left his eyes. He glared from one woman to the other, then seized Morven by the wrist and yanked her roughly aside.

'Holy God!'

He stared at the lifeless forms of his wife and wizened infant, then turned and levelled a murderous glare at Rowena.

'She was beyond saving,' Morven blurted. 'Though Rowena did try her verra best.'

'It's nae as ye're thinking,' Rowena said. 'The bairn was already dead in her belly. I listened fer its heartbeat …' She picked up the tiny trumpet she'd fashioned from a ram's horn. 'But there was nothing and … and I could do naught to stem the bleeding.' She lifted her hands in a gesture of helplessness. 'Oft-times it happens that way, more times than ye might think and … and Isobel was terrible weak already.'

He made an animal sound in his throat. 'Who gave ye the right to come here? With your *witchery*.'

'Isobel did. She asked fer my help. But I've used no witchery.'

'No?' He lifted the flask. 'Two days ago I found this hidden in the chimney breast.' He snared Rowena with his eyes. 'Poison it is. Sorcery. Used to murder my wife, to kill my child. I know it's yours, or are ye going to deny it?'

Morven stared in horror at the flask. Beside her, Rowena spoke mildly, a little wearily. 'Not poison. I gave Isobel that tincture but 'twas to fortify her fer her labours, nothing more. 'Twas likely fear of you made her conceal it.'

The exciseman's mouth clamped shut, his jaw clenched so tightly his head shook, and he looked again at the bed. His gaze fell on the faery charm still tied around his wife's neck and he recoiled with a sharp hiss.

'Witchcraft!' He reached out a hand to touch the tiny charm, then snatched it away as if it scorched him. 'What did you do to her?' he choked. 'What wickedness did you work with that foul effigy?'

''Tis only a charm. Fer her protection.' Rowena bent to untie the tiny bronze.

'*Protection?*' He grasped one of her hands and forced it up to the light. 'From a woman with blood on her hands?' He thrust her hand away and circled the bed, halting to stare at the bundle of soiled and blood-soaked linen half hidden beneath it.

'By all that's holy! I see what's been done here. Murder it is, and by uncanny means.'

''Tis nothing o' the kind,' Morven protested. How to make him see that, though? 'The charm was fer yer wife's protection and … and it wouldna have been decent to leave her like that, bloody and all.'

Unmoved by her protests, the gauger levelled a murderous glare in Morven's direction.

'Yer wife bled to death,' Rowena said softly. 'I'm so verra sorry. But 'tis what can happen when a woman is brought to childbed so often, and wi' each labour so verra close upon the last.' She frowned apologetically and pressed her lips together. 'Her womb was simply too weak to compress the bleeding vessels …'

McBeath gaped at her. '*You're blaming me?*' he choked. 'You've the gall to censure me! To question my … my personal relations with my own wife? Lord, but ye're brazen!'

Unconsciously, Morven had backed up hard against the iron of the bedstead, but with a stab of admiration saw that her companion stood her ground, defiant and collected.

Desperately, she cried, 'I swear to ye, sir, yer wife's death was nae Rowena's doing. She came here to help her, even knowing 'twas likely useless, that yer wife was beyond her help.' She wrung her hands, seeing in his cruel expression a blank refusal to consider any judgement but his own. 'She's the most gentle-hearted and selfless of women, I know of none finer. The most Christian –'

'*Christian!*'

'Bless ye, lass,' murmured Rowena. 'But I speak the truth as plainly as I see it. And see it as 'tis so.'

The gauger appeared thunderstruck. 'The words of a known witch!' he choked. 'Uttered to conceal her guilt. To deflect it onto another. Onto the innocent.'

'Not so!' Morven cried. 'Dinna dare call her that!'

McBeath turned savagely on her. 'D'ye think I didnae hear what you were saying when I first found ye?' He grasped her by the upper arm, viciously pinching her skin. 'I heard ye plotting. You planned to take the child for yourselves – for *her* devilish purpose.' His face was close now; she felt the hot sweatiness of him, could smell his breath, overlaid with liquor.

'I dinna ken what ye mean.'

'Had it lived, you'd have taken the child, used it for devil knows what fiendish purpose.'

'Ye're hurting me!' But he merely gave her arm another vicious twist.

'Let her be, Hugh, please – let her be.' Rowena spoke calmly, and he loosened his grip a fraction, more in surprise that she'd used his first name, Morven sensed, than for any other reason. 'This is atween you and me. Ye ken it as well as I. The lass has no part.'

He surveyed Rowena in quivering silence, then rasped, 'Aye, you and me. We've unfinished business.' He whirled on his heel and propelled Morven across the room. Her feet skidded on the polished floor, and she writhed to free herself, but his grip was fast on her arm, impossible to dislodge.

'Get out!' he roared. 'Get ye gone from here!'

She twisted to catch a glimpse of Rowena's face, silently pleading for guidance. The widow nodded, a minute acknowledgement that she should do as the exciseman bid, but her face was rigid with fear.

For an instant, Morven thought he'd hurl her down the stairs. He dragged her to the landing, wild-eyed and panting, then thrust her forcibly from him.

'Get out! OUT!'

She didn't wait to argue the point, but clattered down the stairs and ran, her heart hammered hard against her ribcage, down the long hallway. She burst from the house, almost tripping down the stone steps, and blinked in the brightness. Outside it was a balmy day. She blinked at the brilliance, the blue of the sky marred only by a few tails of high cloud riding the warm air. The grass on the bank opposite moved a little, stirred by a gentle breath, and a low rumble drifted up from the hubbub at the foot of the brae. 'Twas another world.

Sobbing, she gathered up her skirts and sprinted down the earthen road. But what to do? Get help, but how and from where? The Balintoul Inn was the first building she came to, its chimney belching smoke, a trail of ponies tied outside. It was strictly men-folk only. Men and women of loose morals. Her father would likely commit murder, but that hardly mattered now. She shoved the door open and stumbled inside.

A grubby hand clutched at her sleeve and she whirled around, disorientated by the clouds of tobacco smoke, the reek of pot-ale, and the press of faces leering at her out of the gloom. An ugly heavily-whiskered face grinned at her, displaying a single brown tooth.

'Have ye a spare hour or twa, ma quine?' A filthy hand tugged at her bodice.

'Get away!' she snapped, pushing him off.

'How much?'

'I need help!' She pushed her way further into the room.

'Oh, aye? I could help a'right. What was it ye had in mind?'

'I'll help ye out o' yer gown!' guffawed another.

She shuddered; the inn had been a mistake. Turning to go, she lashed out at the drovers blocking her way, ruthlessly elbowing them aside.

'Morven! Wait, Morven!'

Incredibly, it was Ellen MacPherson who squeezed her way through the press, her face white and pinched-looking. There were two men with her; a red-haired lad little older than Morven herself and an older man with a kindly face.

'Thank heavens ye're alright!' Ellen's voice rose shrill above the general rowdiness of the inn. 'I heard the gauger come hame and kent there'd be trouble. When he made straight fer the stairs, I ran fer my man and this here's my lad, Angus.'

Morven could've kissed the woman. 'I'd to leave Rowena with him,' she blurted. 'And him in a towering rage, claiming she's murdered them both. What he means to do I dinna ken, but 'tis something fearful.' She clutched at the older man's sleeve. 'Will ye come back to the house wi' me, sir? Help me get her away?'

'*I'll* come back to the hoose wi' ye!'

A chorus of bawdy cheers followed this ribald remark, but the man nodded without a murmur and led the way out.

Ellen waited outside in the courtyard for her sister returning with the silvered water while Morven and her men-folk stormed the exciseman's home. From the foot of the stairs, they could hear an eerie sound. A keening that chilled Morven's blood. No words, just a harrowing wail abruptly choked off. The two men exchanged a look and charged up the stairs.

When Morven reached the doorway, Ellen's men-folk were grappling with the exciseman, attempting to haul him over to the hearth, as far from Rowena as they could. He bellowed his rage, struggling furiously, his face livid with angry blood.

'He's getting awa' from me, Da!' shouted Angus, and his father dealt the exciseman a swift blow to the groin, doubling him over. Angus quickly pinioned the gauger's arms behind his back.

''Tis fer yer own good, man,' grunted the older of the two, though plainly he'd derived considerable satisfaction from the blow himself and delivered another for good measure. 'Whatever's she done, this isna the way.' He stepped back and motioned for his lad to stand the exciseman up. 'And 'tis hardly the place fer it,' he added, glancing uneasily at the lifeless figures on the bed.

McBeath glared at him, wheezing, his face purple, the sinews of his neck taut and straining.

Rowena was sat at the edge of the bed, rocking back and forth, staring dazed-like. Her face looked deathly. On seeing Morven, a thin wail erupted from her lips. Morven helped her up, then had to support her weight lest she crumple back down again.

'Did he hurt ye?' she whispered. 'What did he do?'

Rowena shook her head, a ghastly expression on her face.

'Take her home,' cried Rob. ''Tis a sorry business, but whatever he believes has plainly tipped him ower the edge.'

Quickly Morven bolstered Rowena under an arm and led her stumbling from the room. The exciseman heaved and strained in the grip of the two men, glaring at them. Defiantly, she returned the glare, twisting her head to maintain her challenge until the very last moment.

CHAPTER NINE

THE EARLY CHILL OF the day had lifted, and the sun shone warm on Jamie's back. He straightened and eased the ache in the base of his spine, then began piling the rocks he'd cleared onto his aunt's hand-cart. The rain clouds threatening since dawn had come to nothing, and he shaded his eyes as he looked up to the misty foothills of the Cairngorms.

The beauty of the place could still catch him unawares, could tighten his chest, and he stopped to breathe-in the rugged grandeur of the place. There was a timeless quality about Strathavon, a remoteness certainly, but it was far from the Godforsaken land some believed it, and instinctively he considered it home in a way Inverness had never been. Here, among the heather-clad hills and ancient birk and pinewoods, he could take his fill of life and let it feed his soul.

He briefly closed his eyes, feeling at peace, then looked around at his kinswoman's scrape of land. There was still much to do. He must grow more oats to see them through the winter along with the new crop, potatoes, which was still viewed with suspicion by most in the glen. But first, he must clear more land, put heather and whin to the plough and break the granite backbone of the land, then unearth it to build dykes. As he worked, he thought over possible sites for his whisky-making. A safe location was needed for his bothy, a place no-one would think to look. The secret place Morven had taken him to was perfect, but 'twas hardly fair to push her father's generosity further. And he knew not whether to trust the man.

Bending, he drove his spade under a half-buried rock, pressing his entire weight onto the spade and rocking it from side to side until, at last, the ground relinquished the mass and he could roll it away. The ache in his spine returned, although he carried another more private ache within him. This was entirely separate from the agony of losing his family. The bitterness of that, of finding no-one to blame, no-one to hold accountable, save God, was less raw now, although the sorrow was as profound as ever. 'Twas hard to understand, he doubted he ever would, but the Lord had chosen to take them and leave him untouched. God's will, the priest had said, nae his fault, though he'd believed it was for a time.

Only the private hurt was another matter. This he *had* caused. His thoughts turned to her now, unbidden, as they did at almost every opportunity. Whenever he thought of her it was always the impression of a young cat that sprang to mind, the fluid grace, the instinctual caution, sensitive to any threat, yet self-contained and direct. He lifted the edge of the rock up onto the front of the cart, and, squatting beneath it, managed to lever it up until he could slide it to rest with the others. Rubbing his eyes, he pressed into the tense flesh at the bridge of his nose. He'd taken advantage. And nae content with that, he'd then insulted – nay, accused – her father wi'out thought or proof. Morven had needed comforting, had been angry and vulnerable, yet had he done that? Had he gentled her fears? Hardly. He'd seen an excuse to touch her, kiss her, and been unable to stop himself. And then foolishly maligned her father, disclosed what he should not have done, riling her further.

He began to dig into the earth once more. She was the most fascinating woman he'd ever known. Indeed she captivated him so much he could not stop from looking at her, discovering each time something new that drew him further under her spell. Perhaps 'twas her directness that disarmed him so, for when she looked at him, he felt as if he'd come home, did belong again. Yet she was young and vulnerable, and his yearning to protect and keep her safe was so strong, he sensed it frightened her. For she was loyal to a fault, he knew that now, perhaps to his cost. 'Twas but another part of her that drew him.

Only, to hold her. Lord, to touch her skin, feel her small and tender against him. And her mouth …. He groaned and turned to attack the ground once more. 'Twas unforgivable. She'd given him nothing but friendship, even when he shamefully spilled his heart out, she'd given him no encouragement. Likely been horrified. The ache in his chest deepened. He worked furiously at the ground, waiting for the ache in his muscles to lessen the more private hurt inside. Her friendship was precious, far too valuable to misuse. Only, was it nae right to tell her the truth? To warn her about her father? His da would have said so, what would his mother say? He wished he knew.

A cloud of midgies closed in, and he swiped at the air above his head. He'd nothing to offer Morven even given she felt the same, and plainly she did not. She felt beholden to him, and likely despised feeling so, for she was her own woman and clearly made her own choices. He'd never made mention of that night of flames, but the indebtedness was there between them, a ghostly presence, one he could never seem to exorcise, no matter how hard he did try. And here in this place, he was still an outsider. Whispered about. Held in distrust. The instrument of their undoing? He sincerely hoped not.

As he remembered, there'd been superstitions aplenty in Inverness too. Father Tobias, the old priest who'd taught him to read, had declared superstition a religion of feeble minds. Yet belief in the supernatural ran deep here. Naught to do with feeble minds, just simple reliance on traditions handed down through the ages, and 'twas mighty difficult not to be affected by it all.

He drank from a leather flask, savouring the sweetness of the spring water. At Tomachcraggen, they drew their water from the *Tobar Fuar*, the cold well, a haunt of faeryfolk he'd been told on Tomachcraggen land. Here, three springs brought ice-cold water to the surface from rocky underground deposits, each tasting remarkably different. Sarah had explained the springs were said to cure blindness, deafness, and lameness and were watched over by a guardian spirit and this accounted for the difference in taste. She'd been sober about it, though he'd known 'twas all meant to impress him. She liked to do that; to try and shock him, to appear worldly, though beneath it all he sensed a confused young lass and felt for her.

Sarah could be difficult, 'thrawn' Rowena called her, and his aunt fretted over her. She'd no father and a purported witch fer a mother, nae wonder she was difficult. Sarah had need o' some steadiness in her life. She needed a father. 'Twas his duty to guide her, to listen to her as an older brother might, nae a father. He could never be that.

Looking around, he regarded the forest of tree stumps left from his woodcutting work of a few days ago. He'd need to dig them all out – every one. The land was needed. He caught sight of a small figure making toward him. William, was it? He squinted into the sun, warmed by the thought of William's company. The lad was likeable in a quiet way. But no, had Rowena nae sent him and Sarah to the dominie that forenoon? The schoolmaster was in the glen again teaching the glen bairns their letters. He followed the progress of the figure, perceiving a certain reluctance, a preoccupied air to the figure's movements.

As the figure came closer, he realised with a jolt it was Rowena, but a diminished almost hunched Rowena barely recognisable as the spirited woman he held in such regard. She winced at his scrutiny, and he felt a twinge of conscience. He'd thought her uncommonly quiet the night before, only he'd been sunk in his own thoughts too. After finishing the second run of spirit through the still, he'd worked long on the land, giving himself up to the work, numbing himself with it, and returning late and too weary for anything but sleep. He'd seen her ashen face and troubled eyes but paid little heed. Now he was shocked at her appearance. Her face was drawn and lined, her eyes over-bright with the quick darting movements of someone deprived of sleep, and there were dark circles under them.

'Rowena!' He dropped his spade. 'Ye're unwell, ye –'

'I'm nae unwell,' she said grimly. 'But I would speak with ye. Nae here, though. I need the feel of the forest about me and to know *na daoine sìth*, the faeryfolk, will hear me and may help.'

He blinked in bewilderment, but she merely nodded and gestured for him to follow her. She set off toward Dun Sithean.

'Has something happened?' He glanced sidelong at her, matching her steps over the ground he'd cleared. Her face was drawn and pinched, but when she turned to look at him, her eyes burned fiercely.

'Something ill. Isobel McBeath and her infant are dead.'

In the shock of the moment, all he could think of was Morven. 'And ye were there – you and Morven? 'Twas *his* wife ye were called to yesterday?'

She gave a brief nod.

'God's teeth! What on earth made ye do such a thing?'

'Isobel did.' She frowned at him. 'Never would I forsake her. Though ... though she was beyond my help.'

'But,' he croaked, 'd'ye nae see how this will look? The gauger might believe ye were involved in their deaths, maybe even responsible.' He puffed his cheeks out, struggling to grasp the enormity of this.

'Aye, 'tis what he believes, but it's what I ken of him that matters now, and what I must do wi' that knowledge.'

She refused to be drawn further until she reached what she called the sanctity of Sìthean Wood, and one look at her closed countenance told him it was useless to coax her. She was trembling, but he sensed not from fear. 'Twas perhaps anger, or something even more disturbing.

From the western slope of Dun Sithean, the hill of the faeries, a small track led into a dense wood. The wood seemed dark and impassable and overly silent. Jamie had seen the path before and wondered who could have made it. It led from the wood to the oddly rounded summit of the hill with its crown of pine trees and then ended. Yet it was clearly well used – hard-packed with no covering of deergrass or bracken. He'd never observed anyone enter that wood and had never felt inclined to do so himself. There was something forbidding about the place, but it was clearly where Rowena was headed. Too disturbed by her revelations and anxious to know more, he didn't question the wisdom of her actions but silently followed her.

Immediately they entered the wood, he felt the chill. An iciness seeped into his bones, drawing his warmth away despite his thick plaid, and he shivered. There was not a sound in the denseness of the forest, the silence was oppressive, and an overwhelming urge to flee from the place came over him. It was only possible to walk bent double with the grasping branches of blackthorn and briar scratching at his face and in the darkness, he stumbled over the tussocky ground. The pale scrap that was the kertch Rowena wore to cover her hair bobbed in front of him through the trees, and he gritted his teeth and followed it. The sound of his own blundering advance seemed deafening, yet, oddly, Rowena made barely a sound.

His back began to ache at his uncomfortably crouched position, and there was a dull pain in his jaw and neck – he was so tense he'd been grinding his own teeth. He took a deep breath. How long had they been floundering in this Godforsaken place? Long enough. He drew breath to tell Rowena as much when the distinctive sound of children's laughter rang out. He froze, then whirled to pinpoint its source. 'Twas gone, and the silence closed in again. The hair on the back of his neck rose.

Rowena's white kertch vanished into a dark tunnel in the trees ahead, and he blundered after it, emerging suddenly into bright light. He stretched to his full height, blinking in the brightness, almost deafened by the clamour of birdsong and stared at his kinswoman.

'What is this place?'

'D'ye not know?' she said with a soft smile. 'Does it look like any place ye've ever seen afore? Like a human place?'

He blanched and stared about him. Here the trees had room to spread and were evidently of great age. Twisted into extraordinary shapes, their branches draped to the ground and also climbed to incredible heights. Hung with mistletoe and crisped over with lichens, he realised they must have stood here untouched since ancient times. A great oak tree stood guard at Rowena's shoulder, smothered in curious panicles of blossom, and a warm breeze ruffled his hair. The air was gently perfumed; a familiar scent, yet one he knew he'd never encountered. Birds sang from amongst the leaves of every tree, and he thought he heard again the faint sound of children's laughter. 'Twas a peaceful place and seemed to welcome him, for he felt no fear, only an immense curiosity.

'A faery glade?' he ventured.

'Sacred to Brigid. Or St. Bride as they call her now.'

'But ...' He'd never really believed in such things, although he'd never been able to entirely deny them either. Nor had he ever ventured near the faery hillock of Tomnahurich in Inverness, though he'd been dared to often as a boy. And he knew every night of his life his mother had faithfully left out milk in a special cog for the faeryfolk in the hopes they'd leave their own churn untouched.

'Dinna question it. I can speak here, think clearly wi'out the anger clouding my judgment, and I hope ye'll be able to guide me. Never forget whatever we say here may be listened to and the guidfolk may help.'

He glanced uneasily around as if expecting to see eyes glinting from among the trees, but there was nothing. 'Will ye tell me now what happened yesterday?'

She nodded, appearing less drawn and to have recovered some of her vigour. 'But,' she warned, fixing him with a shrewd look. 'I ken how like yer father ye are, Jamie, and nae just in yer looks but in yer nature too. Ye must promise me nae to let yer temper get the better of ye, no matter what I tell ye. I seek yer guidance, but clear thought is needed here, nae a rush o' blood to the head.'

He blinked, nonplussed.

As she talked, Rowena paced the clearing, her agitation growing, her gaze rarely resting on one spot for longer than a few seconds. Jamie watched her and felt his own unease rise, although he did not understand it. He listened in silence as she recounted the details of her ride to Balintoul with the two sisters, of the dead infant and her desperate attempt to save the child's mother. The woman's life had ended in a rush of blood, a catastrophic loss, but Rowena had tried her best, had employed every practice known to her in a bid to save the woman's life. When she spoke of Morven's anxiety for them to be gone before the gauger returned, his heart hammered in his chest while his stomach lurched at the man's wildly unjust accusations.

'If only I'd been with ye,' he choked. 'I doubt he'd be so quick to accuse ye wi' my dirk at his throat!'

'Maybe not. Yet we must be wiser than that, must put aside our anger.' She firmed the slight tremble to her jaw. 'Only I've more to tell.'

He took a quivering breath. 'Go on.'

She seated herself on a hummock of moss beneath the oak tree, hands clasped fast in her lap and looked up darkly. 'He thought we planned to take his child fer some hellish purpose, fer ...' She shook her head. 'I'm nae rightly certain what he imagined.'

Jamie gritted his teeth. Was the man such a clot, he couldna see Rowena's goodness, her humanity, that her only desire was to help?

'He said we'd unfinished business, me and him, and he threw Morven out o' the house. The lass ran fer help, but while she was gone ...' The muscles in her throat convulsed, and she struggled to keep herself under control. 'He wished to hurt me, as I wounded him years ago. I did crush his pride and still torment him yet just by living in the glen. He believes I've cursed him to be childless, occasioned the death of every one of his unborn infants and now brought his wife's end too.' A cracked little sob escaped her lips.

'What did he do?'

Her face crumpled, then she seemed to draw herself together, dredging up every scrap of strength to haul herself back from some chasm. 'He told me he killed Duncan. 'Twas an execution. Done in deliberate cold blood. He said he gained pleasure from it.' She made no movement, yet an involuntary spasm rocked her body, the tremor shattering the stillness of the glade. 'I always knew it didna happen as they said, but never did I consider fer a moment that he'd planned it all. Knew where Duncan would be, and when, then laid a trap fer him, taking deliberate pleasure in his killing.' She ran trembling fingers over her dry lips, then slowly brought her gaze up to her nephew's face.

'The bastard,' he growled. 'He actually told ye all this? Bragged about it?'

'He said beating Duncan was rare entertainment. My man pleaded fer his life, and they jested with him, letting him think they'd release him once each had tired of kicking and beating him. The gauger then sat him up against a rock and took aim wi' his musket.' She pressed her eyes shut and took a quivering breath. 'A musket ball will smash a hole the size o' a clenched fist through a man's chest. I've seen it afore and 'tis something I'm nae like to forget. 'Tis a terrible way to die.'

'Dear God!'

'Yet fer Hugh McBeath, 'twas an amusement. He said 'twas rare sport to listen to my love struggling fer breath, his chest filling wi' his own blood, and that ... that it took ower an hour fer him to die.' Her shoulders shook, and she hid her face in her hands. 'They took wagers, him and his hirelings, bet at how long 'twould take fer my man to drown in his own blood.'

Rocked by her words, Jamie stared at her, white-faced. He wished to comfort his kinswoman, but what in God's name could he say after that?

'He'll hang,' he said with quiet certainty. He'd never witnessed a public hanging, had never felt a desire to do so, but this was one neck he'd take satisfaction in seeing stretched. 'As God is my witness, I swear, I'll see him hang!' He clenched his fists, the thrumming of his blood filling his ears. 'If he gets to live that long.'

Rowena's ghastly expression was one he'd never witnessed before and sincerely hoped never to see again. 'Ye dinna understand. He's a murderer, but I canna prove that. No-one will believe me, he took pleasure in telling me so, and … and he was right.'

'But surely the evidence at the time pointed to –'

'To nothing. 'Twas all twisted around. He made out Duncan attacked them. Acted like a madman he said, and they'd to fire at him, but,' her mouth twisted bitterly, 'didna mean to kill him.' She looked at Jamie with a dreadful desperation in her eyes. 'Ye see how useless it all is? Knowing what he did, the cruelty of it. Knowing he's still free to … to brag about it, I canna bear it. 'Tis all ower me, the hatred, the …' she searched for the right word, 'the *obsession.*'

She rose and swayed a little on her feet, a hand held to her throat, then began to pace back and forth between the trees. Not knowing what to do, Jamie reached out and squeezed her hand as she passed. She halted and looked steadily at him, then sat back down on the mossy mound and pressed her lips together; he had a horrible feeling there was still worse to come.

'Revenue Officers are held in high regard,' she said. 'At least by magistrates and the like. Common folks see things a wee bit different. We do hold them in the grossest contempt. As for myself, as I live and breathe, I do despise that man like no other.' Her eyes, dark now with despair, moved to his face. 'Yet I must accept him, or he'll see me arrested fer the murder of his wife and child.'

'Accept him?' He stared at her. 'Ye dinna mean … *as a husband?*'

Miserably, she nodded, then clutched her head in her hands.

He gasped in disbelief. But no, for certain he'd misunderstood her. Yet staring at the crumpled figure, her despair was so profound it was difficult for him to look upon, and he realised he'd misunderstood nothing. He knelt awkwardly at her feet. She turned her face away, holding a trembling hand up against him. Even in the circumstances, the gesture struck him as somehow more troubling than her words. He blinked and sat back.

'After he told ye he slaughtered yer man? And with his own wife nae yet cold from the birthing bed, *he actually expects ye to wed him*?'

She gave a wretched nod.

He thought he might be sick. The man was inhuman; he was … he didn't know what he was, 'twas unthinkable. Realising he was still gaping at his kinswoman, he snapped his mouth shut and rasped, 'Then I hope ye told him to go to hell, where he most surely belongs!'

'I have three months to accept him, or he'll have me arrested fer the killing of his wife and child. And fer practising witchery.'

'But, he could never bring those charges … there are witnesses, those who'd swear ye were only there to help.'

'Aye, mebbe, but doesna matter.' She looked up bleakly. 'The scandal will be enough to see me evicted. His Grace willna tolerate the likes of me as a tenant. Nae wi' the whiff o' witchery and child-killing. My murderous ways will be brought to the Duke's attention, so I'm damned either way.' She began to weep.

'But I'll not let that happen!' Still on his knees, he cautiously took her hand and stared down at the small perfection of it as his mind whirled. They sat like that for some time, Jamie searching in vain for something comforting to say to her, some way of easing her anguish, but finding nothing to offer but his own presence, utterly inadequate as he knew it to be.

After a time, Rowena's grief exhausted itself, and he dried her face with his plaid.

'Forgive me.' She gestured with her hand, encompassing her red swollen face and crumpled appearance. 'I meant to be strong. Thought maybe wi' your help we could, I dinna ken exactly, take a stand against him.'

'And we will, I swear it.'

She nodded and pulled herself straight, sniffing and trying vainly to smile at him. 'But I dinna see how.'

Neither did he, but he wasn't about to let her know that. 'Ye must tell me everything ye know of that day,' he said. 'The day Duncan died. Everything ye can so we can think o' something.' He squeezed her cold hand. 'We'll nae let the bastard away with this.'

She frowned, and her dark pupils dilated.

'He was a quiet man, Duncan. You'd not the chance to meet him Jamie, but I'm certain ye'd have liked each other. I see a lot o' him in William, the same seriousness, the thoughtful nature, and I hear him speaking through his son wi' that same soft-spoken voice.'

She sighed. 'It would've been profitable fer us that consignment, the result of a whole winter's distilling.' She wet her dry lips with her tongue. 'Duncan didna speak of the smuggling like some in the glen, didna boast ower it, but kept the details secret, kenning full well the gaugers were aye listening fer word of a convoy, most especially McBeath. But someone knew. Someone told them what Duncan was about that day.'

'It couldna have been a chance encounter?'

'With McBeath the idlest gauger north o' the Highland Line? I dinna see how. And anyhow, he said he knew where Duncan would be – that he'd been informed.'

'By who?'

'That I dinna ken. Only those closest to us knew; myself and the bairns, Grace, Malcolm.'

'None of them would turn informer.' He frowned, his eyes flicking over her face.

She fixed him with a dark look. 'Someone did. A traitor. Someone from the glen betrayed us.'

''Twould seem that way. Someone informed and likely profited from it. And you … you have yer suspicions?'

She regarded him for a long moment. 'I think we both know who I suspect.'

'Malcolm. Morven's da.'

'Oh, I dinna ken! I canna believe I even said that never heed thought it.'

'But ye did think it.'

Wretchedly, she nodded. 'I've gone ower it in my mind as often and can find no other earthly reason fer the change in Malcolm. Though scarce can I believe it. The two o' them were as close as kinsmen. As close as Duncan once was to yer father, Jamie.'

'And Malcolm knew every detail?'

'He did. But then, he's kent every detail of every shipment o' whisky Duncan's ever smuggled. 'Tis many a time they banded together and smuggled their mountain dew south lashed to the sides of the cattle as they drove the beasts to market at Falkirk or Crieff. That at ease were they with each other.'

Jamie massaged his brow, trying to make sense of it all. 'Yet there does seem a powerful hatred between Malcolm and McBeath. 'Tis hard to believe he'd be content to work fer the gauger and in so doing betray his neighbour and his friend. Indeed, betray everything he believes in.'

'I know. There's more to this than I can see.' She shook her head. 'I do fear I've made a terrible mistake. At times I can scarce look

Morven in the eye, fer fear she'll see what I'm thinking and 'twould hurt her so. 'Twould come atween us.'

He nodded slowly, thinking much the same.

'Only,' she asked, 'who else could it have been?'

More troubled by this than he wished her to know, he said, 'Can ye tell me what happened that day? The day Duncan died. As much as ye know.'

Grimly, she nodded. 'He'd only been gone half the forenoon when his pony came back wi'out him. William came with me to look fer his da.' She paled at the memory. 'If I'd known what we'd find, I'd never have taken him, poor lad. We found Duncan in a ditch nae two miles from the bothy, beaten and soaked in blood, a great hole opened in his chest. 'Twas plain he was –' She swallowed.

'Take yer time,' he said, squeezing her hand.

'I kent he was dead. William found his dirk in a clump o' heather and the garrons we found straggled ower the hillside. The ankers were gone but 'twas only later I realised my ring was gone.'

'Yer ring?'

'Forgive me, I'm getting ahead o' myself. 'Twas given me by Morna, an uncanny woman wi' magic skills – the woman that taught me to heal – many years ago. Silver it was, the most delicate work, wi' strange markings and trailing ivy leaves, verra ancient I believe. When Duncan and I were marrit I gave it him as a gift, a token of my love, and he wore it on a lace about his neck, it being too wee fer his finger.' She smiled a ghost of a smile as if remembering something.

Jamie felt a flicker of hope at last. 'Then the killer must've taken the ring. If we could find the ring we could point to the killer, in the eyes of the law, I mean.'

She glanced up sharply. 'If the man's nae sold it already.'

'Aye, but something makes me think he's not done that. His obsession with you might make him keep it. Maybe even keep it on him, as Duncan did.'

She stared at him, plainly sickened by that thought.

'Forgive me,' he stammered. 'I didna mean to distress ye.' Lord, but he wished to kill the bastard. Squeeze the life from the miserable obscenity with his bare hands. He cleared his throat.

'There must have been some manner of investigation though, after the kill … the death?'

'Oh aye, there was a hearing.' She gave a short laugh. 'They held it at the Craggan Inn in front o' the Sheriff Officer. Half the glen turned out to watch.'

'The Craggan Inn? That hardly seems the place.'

'Duncan was a smuggler, mind,' she said bitterly. 'A man of poor character and little consequence.' She massaged her brow. 'There were only the three witnesses called. McBeath and two cottars from Balintoul, his hirelings: Charles Stuart o' Wester Lynatoul, Ghillie he's known as, and Dougal Riach of Laggan o' Campdell.'

'And I suppose the two told the story they'd been paid to tell?'

'Both swore Duncan attacked them wi' his dirk. Said he struggled fiercely when they tried to seize the whisky, but McBeath's testimony was most damning. He swore Duncan threatened them wi' a pistol. Said he was forced to fire at him, but Duncan made flight and they'd nae been able to find him. They'd nae been overly worried though, thinking him just nicked.'

She looked darkly at her nephew. 'I knew 'twas all a lie. Duncan had no pistol – he's never owned one. But no-one else could speak at the hearing.'

''Twas all a sham, then.'

'The sheriff said the death was unfortunate, but a desperate disease must demand a desperate cure and the gauger was only doing his duty fer the Crown.'

'A pat on the back, no less!'

Jamie began to stalk back and forth. But what, if anything, could he do? In his mind, he turned over the events as Rowena had told them, exploring possibilities, carefully considering options and assessing the risks involved only to reject his fledgeling ideas in favour of others. After a while, he frowned and looked down at his aunt.

'He's cock-sure o' himself. Convinced he canna be touched, or he'd never have told ye all this?'

She considered for a moment.

'I dinna believe he planned to tell me it all but in the heat o' the moment, riled by anger and fear – fer he's more than a little afraid o' me – a kind of madness took him, a …' She shook her head, and a violent shudder ran through her. 'A bedevilment.' Abruptly, she stood and stalked a few paces before turning back, her eyes blazing. 'But if there's any in this glen possessed by the divil, then it's surely that man!'

Jamie looked uneasily at her. Her hands were trembling, and unconsciously she traced the neat rows of stitching that crisscrossed the bodice of her gown. 'Possessed, ye say?' He lowered his voice. 'He didna hurt ye, Rowena, bodily I mean?'

She turned away. 'He didna hurt me. But he plans to have me fer his wife and … and failing that he'll see me gaoled and evicted.

Thereafter I'll be homeless – landless and penniless – me and my bairns at his mercy. In the end, he knows full well I'll have no choice but wed him.'

'Nae as long as I draw breath!' He'd not allow it. The certainty of that settled in his core, buoying him a little. 'He carries the knowledge of this deed with him always,' he said gruffly. 'It must burden him some, God-fearing soul that he is.'

'I doubt it.'

'But if he'd someone like-minded he could confide in, or better yet, if there was someone of little consequence close to him, listening, keeping his eyes open, searching fer the ring, that might prove the way to ensnare him.'

A spark of hope ignited in Rowena's eyes. 'Who d'ye mean?'

He smiled grimly but with a sickening lurch felt his guts turn over. 'There's only one man could do it. I must join the Board of Excise, seek work in Stratha'an, and then wait fer the miserable bastard to slip up.'

'God, no, Jamie! 'Tis too much to ask! If he should find ye out, why he'd kill ye fer certain. He'd no more trust a kinsman of mine than sup ale wi' his Holiness the Pope.' She sat down abruptly and dipped her fingers into a dark pool Jamie hadn't noticed before.

'Ye mightna ken this lad, and I hadna the heart to tell ye afore, but you're mistrusted here, in the glen, nae accepted yet, though I dinna doubt ye will be in time. Only this, this would just confirm their worst suspicions. The Stratha'an smugglers will never accept ye after seeing ye in the gauger's garb.'

'To blazes with them!' Seeing his aunt's shocked expression, Jamie softened a little. 'You and yours are all that matter Rowena. You're my blood, my kin … I canna let this happen.' Kneeling before her, he willed her to understand and accept his gift. 'I wish ye to know how dear ye are to me – far dearer than my own safety – and … and knowing it, will ye not let me do this fer ye? At least try?'

She regarded him for what seemed an age, unblinking, then finally dropped her head into her hands and whispered fiercely, 'God forgive me, but aye. Aye, I will.'

'Thank you. I'll leave at dawn. Go to Elgin. To the Collector there and offer myself. I can send ye my wages to help with the croft and … and I'll come and see ye whenever I can, when it's safe, and tell ye what I've learned.'

When she gave no answer, he continued to speak to the top of her head, hoping that if he talked through his fears and doubts, they might somehow cease to exist.

'I'm certain McBeath kens nothing of me. I saw him only the once, at the *ceilidh* if ye mind when he tried to arrest Morven's da, but he paid me no heed. Nor does he know who I am.' He thought for a moment. 'We must tell no-one about this. With a traitor in the glen, the bastard could well get wind of our plan. And that would mean the end of it.'

'Aye,' she agreed. 'I'll nae tell a soul. If I must, I'll say ye've gone back to Inverness, gone to make sure folk ye're acquainted wi' survived the sickness.'

'You can tell Morven,' he added hastily.

'We canna do that, Jamie.' There was hurt in her eyes as she said it. 'Canna be taking the risk. If 'twas her father betrayed us …' She swallowed, an anguished expression twisting her face. 'Ye must promise me.'

Rowena was right, but still, his heart sank. What if he should discover Malcolm MacRae was the traitor? How could he tell Morven that? He nodded briefly and summoned the closest thing to a smile he could find. 'Ye have my word on it.'

Rowena looked tenderly at him. 'Come, lad, we'll ask Brigid to protect ye. I need yer dirk.'

He handed it to her and watched curiously as she cut a strip of cloth from his sark and dipped it into the pool. Chanting softly in Gaelic, she tied it onto a branch of the oak tree. He looked more closely at the tree. What he'd at first taken for blossom he now realised was a great number of cloth strips just like the one Rowena had cut from his sark but all obviously of great age. Desiccated by the winds of time, they looked as though they might disintegrate if he as much as breathed on them. The dusty remains of many were littered around the tree.

'What is this?' He peered into the dark water.

'A clootie well. And a verra ancient one at that.'

'A what?' But he did know. As a child, he remembered seeing the bedraggled procession wend its way to the clootie well at Clava. His mother had tried to explain.

'A place o' healing,' said Rowena, and he nodded. 'These cloots or pieces of cloth represent the heartfelt pleas fer help of many souls over a great many years. No-one comes here now, but once this place was sacred to the Celtic Church. A place o' pilgrimage. They'd pray to Brigid, the White Woman, and cut a strip from the clothes o' the afflicted, or the one to go to battle, or into danger, and tie it onto the tree. Brigid would watch ower them as she still does today, only she's kent as St. Bride now.'

'She's like Our Lady, then?'

'One and the same,' Rowena confirmed.

'Thank ye,' he said, watching his cloot move gently with the others.

'No, lad. 'Tis me should be thanking you. I pray Brigid keeps ye safe.'

'I pray she keeps you safe,' he whispered. 'You and my cousins.'

Turning, they made their way out of the clearing, Rowena leading the way and an air of peace returned to the sacred place. Birds called to each other from amongst the trees, and a pair of tree pipits parachuted down from the treetops, giving voice to their joy in loud musical trills. They settled on the ground, then rose again in alarm as the branches of the old oak tree began to shake violently. There came a loud snapping of boughs, and a shower of rags rained down in a cloud of dust. Eventually, a pair of legs appeared, dangled for a moment, and then dropped down in a ball of skirts.

Sarah picked herself up and rubbed her neck and shoulders. She was stiff from her long-cramped concealment in the tree, but it had been well worth it. Whoever would've guessed her playing truant from the teachings of the dry auld dominie would be so rewarding? She hadna heard everything they'd said but enough, enough she supposed for her purposes.

So, Jamie was to join the Excise. Why he couldna just stick a dirk in the Black Gauger's back, she couldn't quite fathom, but she hoped McBeath would hang. A slow lingering death with the knot nae positioned right so he would choke, a quick death was too good fer him.

She brought out the parcel of bannocks and cheese her mother had made for her that morning and made herself comfortable by the well at the foot of the tree. A knowing smile stretched her pretty lips. Poor Morven, she snorted aloud at the thought. What rare entertainment she'd have with her mother's devoted apprentice. Anticipation warmed her breast, a welcome exchange for the more confusing feelings her mother's words had aroused within her.

She'd not think on her da's unspeakable end, wouldna dwell on the shock of it. Only in the depth of night, alone in the darkness would she think on that. Then the tears would come. She screwed her face up, lest they come now and spoil her fun.

'Twas only fair she should have some sport with Morven. Compensation, so to speak, fer her stealing her mam away. For that gnawing wound that ate away at her innards. And she was stealing Jamie too, she could feel it. A fearful bitterness smarted in her heart.

What was so special about Morven anyhow? Naught that she could see. And soon Morven would see it too. And Jamie? She considered him for a moment. She'd still to decide about Jamie.

She stretched herself out to wait in comfort until it was time to meet up with William returning from his lessons. So, no-one ever came here anymore? That only proved how little her own mam knew about her. She cracked her knuckles. Or cared.

CHAPTER TEN

A LITTLE AFTER DAWN on the morning after Isobel and her infant died, Morven sat with her kinfolk as they broke their fast. She had no appetite. She'd passed a restless night thinking long and hard how best to tell them of the deaths, thinking on the words to use and how much to divulge of the gauger's accusations. Disturbed by what she'd witnessed, she finally delivered the tidings in a forthright manner, then sat back, her stomach churning. She'd meant to soften the news somehow for her mother's sake, but 'twas done now.

Her mother's eyes filled with tears, and she dropped a protective hand to her abdomen. 'Poor Isobel. After all she's been through, 'tis so pitiful unfair.'

Morven turned to her father. He'd stopped chewing and now glowered critically at her, his spoon suspended in mid-air.

'The woman was aye a weakling, but ye should've kent better than to go there … and wi' Rowena Forbes. God's blood! Ye'd no business involving yerself wi' the gauger's wife.' He brushed the crumbs from his beard and fixed her with a black look. 'There'll be hell to pay, see if there's not, and we'll all have to pay fer yer foolishness!' Grunting, he resumed ladling porridge into his mouth.

Stung, Morven raised her chin. 'We went there to help her. To be Christian!'

'Aye, and failed.'

'Maybe so, but Rowena brought her some comfort – at least she tried!'

'Rowena! I'll tell ye what Mistress Forbes has brought.' He leant across the table and locked eyes with his daughter. 'More tyranny. More hardship and suffering fer us all.' Standing abruptly, his breath whistled down his nose causing the protruding hairs to quiver. 'There'll be reprisals. He'll be wanting to take an eye fer an eye. 'Tisna hard to see where he'll be wanting to take it. Stay away from Rowena!'

'What?' Her mouth dropped open. 'Rowena's the wisest, most

selfless …' But he'd not see that, being hellbent on opposing his daughter. He'd merely judge this another opportunity to curb Rowena's influence over her.

He made an exasperated sound in his throat. 'She's seen as blasphemous, profane. She be deemed wicked!'

'By who? Nae by me!'

'By those that matter, those we need to cultivate good relations wi' that we might keep a roof ower our heads!'

'Ye mean the factor? As if he even kens ye exist!' She tilted her head and looked askance at him. 'And he means more to ye, does he, than yer own kind?'

'He does not!' A storm of indignant blood boiled up Malcolm's neck and steam near blew from his ears. 'Upon my honour, he does not!' He drew several short breaths to calm himself, then hissed, 'Stay away from her.' He thrust his bowl at Grace. 'Swear it!'

Morven's eyes ignited mutinously; deliberately she pressed her lips together.

Malcolm nodded once to verify his understanding of the facts, then with a disgusted glance in her direction stuffed his bonnet onto his head and banged the door on his way out. Alec coughed apologetically into the silence that followed and gave her hand a quick squeeze.

'Never heed him. He doesna mean anything by …' his hand fluttered, encompassing the volatile idiosyncrasies of their father's manner. Ever her champion, Alec would remain loyal to his da no matter what. Giving her a rueful smile, he took his leave to catch him up.

'He means nae harm,' Grace said defensively. ''Twill be alright, I ken it will.' She sat back in her chair and looked steadily at her daughter. 'I mind how earnest he was the day Duncan and Rowena were marrit. It did swell my heart. He swore to take care of her, swore it to Duncan, vowed should anything ill happen he'd look after her as if she were his own blood. He's nae forgotten, I ken he's not, nae matter how it seems.'

'Twas hard to believe, yet Morven could also remember a different man, a father she'd once been proud of, before this crabbit stranger. She glanced at her younger brothers; both were staring at her, even Donald recognising the significance of Isobel's death. She took a calming breath. She'd made no mention of the Black Gauger's behaviour, of his wild accusations, that could come later, maybe, if she deemed it wise.

'I'll be away to the spring fer water.' She rose from the table and her untouched bowl. Fetching water was generally Donald's chore, she winked at him, but she needed time on her own.

'If ye like. Ye did right to go to her, though.' Unconsciously Grace cupped the still flat plain of her own belly. 'I'm proud of ye fer trying, nae matter the outcome.'

Morven smiled faintly; 'twas good to hear her say so, even be it out of her da's ear-shot.

The spring their water was drawn from was only a few minutes' walk from the shieling hut. Here, Morven washed in the icy water and filled two staved wooden pails ready for the day's cooking and chores. The rocks around the spring were sodden and slippery with weed, although it looked drier under the stand of pines clinging to the hillside above. She climbed up to them. It was peaceful among the trees, the silence broken only by the dry crunch of pine needles beneath her boots and the haunting cry of a curlew. She sat on the ground, feeling the sharp prickle of the needles, and stared out across the glen. The clouds were thin and high, mere smears of mist, and she could see Ben Avon in the distance, wild and barren, still wearing her bonnet of snow. In a good year it might melt by August and stay clear until October, but she hadna come to admire the view. 'Twas Rowena that worried her.

The widow had uttered not a word during their frantic ride from Balintoul, her expression ghastly. She'd been shocked by the gauger's violent behaviour as much as her failure to save Isobel and the child, but Morven had never seen her look so stricken. She'd helped Rowena onto her pony, hastily packing her things around her, then urged the garrons into a frantic gallop. Taking Rowena's reins together with her own, she scattered the merchants at the marketplace, inciting several to run cursing after them, and drew a sharp challenge from two redcoats loitering in the square – she lent them scarce a glance.

As they left the tumult behind, she mouthed a silent prayer for the ponies' sturdy hearts as they tackled hill after hill without complaint, breath snorting from dripping nostrils. Turning the garrons toward Strathavon, she glanced sidelong at her companion, wishing to ask what had happened while she ran for help but deterred by the dreadful look on her face.

On reaching their own glen, she slowed the garrons to a walk, allowing them to recover. Her own breathing was ragged, and her heart pounded hard. She gave Rowena back her own reins, and they walked silently in single file. At the fork in the track that led to Tomachcraggen, she at last ventured to ask what had taken place in that room. Rowena swayed in the saddle, then tumbled to the ground and staggered a few feet before retching into some bracken.

'Are ye alright, Rowena?'

Her sickness over, the widow dropped to her knees and rocked herself back and forth emitting an unearthly keening sound. Morven faltered at her side, then shrugged off her arisaid and wrapped it around Rowena's shoulders.

'What's happened?' she said again. 'Can ye not tell me, Rowena?'

'I'm alright. This is … just a bit o' foolishness.'

'But something's happened. I ken it has.'

The widow ran an unsteady hand up the side of her neck, massaging the tense flesh at her nape. 'Nothing's happened. The man was demented wi' grief … 'twas understandable.' She gave a grim nod, indicating she was restored enough to continue and climbed back into the saddle.

'Are ye certain? I mean, he didna threaten ye?'

'I just took it hard being so … so powerless to prevent that gentle soul from bleeding to death afore my eyes.' She smiled a crooked smile. 'But I'm accustomed to being branded a witch.' She averted her eyes from Morven's continued study of her face and stared patiently ahead, waiting for Morven to remount.

'Twas plain she was hiding something. But what? And why? Morven stole another glance at her, but the widow planned to give no more away; she'd withdrawn into herself, her face a careful blank.

They went their separate ways then, Rowena mumbling her thanks, and Morven pressed her no further. She held the bay mare in check for some time though, watching until the small mounted figure merged with the moor, and her disquiet continued.

She felt that same disquiet now as she gathered up a handful of dry pine needles and crushed them to dust. Lord, that the bairn had thrived, that Isobel had lived to tell the truth of the matter, but the Lord hadna seen fit to work things that way, more was the pity.

She thought it likely McBeath had threatened Rowena, and his threats were anything but idle. He was able to draw on the redcoats or Black Watch if need be. She remembered Sergeant Shiach's irritation with him; perhaps the sergeant would be less than eager to do McBeath's bidding, but that still left an entire garrison of English redcoats stationed at Corgarff. Charged with keeping peace in the Highlands, arresting a murderess would certainly fall within the scope of their duties. Whether McBeath could have Rowena charged with witchery was another matter, but this would be serious kindling for the fire that already raged about her in certain quarters, notably with the factor and his band of acquaintances. And the risk of eviction already hung over Rowena's head.

Yet she sensed 'twas more than McBeath's threats that sickened Rowena. Her friend was accustomed to being branded a witch, she'd said so herself. 'Twas something else. Something grave. But who could she confide her fears in? Not her da. She picked up a pinecone and threw it into the air, watching it arc down and bounce off a rock with a resounding thud. He wouldna care one way or the other. She could speak to her mother about most things, barring her father, but with her mam poorly and carrying another bairn, she daren't risk worrying her. And it wouldna be right to trouble Sarah, nae about her own mam. Jamie, then? She dismissed the blaggard. 'Twould need to be Rowena herself, if she would speak.

She brushed off the pine needles and bits of dry bark clinging to her skirts and returned with the water, heedless of her mother's questioning glance at the length of time she'd taken to fetch it. Once the chores of the day were done, she headed to the bothy where her da had stashed fresh sacks of malt for her to turn into whisky.

The bothy felt cold after the warmth of the open air and smelled sourly of damp ashes. As she bent to clear away the remains of the fire, she gave a little start, her gaze falling upon a strange sight. Set to stand upright and enclosed in a ring of evenly sized pebbles, she found a clutch of harebells arranged upon the fire-cairn. She blinked. Faeries' thimbles they were known as, dainty mats of leaves bearing tiny blue dangling bells. On rare occasions, she would find them growing in clefts in the gorge, and always they did charm her. But these had been put here. Plucked from their hollow with some end in mind. They were meant to signify something, or were mebbe an apology of sorts.

She knew well who'd left them, and the thought didn't altogether warm her. Jamie's claims about her father felt like a barb twisted into her flesh, and that barb held more than one thorn. For in the secret reaches of her heart, she did doubt her father too. The bond between them was one of blood, of kinship, and there was none stronger. Yet her father's hostility toward her learning from Rowena was a mystery, one that shamed her, for something was changed between her father and Rowena, she'd long sensed it and knew Rowena did too. But what Jamie claimed was foul and scurrilous. The imaginings, nay, the ravings of a stranger, one who'd likely damn them all just as Achnareave foretold.

She snatched the posy from its altar and flung it to the ground, scattering the pebbles and bringing the heel of her boot down upon the delicate flowers, crushing them into the ground. Quivering with rage, she sank down beside the desecrated offering. She sat there for a time, breathing hard, but her rage soon ebbed away, and she found herself shivering and confused.

She rose and hauled the mash-tun through from the cave and began filling it with water. In the morning she'd speak with Rowena and hopefully would find some answers. She thought fleetingly of her father's unjust command to stay away from the widow and dismissed it out of hand.

***

Morven woke early the next morning, the raucous cries of sparrow chicks in their nest beneath the eaves drawing her from a shallow sleep. She lay a moment, imagining the frantic jostling in the nest. Another half-hour or so of oblivion would have been welcome, but the events of the last two days would not allow it. Rising, she smoothed down her shift, trying to press away the outward signs of her restless night.

Alec was still asleep, a tuft of brown hair all that showed of him above his pile of blankets, and there was no sign of life from her younger brothers either. Both still slept in their shared pallet by the fire. Her mother's face was peaceful, her body sheltering in the lee of the great mound her father created beside her.

She dressed quickly and poked the fire into life, fuelling it with fresh peat. It was never allowed to go out, except at Hogmanay when a fresh fire was kindled to welcome in the New Year. It began to hiss and spit loudly, threatening to rouse the rest of the household. It was still early, the greyness of dawn seeping through the gaps in the stone walls and beneath the door. Better not to awaken anyone, she needed to see Rowena first before the tasks of the day drew her away. Cupping her hands into the pail of water by the fire, she splashed her face, a rash of gooseflesh breaking out on her body, then quickly brushed her hair, twisting and tying it up out of her way.

She stole a quick glance at her father. His hairy shoulder protruded from the mound of blankets meant to be covering both him and her mam, and a fleeting frown furrowed her brow. His presence unsettled her. He rarely slept at the shieling in the summer months, preferring to stay at Delnabreck and tend the crops, but now the sowing was complete, he'd returned to the high pastures with Alec and Rory. It wasna right to resent yer own da, yet part of her did. Turning away, she rummaged for her arisaid, then, remembering she'd given it to Rowena, picked up her boots and tiptoed out.

The morning was cold and damp, the heavy rain of the night now thinned to a fine drizzle, and a dawn mist rose pearly grey against the purple of the heather. The sky was still laden, rain clouds banked atop of each other their greyness tinged with streaks of dawn, and the air was heavy with the scent of damp earth. The eaves were dripping, and a cold droplet slithered its way down the back of her neck. Shivering, she pulled on her boots and picked her way through the puddles and mud to the ponies.

She would take one of the other ponies and leave Shore to rest, perhaps Fergan, her father's black gelding. She spoke soothingly to him in Gaelic, trying to calm his nervous snorting, and enticed him over with some sweet cicely roots. A powerful garron, she ran her hands over the smooth plains of muscle beneath his wet flanks and felt the solid bulk of his shoulders, but he was nervous of any but Alec or her father. A sense of sudden urgency quickened her pulse, and she checked her rough breathing before her strange panic overtook the pony.

The garron accepted her, and she quickly bridled him and guided him, bareback, down the slope of Carn Odhar, avoiding the jagged rocks of the hillside and the dark shapes that emerged from the mist with an indignant moo. Less sure-footed than the bay, Fergan was inclined to be rash, but she kept him in check, not sharing his enthusiasm to run free but dreading an injury to her father's favourite pony.

As they came within the bounds of Tomachcraggen land, she saw sizeable stretches of newly cleared ground. Arable land was scarce in Strathavon, though hill pastures abundant, and much of the soil here was almost useless. Littered with great slabs of ancient granite, it was impossible to work it with a plough, and the surrounding forests and moorland soon encroached. Yet peering through the mist, she saw the stumps of many newly felled trees and great cairns of rock awaiting removal while the heathery undergrowth had also been cleared away. Jamie, she thought.

At the crofthouse, there was no sign of either of Rowena's two ponies, but a thick column of smoke rose into the damp air from the single chimney; plainly someone was up and about. Without her thick arisaid, the drizzle had soaked through her clothing, and she felt chilled to the bone. She dried her face as best she could and tied Fergan to the water trough. Standing at the door, she felt an inexplicable nervousness and tried to swallow it away, though a sense of misgiving persisted.

Sarah opened the door, her pale eyes widening at the sight of her neighbour dripping on the doorstep. 'Morven. There's naught wrong, is there? Ye're half drowned.' Not waiting for an answer, she held the door open. 'Come and warm yerself.'

The room was dim, potions and powders cluttering the window ledge and only the weakest glimmer of daylight managed to penetrate the gloom, yet it was clear Sarah was alone.

'Yer mam's nae here?' Sarah could be good company, wickedly quick-witted at times though less so since her da died, but Morven needed to speak with Rowena.

'They left early.' Sarah removed a bundle of dried herbs from the chair nearest the fire, indicating Morven should sit. 'Her and Jamie.' She sat down in the chair opposite. 'And William's up at the shieling, so ye'll have to make do wi' me.'

She gave Morven a half-hearted smile and turned to warm her hands at the fire. 'Mam said she'd go as far as the ford at Fodderletich wi' Jamie and then come hame.'

Morven looked blankly at her. 'Fodderletich? Jamie's going northwest, then? To …?'

'Aye, did he nae tell ye?'

'No. Yer mam didna mentioned it either.'

'I thought one or t'other would've told ye,' Sarah said, puzzled. 'Ye being so close to them both. But Jamie's going back to Inverness.'

'But …?'

'Back to where he came from.'

'But he comes from here. Whatever d'ye mean?'

'I mean he plans to bide in Inverness now. He misses the sea and the hurly-burly o' the auld town – he misses his old life. He didna tell ye?'

Morven felt herself go cold. Why would he keep that from her? It could hardly have been a sudden decision. And why leave now? 'When did he … decide this?'

'I'm nae rightly sure. Yesterday, I think. I thought he'd have said.' Sarah frowned, evidently trying to find some explanation for this. 'But he seemed to make his mind up real sudden-like, and then was terrible anxious to be away.'

Stunned, Morven sat back. It hardly seemed possible Jamie would leave like that, without a word. 'Ye're certain of this?' She studied the girl's face, a look of extreme scepticism searing the air between them. 'He doesna intend coming back to Stratha'an?'

Sarah's pale eyes moved to meet Morven's darker ones. 'Aye, 'tis what he said. We all tried to make him change his mind, God knows we need him, but he was set firm on going.'

'But, I thought he meant to stay and help yer mam wi' the croft?'

'We thought that too.'

'He seemed that fired-up about it … learning the whisky-making. I dinna understand.'

'Nor me.' Sarah chewed her lip. 'I ken he thought folk here didna like him; they were surly to him. He thought they didna want him here. That might've made him want to go, I suppose.'

'Aye,' Morven conceded. 'Few here trust him.'

'But I wonder myself if there was maybe not a lass involved,' Sarah said half to herself. 'Someone he left in Inverness. I mean, is that nae why most young lads do anything? I dinna ken,' she added hastily. 'But 'twould explain it, no?'

Morven stared at the girl. In her mind, an image of Jamie took shape; his face close to hers as he cradled her, his jaw tight with emotion, dark eyes aglow. She felt again his fingers on the back of her neck as he guided her mouth to his, and she breathed again the scent of him. 'I care fer ye,' he'd said. And like a fool, she'd believed him. Now she saw him holding some other lass, some nameless beauty, looking at her just as tenderly, bringing his mouth down on hers. Her eyes stung with sudden tears.

She blinked them away, along with the image, and struggled to gain mastery of herself. He couldn't have said those things, kissed her the way he did, nae if he cared fer another. He thought too much on his honour fer that. Or did he? Could he have done those things? A man he was, like her da, were they nae all much the same?

'Ye liked him, didn't ye?' Sarah said softly.

Morven had no answer, and stared back mutely.

Sarah rose and poured out a draught of ale and silently offered it.

'How did yer mam take it?' Morven managed. Rowena had been that proud of her young kinsman, that keen to help him; on top of everything fate had thrown at her, she was bound to feel crushed now.

'Bad, I think. But ye ken what like she is; she'd not let on, not wish to worry us. It seemed fer a time there all would come right fer us at Tomachcraggen, but now …' She sighed. 'Now I dinna ken what's to become o' us.'

Morven swallowed down a mouthful of ale. 'I'm heart-sorry,' she offered, knowing how useless were her words. How could he abandon Rowena like that? After giving his word, swearing he'd allow no more of his kin to be forced from the glen, how could he then callously abandon them? And to steal away wi'out even saying his farewells, like some lily-liver skulking off in the night.

Sarah looked at her with a strange light in her eye. 'Ye ken, it might've been something Mam said that made him go.'

Morven refocused on the girl.

'I dinna ken.' Sarah shook her head. 'Just something I thought on now.'

'What's that?'

'He might've been angry wi' her – wi' Mam. They were speaking of something when I came in from the byre the other night. Jamie seemed riled and Mam looked right funny, like she was sickening fer something and she went away to her bed. I thought mebbe that birthing she went to, the gauger's wife, I thought mebbe it hadna gone well and she was grieving.'

Morven felt a cold finger trace along her spine.

''Twas the next morning Jamie told us he was going. William was fair heartbroken; he's been up at the shieling ever since. Mam was real quiet about it, but she said she'd go with him as far as the ford and Jamie agreed. I heard him say though, 'twould make nae difference. He was going anyhow, and she'd brought it on herself.' She frowned. 'What he meant I dinna ken, but I thought he wasna best pleased with her.'

The blood left Morven's face, then flooded back as sudden comprehension hit her. Rowena had doubtless told Jamie of Isobel's death. Likely he'd seen her return dishevelled from Balintoul. He maybe even knew more of what happened in that room, and what was said, than she herself did. And fearing McBeath's reprisals, like some spineless rat, he'd chosen to leave the glen before they could be carried out!

Her breath came in angry spurts now. He'd no wish to be associated with his aunt, not now 'twas likely she'd be seized by the authorities, put under examination, mebbe even condemned as a murderess. She reeled at the thought. He was afraid to stay, likely thought they'd all be put out anyhow. She'd thought Jamie honourable, driven by love and respect for his kin, when all along he'd been plain gutless.

Sarah was still watching her, waiting for her interpretation of Jamie's strange words. She looked young and vulnerable, and there was now a trace of alarm in her eyes, prompted, Morven imagined, by the expression on her own face. She struggled to restore some calmness to her features while inside she reeled.

'I'm sure he wasna angry.' She attempted a reasonable tone. 'He'd no reason to be. Yer mam showed him nothing but kindness, was a true kinswoman to him. Doubtless, he just … missed town life,' she suggested lamely.

Sarah nodded, looking thoroughly wretched.

'Can ye tell yer mam I'll speak wi' her later?' She needed time to think. It hardly seemed possible she'd misjudged Jamie so badly, but what else could all this mean? Morven felt a stab of guilt at leaving Sarah alone, so obviously miserable, but her head was spinning. 'The morn mebbe. Aye, tell her I'll speak wi' her the morn.'

At the door, Sarah handed Morven a thick woollen bundle carefully folded. 'Ye'll be needing this,' she said. ''Tis yours, I think?' It was her arisaid.

The rain was much heavier now, sheeting down in icy blasts, and the wind had picked up. She happed herself in the woollen garment and ran through the puddles of the yard to where Fergan stood, braced against the elements. Looking back through the downpour, Sarah made a forlorn figure in the doorway.

Morven stopped only once on her way home. As she came again on the piles of rock cleared from the ground around Tomachcraggen, she slid from the garron's back and gave savage vent to her anger and disgust sending the rocks rolling in all directions with her boot. Through the rain and mist, she saw another cairn a short distance away and, cursing Jamie Innes to hell and damnation, gave vent to her fury there too.

CHAPTER ELEVEN

THE FOLLOWING DAY, Mass was held in the glen's makeshift chapel. For the past eighty years, the Catholic faith had been outlawed in Scotland, and even attending a Catholic service carried the penalty of banishment followed by death should the offender return. As Morven filed into the little blackhouse that functioned as a place of worship for the many Catholics of the glen, she glimpsed Rowena sitting at the back. William and Sarah were at her side; Morven scoured the interior for Jamie, but sure enough, there was no sign of him.

'Something wrong?'

She shook her head at her mam's innocent question, wincing at the pain the movement produced at her temples. A sleepless night had done nothing to alleviate her confusion, and her nerves were raw. She'd spent it re-examining everything minutely, objectively, but come morning knew only one thing – she wasn't objective. She'd little wish to make sense of it all, for the only sense she could see was shameful. She longed to believe in Jamie, had hoped he'd be in chapel today sitting tall beside Rowena as he'd been at every Mass since he came to the glen. His absence was almost painful, so significant was it.

Twisting in her seat, she watched Rowena from the corner of her eye. Her friend's face was pale and tense, her lips moving over some private prayer although the Father had yet to begin the liturgy. Outside, the rain still fell, and her kertch was stuck limply to her hair, droplets of water clinging from the corners.

Her gaze flicked to Father Ranald, a spare little man gentle in manner and bald save for the wisps of white hair that ringed the back of his head. He made his way to the altar and then indicated with his hands that they should all be silent for the Penitential Rite. The Latin words were delivered with solemnity and respect, the rising and falling pitch of his voice betraying his Gaelic ancestry while also revealing something of his benevolent nature.

Morven stood obediently for the Bible readings, then knelt to pray when directed and responded in the correct places to the Father's familiar prompting. It was warm in the chapel, the air vaporous with the breath from many bodies crammed close together, their woollen clothing sodden with rain. The scent of incense and the flicker of altar candles brought a drowsiness that reminded her of her lost hours of sleep. She shifted uncomfortably, pressed against wee Donald, and fixed her eyes on the statue above the altar where Our Lady of Perpetual Succour smiled down benignly. The languid air lulled her again and her vision blurred, her eyelids heavy with weariness. She half wished she could sleep, that way it might all prove to be a dream.

Instead, she stared at the charred chapel walls, their blackness bringing a familiar pang of horror. Belying the glory of the chancel, the blackened stones of the chapel walls bore testimony to the passage of the British army on route to Culloden, when they burned not only the old chapel but also the homes of the Catholic Highlanders they found in the glen. Faithfully rebuilt to the same inadequate proportions as the original, the building now leaked copiously when it rained, the walls slick and slightly green-tinged, and bulged at the seams, each seat accommodating at least two people.

She shook herself but could find no solace in the Father's words. Rather, his voice set her teeth on edge and the dimness and pressing warmth seemed to suffocate her. The gospel reading and epistle left her untouched, and uncharacteristically she wished the service to be over and to feel again the freshness of rain on her face.

People began to file past to receive Holy Communion, and Morven watched Rowena carefully, yet there was nothing to be read in the widow's pale countenance. Rowena remained as enigmatic as ever.

Soon, Morven also received the consecrated bread. 'Go in peace,' the Father mumbled, touching the top of her head, but she could find no peace in her heart, only bitterness and confusion.

At length, with the solemnity of the service over, the Father's weatherworn face, hardened and ruddy through the assaults of wind and snow, creased into a kindly smile and his eyes watered.

'I have heartening news,' he declared, surveying his flock with unconcealed pride. He dried the top of his head where rainwater had been dripping through the roof. 'This very day I received a momentous communication from Rome.' He picked up an elaborate scroll, his hand trembling a little, and held it up before continuing. 'The Papal Administration has generously presented funds to the faithful of this glen. These funds are fer the building of a new more commodious chapel, one that 'twill serve the steadfast and devout of this land.' He clutched the scroll to his chest, beaming as a gasp echoed around the blackened building, and nodded his head delightedly. 'It's nae quite enough, I fear,' he added hastily. 'But I'm confident we'll be able to raise the remainder ourselves.'

There was a cheer at this, and the congregation broke into spontaneous applause, the little priest bobbing jubilantly. 'I thought,' he went on, holding his hand up for calm, 'that the Stratha'an Gathering in a few weeks' time might afford an opportunity fer fund-gathering, there being generally many visitors to the glen. And perhaps His Grace, whom I know to be sympathetic to our cause, might also be persuaded to donate.'

This last proposal clearly held even greater support, and he again signalled for calm. 'I had hoped,' he went on, 'that the hated, Act for Preventing the Growth of Popery, might soon be repealed, and we might be free to design our new chapel to look quite openly like a church. However, 'tis not to be, dear souls – nae yet – but our day will come, dinna doubt it. Until then, we'll keep the faith, and I pray ye all remember what the Lord himself preached – that the meek shall inherit the earth.'

At that, the congregation rose to their feet amid a mighty clamour, a collective outpouring of devotion. Father Ranald shook his head self-effacingly, motioning for them all to be seated again that he might conclude his announcement.

'Anyone with suggestions fer raising funds can speak with me outside or see me at their convenience, and of course all those fit and able to perform their portion of the necessary building work will be expected to do so.' With that, he brushed away a stray tear and sat down abruptly on the chancel step, his robe trailing in a puddle.

Grace grasped Morven's hand and gave it an excited squeeze. 'Is the Lord nae bountiful? And methinks,' she added conspiratorially, 'that our littlin when it comes might be the first bairn baptised in the new chapel!'

Morven smiled weakly at her, her eyes unconsciously straying to the flat plain of her mother's midsection where the new life quickening in her was still indiscernible. Grace was far from glowing, Morven often wondered how such a slender neck could support her head with its weight of hair, yet she was undoubtedly euphoric to be once again swollen with the fruit of Malcolm MacRae's loins.

They gathered outside on the heath, Grace instinctively seeking out Rowena to share in her joy. 'But, where's Jamie?' She looked past

Rowena to the last few people emerging from the chapel into the rain.

Rowena's hesitation was so fleeting it might have gone un-noted by any but the shrewdest observer. 'Inverness,' she said cautiously. 'He wished to go back ... to see folk, see how they fared the sickness. I'm nae rightly sure when he'll return.'

'Aye, poor lad.' Grace dismissed it, turning to blether excitedly to the boys.

Sensing Morven's scrutiny, Rowena glanced into her face, a flicker of contrition darkening her eyes before she turned away. She was lying. Morven knew her far too well to mistake her discomfort. Jamie had never mentioned folk in Inverness. There'd been acquaintances, aye, and an old priest he'd spoken of, but no-one he'd been close to, nae that he'd mentioned, nae enough to make him wish to go back, she concluded. 'Twas true then, Jamie'd forsaken his kinfolk.

Yet such was Rowena's desire to protect his honour, to shield her nephew from shame, she'd attempted to cover his contemptible behaviour with a lie. Morven tasted gall on her tongue, but above all, it was a terrible sadness she felt. Grief for Rowena. And feeling it, she realised she must uphold his worthless honour too, for Rowena's sake, though the miserable cur had no right to such a kinswoman.

Her father was less charitable. 'Nae muckle use to ye in Inverness, is he?' he grunted. 'And what o' the crofting and the whisky-smuggling he was so eager to get into? He's surely nae expecting me to sell his liquor fer him, or has he forgotten the ankers he's stashed at my bothy?' The shrewd green eyes disappeared under lowered brows.

'We could mebbe carry Rowena's whisky south fer her,' Alec interjected. 'Along wi' our own. After all,' he added, seeing his father's expression, 'another couple ankers will make little odds. Rowena could mebbe spare a pony to carry them?'

'If it's nae too much trouble.' Rowena eyed Malcolm dubiously.

He grunted without enthusiasm, then, realising all eyes were turned on him expectantly, grumbled, 'God's blood! Am I never to be done wet-nursing that lad?' Glowering at Alec, he puffed his cheeks out. 'If the lad's truly gone, then I daresay I've little choice.'

'That's real Christian o' ye.' Rowena's relief was pitiable. 'We're indebted to ye.' Her gentle hand gesture included William, standing silently beside her in the rain, and Sarah, slightly removed from their little group and watching with an odd air of attentiveness.

'Och,' said Grace. 'There's nae need to thank him. 'Tis what any decent man would do.'

Malcolm turned away sourly, making a great show of greeting Craigduthel, who loitered nearby. He was glad of an excuse to extricate himself, yet once he'd have helped Rowena without a second thought, there'd be none o' this sullenness. Yet he was a man, Morven thought with a measure of scorn, and like the rest o' the breed utterly beyond comprehension.

Droplets of rainwater were beginning to gather on her eyelashes and to drip from the end of her nose. She tilted her head back and let them trickle down her neck. Alec was the only decent man she knew, excepting perhaps fer Father Ranald, who, being a priest, hardly counted. She turned to catch her brother's eye, but he was far too busy gazing at Sarah. He was trying to cheer her with one of his quirky grins, that whimsical look on his face, the one he used to win over wee Donald when he was crabbit, the one he sometimes gave her.

Sarah remained unmoved, her eyes surveying Alec with apparent disinterest before dismissing him. Yet a flush at the base of her throat betrayed her pleasure. Alec whispered something into her shoulder and brushed her arm as he drew her closer, his eyes soft and coaxing, and she rewarded him with a throaty laugh. His sensitive young face lit with elation. With a jolt, Morven realised her brother was smitten. Conscious of prying on something private, she turned away.

'… wi'out Jamie, then?' She caught only part of her mother's enquiry but observed Rowena's immediate discomfort.

'Aye,' answered the widow, 'but we'll manage.' Swiftly changing the subject, she turned to Morven. 'I'm thinking about reading fortunes at the Gathering. To raise funds fer the chapel, I mean. And am wondering would ye like to help. Ye've a gift fer such things. What d'ye say, lass?'

Taken aback, Morven glanced instinctively at her father. He snorted without looking at her, but nodded minutely. 'But, would it nae be unseemly?' She lowered her voice. 'An ungodly thing to do, given the money's fer the chapel?'

Rowena considered for a moment. 'I'll need to ask Father Ranald first, but he's kent me long enough to know I mean nae disrespect. I doubt he'll object. 'Tis fer the new chapel after all.'

'Then, aye.' Morven felt a slight lifting of her gloom. It was the first pleasant sensation she'd had for some time. 'I'd be liking that.'

Rowena was skilled in the art of soothsaying, a spaewife folk called her, and had already shown Morven a little of what she knew. Yet there was still much to learn; Morven felt a tingling in her belly at what was to come.

***

Isobel and her infant were laid to rest in Balintoul kirkyard the next day. They were buried beneath the yew tree that already sheltered the graves of her other infants. None of the Catholics from the glen attended, the service being held in the Presbyterian Kirk with a heavy presence from the Board of Excise, but Grace offered a prayer for her soul and that of her infant at breakfast on the day of the funeral, and Morven knew many in the glen remembered her fondly.

It was rumoured McBeath was that drunk on the day of the funeral, he stumbled bearing Isobel's coffin and pitched forward, tipping it headlong into the grave. But as time went by, no dragoons came to arrest Rowena, and there were no reprisals exacted on her or any of the glen smugglers. McBeath was rarely seen in the glen, spending his time, 'twas said, the worse for drink at his home, or, more often, 'mortal fou' at the Balintoul Inn with his equally idle assistants. Morven began to breathe a little easier.

Her father and Alec made full use of this slack period, smuggling their mountain dew south into many Lowland cities, even Edinburgh itself. They'd meet up with agents Malcolm dubbed 'blethermen' some miles from the town where their rough Highland appearance and laden ponies would draw less notice.

Morven worked herself ragged at the still, keeping them supplied with whisky, and for the first time she could remember knew her father was confident of paying his rental at Martinmas in the cash demanded by the articles of his lease agreement instead of precious cattle. He even spoke of having silver left over to go toward next year's rent and joked he'd become McGillivray's best customer. It failed to lighten his mood any, and he warned the Black Gauger was surely plotting something.

Morven's days were full, but at the same time, she felt her life to be empty. She spent long hours alone at the bothy, Donald bringing her parcels of food and ale, and although she was needed more and more by her mother as Grace's health deteriorated, despite her father's command to stay away, she still managed to spend every spare moment she could with Rowena.

The widow mentioned Jamie only the once. A few days after his departure, alone together at Tomachcraggen, Morven sensed a rent appearing in the widow's mask of composure. They'd been discussing the behaviour of egg whites dropped into cold water, interpreting the writhing of upright oat straws thrust into the ashes of the fire and other such methods of divination for what seemed an age, although was likely little more than an hour, the atmosphere in the room stiff with tension, when at last Rowena sighed and turned to Morven.

'Ye'll be wanting to know why Jamie's gone, I expect.'

Morven had been skirting around the subject, at pains to avoid anything that might bring back a memory of him and sensed Rowena had been doing the same.

'It's nae my concern,' she said gruffly. 'Twas enough that the coward had deserted his kinswoman without Rowena needing to explain what so plainly shamed her. 'Anyhow, I ken why he's gone,' she said without looking up.

'What d'ye ken?'

'That he's ... away seeing folk in Inverness. 'Tis what ye said, isn't it?' Acutely aware of Rowena's attention to her answer, of the air of sudden stillness about her, Morven kept her tone light.

'Aye.' Rowena released her breath. ''Twas his reason.'

Morven observed the tension leave her companion and was glad. Rowena had plainly sensed she didn't believe her story and had felt the need to explain, though the thought of revealing Jamie's real reasons clearly pained her. Well, there was no need. If Rowena had no wish to speak of Jamie's shameful desertion, then that was fine – neither did she.

'Are ye going to show me how to use thon magic stone?' she coaxed, picking up a small wooden box Rowena kept on her dresser. It contained a cairngorm, a semi-precious stone from the Cairngorm Mountains, a fascinating thing of translucent umber that caught the light of the fire and then burned with its own fire. She opened the box and held up the gem, watching it gleam slickly as she turned it in her hand.

Rowena chuckled. 'Ye've been fair taken wi' that since ye were a wee sprout, but it can tell ye things if ye really look.'

Morven smiled. Rowena was at ease again, and 'twas as it should be. 'Will ye teach me how to look?'

***

Having given his permission for the fortune-telling, Father Ranald suggested a small hut be built for the purpose on the ground where the Gathering would be held. This, he felt, would accord a degree of privacy to the proceedings and would hopefully encourage more to part with their money. Alec built the hut, and with William and Rory as eager apprentices, had spent the last two days thatching it with heather. Morven now surveyed the neat windowless structure with a mixture of both pride and embarrassment that he'd gone to so much trouble.

'Ye've done a grand job,' she told him, pushing open the rough-timbered door. 'You as well,' she added, seeing Rory's crestfallen expression. 'Let's just hope there's many willing to part with their siller fer the curiosity of it all if naught else.'

'I doubt many hill-folk will,' Rowena observed. 'They've nothing to spare. But maybe the visitors.'

It was dark inside the hut, the chimney little more than a hole in the roof, and the interior smelled strongly of fresh-cut pine. Morven thought a few fir-candles would be enough to supply the correct air of mystery.

'The factor should be paying ye fer this.' Rowena spoke to all three boys with equal measure. 'He's bound to find some use fer the building once the gathering's over.'

For many years now the Strathavon Gathering had been held in the grounds of Inchfindy Hall, home to William McGillivray, and they were all aware that acting as host with the position and privileges that entailed was very much to his liking.

They emerged from the hut into the sunlight again to see a group of men standing at the entrance to Inchfindy Hall. All were dressed in fine hunting clothes, carried muskets, and were apparently watching them with considerable interest. A stocky well-dressed figure in bronze doublet and feathered bonnet broke away from the group and advanced purposefully toward them across the lawn. The bloated figure was unmistakable, as was the swaggering gait.

'Hell, no,' swore Alec.

The factor cocked his head suspiciously to one side as he neared, his face darkening, jowls wobbling in rhythm with his snatched strides. Morven was conscious of Rowena tensing at her side.

By the time he reached them, he was breathing hard, whether through anger or exertion she couldn't tell, but the murderous glare he levelled at Rowena was impossible to mistake. His lips thinned in distaste.

'What in the devil is this *woman* doing here?' He directed his bark at Alec, evidently dismissing Morven and the two boys as beneath his attention.

'My neighbour, sire,' Alec replied evenly. 'Mistress Rowena Forbes. His Grace's tenant at Tomachcraggen.'

'I know full well who she is!' he boomed. 'What's she doing on my lawn, that's the question?'

'She's here to inspect the hut I built fer her, sire. She and my sister are to use it during the Gathering. 'Tis fer the fortune-telling. But … but I thought ye'd be knowing that already, sire.'

McGillivray's eyes widened incredulously. 'You mean to tell me this … this,' his mouth worked furiously, searching for a fitting phrase to describe Rowena given the presence of the youngsters. 'This *disciple of Beelzebub,* this false prophetess, is to practise the sin of divination here, on my land?'

'She'll try to raise funds fer the chapel, sire. But she's hardly a false prophetess, or … or thon other thing ye called her.'

'Mam's a healer,' William informed him.

'I know exactly what she is,' McGillivray snapped. 'I've heard tell of her. If she's your mother, then you have my sympathies laddie, but she'll not be carrying out her evil practice here. Not on my land!'

'We have permission —' Rowena began.

'What've ye heard?' Morven cut in. 'And from who?'

'I have my sources.' He rounded suspiciously on her. 'And they're entirely reliable.'

'Are they? And ye're certain o' that?' McBeath, she thought in disgust, he'd not miss an opportunity to blacken Rowena's name, particularly where it mattered. ''Tis unwise to believe every scrap o' idle gossip ye hear, sire,' she said scathingly. 'Most especially wi'out first attesting to the virtue o' its source.'

McGillivray gaped at her. 'I've no earthly notion what you're suggesting, nor do I care for your tone. You've exactly one minute to remove that woman from my lawn before I have her removed.' Deliberately, he shifted his gaze back to Rowena. 'Permanently removed. Do I make myself clear?'

Alec's jaw tightened, and a spark of anger lit his eyes, but he nodded and drew his kin around him, then silently guided them away. He turned back to look at the factor and caught Morven's eye. A warning flicker crossed his face. She indicated her acceptance with a weary nod.

They'd left their ponies tethered to a wych elm by the river's edge. Morven mounted with as much dignity as she could muster and pressed her garron into the ford.

'Dinna go fashing yersel' ower that jumped-up wee lairdie,' Rory advised Rowena. 'Da says he's got crowdie fer brains and tends to speak through his arse!'

Alec snorted with laughter, and William, generally more reserved, also began to giggle, then they all collapsed in fits of laughter, the tension of the encounter quickly swept away. He *would* say that, Morven thought with a rare twinge of fondness for her father, but then he still insisted on referring to the king in London as, 'thon wee-bit German Lairdie,' and the other in Rome as, 'oor Rightful King.'

'You may speak more truth than ye know,' Rowena told Rory with a slow smile. She settled William more comfortably in front of her on the pony. 'Fer when I said we had permission, I didna just mean from the Father, I meant from His Grace himself.'

Alec turned to stare at her.

'The Duke's opening the Gathering this year and Father Ranald tells me he's keen to see a new chapel in the glen fer those that still follow the auld faith. He's agreed to the fortune-telling and anything else that might bring in funds.'

'One in the eye fer auld McGillivray,' chuckled Alec. 'He'll likely choke on his French claret when he hears o' this.'

'Though I dinna suppose 'twill make him any fonder of me.'

That was true, Morven reflected, though it felt good to savour this one small victory, this would do nothing to further Rowena's standing with the factor.

***

The day of the Gathering finally dawned; one of those rare July days when the sun shone from the moment it slipped over Carn Daimh. The wind was nothing but a breath carrying the rippling cries of golden plover over the hum of bees busy among the heather. Alec was up early, cleaning his pipes in noisy experimental skirls until Malcolm put a stop to it with a harsh reminder that there were still beasts to be seen to. But even Malcolm had a spring in his step, taking pride in unpacking his father's Highland dress from the kist beneath his bed.

The wearing of highland garb had been proscribed since 1746, since the disaster of Culloden, and the law had yet to be repealed, although many in the glen, her father included, still owned fine examples. Confident that under the protection of the Duke he was unlikely to be transported to the colonies for wearing his father's plaid, Malcolm took pride in donning the richly coloured tartan *fèileadh-mòr*. The pattered wool was still as vibrant as it had been the day his father last wore it; Malcolm gathered and belted it around his waist, the length mantled over one shoulder, and secured it in place beneath his belt. His silver-buckled sword belt, minus the weapon itself, he strapped across his chest. Pleased with himself, he looked over at his wife and daughter.

Morven couldn't help smiling. There was nae doubting he was still a fine figure of a man, his red hair newly washed and tied back behind blue bonnet. Grace was quite beside herself, praising her fine man with his bonny looks.

'Hold yer tongue, woman,' he snarled, face crimson.

But Morven sensed he was secretly pleased by his wife's obvious adoration.

When they arrived at the Gathering, the MacRaes found the grounds of Inchfindy Hall already aswarm with folk. Tinkers had come to ply their wares and many powerfully built men, both militiamen and hill farmers from neighbouring glens, were strutting about preparing for the strength competitions. Everywhere she looked, Morven could see Highland dress being worn with pride and dignity, the folk of the high glens clinging stubbornly to their traditions and cocking a snook at the handful of redcoats in nervous attendance. Many poor cottars who only the day before had worn shabby remnants of hand-me-down trews, now stood upright in fine belted plaid with gartered tartan hose, sporran and targe.

The Duke was present and housed in a raised enclosure with the other members of his family and household. McGillivray hovered in the background, face purple and corpulent, relaying orders to a string of scuttling servants. It was only the second occasion Morven had seen the Duke of Gordon, and despite the display of glittering finery around him, he seemed very much an ordinary man, nothing about his face suggesting he was, in fact, one of the wealthiest men in Scotland owning vast tracts of the Highlands.

'Naught but a common-enough looking man,' murmured Rowena, materialising at her shoulder.

'How d'ye manage to read my mind like that?' Morven laughed.

''Tis nae so difficult with *your* face,' Rowena chuckled. 'Maybe more so with some we'll see today.'

They waited for the Duke's short opening speech, which he delivered in clipped English, much to the disgust and general incomprehension of many of the older folk in the crowd who understood barely a word.

'Has he nae any Gaelic?' grumbled Granny Muldonich, shaking her head. 'All my sons have the Inglis *and* the Gaelic. Ye'd think a educated man like himsel' would hae more than the one tongue.'

'He can likely speak French and Latin and all sorts else,' muttered Sarah from somewhere behind Morven. 'But nae the tongue of his ane land.'

The sharp crack of a pistol firing rang out, and then the hill racers were sent off in the direction of Carn Meadhonach, the rangy runners leaping over boulders, kilts flying, bare legs quickly stained with bracken juice. They'd be gone for many hours.

'That's more like it!' cried Granny Muldonich as the Duke's footmen rolled out casks of ale from the Duke's own stock. A great cheer went up as the Duke's personal piper piped in the *uisge-beatha* and flasks appeared from sporrans like midgies at dusk.

'We'd best go see if there's any desperate to hear o' their future.' Rowena took Morven's arm.

When they reached the little hut, a group of bedraggled people already waited outside, although it soon transpired they were mostly folk from further up the glen who, having heard Rowena would be here, had come with various ailments ranging from toothache to an ingrown toenail in the hope she could ease their suffering. Rowena had half expected this and had brought along a basket of potions and salves in readiness. She turned to Morven.

''Tis my belief *you* should tend these folk,' she said with an air of quiet certainty.

Morven's eyes widened.

'Ye're more than ready, and I'll be here if ye need me.'

'But they'll nae be wanting me,' Morven said in an urgent whisper. ''Tis you they've come to see.'

'Maybe so, but they know ye've a gentle touch, and they trust ye. It's near three years I've been teaching ye. It's time,' she said firmly.

That much was true, but Morven couldn't help experiencing a stab of doubt. 'Ye think?' she said uncertainly.

'Aye, I do think.'

A giddy sensation swooped through Morven's midsection, and the corners of her mouth twitched into a self-conscious grin. It was a moment she'd long waited for. 'Lord!' was all she managed to say.

Among the line-up of sufferers, there were no ailments Morven hadn't seen before, and she soon found herself settle into an assurance born of sound teaching, her stomach un-knotting as her confidence grew. Only once did she need Rowena's help. Archie Chisholm had dislocated his shoulder and whimpered like a puppy whenever she tried to touch him. He carried himself stiff and awkward, his face greased with a thin film of sweat.

'How long've ye been like this?' she asked him.

'A while,' he grunted through clenched teeth.

'More than a while,' put in his wife. 'But 'twas the jolting o' the pony on the way here that did fer him mair than anything.'

Morven winced at the thought of Archie's bone-jarring ride; 'twas near fifteen miles from Clachfuar croft. 'I'm thinking a drop of the Duke's whisky might help,' she suggested.

Archie broke into a grin at that, revealing several rotten teeth stagnating in a mouth that smelled like a midden. She reached for the whisky.

Away from the area near the hut where she'd been dispensing aid, Morven saw a number of men, both young and old, waiting to try their hand at lifting the *clach làn-aois*, the manhood stone. Among them were a few lads she recognised, although she imagined her father would wait for the caber-tossing, which he was well skilled at. She glimpsed him nearby with Craigduthel knocking back the Duke's whisky and laughing at the old crofter's jokes. He mightna last till the caber-tossing if he kept his right elbow so well exercised.

In the end, it took more than a drop of the Duke's whisky before Archie would let her manipulate his shoulder joint back into its socket, and he bellowed like a bull before passing out cold on a patch of clover. Morven took the opportunity to remove his rotten teeth while he lay unconscious and he awoke pathetically grateful.

While Morven was treating the ailing, Rowena had been scrying using her knowledge of hidden signs and omens. Now that the last patient had been attended, Morven was free to join her. Two giggling girls from Ballindalloch were the last in line. Both, it emerged, were servant girls from Ballindalloch Castle and had lads they were uncertain of. They wished to know if these lads would stay true and wed them.

They paid their dues and settled themselves at Rowena's makeshift table, nudging and tittering nervously. Humming an old Gaelic charm under her breath, Rowena passed a smoking brand of hazel beneath the girls' noses, and they settled instantly, eyes glowing. She managed to extract from them the names of the offending lads and Morven placed two pairs of hazelnuts, symbolising the couples, into the fire. When the nuts were glowing around the edges but not yet alight, she removed them with iron tongs and set them in pairs on the firestone while Rowena murmured a love charm over them. As they cooled, both pairs of nuts jumped violently apart.

'Aye,' Rowena noted. 'Neither the two of ye are well-enough acquainted wi' yer lads. They've not been true to ye, but are still after sowing their wild oats, aye?'

The girls looked at each other in horror and Rowena drew out the cairngorm stone from its wooden box. She chanted some faery words over the stone, then tapped it three times with a switch of rowan. 'Now, each of ye look into the stone and tell me what ye see.'

The girls did as they were bid, then again looked at each other. 'You go first,' prompted the smaller, prettier of the two.

'If ye like,' sighed the other, running her hand nervously through her hair. 'I ken the stone's brown, gold almost, but I see a great stretch o' blue inside.' She shook her head. 'Just that – a stretch o' blue.'

''Tis what I see too,' gasped the other.

Rowena nodded. 'Blue as the sea. And from where do these lads hail, now tell me?'

'From Skye,' the girls chorused.

'Then that's where they intend to return. To Skye. But nae, I fear, with either of you.'

Both girls then launched into a hostile tirade accompanied by a deal of savage cursing, shocking Morven with their language, then whispered together urgently.

''Tis just, we might be ...' faltered the small pretty one.

Again, Rowena nodded. 'Ye'll be wanting to know if they've left ye with more than just promises.'

Blushing, the smaller girl slid her gaze to the ground, while the other scowled darkly, her gaze similarly occupied.

'They came to the castle wi' thon Sir whits-his-name,' the taller girl blurted. 'MacDonald o' Sleat. His bodyguards they are. Said they'd take us wi' them to the isles when 'twas time fer them to go.'

'They're men!' Morven said scathingly. ''Tis what they'd say. They'd say anything to bed ye.'

Rowena glanced sharply at her and shook her head. The smaller girl began to sob.

'I'll need to examine ye both,' Rowena said gently. 'Ye might wish to watch the caber-tossing, Morven? Fer a while, aye?'

Thankful, Morven scrambled to her feet and left the two girls with Rowena.

Outside, she spotted her mother with Alec, Sarah, and the three boys settled on a small hillock watching the sword-dancers; she made her way over. Her father was close by, still jesting with Craigduthel but looking a bit more bleary-eyed.

'Have ye no more takers fer the fortune-telling?' Alec teased. 'Ye'll be able to listen to my playing, then. I'm told I'm to play with His Grace's piper.'

'A rare honour!' Morven was pleased for him. 'I've not to sing, have I?'

'I didna volunteered ye, no.' He turned to whisper something to

Sarah, who sat slightly stiffly beside him.

Morven caught the name McBeath spoken somewhere behind her and immediately turned to locate the speaker. Her father was markedly louder in both manner and speech now as he relayed the tale of Hugh McBeath's brush with *Am Fear Liath Mor*, the old man of Ben Macdhui, to Donald Gordon. She'd heard the tale many times and felt sure Donald had too, but her father never seemed to tire of its telling.

'And he was just settling himsel' fer the night,' Malcolm said in a loud attempt at a hushed voice. 'When he heard footsteps whooming and crunching through the heather.' He failed to keep his face straight as he continued. 'Fair shivering wi' fright he was, near fillin' his breeches, when oot the mist loomed a great grey shape. 'Twas the giant himself.' His voice cracked, but he sobered enough to go on. 'Fair made his blood run cold, and like the woman he is, he upped and ran fer his life, leaving six ponies and a dozen ankers of confiscated whisky behind!' He snorted with laughter. 'Many the poor soul's seen that creature, but none's run so fast as the Black Gauger!'

Her father had drawn a small group of interested listeners around him and all now creased over with hilarity. He nodded delightedly as they scoffed along with him. There were no excise officers present today, the Duke happy for his tenants to enjoy themselves in peace on this one day, and with McBeath's strange absence from the glen many had begun to view him as more an amusing figure than an alarming one. Morven excused herself and returned to the hut.

The door was shut fast. Half expecting to find one or other of the girls still inside, perhaps tearful, she opened it cautiously. 'Twas a stark warning of what could happen if ye allowed yerself to care fer a bonny lad wi' fine words but nae backbone. It took a second for her eyes to adjust to the gloom, the only light coming from the small fire and a single fir-candle, then she jerked back, drawing her breath in with a hiss.

Talking quietly with his kinswoman, Jamie Innes was now turned toward the door, his face pale and perturbed. She took in the striking red plaid, the strong jawline and dark eyes, widened in surprise, the lock of loose hair hanging roguishly over one eye, then abruptly turned on her heel and bolted, her heart leaping in her chest.

CHAPTER TWELVE

'MORVEN! WAIT, MORVEN!' Stricken, Jamie glanced at his aunt, then plunged toward the door.

'Let her go, Jamie.'

He halted and turned to stare at her. 'But, the way she looked at me. Wi' contempt. She thinks me false … dishonourable.'

Rowena's eyes softened. 'Morven's confused, nae understanding why ye left. But, 'tis how it must be. She'll calm down soon enough, and that's the time to speak wi' her, not when she's that riled she hardly kens what she's saying. Though ye must be guarded in what ye say.'

Still doubtful, he continued to regard his kinswoman intently, his hand poised on the door.

'Morven's long been fiery,' Rowena said with fondness. 'Seeing ye was a shock. She'll nae ken how to react – this is her way.' Her voice was calm and full of reason. 'I know her well, she'll nae go far, and when she's mastered her hot blood, she'll come looking fer ye.'

He sat down again, pressing his fingers into the hollow between his eye sockets. He'd thought he might see Morven, had hoped he would, only the way she looked at him – it had felt like a dagger strike.

'Are ye alright, Jamie?'

'Aye.' He shook his head with the closest thing to a smile he could raise. ''Tis just, after what I said to her … the things I swore to, she must now set little value on me.'

Rowena looked oddly at him and poured him a stiff dram from the flask she kept for medicinal use. 'Here,' she offered, 'ye look as though ye need this.'

He murmured his thanks and took a mouthful of the whisky, feeling the familiar fire seer through his innards. Dread had been his constant companion on the road from Elgin. He'd not broken his journey to rest but had made the ride in two gruelling days, guilt at leaving his kinfolk alone all this time driving him on. Along with a fear of what he might find when he reached them.

He'd found the cot-house at Tomachcraggen empty, yet his kinfolk's belongings were still there, herbs and the like still hung from the roof-beams. He'd tormented himself with the possibility Rowena was arrested, his cousins taken and cared for by others. Sick at heart, he rode on. But at the forge and every croft-house he came to it was a similar picture, beasts left unattended, homes empty. In the end, a strange panic overtaking him, he followed a band of genial cottars, keeping his distance, observing their extraordinary high spirits, and at length came upon the Gathering. The first person he asked pointed him in the direction of a small wooden hut, and he waited out of sight in a copse of aspen, anxious to speak with Rowena alone.

Two girls emerged, and he watched them embrace and make off across the grass, then slipped inside himself. His kinswoman's joyous face chased away his fears, and he'd near wept with relief. Now weariness crept over him, such a deep boneless exhaustion he could gladly curl on the floor like a dog.

He shook himself and looked more closely at his aunt. She appeared well enough and was sitting in the shadows contemplating him with that stillness of hers. As always it unsettled him, made him feel she could read his very thoughts, though she made no judgments. Not for the first time, he wondered if she *was* a seer. He'd always considered his dark eyes and countenance fairly unreadable, had been told so on occasion, but likely 'twas as gazing in a looking-glass for a woman like Rowena.

Completing her study of his face, a troubled frown drew Rowena's brows together. 'You and Morven,' she ventured. 'Ye've feelings fer each other? It's nae my business, but I canna help –'

'I have feelings.' A tone of desolation crept into his voice. 'But she doesna return them.' He made a dismissive gesture with his head. 'And in truth, I can hardly blame her.'

Rowena digested this information in thoughtful silence, then looked at him again, a light of pity softening her eyes.

He took another mouthful of the whisky. 'But I need to know what's been happening here.' In an instant the frustration of his time in Elgin, the enormity of what lay ahead, engulfed him and he railed against his own impotence. 'Such a time the Excise Board kept me in Elgin. 'Twas my own doing, I should never have let on I could read or write. Once they kent that they took me on forthwith but put me to work as a clerk. I'm shamed to say I've spent the last few weeks compiling records o' seizures and writing out accounts fer the courts.' He cursed softly. 'All this time I've been fretting ower what might be happening here, imagined ye arrested and thrown in gaol and me trifling wi' paper and pens!'

'Hush, nothing's happened. There's no need to fash yerself.'

'Then, he's not accused ye?'

'I've seen neither hide nor hair of McBeath since that day in Balintoul. And I'm nae likely to either, fer he said three months and I'll wager that's what he'll give me – to the verra day.'

'Generous o' him. But aye, 'twould be like the miserable creature to find some misbegotten honour in upholding his word in that way.' He cleared his throat. 'Word came to the authorities of his wife's death of course, and 'tis rumoured he's neglecting his duties, drinking himself senseless wi' the contents o' seizures and passing on nothing to the Treasury. 'Twas only on account o' this idleness, along wi' my constant chivvying, that I was given leave to come here.' He looked grimly at his kinswoman. 'As of the morn, I'm to be a revenue man. An officer of his Majesty's Excise – Assistant Riding Officer to Hugh McBeath.'

Rowena's eyes widened, and a ghost of a smile flitted across her face. 'Then ye did it. Just as ye said ye would.'

He nodded, a trace of grim humour lurking at the corners of his mouth. 'Fair flummoxed they were in Elgin, thought I'd taken leave o' my senses. Who in their right mind would give up decent town work, they said? Only to ride the glens sniffing out smugglers and ruffians.' He laughed shortly. 'The Collector himself advised me to reconsider.'

Rowena's face sobered. 'Then maybe ye should, Jamie.' She laid her hand over his and held his gaze uneasily. 'I've nae right to ask this of ye. Giving up a decent future, putting yerself in danger, and fer what?'

He stared at her. 'To stop this man, this … *predator*, to have justice fer Duncan. Surely yer nae forgetting what's to happen in barely four weeks if we do nothing?'

She flinched. 'I've not forgotten.'

'Forgive me. I know that.' He watched her turn and add more peat to the fire, her graceful neck bent to the task, a slender wisp of dark hair trailing from beneath her kertch. 'Twas the same blood flowing through her veins that had flowed in his father. They *were* the same blood. He pictured her wed to McBeath – the man's crude hands upon her, his outlandish eyes stripping her of her dignity. Swallowing, he pushed the image away.

'What good is decent town work when my kin are here, in this glen? I could no more turn my back and leave ye to be dispossessed or … or worse, than I could do the deed myself.' He reached out and touched her hand, trying to convey to her the great need in him to do this for her.

'I ken that. And I thank ye.'

'Only,' he squeezed his eyes shut and waited while a wave of exhaustion swelled up over him, then ebbed away. 'I didna think on it taking such a time to get this far, didna imagine I'd waste so much time just getting the chance to watch the man.' He breathed out heavily. 'There's still much to do and little time left to do it.'

'Ye mustna chide yerself. 'Tis a wonder ye managed to do this much. It hardly seems possible of all the glens the Elgin collection covers ye did manage to get work here, in Stratha'an.'

His mouth twitched again at that. 'Let's just say I made a good impression wi' the Board o' Excise.' He felt a slight twinge of guilt at deceiving them the way he had, letting them imagine him some manner of zealot bent on stamping out all illicit stills on the Duke's land, but it couldna be helped. He shrugged off the feeling and caught his aunt watching him with a look of such tender sincerity his throat immediately tightened.

'I'd have ye know, Jamie,' she said softly. 'There are more forces at work here than just you. Ye are one man. If things go badly, you're nae to blame. I dinna wish ye carrying the weight o' my eviction on yer shoulders, nor do I hold ye responsible fer the course my life must take.' She smiled a bright smile at him. 'That's down to the Creator … and to me. Mind and heed it.'

He nodded, feeling a trace lighter, grateful for her attempt to relieve him of his responsibilities. Yet the cold fact remained: *he* was the only one who could prevent his kinswoman's arrest and ultimate eviction. Or, if she chose the other course, her enforced union with her husband's murderer.

He finished his dram, draining the last of the golden liquid, and eyed her surreptitiously over the rim of his drinking vessel. As always, she maintained an outwardly calm appearance, nothing in her face or manner indicating the crisis that awaited her. Which would she choose, he wondered for the thousandth time? To be put from the land of her forefathers? The place where she and his father had been born? Or to submit to a union with the man who slaughtered her mate? A man who was scarcely a man at all, a creature who believed himself cursed, but was that consumed by her he'd do almost anything to make her his. He didn't know. She'd never spoken of either course; both were too loathsome to contemplate. 'Twas his duty to stop the devil before then, to ensure neither alternative need be considered.

He set the vessel down reluctantly. 'I fear I must be taking my leave, must report to my new master in Balintoul.' He smiled with a brightness he didn't feel and pressed a heavy leather pouch into his aunt's hand.

She uncurled her fingers gingerly, staring at the pouch as though it might bite her. It contained his earnings from the last eight weeks, or at least the best part of his earnings; he'd had lodgings to pay for. 'Twas no great fortune, but still, a useful-enough sum slid from the purse into Rowena's hand. She turned the softly clinking coins, marvelling at them, weighty and flat in her small fingers, then slipped them back into the pouch.

'I canna take this. 'Tis yours and likely ye'll need it.' She tried to push the pouch back into his hand.

'I'll not,' he said with equal insistence. 'Your need is greater than mine. I've been no use to ye on the croft these last weeks, and I've taken yer good pony. I mean ye to have this.' His dark eyes locked with hers, then softened a degree. 'Or I *will* go back to Inverness.'

She swallowed and considered the purse before laying it carefully on the table. Unable to speak, she reached out and touched his hand, a small gesture of thanks, and he was stricken to see pitiful appreciation brimming in her eyes along with a sad acceptance that he'd likely change nothing.

He placed his hand over her smaller one and squeezed it lightly, trying to impress a sense of his resolve upon her, his sincerity, then, as a surge of bitterness rose in his gullet, stood and took his leave. He *would* change things, one way or another he must.

Outside, he glanced around. He was trembling, and weariness dragged at his bones, but he ducked back into the copse of aspen and again prepared to wait, this time for Morven.

Morven thought badly of him. His behaviour would seem questionable, shameful, she might even believe he'd forsaken the oath he made to her. Yet the weight of her contempt would be worth it, anything would to keep her safe, for she was precious to him.

A tiny shiver ran through his heart at the thought of her. His kinswoman was already involved, and her eviction was also his, but there was no need to implicate Morven. She'd been present at that poor woman's deathbed, but that's where her involvement ended. Telling her the whole truth would serve no purpose, even had he not given his word. And he knew not the whole truth, only hoped to discover it. A shadow crossed his heart. What if he found the traitor was her father? He'd need to be truly convinced of the man's guilt before attempting to expose him.

He leaned wearily against a tree-trunk, too tired to think clearly. Sleep was what he needed, but more than that he needed to see Morven. After all this time, he yearned to look at her again. He felt the pull of the mossy ground at his feet drawing him down to curl like a dog on the nearest tussock and, with a groan, knocked his forehead sharply against a tree. He sincerely hoped his aunt was right and Morven's hot blood had cooled enough for him to speak with her, though what he'd say he had no notion.

***

Morven fled the hut only to crash headlong into the factor just steps from its door. McGillivray had been muttering with Alexander Grant of Achnareave, she realised with some irritation, passing judgment nae doubt.

'Ye see!' grunted McGillivray. He snatched his feathered bonnet from the muddied grass at his feet and replaced it slightly askew on his head. 'As uncouth as they are ungodly!'

She pushed past him.

'Aye,' muttered Achnareave. 'Nae good will come o' this tampering wi' the natural order o' things …'

She stumbled away, the sound of her thudding heart drowning out their words. Why had Jamie come back? Did he think himself safe now? With Rowena neither arrested nor accused did he think he could worm his way back in again as if nothing had happened? She blundered across the grounds of the Gathering, oblivious to what went on around her, almost struck by the *clach neart*, stone of strength, as it thudded into the ground beside her, deaf to the curse hurled after her. Squeezing through a knot of rowdy drinkers, she choked as she entered their cloud of tobacco smoke. It still hurt. The pain of his betrayal was still as raw, as deep. Her hands were cold and trembling, and she pressed them to her cheeks, feeling the heat radiating from her flushed face. Everyone must surely see it, must know of her humiliation.

The small hillock where her mother still sat with Rory and Donald reared up in front of her; she shied away. They would see her distress, ask questions she'd no wish to answer. She whirled around. The river, then. She could maybe quell the agitation in her heart at the riverside.

The caber-tossing area was in front of her now. She watched the next contestant make his run, shorn tree-trunk balanced within cupped hands. There was her father, staggering slightly but stripped to the waist and dusting his hands with dry earth. She gave him a wide berth.

She could hear the Avon, feel it almost before she saw it. A breeze oft-times arose from the river, from the turbulence of the currents, the air disturbed by the seething of the water. It drew her to it, a match to her own turmoil. She sat on a boulder at the river's edge and breathed-in deeply, feeling the delicate mist from its passage cool her face. What was wrong with her? She stared into the swirling pool at her feet. She'd forgotten about his eyes, deep and serious they were, thoughtful. They made ye think ye could trust him. She cursed softly.

Yet Rowena wasna angry with him, it struck her now. Even in that brief glimpse, she'd recognised her friend's joy at seeing her kinsman again. Rowena was far too generous-natured to bear him any ill-will. Was *she* the only one cursed with a temper, then? A gift from her da — the hot MacRae blood. And Rowena had given Jamie one of her two ponies; the grey mare. The willing wee garron that carried her from Balintoul on the day of Isobel's death. She'd never said as much, but from the day of Jamie's going 'twas evident Rowena had given him the mare, leaving only old Trauchle to help her work the crop rigs. Doubtless he'd been an eager-enough garron in his day, but as her da had scornfully put it, the poor creature was scarce fit to pull the skin off a milk-pudding. He'd been quite beyond words when he discovered that was the only mount Rowena could spare him to carry Jamie's whisky, though his scathing expression had said it all.

But then, 'twas like Rowena to be selfless — she would turn the other cheek. Was it sinful, then, to feel bitter and betrayed? If so, then Morven knew herself to be such a sinner, for she felt as consumed with rage at Jamie's betrayal now as she had when she first learned of it. Yet, if she were honest, was it not her own hurting that really fired her anger? He'd inflicted a deep wound and 'twas the sting of that wound that gave life to her anger. Nae verra noble considering the person he'd hurt most had clearly forgiven him already. If she ever blamed him at all.

She gazed across the Avon to the birches growing on the far bank. A froth of meadowsweet moved in the breeze. Her mother loved meadowsweet, the scent o' summer she'd often say. At her feet, chamomile blooms nodded among the grass; she bent to pick some. She could make a soothing infusion with them. Chamomile was known to promote sound sleep, and Grace slept only fitfully now, the weight of the child causing her much discomfort. She piled the blossoms in her lap. But no, this wasna helping. She needed to face Jamie, running off was *his* way, nae hers. 'Twas stalwart MacRae blood that pulsed through her veins, nae the mealy-mouthed kail bree that likely dribbled through his. Anyhow, she needed to show him the contempt he deserved.

Her decision made, she wrapped the blossoms in a corner of her arisaid and tied it securely, then hurried back to the Gathering, her jaw clenched defiantly. Only her heart betrayed her, its rapid fluttering beating a nervous tattoo against her ribs.

It was the grey mare she spotted first, Rowena's pony, tethered among a copse of aspen. Her heart gave a series of wildly erratic thumps; Jamie was still here, then. McGillivray and Achnareave had evidently moved on, and there was no sign of either of them. As host, McGillivray was to judge the piping competitions, though what he knew of masterly piping ye could likely crush into a fine snuff and snort up yer nose, she thought scornfully.

No-one appeared to be waiting outside the hut, although Rowena's little sign with the picture of a hand palm up and crossed with silver was still nailed to the door. She approached warily, listening for the sound of voices, reluctant to burst in again in case the scoundrel still loitered within. But as she leant to press her ear to the door something struck her on the back and then dropped at her feet. She spun around. And there he was, half hidden among the trees, another pinecone poised in his hand.

He beckoned her over with an urgent gesture and then stepped back behind a tree. Holy God, he was hiding! A prickle of irritation raised the hackles on her neck, and she muttered, 'Spineless rat,' under her breath, but found herself checking to see if she was observed, then slipping into the trees herself.

As she approached, Jamie put his hand out to her as though to draw her to him, perhaps to draw her further into the concealing brush, his eyes dark and intense, and she recoiled with a hiss. 'Dinna dare touch me!'

His hand dropped, and he winced as if she'd struck him. 'Forgive me. I meant only –'

'I ken what ye meant.' She eyed him coldly. 'But I think I can manage to resist ye.'

He swallowed, the lump in his throat dipping sharply. 'Ye're angry. I knew ye'd be and ye've every right. Perhaps 'twas wrong o' me to want to see ye.'

He was unshaven, several days' growth darkening his chin and throat and he looked slightly wild-eyed, his dark hair escaping from its lace to hang disreputably over one eye. The effect was oddly magnetic on the dark gravity of Jamie's face, and unconsciously she took a step toward him. 'What was it ye wanted to see me fer?' She slanted her eyes in suspicion.

'I wished to explain.' He took a deep breath, and his jaw tightened. 'Only I canna. I can only ask ye to trust me – though I realise 'tis nae so easy.'

'Trust ye!' She gaped at him. His gall took her breath away, and for a moment she was without words, then her voice squawked incredulously. 'I doubt I've met anyone I trust less.' She could think of a few, but the brazenness of his request struck her afresh, and she gave a choked little laugh. 'Ye must be the most shameless nae to mention gutless excuse fer a kinsman I've ever met. How Rowena can …?' She bit back the rest of her words, not wishing to reveal how much his callousness had hurt. Cold contempt was needed.

He seemed genuinely startled by both her words and the force of her scorn. 'I've distressed ye, I can only say 'twas not intended.' He lowered his head and, remembering his bonnet, snatched it from his head and twisted it in his hands. 'I pray ye can forgive me.'

He wore a sprig of broom on his bonnet, the age-old emblem of the Forbes clan, and she wondered fleetingly if Rowena had given it him. 'Ye've caused me nae distress, though I canna speak fer those others ye abandoned.'

His politeness was vexing; she wished to tear it away, to expose what lay beneath. Even stronger was the urge to rage at him. She wished to name him for the miserable milksop he was, demand to know why he'd wanted to learn the whisky-making when he'd been too afraid to smuggle. Most of all, she wanted to know why he'd told her he cared for her when so plainly he did not. But she found his courteousness frustrated her, and she dug her nails into her palm to prevent herself losing control. Once she did that, she'd be lost.

With an effort, she assumed a detached manner. 'So, will ye be bideing in the glen this time? Or can we expect ye to flee again at the first sign o' trouble?'

He hesitated before answering, and she noticed for the first time how tired he looked, his face lined with weariness. She couldn't be sure if it was exhaustion or just plain reluctance that made his answer sound grudging.

'I'll nae be staying at Tomachcraggen, no, but I'll be … close by.'

'Nae help to Rowena, then. And I wouldna say Inverness was close by, would you?'

He looked blankly at her. It seemed he was going to accept her withering reproaches without a murmur. Not much of a man at all and certainly nae the man she'd once thought him.

'Maybe belonging to Inverness,' she continued, deliberately ignoring the fact of his birth at Druimbeag. 'Ye're nae familiar wi' the morals o' Highland kinship. But here in Stratha'an, Highland clan customs hold strong, and kinsmen here protect their kinfolk or risk the scorn o' the glen.' She thought of Rowena's shame at his desertion and the lies she'd been forced to tell to protect his honour and a pulse began to throb in her throat. 'Maybe those customs dinna hold in Inverness. Or is it just ye're nae the man o' principles ye had us all believe?'

Anger was putting bitter words in her mouth, and she wrenched her gaze from his face before she gave too much away. She'd not reveal how hurt and confused she was, she'd not give him the satisfaction, but recognised too late just how openly her anger betrayed it.

A muscle along his jawline flexed, but there was no answering flash in his eyes. 'I understand ye think badly of me. But … I didna appreciate just how much I disgust ye.' There was a note of regret in his voice, and she shot him a puzzled look. His face was pinched and wretched-looking, though he still wore that air of quiet authority she'd once found so fascinating. He held her look with a disconcerting directness. 'I wish to explain my leaving, but that's nae possible. As fer my kinfolk, I've not forsaken them, I'd never do that, and I do plan to bide in Stratha'an, only there's something I must do first.'

'Oh aye, and what's that?'

'That I canna tell ye.'

She turned away, but something still bothered her. Without turning back, she said, 'Why did ye come here, Jamie? And why were ye waiting fer me? Ye were waiting fer me, weren't ye?'

His hesitation lasted so long she abandoned hope of receiving an answer and moved to walk away, when he said gruffly, 'I wished to look at ye again.'

The muscles around her heart contracted sharply, and a little shudder ran down her spine. Every fibre told her to walk away, not look back, but she couldn't help turning back to him.

He was watching her intently, his dark eyes fixed upon her face. He looked neither cowardly nor dishonourable it struck her then, his expression more haunted than anything. For a moment it seemed her feet had grown roots into the mossy undergrowth and she was anchored fast, unable to break away.

'Dinna hate me,' he said softly. 'Have faith, aye?'

She stared at him.

'And, I beg ye, have a care. I say this as ye mean that much to me, I'd not say it otherwise. I'd not come atween you and yer sire.'

More confused than ever, she turned and stumbled her way out of the trees.

CHAPTER THIRTEEN

'WHERE ARE YE, WOMAN?' Malcolm roared, swinging his head ponderously from side to side. 'I feel like haeing a wee fling.'

The Gathering was in full swing now, the firelight leaping on the revellers and the shadows long upon the hills. Morven sat with Rowena and her mother listening to the silvery sound of a *clarsach*, a Highland harp, though her thoughts were elsewhere, scattered and confused. She threw her father a scornful look. Swollen with drink and the glory of winning the caber-tossing for the third year on the trot, he'd only remembered his wife now that the need to dance was upon him.

'Dance wi' me, then!' he bellowed, jerking Grace from the music's spell.

'Away,' she laughed, indicating her swollen abdomen. 'Ye dinna want to be dragging this great side o' a mountain about the dancing ground.' The prospect appeared to bring her little pleasure; it had been a long day, and she'd complained of a nagging pain in her lower back.

'I do that.' He stood with bent arms on hips, his body leaning forward a degree as if he needed to weather some fierce gale. He squinted down at her, perhaps attempting to steady her image as the world reeled drunkenly by, or more likely dimly trying to mind what it was she referred to.

'Ye're well fou, Da,' Alec warned.

But Grace rose heavily and without a murmur and submitted to his riotously drunken attempt at a highland fling, the typically solo dance transformed into a vigorous duet lacking any elegance or form. It was once she'd sank gratefully onto the grass again that the extent of her distress became apparent.

'Merciful Lord!' she gasped, stiffening in pain.

'What is it, Mam?' Morven took fright at her ghastly appearance, seeking out her father in silent accusation.

Rowena took immediate charge of the situation, ordering

Malcolm roughly out of the way and sending Alec to Inchfindy Hall for blankets and pillows that Grace might lie flat and rest. A hand placed on her belly confirmed the worst. 'Her pains,' she said grimly.

'But, 'tis still ower three months till her time.'

Rowena nodded and pulled Morven to one side. 'There's naught I can do to stop her pains, ye'll ken that, we must pray that lying down still-like they'll maybe cease o' their own accord.'

Morven gave her father a long hard look. Yet she'd made no attempt to stop him herself, hadna given her mam's safety a second thought, her thoughts squandered on Jamie. She joined Rowena by her mother's side, and together they watched in silence as Grace writhed and whimpered, then, as the contraction released her, lay limp and breathless. Morven longed to weep but with fierce concentration quashed the feeling – what good would that do anyone?

After a moment, the pain slackened its grip and her mother could speak. She clutched at Rowena's sleeve. 'Dinna let me lose this bairn,' she pleaded. 'I'm begging ye.' The widow nodded with a tight smile.

As the night wore on, they were able to move Grace to Delnabreck; a painfully slow journey with her stretched out flat on the back of Father Ranald's rickety old cart. Malcolm sat on the board-seat, hunched and silent while Alec guided the pony over the rough track by the light from two oil lamps grudgingly lent them by McGillivray's manservant. In the back, Morven watched the shadows skulk back, swaying and pitching before their advancing light, and felt for her mother's clammy hand.

'Nearly there,' she reassured her, but the answering fear in her mother's eyes extinguished further talk. She glanced at her younger brothers huddled silent and miserable in a corner and felt for the knotted bulge in her plaid that was the blossoms from earlier. She prayed she'd get the chance to use them.

Grace survived the night, the pains that gripped her gradually loosening their hold, the child still living Rowena assured her, but she was on no account to leave her bed. As Rowena prepared to return to Tomachcraggen pale and weary the following morning, she tackled a tense and ill-tempered Malcolm.

'If ye wish her to live, ye must let her do nothing now till she's delivered of the bairn – nothing at all. D'ye understand me? Any movement could bring her pains on again and next time 'tis likely nothing will stop them.'

He nodded, avoiding her eyes.

'Ye must share out the work, make certain she doesna leave her bed on any account.'

Malcolm turned away, his shoulders hunched, but Rowena persisted.

'D'ye nae see how the child's sapped her strength? Her body wants rid of this burden, should she not lie still and rest it *will* rid her o' it. Only her own life will likely bleed away too.'

'We'll make sure there's nothing she need do,' Alec assured her, white-faced. 'Won't we, Da?'

Malcolm nodded curtly, his expression rigid with loathing, though whether it was of himself or the inferred blame that thickened the air, Morven couldn't tell.

***

They all carried out their extra duties willingly, even her father, though Morven found the endless round of chores utterly exhausting. There was no time to enjoy summer's brief burst of bounty, nor, thankfully perhaps, time to linger over Jamie and his parting words to her. Her days were swallowed by the unending pattern of daily tasks. Sleeping at Delnabreck now to be near her mother, there was the twice-daily trek up to the shieling and back to milk the cattle and sheep and to churn butter and press cheese in the tiny dairy room. There were eggs to be gathered, oats to grind, broth to make, and bannocks to bake, not to mention the skinning and cleaning of hare and trout now supplied chiefly by Rory.

Poor Donald, at six he was keen to hunt with his older brother, but it was he who was now saddled with most of the washing, drying, and cleaning; tasks he despised as woman's work, though he did them nonetheless. Morven's heart squeezed to see his wee face alight on the washing tub with a quiet resignation far beyond his tender years. Rory now tended the crops – weeding, spreading muck, and cutting peat – while Malcolm and Alec saw to the selling of calves at trysts in Crieff and Falkirk, the buying of quantities of barley from McGillivray and the secret malting of it in readiness for Morven's work at the still. Alec worked especially hard, even learning to handle a spindle and mend clothes by the fireside of an evening while they each took turn at story-telling to keep Grace's spirits up. Morven was as busy as ever at the still and crawled home too tired and drowsy from whisky fumes to think straight. It seemed her father, however, preferred the company he kept at the Craggan Inn.

Rowena visited Grace at some point every day, often bringing Sarah, and Alec would contrive to be there whenever he could.

Morven watched her brother's efforts at pleasing Sarah with a heavy heart. It seemed he gave such a lot of himself to receive so little in return. But Sarah's presence, even the mention of her name, brought him such unmistakable joy that she could say nothing – what right had she to blight his happiness?

Grace fretted over how idle she'd become, guilt at the extra work she'd given her family weighing heavy. Attempting to ease her mind, Alec confessed to falling asleep in the byre one day when Morven knew full well he'd been hours there bundling great lengths of heather in readiness to re-thatch the roof. But as Grace's belly grew, so the rest of her seemed to shrivel. The delicacy of her finely boned features became a brittle frailty, her eyes the only part of her to retain any spark of her former self. Morven sensed her mother would need these weeks of rest to rebuild her strength if she was to stand any chance of surviving the birth ahead of her. But her great need to give Malcolm another child, specifically the lass he reputedly wanted so badly overrode all else – it did consume her. Atonement for the two wee crosses in the chapelyard, though why Grace should need to make amends, Morven scarcely knew, though the pity of it wrung her heart.

By the time the middle of August was upon them, Morven had a batch of twenty ankers ready for smuggling out of the glen. It had been the best year for the *uisge-beatha* she could remember, and she knew her father had a buyer for them in Aberdeen, a wine and spirit merchant by the name of Joseph Skene who shipped the whisky on by coastal smack to the port of Leith where rich Edinburgh merchants awaited it.

'I'll warrant the man's a rogue,' Malcolm grumbled. 'Tricking me out o' my whisky fer a piffling four pound an anker and nae doubt selling it on to them dupes in the Lowlands at ten, maybe even eleven pound a cask.'

'It canna be helped,' Alec soothed. 'He's taking a risk as well, mind. There'll be gaugers at Leith the same as there are here and he'll be carrying mair than just oor casks.'

'Aye.' Malcolm acknowledged this with a curt nod and stashed the kebbock of cheese Morven handed him into his pack. 'They tell me at the Craggan he's a muckle fish, this Skene. All the more reason to pay decent prices, I say.'

Grace rose on one elbow from her bed. 'Just come hame safe to me, Malcolm, never heed the price this Skene gets in Leith. Faith, it hardly matters to us here in the glens!'

Malcolm considered her for a moment, his beard quivering with some unspoken emotion, then muttered to no-one in particular, 'But I'd plans fer that money. Seeing it snug in Skene's pouch wasna one o' them.'

'What plans?' Morven queried. Supping it at the Craggan Inn seemed the most likely plan.

He shook his head irritably and continued his packing. Without looking up, he moved onto another course, neatly deflecting her interest. 'There's fresh word in the glen of the Black Gauger.' The ease of his manner belied the seriousness of this news. 'They're saying he's active again. Craigduthel saw him the other day in Glenlivet, and he'd a Riding Officer wi' him, a big brute by all accounts – seems to have shaken the bloodsucking leech from his sloth.'

'Damnation!' swore Alec. 'Just when we were doing so well, that cursed snake had to slither from his nest!'

'It had to be, lad,' Malcolm said softly. 'Ye didna think he'd aye be in mourning, did ye? Nor that fou he'd never crawl from his bed again? He might be fair vexed though I'm thinking, kenning we've all had a free hand – might wish to make an example, ye could say.'

Grace rose from the bed again, her eyes round with fright, and crossed herself. 'Ye should be taking the greatest o' care then, Malcolm. Should be waiting fer nightfall, surely.'

'Hush, woman. Ye're meant to be resting. Ye'll have Rowena scolding me again. I ken what I'm doing.' He scowled at her until she slumped back on the bed. 'We've a wee coaster to meet at midnight two days hence, eh Alec. We dinna want to be entering the town in daylight. But 'twas more Morven I was thinking on.'

Morven nodded uneasily. Her father was right. McBeath's absence from the glen had been welcome, but they could hardly expect it to last. 'Twas Rowena's safety that worried her. What if he still wanted revenge fer his wife and bairn? What might he do now?

'I can look after myself,' she said curtly. Her father's misplaced concern had stifled her all her life; she now recognised it made them both uncomfortable.

'Mak' sure ye do, then.'

By the time the ponies were laden and the men ready to leave, dawn was spreading its milky lustre from the east, burnishing the top of the in-field dyke and silhouetting the crown of Carn Liath. Malcolm was several minutes taking his leave from Grace, their voices surprisingly tender, while Rory and Donald clustered around Alec, their eyes bright with envy. But they knew full well they couldn't come; even if they weren't needed at home, their father would never allow it, not until they reached manhood.

'Be on yer guard, Morven,' Alec called to her as she checked the ponies for the umpteenth time. There were ten ponies in all, each rigged with a timber harness from which two ten-gallon ankers were slung, one on either side of the ponies' flank.

''Tis you needs yer wits aboot ye,' she answered him lightly. But as he came to kiss her softly on the cheek, she whispered, 'God protect ye, Alec. Mind and come hame safe, aye?'

He nodded, his jaw tightening a fraction, and they shared a brief look that spoke of Alec's anguish at leaving his mother and Morven's unspoken promise to look after her.

When Malcolm appeared in the doorway, the boys scuttled inside, and he shook Rory briefly by the hand, a small acknowledgement to his growing maturity, and patted Donald fondly on the head. With a brusque nod in Morven's direction, he led the convoy away. They'd take the Ladder Trail to Glenbuchat, then follow the river Don on its way through the Grampians and eventually down into the old town of Aberdeen.

It was almost mid-day by the time Morven reached the Lochy Gorge and the still. The milking up at the shieling was done, and fresh butter and eggs were stored in the aumry for supper. As she lugged the mash-tun through from the cave, her belly rumbled softly. Being up so early she was ahead of herself today, at the still already and nothing in her stomach since the porridge she'd eaten before dawn, but it couldn't be helped. She paused for a moment as a thought struck her: she'd meant to warn Donald not to come to the bothy with food for her now that McBeath was patrolling again, but it had slipped her mind. Maybe he'd realise the danger himself and stay away. After all, a wee bit hunger would do her no harm.

But later, as she was draining the first batch of worts into the fermentation cask, Donald dropped onto the rocky ledge in a tangle of kilt and beamed in at her, a bundle of food slung over his shoulder.

'Did ye think I was never coming?' He tossed the bundle of food over to her and took hold of the rope again. 'I've tinder and kindling fer ye at the top o' the gorge, I'll shin back up and get it. It's lichen and birch bark, bonny and dry like ye showed me –'

'Wait, Donald.'

'Aye?' He looked curiously at her, green eyes peeping from beneath a fringe of dark lashes.

She shook her head. 'Never heed.' He was here now, and the tinderbox *was* nearly empty.

Half an hour later though, as they were eating their meal together, she warned him of the reasons he was not to come here again so openly, and he nodded at the wisdom of that, his eager wee face downcast. 'Twas likely the high point of his day, she thought meanly, and she'd now deprived him of even that, but he convinced her he didn't really mind, and she watched him go with a tight little feeling in her chest.

***

Jamie pressed his knees into his mount's flank, edging the twitchy mare closer to McBeath's mount. He didn't like McBeath any more than the animal did and understood the creature's desire to shy away, nostrils flared and eyes rolling. The man was utterly noxious, a thoroughly foul example of humanity and it had taxed Jamie's endurance these last few weeks not to show his loathing of the exciseman in any way. Rigid self-control had paid off, however, and he felt sure McBeath had no notion how much he despised him.

After three weeks as McBeath's assistant, this was his first patrol into Strathavon, and his apprehension was tangible. He'd now seen precisely what McBeath was capable of, and the man's casual cruelty had sickened him. The thought of his aunt wed to such a man had begun to haunt him, and he now knew he'd do almost anything to prevent it.

At Balintoul, Jamie had found the creature wallowing in a mire of his own creation, still bedded at gone ten of the morning and so drunk raw spirit seemed to ooze from his pores. He'd stunk that badly, Jamie had been able to smell him from the foot of the stairs – a rank cocktail of unwashed flesh, congealed vomit that lay in sticky streaks on the bed, and an indefinable whiff of decay the man carried with him always, originating from his breath, Jamie thought. An indication, if any was needed, that the man was rotten to the core.

At his assertion that he was a fellow Excise Officer, a nervous maid had shown him upstairs and then promptly fled. McBeath lay prone on the bed muttering incoherently. Jamie cleared his throat, introduced himself in a loud but respectful tone, and waited.

Cursing, the exciseman jerked his head and shoulders off the bed, then lurched into an upright position, his eyebrows raised but eyelids still gummed shut, then reeled back down again, this time on his back. He proceeded to snore; an objectionable sound Jamie likened to pigs being driven to market, his breath so rank with stale whisky 'twas likely he could ignite touchpaper at a hundred paces. In the end,

Jamie was forced to straddle the creature, his gorge rising, while he shouted over and over that he'd been sent by the Board of Excise in the fight against smugglers.

The exciseman surfaced enough to prise one eyelid open and focused with a look of open disbelief on the giant Highlander atop him. Breathing hard, Jamie compelled himself to adopt a deferential manner with the drunkard, a demeanour he hoped would flatter the exciseman into accepting him quicker and lull him out of any inherent suspicion. He climbed off the bed and straightened his plaid, his bonnet clutched respectfully in his hand. His eyes roamed the bare room. It was likely the room where the gauger's wife had died and the devil had taken pleasure in describing to Rowena exactly how he'd killed her man. He swallowed hard but with masterly control pushed the thought away and kept the disgust from showing on his face.

McBeath seemed to sober surprisingly quickly and levered himself upright, squinting at Jamie and absently brushing at the congealed matter plastered to his sark. Jamie wondered fleetingly if it was perhaps the man's own guilt and torment that prostrated him so, rather than plain drink. But no, that would indicate a trace of remorse he sensed the exciseman did not possess.

Without comment, McBeath read through the accompanying letter from the Board of Excise, then lowered the sheet, his hand shaking slightly, and regarded Jamie through bloodshot eyes. His squint was disconcerting, but Jamie sensed the exciseman's vision was as keen as any, and he was searching for signs of trickery and guile in his face. He gazed back openly, forcing a blankness to his eyes, a vacuousness to his expression. If the devil felt more secure with a fawning empty-headed fool, then that's just what he'd give him.

'James Lang.' McBeath rolled the name around his mouth as if tasting some potentially poisoned morsel. 'And where de ye belong, James Lang?'

'Inverness, sir.' Jamie held his breath. He'd given his mother's name to the Board in Elgin, knowing full well his own name would likely spark some recognition with McBeath; a memory of his father and that might then lead him on to Rowena.

'Which part?'

'I bid above the forge on Market Street, sir. Next Urquhart's coaches and stables.' The truth always sat easier on the tongue, but McBeath showed no suspicion of the name, or, for that matter, his face, Jamie was relieved to see.

The exciseman grunted that he knew of the place. 'And what brought ye here? And to the notice o' the Board in Elgin? For you've surely caught their notice, I can see.'

'Nothing in particular,' Jamie replied vaguely. 'After my folks died I wandered fer a time, wound up in Elgin. I heard say smugglers brought the morbid throat to Inverness. Thought if I could mebbe get work putting an end to the filthy business, so much the better.'

'I see.' McBeath belched softly. 'And you were a clerk in Elgin? What made you want to give up such soft employment in favour o' the real work?'

Jamie grimaced, then shrugged foolishly. 'I dinna ken. Only 'twas real dull work. I like it well being ootdoors doing something mair exciting.'

McBeath laughed uproariously at that, a deep belly-busting laugh that brought water to his eyes, and Jamie grinned back, waiting to see if this was the gauger's way of accepting him or whether the man was still unconvinced.

'A half-wit they've sent me! And me thinking ye educated!' McBeath wheezed some more and then sobered, his eyes narrowing. 'You can plainly read, write, and add-up though. Now tell me, how did ye manage to learn that while ye *wandered*?'

Jamie nodded admiringly. 'They telt me in Elgin ye were a shrewd man, but no, I was taught as a lad ye see, by a priest in Inverness.'

'Ye're a papist, then?' McBeath made no attempt to hide his abhorrence.

'Nae a practising one, no,' Jamie added hastily. Being an outlawed faith, any connection to popery would immediately bar him from His Majesty's employment, not to mention risk his arrest. 'But I'd the misfortune to be brought up that way.'

'Well see here, there'll be no foul praying to saints and the like while you're working for me, have ye got that?'

'Aye, sir. Whatever ye say, Mister McBeath.'

'Come back the morn then.' McBeath slumped back on the bed. 'And make sure you're dressed decent next time – none o' that heiland garb, d'ye hear?'

'Till the morn then, sir.' Jamie gave a servile bow and turned to leave.

'Lang, ye say?' The exciseman didn't bother to lift his head, but there was an unmistakeable sharpening of his interest. 'That's a Strathavon name, is it no?'

Jamie didn't turn back, afraid his apprehension would show upon his face. 'I wouldna like to say, sir. My folk a' came from the Black

Isle way.'

'Damn good name for ye, though. Ye must be the tallest man I've seen in many a long year.'

The next day, Jamie returned wearing the hateful clothes he'd bought in Elgin. Each Riding Officer was entitled to a small allowance to cover the cost of the exciseman's garb: respectable black clothing in the Lowland or English style, along with a pistol, a sword, and an axe. He felt constrained by the close-fitting breeches and tailed black coat, but it was the black lum hat that sat most uneasily with him, its stark Calvinism somehow deeply offensive.

McBeath had cleaned himself up and was again reading through the letter Jamie had brought with him. He looked up blackly at Jamie, but it seemed without really seeing him. Jamie wondered again what exactly was in the letter, he'd thought about reading it himself before handing it over but would have been unable to re-seal it. He hoped it didn't describe him in too glowing terms. He didn't want McBeath to feel threatened by him in any way, or resentful. In fact, he'd no wish for McBeath to think about him at all. He wished to blend with the surroundings in such a blandly benign way McBeath would barely notice him. Nae so easy when he stood six-foot-three in his bare feet, but he'd need to accomplish it somehow.

Over the next three weeks, McBeath was more active than he'd been in years, or at least he was according to his two regular henchmen: Charles Stuart, known as Ghillie for the other work he did, and Dougal Riach. These were the two hirelings Jamie knew had been present at Duncan's killing and had been well paid to say the right things at the hearing. He cultivated a relationship of sorts with these two men, they spoke the same tongue and secretly held the same faith, but their ruthlessness toward Duncan meant he kept them under constant observation.

For all he was reputedly more active, Jamie soon discovered McBeath's primary business was carried out not in the glens, but at the Balintoul Inn or at his home. Here he'd accept bribes he called 'passages' in return for the smugglers' safety while they distilled and for free conduct through his district. At first, McBeath was clearly uncomfortable with Jamie's presence at these transactions, but after a few drams, he'd relax his guard and ostensibly forget Jamie was there. By the end of the first week, when Jamie had made no comment, either way, he appeared to accept his presence as harmless.

But it was in Glenlivet, a neighbouring glen, that McBeath's true character was exposed. It seemed there had been no regular patrols into Glenlivet since the day of Isobel's death, and the glen folk had let their watch slip. Early one misty morning as Jamie rode into the head of the glen with McBeath, they observed the pungent smoke from many peat fires, the tell-tale wisps curling into the air from dozens of rustic bothies lining the banks of the Livet.

'Well, well.' McBeath grinned at Jamie with obvious relish. 'At last Lang, here's yer chance at some real work. Let's at them!' With a roar, he charged his horse down toward the nearest bothy.

A small boy was filling a pail at the river and stared up at them in horror.

'The gaugers!' he shrieked, dropping the pail. McBeath scooped him up, threw him over the saddle, then holding the boy by the ankles dangled him over the side of his horse so that the boy's head and shoulders were rattled and bounced along the rough ground of heather with its hidden rocks. The boy's head and torso jerked and twitched in a silent jig, he was too terrified to make a sound, and then with a sickening thud went still. McBeath threw the legs down on top of the still little bundle and charged on.

As Jamie came upon the small folded form, he saw blood trickling from the boy's ear, although his lips were moving a fraction. Shocked, he drew his mount up, stamping and whinnying, but screams from the nearest bothy drove him on again. When he reached it, McBeath was savagely roping together the two women who'd been operating the still, one screaming frantically in Gaelic. She was the boy's mother, he realised.

'He still lives,' he told her in Gaelic, but she cursed and spat at him.

'You're wasting yer breath,' grunted McBeath, and then he was racing on to the next bothy. 'Come on, man! We'll come back for this.' He nodded at the kegs and still equipment littering the ground. 'But the others'll be away into the hills if we dinnae move fast.'

In a little over an hour they destroyed eight bothies, smashing the rough-timbered huts, the casks and barrels with their axes and confiscated over a hundred gallons of whisky. Yet McBeath was less than pleased; most of the smugglers had vanished into the mist, taking their precious copper cooling worms with them, and in the end, they had only the two women and a half-blind old man in their charge.

A number of the little bothies remained untouched, the folk going about their illicit business unmolested, though white-faced and shaken. These had paid their passage, Jamie surmised. The child was with a group of these folk, and a man was trying to force water between the slack little lips. The lad was alive, but 'twas questionable whether he'd ever be the same again.

'You dinnae seem to have much stomach fer the work,' McBeath observed. 'For someone who wanted to put an end to the filthy business.'

'No, no, I like it fine.' He felt sickened by what he'd had to do, soiled by the brutality of it, the unnecessary cruelty, and could have gladly shot McBeath there and then.

They confiscated as many ponies as they could find to carry the whisky away, and with them tied together in a line made a sorry trail wending its way back to Balintoul. The two women watched Jamie through grief-filled eyes. He could feel their gaze upon him but hadn't the courage to meet it levelly, such was his utter shame. On top of their agony at leaving the battered boy, McBeath had lashed the rope around their breasts, the bindings cutting mercilessly into tender flesh, and he instinctively knew the gauger had gained some depraved pleasure from that. Their despair was palpable, he could feel it in the air and had to press his mount to the front of the line to escape the suffering in their eyes.

'Lord,' he muttered through clenched teeth. 'Give me the strength to endure this.'

At Balintoul, McBeath stopped at the Inn, leaving Jamie to carry on to Elgin with the trail of ponies. But he'd barely reached the kirk before the gauger caught him up again riding a fresh mount.

'*I'll* take this load on to Elgin,' McBeath announced. It mightnae look so well for him with old Farquarson, the Collector in Elgin, if this bright-eyed young upstart brought in such a sizeable seizure. Farquharson had been scathing about his recent laxness, had shown no compassion regarding his bereavement, and had even ludicrously suggested in his letter that Lang might be the answer to the general lawlessness in the Balintoul area. The Collector was known for his taste in young men, and McBeath supposed this particular young man, with his hard young body and clean-cut features would be much to his liking. The letter was worrying enough without letting Lang take the glory for this little tally as well – the man was less than useless anyway. But the penny had now dropped, and McBeath thought he knew exactly why Farquharson had been so enthusiastic about Lang.

'Whatever ye say.' Jamie nodded affably. 'D'ye want me to come wi' ye?'

McBeath thought for a moment. It might be sore work for one man, but no, witless though he was, Lang was definitely no' the man to take.

'Ye'll find Dougal and Ghillie at the Balintoul Inn,' he muttered. 'Tell them to catch me up, they'll be well paid.'

Jamie accepted McBeath's change of mind gratefully. He'd no heart for carting those three country folk off to the gaol; they'd done nothing that circumstances hadn't forced upon them and nothing that he himself hadn't done.

McBeath returned several days later and made no mention of what became of the three Glenlivet folk. Jamie supposed their fate held no interest for him. But he seemed better pleased with himself and drank the best part of four quaichs of whisky before announcing they'd raid Strathavon the next morning.

Jamie covered his sudden alarm with a swift movement toward his own quaich and downed a large mouthful of raw whisky. 'Aye,' he croaked. 'Whatever ye say.' The blood drained from his face, but McBeath appeared to notice nothing in his beatific whisky-induced state.

To Jamie's profound relief, the next morning's raid on Strathavon was much less eventful, word having spread of McBeath's renewed activity, and they saw nothing more suspicious than two men travelling with a covered cart near Clachfuar Croft. These turned out to be Chisholms with a load of limestone for Gordon Castle.

McBeath was intensely irritated by what he saw as the wily Highlanders' efforts at deceiving him. 'There's barely a handful in the whole o' Strathavon pay their passage,' he grumbled. 'Yet I ken fine they're all at it.'

Jamie grinned his agreement at this and then attempted to dispel McBeath's displeasure with some inane chatter.

'Can ye no hold yer tongue, man?' the gauger growled, and a thick silence had fallen between them.

Now they were concealed among the hawthorn and dog cherry on the ridge of Carn Daimph, still mounted and watching the glen carefully. Jamie murmured softly to his nervous mount and stroked her neck. 'Twas partly his own apprehension causing the animal's jitteriness, not just McBeath's proximity, but watching from that ridge, so close to the MacRae bothy and with nothing to do to dissipate his growing tension other than wait, he could feel his heart rate rising inexorably and his stomach churning.

He glanced sidelong at McBeath. The devil showed no sign of the vast quantity of whisky he'd drunk the night before but surveyed the southern end of the glen, hawk-like, from the back of his horse. Yet Jamie knew better. For all they had an excellent view of great stretches of the glen, 'twas the crofthouse at Tomachcraggen that lay directly in their sight, even be it some way off, and he sensed that's where McBeath's real interest was directed.

He thought of Rowena, likely inside the cot-house and going about her daily tasks. What would she be doing at this moment? Preparing healing potions? Seeping leaves fer poultices? 'Twould likely be something of that nature, something fer the benefit of others, while they, like wolves in the woods, skulked and prowled. As always, his thoughts crept back to Morven. He couldn't bring himself to wonder if she was at the bothy at this very moment, curled like a kitten by the firestone as she'd been that day he'd kissed her, the thought of her in such close danger was simply too much to bear.

McBeath climbed down heavily from his horse, fumbled with the fastenings of his breeches and then urinated noisily against a tree. Jamie looked away. It was only with the aid of whisky that he could hope to get inside the creature's mind, learn of a way to ensnare the man; 'twas whisky that loosened the creature's tongue and he resolved to begin some delicate whisky-laden probing later that night.

McBeath clambered back into the saddle and then breathed in sharply up his nose. Jamie turned in time to see the exciseman's face twitch with sudden interest and followed the direction of his gaze. At what he saw his heart near skipped a beat. A small figure was climbing over the lip of the Lochy Gorge. It stopped to sling something over its shoulder and then darted off through the trees. As the figure emerged again, much closer to them now, he knew without a shadow of a doubt it was wee Donald and the boy could only have been at the bothy for one reason.

McBeath let out a little gasp of excitement. 'Is that no one o' the MacRae litter?'

'The MacRae litter?'

'Aye, the MacRaes of Delnabreck. The faither's a cunning auld fox. It's many a time I've caught him smuggling out his whisky, but I've never yet found his bothy.'

'I wouldna ken,' Jamie croaked.

The gauger was breathing faster now, quivering with excitement. 'I want to take a closer look – see what the lad was doing down there. Stay here, Lang.'

'But, should I nae be coming wi' ye?'

'There's no need for that. 'Tis likely nothing.'

Lang wasnae getting any part o' this. Likely it was nothing, but still, by God, this could just be it – fifteen years of searching and this could well be Delnabreck's hiding place, insidious thorn in the flesh the man was. If so, this was far too good to give away to a foolish young upstart like Lang. If this was what he thought it was, and already McBeath's nose was twitching at the scent of victory, 'twas rightfully his and his alone. He wrenched his horse's head up. 'Stay here, Lang!'

Jamie watched in horror as the mounted figure descended the ridge, tailed black coat flapping in rhythm with his horse's movements, the column of his hat ruthlessly rising and falling.

'Dear God,' he breathed.

CHAPTER FOURTEEN

AT FIRST, THE EXCISEMAN baulked at the sharp drop in front of him. The Lochy Burn, channelled through a narrow gully, seemed to plummet over the edge of the earth. Cautiously he peered over the lip, watching water thunder and crash on many razor-edged ledges below. He stepped back, wary of the roiling water, mist rising around his feet. The lad could hardly have climbed up there. But ... he drew a sharp breath. Was that no a rope looped around a tree? He knelt in the wet bracken and reached out to touch it, then gasped with excitement. Almost indistinguishable from the twisted roots snaking from the rock-face, he felt the pliant but unmistakeable roughness of rope and an unguarded whoop erupted from his lips.

Morven didn't hear McBeath clamber down the gorge, the roar of falling water was too loud. She didn't hear him curse at the slipperiness of the narrow moss-furred ledges, nor mutter, 'At last, at last,' under his breath. As she drained the worts through the heather filter and into the waiting fermentation cask, some wash slopped onto her hand scalding her, and she winced at the pain, but it was the abrupt darkening of the bothy that brought her head snapping up.

Hunched on the ledge and blocking out the light, McBeath had drawn his pistol and peered in at her, a feverish excitement burning in his eyes.

'Well, well.' He stooped through the opening and straightened, a quick glance confirming she was alone. He replaced the pistol among the folds of his coat and sneered at her.

'So, this is it?' He stared around him a mite incredulously. 'This is Delnabreck's hiding place, this damnable hole in the hillside.' His sneer widened as he eyed the empty ankers stored in readiness by the cauldron, the sacks of malt piled high against the walls.

It wasn't quite as he'd imagined it, for he'd dreamed of this moment more times than he cared to recall, but always at the moment of discovery, at the very point of sweetest success it was Malcolm MacRae's startled and fearful face he saw before him, no this lass with the hint of ice in her eyes. No' the witch's apprentice. And he'd have enjoyed the look on Delnabreck's face, would've taken untold pleasure in smashing the petty symbols of his defiance, trampling them into the ground. But no matter. He drew his axe from the loop on his belt and raised it high above the fermentation cask. For a brief exultant moment, he felt like a kirk minister exorcising a demon. 'May the devil take back his own!'

He scarcely knew what happened next it happened so fast. The witchling launched herself from the fireside, lowered her head and charged butting him hard in the stomach. As the breath fled his lungs, he uttered a shocked little grunt and reeled backwards, ending sprawled on his back.

'You're the only devil I see!' Scrambling on her hands and knees, Morven made a desperate lunge for the axe trying to wrench it from his grasp. He was a powerful man though, and his grip was iron-hard.

Strangled whooping and wheezing sounds were coming from his throat; there was only the time it would take him to drag some air into his heaving lungs and he'd be upon her. The axe seemed set in stone, she gave it up and made a grab for his dirk, sliding it from its sheath.

His eyes fixed on her in shocked surprise, and she saw a flicker of ruthless intention take shape, and knew she'd made a mistake. Before she could think what to do with the dirk, he drew his knee up and kicked her squarely in the face. His boot connected with her cheekbone and jaw, snapping her head back, and splitting her lip. An explosion of pain flared out over her face bringing tears to her eyes, and she gasped in shock.

In the second he'd raised the axe, rage had overtaken her, and she'd acted without thinking. Now, as he rose to his feet with elaborate leisure and collected the dirk from the ground where she'd dropped it, fear curdled her innards. He was grinning again, but something dangerous moved in his eyes.

'I might've known. Ye're Delnabreck's getling ... the witch's apprentice, defiance must flow in yer blood.' He snorted. 'But ye're still naught but a muck-the-byre's daughter.' Bringing the point of the blade up to the soft spot on her throat just below her left earlobe, he canted his head, openly raking her with his gaze, assessing her as a breeder might an untried filly. For all she was a common muck-the-byre, she did look young and ripe. And the familiarity she enjoyed with the dark-eyed witch who tormented his dreams, somehow made her immeasurably attractive. His breathing quickened. Deflowering her would be yet another way to strike at Delnabreck. A pleasurable means to bring the most vexing smuggler he'd yet pitted himself against to his knees.

'Aye,' he said slowly. 'Yer faither did me a great service, he played the witch's man right into my hands. But I believe I've found a better way to bring that bur in the breeches to his knees.'

'Liar!' she gasped. 'Ye're a damned filthy liar.'

Her mouth had dried, despite the blood, but she spat as hard as she could directly into his eyes. He recoiled as a bright red spray splattered his face, and she bolted for the opening.

He was quicker. A hand snaked out and caught her by the hair, viciously yanking her back, and she screamed and lashed out with her fists.

'Scream all ye like.' He slammed his fist into her stomach, then as she doubled over, kicked her again in the face. 'There's no-one to hear ye but me, and I dinnae mind a bit.'

Momentarily blinded, she saw the bright pinpricks of light behind her eyes and instinctively raised her hands to shield her face. She'd had thrashings before, but nothing compared with this. Blow after blow slammed her to the ground and she crawled backwards into the cave whimpering and praying. It was dark in the cave but she could hear him coming after her. Choking on her sobs, she prayed he'd had enough, but he'd not finished with her yet.

It was the dirk she saw first, the dull gleam of its blade. The blade swayed before her eyes, winking in the meagre light. No more than a dark shape now, crouched and panting, the exciseman obliterated the light, plainly seeing her better than she could see him. The blade flashed. She gasped, then clenched her teeth for the blow.

Her gown opened with a zipping little rip, and he thrust her backwards, falling upon her, sucking and nipping; gorging himself with indulgent little grunts. She cried out in revulsion, thrashing to dislodge him, then turned her head and sank her teeth into his ear, hearing the raw crunch of gristle. He yelped like a dog, twisting his fingers into her hair to savagely yank her head away. Still thrashing, she desperately tried to throw him off, but he was built like a buttress and just as unyielding. Writhing her hips, she rained blows on his back and shoulders, but he merely groaned,

'Struggle all ye like, 'tis more pleasurable.'

Wrestling his coat off, he hurled it away and tore his sark open to press his grizzled chest against her. The rancid stench of unwashed male rose in her nostrils. Then he was pushing her skirts up, spreading her thighs with his knees, his weight pinning her down. His free hand pawed at her linens, and she felt the pain of his blunt fingers probing and jabbing.

'Ye black devil!' She groped for his eye sockets. 'Ye'll not have me.'

Ignoring her, he sat up and fumbled with the fastenings of his breeches. She made a wild scramble for her feet, but he jerked them from under her.

'Be still, ye vicious wee vixen. I like to take my time ower these things. Be still!' He struck her hard across the face, her head hitting the rocky cave floor, and spat into his hand. 'I mean to rut with ye. Fight me if ye will, 'twill only make the rutting more lusty.'

The last blow struck her senseless, and her vision swam. She no longer had a firm grasp of her surroundings for there seemed to be another dark shape now, even bigger and more menacing bent over the gauger. Something slim was being pressed to the devil's head.

'One more move and I'll send ye to hell,' said a murderous voice. The voice was acutely familiar. 'Take yer foul hands off her and let her up.'

The gauger's weight abruptly left her, and she scrambled from the cave, sobbing and shivering and snatched up an empty malt sack to cover herself.

'God's teeth! What d'ye think yer daeing, ye great mutton-head!'

The answering voice was cold with fury. 'No-one told me the work involved attacking defenceless women. Nor rape. Naeone at the Board mentioned that when I joined up.'

There was a stunned silence. 'Jesus God, she's a smuggler! The witchling attacked me! What am I explaining myself to you fer? A pox on ye. I told you to stay where you were. This has naught to do with you.'

'Then complete the seizure. And let the lass be.'

The voice swirled in Morven's battered head as she searched for the face that matched it. Vague shapes formed, then dissolved in the aching blur. As Jamie stooped from the cave, the voice joined with the face in a jolting impact that sent her hands flying to her face. She stepped back in disbelief. 'Twas Jamie, but…she stared at his clothing. He was dressed in the same tailed black coat and austere black hat as McBeath. He was dressed as a gauger.

'Brathadair!' she hissed.

Jamie recoiled in shock. Not her word, betrayer was truthfully what he felt himself to be and she could hardly see him as anything else. He'd expected that. But the sight of her. Her face was swollen and bleeding, horribly disfigured, her lip split and oozing bright blood. The bastard had beaten her. The imprint of a boot buckle rose livid on her cheekbone.

'Dear God!' His features contorted, and he dropped his gaze from her face as a violent shudder ran through him. *He'd* let this happen. Dithered on that ridge at a loss what to do. He raised his gaze but couldn't meet hers, staring instead at the curve of her neck, discoloured with bruises, the sweep of chestnut hair he'd never seen unbound. She was shivering and unsteady on her feet, trying to conceal herself behind an empty malt sack as if the sight of her might incite him to the same kind of behaviour as his companion. White-faced, he moved his gaze up to briefly meet hers, longing to cradle her, to take away her hurt, but knowing she'd never let him do that again. He made an anguished sound and dropped his gaze.

'*Dè tha ceàrr,* Jamie?' she asked him in Gaelic. 'Can ye nae look me in the eye?' Her voice broke, but she continued in a cracked hiss. 'After betraying the bothy … and me … to that … that devil, can ye nae bring yerself to look at what he's left?'

Reluctantly, he lifted his eyes to meet hers. Above one brow an angry gash gaped, but from the look in her eyes 'twas plain he disgusted her. He gave an agonized little groan, knowing his words of affection to her had only heightened the betrayal.

'Trust ye, ye said. Have faith.' Her swollen mouth twisted bitterly. 'And then ye do this. Become … *this*.' She made a distressed gesture at his clothing. '*Why?*'

He could hear McBeath cursing inside the cave, searching for his discarded coat. 'Things are nae … as they appear,' he said quickly.

'No?' A tear slipped down her cheek. 'How are they, then?'

He swallowed, his heart crammed high in his throat, but there was no time to explain. Even if 'twere possible, he'd no words to justify this. Her gaze was still upon him, shaming him, while his hands itched to throttle the base creature responsible. To heave his worthless bulk into the falls.

Cursing, McBeath emerged from the cave, crumpled garment in hand. His sark still gaped and his face was speckled with Morven's blood, but his fit of lust had evidently passed, and she was of little interest to him now. His anger was focused on his assistant.

'Is that what those priests of yours taught ye? To disobey orders and turn on your own kind?'

'I thought ye were killing the lass.'

'A lesson was being taught,' he growled. 'Some respect introduced. But it's hardly business of yours how I choose to apprehend lawbreakers. You were told to stay where ye were.' He stooped to leisurely fasten his breeches and glared up at Jamie.

'What was the witchling saying anyhow? Cursing me, I'll warrant. I'd forgotten ye speak the tongue of the savage, but if ye must know, I caught her in the very act, crouched over yon cauldron stirring her illicit brew. When I made to destroy it, she attacked me.' Clearly incensed, he continued to berate his interfering assistant for all the maggot-brained half-wits, but Jamie heard barely a thing.

He was staring at a small bright object nestled within the hoary pelt growing on the exciseman's chest. 'Twas undoubtedly a ring. A small silver band threaded upon a leather cord. He inched closer for a better look. A tiny object, it couldn't possibly fit any of McBeath's beefy fingers. The sark was being fastened now; he took another half-step closer. There was an entwining design upon it, indeed 'twas a piece o' rare beauty. The breath caught in his throat, a rash of gooseflesh broke out on his skin. Entwining ivy leaves she'd said, and there they were twisting around strange unearthly symbols. 'Twas Rowena's ring, he knew it with the same certainty he knew Morven now valued him lower than a louse.

McBeath shrugged on his coat. 'What are you gawping at ye great dunderheid? Destroy the still while I truss the witchling.'

The ring was the way; he knew it now. He shook himself and reluctantly withdrew his axe, looking at the precious still equipment he'd used himself not so long ago. It felt like a lifetime now.

'There'll be no need to tie the prisoner, surely,' he protested. 'How will the lass manage the climb?'

'She can be dragged for all I care.'

'Then let me do the tying, sir.' An image of the two Glenlivet women viciously roped together came to mind.

'Here then.' McBeath pulled a length of hemp rope from his coat and hurled it at him. 'Only get on with it, or she'll be away down the gorge before ye can blink.'

The thought of having a part in handing Morven over to the authorities was thoroughly sickening, yet he felt some confidence he could save her a gaol sentence. Farquharson was a reasonable man after all, and provided the fine wasn't too steep he could likely pay it himself.

'Aye, sir.' He uncoiled the rope. For some reason, Farquharson seemed to pay great heed to everything he said, and he thought it likely he could manipulate her release somehow. If only he could get an opportunity to whisper something of this to her during the ride.

Seeing him advance toward her, Morven's face reddened, heat stinging her smarting cheeks. Her head pounded, and it hurt to move, but her thoughts were now achingly clear. Rowena's reluctance to speak of her nephew made infinite sense now, nae wonder she'd been shamed. A gauger, by God. Never in her darkest moment had she considered such a thing. Swaying on her feet, she drew herself up and, swiping at her cheeks, made a desperate bid to forestall her captors.

'So, ye think me a witch's apprentice, do ye?' she blurted at McBeath.

'I do.'

'What if I said I'm nae that at all, but a fully-fledged witch?'

The exciseman betrayed no apparent reaction to this, other than an imperceptible wariness about his whiskered face, yet she was conscious she now had his utmost attention.

'You're admitting it?'

'I am.'

She laughed then at the absurdity of it all. Jamie's impossibly handsome face looking at her all torn and confused – damn him! And McBeath, ugly face stippled with her blood, a faint quiver to his breathing as he assessed her. She scarcely knew whom she hated more – the exciseman who'd bled the glen dry all her life, or the other who'd so shamefully deceived her.

'Admit it?' Her voice rose menacingly. 'Praise Lucifer, I rejoice in it. Rowena's nae my mistress, ye fools. 'Tis me embraces the black arts!'

Both men stood stock-still now, staring at her. She read apprehension on one face, incredulity on the other. It only fed her fury. If they wished to brand her a witch, then let her be one, and gladly, that'd give them something to cry about. What had she to lose?

McBeath's eyes bulged, the one with the squint near popped from his head. 'You're saying the Forbes woman is no a sorceress?'

'She can perform little more than the simplest of charms, nothing that canna be done by many in the Highlands.'

'Whereas you, on the other hand –'

'Can do a great deal more.' Her voice dropped a notch, becoming sly and insinuating. 'I ken all about you and yer secrets, even yer darkest fears are known to me.'

He glanced furtively at Jamie but couldn't stop himself asking, 'Such as?'

'Such as yer unnatural craving fer the mistress of Tomachcraggen. I ken all about that.'

She seemed to be much closer to him now, yet he hadn't seen her move. He wet his lips. 'I proposed marriage to the woman once, 'tis no secret. She could've told ye that herself.'

'No. She never speaks o' ye. I ken of ye through yer darker deeds. They've come to the notice o' my master, shall we say, and through Him to me. I believe yer acquainted wi' the one I speak of, or do I have to name Him?'

McBeath let out a little squawk of fright, but a most peculiar paralysis had come over him, and he couldn't break away from her eyes, glowing cat's eyes. A fear of the dark arts and their mysteries had been instilled in him from birth, his religion only reinforcing that fear, yet a reluctant mindfulness of his previous sins, now totting up, had begun to prey upon him. He swallowed, knowing he'd good reason to be afraid.

Sensing his fear, she breathed in deeply, drawing strength from it, feeding her rage with it. 'Did ye use the same gentle methods on Rowena as ye tried on me?' She laughed. 'Nae wonder she turned ye doon. But ye'll be wanting to know what dark deeds I know of.' Her voice took on a knowing guile.

'No.' He tried to back away. But instead, he found himself even closer, close enough to see the flecks of gold in her eyes, to see how strangely enlarged her pupils were. 'I dinnae wish —'

'Me to speak o' yer crimes? Pity that as I ken them all so well. 'Tis the hares do the watching and gossip to the faeryfolk, even the rustling aspens spread word to me.' Her expression hardened. 'Mebbe I should summon my master to speak o' yer deeds. I can see yer acquainted wi' Him already. Ye've met Him in one o' his guises afore, I can tell.'

The exciseman's face was grey now, twitching and convulsing in fearful spasms as he tried to form words. She pressed ahead, conscious only of her advantage, of the crumbling of McBeath's authority, the disintegration of his command and eager to capitalise on it. She stole a glance at Jamie, but he too was watching the gauger with a look of fascinated loathing on his face.

Remembering her father's mocking tale, she found herself driven to go on. 'In the form o' the Grey Man, was it not? On Ben MacDhui? *Am Fear Liath Mòr.*' She gave the entity its Gaelic name, knowing the gauger had not a word of the Highland tongue but regarded it with the typical superstitious suspicion of the ignorant.

He gasped at mention of the entity. How could she know of such a thing? Of his meeting with it on a frozen mountaintop? A chill stole over him, a cold so biting he felt the sting of snow driven in his face, heard the crunch of it beneath his boots.

'Help me.' He was giddy with the effort of trying to tear himself from her hold, as weak as a new-born. She was gripping him with her will, summoning something; the abomination he'd come face to face with before and prayed never to see again.

She closed her eyes and quite suddenly he was released, staggering backwards. 'Help me get away!' he yelped at Jamie. 'Fer pity's sake, man, leave the still just help me get away!'

Focusing a deadly stare on a point beyond the gauger's head, Morven began what she prayed he'd believe was some manner of summoning:

'By slip of moon and grove of oak. By cleave o' hoof and curve o' horn. *Ghairm mi mo mhaighstir!*' Slipping instinctively into Gaelic, she cursed every fibre of his body, but he didn't wait to hear it.

Scrambling onto the ledge, he dropped to his hands and knees. 'Save me, Lord,' he bleated, groping frantically for the rope. With it in his grasp, he slithered almost snakelike down the gorge, his breathing so violent he near choked himself.

Morven's knees buckled, and she crumpled to the ground. When she dared lift her head, Jamie was also gone, and it was as if neither had ever been there. She let out a desperate little sob and rocked herself back and fore until her heartbeat slowly returned to normal, and her body ceased its trembling. She felt giddy and drained, unable to think clearly, and cold, so cold.

What would be the consequence of the things she'd said in her desperation, she dared not think, though the echo of her act would reverberate, she sensed. Yet it had been so simple, the gauger's terror already coiled beneath the surface and so simple to awaken.

'Forgive me,' she whispered, but she doubted such wickedness could ever be forgiven.

After a time, she forced herself to rise and think hard what to do, not think of McBeath and his obscene intentions, and not, dear God, think of Jamie. Slowly, a matter-of-fact practicality gained control over the chaos in her mind, and she knew what she must do. She strapped a sack of malt to her back and made the slow climb down the rock-face, then returned for more. At length, she removed all six sacks and concealed them beneath an overhanging rock at the foot of the gorge. The copper worm was the last item she removed, and she wrapped it in her arisaid. The rest of the equipment could be sacrificed.

She crawled onto a slab of rock at the foot of the falls and peered at herself in the water. Self-pity welled in her throat, but she ruthlessly swallowed it down – there was her mother to think on. The water was icy, but she plucked a handful of moss and dipped it in, then pressed it to her swollen face. Meticulously, she washed away every trace of blood and then smoothed down her hair, twisting and plaiting it into some semblance of normality. Next, she stripped off her clothes and washed, scrubbing every part the gauger had touched to rid herself of his foulness. She sobbed at the memory of his fingers, shivering with both horror and cold, and then dressed again. The bruising to her ribs was severe, but she thought the bones themselves intact, while a sharp hawthorn needle and some scurvy grass would repair her torn gown. The most obvious damage was to her face and would be instantly noticed.

It was unthinkable her mam should see her like this and learn of the attack. Grace was too weak for such an upset. If she was honest, Morven knew she'd never really wanted the child her mother carried, had thought it a parasite, something her father had carelessly put there, and her mother could not bear to part with, given it was from him. Now though, for some inexplicable reason, she felt a furious burst of love for the tiny soul and a desperate desire to protect both the infant and her mother. Jamie and that part of her he'd occupied since the Beltane night was now dead to her.

It was nightfall by the time she returned to Delnabreck, but her hours of industry with leeches and a mixture of witch-hazel, arnica, and mountain mint had done its work, and her face appeared no puffier than if she'd spent the hours weeping. She held herself stiff and awkward and felt herself to be changed in some fundamental way, but that, she tried to convince herself, mightna be evident to anyone else.

Curiously, the lambs had yet to be penned for the night, and at her approach they cried piteously and followed her into their fold. Immediately she entered the cot-house, she sensed something was wrong. Stilling her breath, she stood a moment in the long shadows, recognising a tension in the air, then cautiously called, 'Rory? Donald? Are ye there?'

'They're both out looking fer ye.' It was Rowena who answered her from the threshold of her parent's bedchamber. 'Where is it ye've been?'

Something in the widow's voice churned fresh fear in her belly, and she clutched at the back of a chair. 'Nowhere … that is … something's wrong, I ken it is.'

'Yer mam's pains came on some hours ago and quicken swiftly now. She's been asking fer ye.' Rowena clasped Morven's cold hands and then drew her close, enclosing her aching body within her arms.

'I felt it,' Morven whispered. 'But … but hoped I was mistaken.'

For a moment, she clung to Rowena, breathing in her familiar scent, taking comfort in her inherent tenderness. Kindness was a quality she'd almost forgotten existed.

Rowena drew back a little and lifted Morven's chin, studying her face, but whatever it was she saw there she chose to make no comment on. 'There's nothing can be done now to stop the child coming, ye ken that, don't ye?' she said gently. 'We can only pray yer mam's strong enough to endure another labour. The bairn though … at ower two months early …' She shook her head.

''Twill finish her.'

'We'll nae let it. But she's this night to endure, and she's pitiful weak.'

Grace's face was colourless, her eyes closed tight against the pain. She put out a clammy hand to Morven and squeezed so hard Morven had to clench her teeth to prevent herself crying out. Even after the pain had passed, Grace managed only a few breathless words, her thoughts as always with Malcolm.

'Rowena doesna believe 'twill live. He'll nae even see it … 'twill be dead and buried afore he gets hame.'

'Ye dinna ken that,' Morven whispered. 'None o' us do.' She traced the spidery veins on the back of her mother's hand and blinked back her tears.

The door opened to admit Rory and Donald, both white-faced. Seeing Morven, Rory's eyes widened, then he swallowed and looked down at his hands. Being his elder, she was beyond his reproach, and she supposed he'd weightier matters on his mind. He shifted his gaze to Rowena, and she indicated they should both approach the bed, should see for themselves their mother still lived.

Watching a stark-faced Donald fidget fearfully beside his brother, his childish presence for once not only tolerated by Rory but actively welcomed, Morven felt a stab of guilt, knowing it was she who'd dragged them away at such an hour – she who had sinned. The boys exchanged an uneasy look, then withdrew to the other room to fret and to pace.

Rowena worked tirelessly, plying Grace with a tincture of crampbark to ease the course of her labour and occasional sips of a pale green elixir Morven knew was to lessen her awareness of the pain. She spoke calmly to Grace, bolstering her through each agonizing struggle, massaging her back and speaking of the infant that was so badly wanted.

Grace was drenched in sweat and the period of rest between each wave of pain seemed too short for her to prepare herself for the next onslaught. Morven cooled her face with a damp cloth and prayed. In contrast to her mother's last two labours, this one was almost silent, Grace too weak to produce the spine-wrenching screams she'd uttered in the past. The only outward indication of her pain was a hissing intake of breath through clamped teeth and the endless writhing of her body.

Some time near dawn, Morven drew Rowena away from the bed. 'Should we nae make her walk? Ye did tell me once it quickens the progress, eases the opening o' the way.'

'It does, but I dinna see how she can walk, she can scarce lift her head.'

'We could hold her, she's as light as a wishbone, we could bear her weight whilst she moves her legs.'

Rowena nodded slowly. ''Tis worth trying,' she agreed.

Rory was eager to help, and between the three of them, they eased Grace as gently as they could from the bed where she'd lain for the past three weeks. Her head lolled, and she muttered something unintelligible in Gaelic, but she could move her feet a little to shuffle slowly around the room. For the next two hours, the three of them walked with her in turns, Rory doing the lion's share of the work while Donald watched anxiously, too small to take his turn. When they laid Grace back on the bed, Rowena judged her as ready as she'd ever be. She ushered the boys from the room and took Grace's hand; it burned ominously.

'Ye must bear down now. Fer Malcolm's sake. 'Tis the bairn he wants, a lass … I believe.'

Grace's eyes rolled, but she pushed her damnedest, losing consciousness but being remorselessly brought back.

'Ye're killing her!' Morven cried. But Rowena shook her head.

'It does seem that way, I know, but 'tis the only way to help her live.'

Even so, it was mid-morning before the tiny soul finally entered the world, the tiny head slippery with the mutton fat Rowena had used to ease its passage. Grace let out a bloodcurdling cry, and it was over.

'A lass,' Rowena told her. 'A dear wee soul.'

Grace slumped into the pillow, her chest heaving, but a trace of a smile touched her lips.

Quickly Rowena swaddled the infant and passed her to Morven. 'She lives. At least fer the moment. Take her to meet her brothers, I must work fast.'

The infant had quite the dearest face any of them had ever seen and wisps of delicate red hair.

'She's that wee,' said Rory. 'To have given Mam so much trouble. But, should she nae be crying?'

Morven studied the precious infant, noting the pallor of her lips, the shallowness of her breathing. Her throat tightened hopelessly.

'She's alright though, isn't she?' Donald piped. 'I mean, Rowena said 'twould be dead.'

'Ye could pray fer her,' Morven suggested, and she began to clean the blood and grease from the tiny face.

Grace had slipped into unconsciousness, although there was more colour in her face than there had been in weeks. Still, Rowena was plainly worried. Feeling the heat radiating from the frail body, she frowned at the simples she had to hand and checked again the rapid racing of Grace's heartbeat at a point on her wrist.

Morven watched her fearfully. 'Has she a fever?' But there was no need to have it confirmed, the signs of fever were manifest.

''Tis what I was afraid of.'

'What can we do?'

'Send one o' the boys out to gather wild garlic. 'Twill help fight the infection. I've dried myrtle to hand and … aye, thank heavens,' she rummaged among her potions. 'I've juniper oil. We'll make a solution and bathe her with it.'

'Will she live?'

Rowena's dark eyes were full of tenderness. 'Only God can answer that. But whatever's in my power, I will do.'

Over the next few hours there was little change in Grace's condition, she remained in that deep state to which she'd slipped, drifting between bouts of distressing delirium and lengthy periods of deathlike stillness. They continued to bathe her with juniper water, a potent remedy for fever, and sprinkled her with the silvered water Rory had eagerly fetched. Beyond that, there was little any of them could do, and Morven's prayers joined the chorus of desperate Hail Marys and Our Fathers Donald and Rory recited.

The child was dying, her tiny abdomen barely moving, her lips tinged blue. Morven racked her mind for ways to bring the mite some relief but there was nothing. The little soul's lungs were simply not developed enough to supply her body with the air she needed. She'd uttered not a sound since birth but battled silently for breath, seeking neither to feed nor be comforted.

Lord, Morven silently beseeched, what has this little soul done to deserve such a brief glance at life? Or was the infant's suffering a punishment fer her own wickedness? Her mam's early labour hastened by it? The notion wormed insidiously through her mind. She who'd sinned, who'd sold her soul to the devil to escape arrest and humiliation. What had she done?

The notion was too much to bear. She held the infant close, desperately willing air into the tiny lungs, her own chest constricted with despair. 'Ye are loved,' she whispered fiercely to the little bundle. 'Loved more than …' She swallowed. 'More than I have words to explain.'

But the struggle went on, the infant weakening by the hour, her eyes never once open to see how much she was wanted. Such a fighter she was, but among the folk gathered there was no talk of the outcome of her struggle – the hopelessness was plain to see.

It was nightfall again before the infant's struggle finally came to an end, and, convulsing, she lay limp and still.

Rowena kissed the delicate little forehead. 'She's at peace now,' she whispered.

The infant's struggle was lost, but Morven could see no peace in that. She laid the infant beside her mother – Grace almost as still as the child – and crept away.

It was almost two days since she'd slept, and she longed for oblivion. She took the copper worm from her arisaid and pushed it beneath her bed, then lay down. She was sore and choked with tears that refused to come, but nonetheless, sleep came mercifully quick.

When she awoke, daylight's glimmer was fading again, and she found her mother a little improved and the infant laid in a tiny homemade coffin lined with fleece. Tears blurred her vision and tightened her throat as she looked at the delicate mouth that would never smile, the tiny unopened eyelids, now still and cold. Yet looking at her mother's dear face, she dared to hope.

CHAPTER FIFTEEN

JAMIE CAUGHT UP WITH McBeath floundering in the Fèithe Mosach, a bog half a mile from the Lochy Gorge. At the sound of hooves bearing down on him, the gauger thrashed through the sodden heath and near wept with relief at seeing Jamie and the mounts. Sobbing and wheezing and without a word of gratitude, he scrambled into the saddle and with a blubbering cry flogged his horse mercilessly out of the mire and away.

Jamie followed at a more rational pace, using the time to think through his next move. 'Twas hard to think straight, difficult to focus on what he must do to bring the Black Gauger to justice with the grievous burden of his guilt weighing him down. It gnawed into his soul. He carried with him an image of the lass he loved, crumpled where he'd left her, and the shame of that fired such a rage within him it clouded his judgement. For he now blamed himself as much as the gauger.

He drew a ragged breath. He no longer knew what to say to Morven, his efforts at keeping her safe had failed utterly. He looked down at his calloused hands as they gripped the reins; they appeared brutishly big and clumsy. Too crude to give any comfort, to touch the delicate curve of her shoulder and turn her toward him, then slide down her back and cradle her. He felt unworthy to attempt such a thing, yet yearned to do so nonetheless.

Tightening his grip on the reins, he took several fierce breaths, struggling to keep his loathing of the gauger under control. 'Twas plain the man's considerable sins troubled him. Leaning forward in the saddle, he pressed his mount into a gallop. Time the man unburdened himself.

At Balintoul, Jamie was forced to leap aside as a frightened maid near knocked him down in her haste to escape McBeath's home. The wind had risen, and he watched the girl's arisaid swirl about her as she crossed herself and scurried away. He turned back to the house. The exciseman had simply let his horse loose to wander, still saddled, and he caught the spent animal and tethered it alongside his own. Both doors to the house were jammed fast, but using his shoulder he rammed the rear entrance, splitting the timber doorframe, and landed heavily amid a stack of casks and barrels on the scullery floor.

The house was dark and silent. Straining his senses, he made out a faint but repetitive sound and followed it. As he neared the drawing room, he recognised the gauger's voice, pitched peculiarly high.

'If only I'd known. Dear God, if only I'd known.'

Without preamble, Jamie booted the door open.

McBeath's start was so violent he almost fell in the fire, and he let out a half-strangled cry of alarm.

'Lang!' He pounced on Jamie and drew him further into the room. 'Thank God.'

'Who was it ye were expecting?'

McBeath paid no heed but hastily closed the door. 'I need holy water.' He turned and lurched across the room.

'And ye suppose me to have some about me?'

'No, no.' He ceased pacing only long enough to wring his hands. 'Ye can get some from the kirk. Take it from the font if need be. Tell the minister I sent ye, he'll no question it, only hurry man!'

'I've the mounts to see to.' Jamie made no attempt to move and still less to conceal his contempt as he watched the exciseman's face twitch with agitation.

'The horses can wait, damn it! Can ye no see my life's in mortal danger?'

Jamie swept his gaze around the room. 'There's many a thing I see, but evidence that yer life's in danger isna one o' them. Yer decency now, yer moral behaviour, aye, that I see is plainly in question. As is yer sanity.'

If the frightened maid he'd seen fleeing the house had informed Jamie a freak tempest had just laid waste to McBeath's home, he would likely have believed her. The room was lit up like an altar, candles burning on every surface, cabinets and cupboards raided to find them, and although it was only late afternoon and the day fine and clear, every window was shuttered and draped, the front entrance barricaded with chairs. Bizarrely, the drawing room was ringed with a wavering line of coarse salt and a great heap of it was spread across the threshold.

Gawping at him, McBeath plucked a flask of whisky from the dresser and took a desperate swig. 'I need holy water. 'Tis to protect me from that … that …' He shuddered, and a thin wail rose in his throat.

'From what? Surely ye dinna believe thon frightened lass? 'Twas plain she was trying to evade arrest.'

'But there was substance to what she said. She *knows* things. Uncanny things. Things it isnae possible fer her to know without being a disciple of ...' McBeath dropped into a chair, shaking his head. 'I'll no name Him fer fear of bringing evil upon myself.' Bunching a fist, he pressed it briefly to his mouth. 'But if only I'd an inkling, I'd never have touched her.' He lifted the flask and allowed half its contents to gurgle down his throat.

'What are ye so afraid o'? What dark deeds did she mean, and if only ye'd known what?'

'What she is. What she can *do*. I always believed the Forbes woman was the sorceress.' He got to his feet and wiped his mouth with a trembling hand. 'And so she is. That woman's cursed me near twenty years.'

Jamie looked around at the richness of the surroundings and thought of Rowena's meagre cottage. 'Ye dinna lead the life o' someone that's been cursed. What kind o' curse?'

'One that means I've no issue to follow me, no lineage to mark my passing through this world. Another two weeks and I'd be free of it. My life's no been my own since the matter with the witch's brother near twenty years ago.' He lunged at Jamie, gripping him by the forearm. 'Bring me the minister then. If ye'll no bring me holy water, bring me the minister, he'll protect me.'

Jamie rocked back on his heels. The witch's brother – 'twas his own father! He shoved McBeath away. 'I need to know more.'

'And then you'll help me?'

'If I judge ye need it, then aye ... I might.'

The exciseman drained the last of the whisky, choking as the spirit scorched the back of his throat, and pulled another flask from the dresser. ''Twas on the Ben I saw it first.' His speech was beginning to slur, his eyes widening as he recalled the horror of it. 'A great grey shape –'

'Nae that! Tell me of the curse. And the matter with the woman's brother.'

'A mere misunderstanding,' McBeath replied glibly. 'I was to wed Rowena Innes, but her brother didnae approve. He poisoned her against me, put forward another, a mere cottar, Duncan Forbes, a muck-the-byre, and she took him in my stead.'

'The brother told ye he did this?'

'No, no, but I could tell.' He licked his lips with a flick of tongue. 'Folk say reivers took her brother's cattle, paupered him they say, and so the factor had him evicted from Druimbeag, and never did she see him nor his wife and bairn again.'

'Reivers, eh? And was it reivers?'

'Well, aye, though they did take a deal o' convincing.'

'Ye mean ye paid them?'

'And a pack o' thieving cut-throats, they were.'

Jamie's face darkened, a pulse beginning to pound in his head.

'Since then my life's been blighted by the woman.'

'Blighted? How blighted?'

'After she married I also took myself a wife. Only her curses brought the death of the bairns she bore me and now 'tis my wife she's done to death. I'm left wi' nothing. Nothing, that is, I hadnae before – an unnatural craving to take my pleasure with the witch-woman. A craving that's been in me twenty years, though I know her to be wicked and unwholesome.'

'If ye're such a bull,' Jamie said through clenched teeth. 'There're women aplenty at the Balintoul Inn. Take yer fill there and forget this witch-woman.'

A tic appeared at the corner of McBeath's deviant eye, a nerve in his cheek twitched. 'This burning's no natural. Nothing will douse it. She's put a curse upon me.' He calmed his errant nerve with a trembling hand. ''Tis the kind o' curse that makes me burn with the wanting of her. Even though I ken she's unholy, I've sinned to have her.'

Jamie gripped the back of a chair, sensing the kernel of a confession forming. 'How,' he asked, 'have ye sinned?'

The exciseman's eyes dulled momentarily before taking on the look of a hunted animal. ''Tis as the witchling said. Dark deeds.' He staggered across the room and pitched into a chair.

Jamie could hear the catch in his own voice as he asked, 'Had ye a hand in making her a widow?'

The question hung in the air, then the exciseman leant forward, jaws rigid. 'Every soul close enough to her to afford protection, I have removed.' He bared his teeth. 'To set her apart, make her vulnerable to me.'

Jamie gasped. 'And her husband, how did he die?'

''Twas on the road. Guiding a trail o' garrons loaded wi' illicit whisky. Duncan was a smuggler – every man did know it.'

'But how did ye ken where he'd be to catch him?'

The gauger grinned so wickedly, Jamie recoiled. ''Tis almost the best part. Ye see he was betrayed – by one o' his own.'

'By another smuggler? And ye did kill him in cold blood?'

Sobering, the gauger blinked and sat back, conscious, perhaps, of how much he'd already revealed. Remembering the predicament he found himself in, his face puckered. 'But there's naught douses this burning, fer what can douse the fires o' hell?'

Jamie stared hard at him.

Slumping forward, McBeath clutched his head in his hands. 'Fer pity's sake man, will ye no bring me the minister before whatever wickedness that lass was summoning finds me and brings me torment?'

''Tis yer own guilt and lust does that.'

'Fer pity's sake, man!'

'Do ye mean to confess yer sins to him?'

McBeath threw Jamie a look, one that conveyed his assistant had clearly lost his mind.

Softening his voice, Jamie relaxed his stance a little to become more coaxing. 'What, then, is to happen in two weeks to free ye o' this curse?'

The exciseman drew a deeper more satisfied breath, his nostrils flaring. 'I'll wed her. Bind her to me by the vows she holds dear. To honour and obey. I'll break her that way, or I'll see her removed from Strathavon for good.'

'All this to bed the woman?'

'Aye! Now go to the kirk and bring back the minister!'

Jamie moved to the door, then looked back at his employer, his dark eyes full of scorn. 'I'm a Catholic,' he reminded him stiffly. ''Twould be a wicked sin fer me to go there.' At that, he turned on his heel and stalked from the room, leaving the exciseman to gape after him.

***

Among the many advantages his profession bestowed, Samuel Dearg found the wearing of a powered wig most agreeable. As a law agent, the wearing of a wig was expected and not only elicited a degree of respect from the somewhat uncouth inhabitants of provincial Elgin but also kept his balding head warm. The stout little scribe had his reputation to consider, and God only knew there were penniless unfortunates aplenty in town bent on abusing his good nature. Frowning, he looked across at the young Highlander sat opposite him, instinctively judging the man to be different in some way. This man's respectful good manners owed nothing to the wig, he thought, but came rather from an inner grace.

It was a peculiarity of his, but Dearg liked to think he could glean more about his clients from their manner and bearing than from what they actually said. James Innes possessed the lilting rhythm of speech of the Gael, something his peers in Edinburgh would recoil from, but Dearg found nothing in the least bit underhand about the striking young man. Indeed, he read nothing at all in Jamie's taut face that alarmed him, but rather felt drawn to offer his help.

The trouble was, even if the young man's story was true, and, he reflected, it likely was, there was little could be done. He removed the wig and placed it on a pate-shaped mould on his desk. As was often the case, he was conscious of the other man's luxuriant dark locks and of his own rather obvious shortcomings in that direction but recognised such matters would likely be irrelevant to a man such as this. Frowning, he glanced over the notes he'd taken during his discourse with the man.

The Highlander leant forward in his seat. 'So, will the law help me?'

Dearg adjusted his spectacles. 'I would very much like the answer to your question to be yes, Mr Innes. But in truth, I fear there's little I can suggest.'

'He all but confessed to me.'

'A part confession only, given under unparalleled circumstances. It would seem unlikely Mr McBeath would repeat such a folly.'

Frowning, Jamie dropped his gaze to the polished wooden floor. 'Without the proof o' my aunt's ring, aye, but I thought, what wi' McBeath having the ring in his possession –'

Dearg nodded; seldom had he taken less pleasure in shattering a client's assumptions. 'I can foresee two difficulties. Firstly, Mr McBeath would need to be apprehended with the ring in his possession –'

'Aye, he does wear it around his neck.'

'Yes, yes.' Dearg raised his hand and nodded with a little frown. 'And it would require to be identified by your aunt, of course. But I see nothing to stop Mr McBeath from merely stating he'd bought the ring or been given it by some intermediary. At the very least, it would be his word against that of your aunt.' He paused to awkwardly shuffle through his notes. 'I fear that as the widow of a known smuggler, your aunt's evidence would be deemed flawed and therefore inadmissible.'

Jamie blinked at the scribe. Without doubt, Rowena was one of the most honest and honourable individuals he'd ever met. The thought of her character being compared to the exciseman's and found wanting was beyond comprehension. He opened his mouth to protest, then snapped it shut. Plainly Dearg had more to say.

'I fear the second difficulty, however, is perhaps the more insurmountable of the two. You see, if you were to bring your allegations to the sheriff here in Elgin, he would likely refer you to your local Justice of the Peace, a Mr William McGillivray of Inchfindy Hall.'

Jamie groaned. 'But the man's corrupt. McGillivray's the duke's factor and holds no love for me or my aunt. Is there no other course open to me, Mr Dearg?' He studied the law agent's face, feeling a sick sensation churn his innards. 'The factor's in cahoots wi' McBeath. Between them, they've a stranglehold on every crofter and smuggler in the glen.'

If there was a way of gaining justice for Rowena, the law agent would surely know of it. Jamie searched Dearg's face for signs that the fastidious little man was at least taking him seriously. In the pale eyes behind the spectacles he observed a sharpness of wit that he warmed to, but with a sinking sensation, he also detected an air of genuine regret about the man's softly rounded face. He swallowed. 'Only a matter of days after coming to live with my aunt, McGillivray condemned us both as mischief-makers.'

'I see.' Dearg dipped his quill into the well on his desk and made a further addition to his notes. 'Most unfortunate.'

While Jamie waited on the edge of his seat, Dearg opened a drawer of his desk and removed a carved wooden pipe and a small knife. Frowning, he began to pare small blackened flakes from the bowl of the pipe.

'You see,' he said, his frown deepening. 'If you could convince an officer of the Black Watch of your suspicions, you could perhaps have your man arrested. But I just cannot envisage any Black Watch officer being convinced of Mr McBeath's guilt. As you'll be aware, the dragoons work closely with the officers of excise assisting them in raids. He'll be well known to them all, and, as such, will certainly be viewed as above reproach.'

He blew gently into the bowl of the pipe and a flurry of black shavings pattered onto his desk. Scooping them up, he dropped them into a small receptacle. 'On the other hand, having given a false name to the Board of Excise, I'm afraid you will most assuredly be discredited.'

'I dinna care about that. I no longer intend to work fer the gaugers. I've learned all I can from that guise.'

'You misunderstand.' Dearg looked up through his spectacles.

'When I say discredited, I mean you will not be believed.' He frowned at the pipe and laid it back on the desk, unlit. 'If you can lie about your name, it will be assumed that you can lie about other things too, including perhaps a rather obvious attempt at ridding your glen – a known haunt of smugglers – of its resident excise officer.'

Jamie stared at him. For the first time during their meeting, the scribe felt the full force of the Highlander's presence, intense and somewhat unsettling, focus upon him. A muscle rippled along the younger man's jaw, and he swallowed hard. Dearg sensed the man was attempting to maintain mastery of his anger and bitterness and had no wish to vent it where it was not deserved.

'I do not wish to appear callous, Mr Innes,' he said hastily. 'But to point out how this may be construed. It's my belief you should think carefully before you proceed. I advise you to leave this well alone. It would be unwise to provoke the authorities, for I fear they could merely turn this around and construct a compelling case against you, yourself.'

The young Highlander appeared not to hear his words. He swayed in his seat and stared at the swirling dust motes riding the warm air of the office. 'A case fer what crime?'

'For supporting and abetting smugglers – a crime viewed in a very grave light. If, let us say, you were to find yourself in front of William McGillivray, whom you've intimated dislikes you, then a lengthy gaol sentence would seem likely.'

'And ye think I care about myself?'

'No, I don't believe you do. You strike me as a man of courage and decency. But what use are courage and decency to your loved ones when those admirable qualities of yours languish in gaol along with your good self?'

Jamie glanced sharply at the scribe but could see no trace of mockery in the man's face; he read only pity and understanding in the watery eyes, and somehow that chilled him more than anything.

'Then I've failed.' He dragged his gaze from the scribe and looked over the little man's shoulder and out of the dormer window behind him. From the window, he could see the corbelled stairtower and spire of Elgin's tollbooth, dark against the morning sky. Its parapet and crowstepped roofline housed a clamour of squabbling rooks and its walls, blackened by wood-smoke, held the dregs of Moray's humanity – thieves and killers, the evil and the immoral, the corrupt and the witless, and, he didn't doubt, the innocent.

'That remains to be seen. But you've nothing material for the law to use against this man you describe so graphically, so … chillingly.

He is too powerful and too protected, and you,' Dearg smiled a little regretfully, 'have made too many enemies. You didn't honestly believe the Collector here in Elgin would be gratified to learn you'd deceived him?'

'I didna think –'

'Believe me, Mr Innes, it would be wise to drop this now before he learns the truth.' Dearg fingered the well-loved contours of his pipe, a gift from his late mother, and hoped he'd not crushed the spirit and resolve of the young man but had instead saved him from senselessly sacrificing himself. Nevertheless, he imagined the sheer latent energy of the man would be none too easy to quell.

'I understand the dilemma your aunt finds herself in,' he went on. 'But you'll not help her by going to gaol yourself.' He rose to his feet and extended a hand to Jamie. 'Good luck, Mr Innes. And my regrets I could be of such little service.'

Once the young Highlander had respectfully shaken the proffered hand and taken his leave, Dearg reached into his desk drawer once more and drew out a bottle of French brandy and a single glass. He poured himself a sizeable measure and swallowed it down neat, then rose to the window and watched Jamie, a tall upright figure, cross the High Street and stare up at the tollbooth for a moment before collecting his mount from McBride's stables. There was a black bundle tied at the rear of his saddle, clothing of some sort. He watched the Highlander toss it on a pile of refuse and dung and then ride away.

It was at times like this, he sincerely regretted not following his brother into mundane employment in the woollen mills of the borders. There his impotence would rankle less. He donned his wig again, lest anyone think him grown soft, and with a resigned sigh returned to the pile of paperwork on his desk.

***

Twice Jamie passed the ring cairn and reached the massive shattered walls of Drumin Castle on its strategic bluff at the north entrance to Strathavon, and twice he turned back for Elgin. Twice the crumbling ivy-strangled fastness scowled down accusingly at him, and he stumbled down the slope to look upon the Avon, strengthened here by its confluence with the Livet, and watched it surge scornfully by. At nightfall, he camped on the haughland of the river near Ballindalloch and gave his footsore pony some rest. But he received little rest himself. His head ached, his thoughts dirled in a head grown weary of thinking and, restless, he could not decide what course to take. He shivered under his plaid and went through the choices again and again.

On both occasions, it was the sheriff he'd turned back to see, but on reaching the outskirts of town he'd shied away, Dearg's warning ringing in his head. The law, it seemed, would not help him, though Dearg had genuinely wished to, he sensed. But if Dearg was right, what use would he be to Rowena locked up in Elgin gaol? She'd have no way of knowing what became of him, and each day that passed her reckoning with McBeath drew closer. Yet to give up now seemed shameful and he spent another night racked in tortuous indecision.

By the end of that night, he again turned his pony toward Strathavon, and as the first glimmer of dawn rose over Ben Rinnes, he drove his garron over the rough heather track with single-minded ferocity. Four days he'd wasted, his plan to bring McBeath to justice in shreds around him, but with all thoughts of magistrates and sheriffs thrust firmly from his mind, he knew what he must do.

***

Tomachcraggen was little changed. The cairns of rock he'd cleared from the ground near three months ago were still piled high, and he looked on the oats he'd sown, well grown and ripe now, and prayed he'd get the chance to harvest the crop. When finally the familiar low-lying crofthouse came in sight, he still had no notion how he'd tell his kinswoman that he'd failed her.

Rowena stood and watched Jamie from the whins where she gathered silverweed and bittercress and love for him filled her heart. Through him, her brother still lived, for Jamie was so like his father she oft-times had to pinch herself. He carried himself with the same poise, undertook every task with the same air of intensity, the gallant manner, prompting in her a fierce affection. Yet as he drew close, she could see the change in his bearing that drooped his shoulders and robbed him of vigour, and a crippling fear struck at her. He'd failed. The lines of defeat were etched on his face in bitterness, and she saw plainly how things stood with him. With them all.

'Jamie!' She pushed aside her trepidation. At least he was safe, his eagerness to protect her hadna brought him to harm and that was all that truly mattered.

At her mother's cry, Sarah looked up from her toil among the tattie dreels and watched her mother embrace her cousin with affection. Once again, she was forgotten, but Sarah had long learned not to let such a minor detail deter her. She crept into a thicket of gorse and, wriggling as close as she dared, flattened herself into a natural hollow in the ground.

Stiff with cold and close to exhaustion, Jamie unsaddled Rowena's pony and put the animal to pasture. Silently, Rowena took the saddle from him. The skin of his face felt taut and grimy, and when he looked at his kinswoman, his eyes smarted with frustration.

'Ye mustna blame yerself,' she said. 'Ye tried, and fer that I'm truly thankful.'

He blinked and shook himself. 'But how did ye –?'

She gave a hint of a shrug. 'It hardly takes the gift o' far-sight to see from yer face it bodes ill fer us.' She pushed the cottage door open. 'But come and rest now, and then ye can tell me what it is ye've learned.'

He passed a clammy hand over his face, over the rough growth of whiskers on his chin, the layer of grime around his eyes from his days spent in the saddle, then nodded and followed her inside.

Sarah scowled as the door closed against her but soon realised it was not shut fully. Scrambling from her thorny nook, she settled herself by the crack in the door where she could see one side of Jamie's face, turned toward the fire, and hear quite comfortably his discourse with her mother.

Rowena busied herself fetching broth and bannocks for Jamie, but the composure of her face belied the flush of alarm that rose in her breast at his leaden expression. Her heart beat dully against her breastbone and she watched his face, her eyes drawn to the sensitive lines of his mouth as he selected his words.

'Ye mightna ken this, but not long after I came here an auld herdsman, speaking fer the glenfolk, branded me the instrument of yer undoing.'

With a nod, Rowena acknowledged she knew of it.

'Back then I didna care much fer superstitions …' He stared into the fire. 'But now I see I've brought affliction on everyone I've ever cared fer.'

'Ye mustna speak like that,' she said a little sharply. 'Achnareave doesna speak fer the glenfolk, merely himself. Ye've brought no affliction. What was done to Duncan … what may yet happen to me, all the bad feeling, that was born long afore ye came here.' She sat on the stool opposite and looked darkly at him. 'Ye've doubtless heard the tales told of me?'

He looked uneasily at her but made no comment.

'I should've explained it afore.' She took a deep breath. 'But ye see, Jamie, I have gifts beyond the natural. Gifts I believe are from the Creator, though they did come to me by uncommon means. My healing, my … my sensing things. Yet it's in my choice to use these gifts as I judge I should to benefit others, that McBeath has found the means to punish me.' She narrowed her eyes as she spoke, seeing clearly the way of men, despairing of their intolerances. 'Few men are wi'out prejudice, enlightened enough to recognise and understand my gifts. So in a way, I've brought this upon myself, nae you. 'Twas never *your* doing.'

He made a dismissive gesture with his head, and she sensed he was too weary to argue with her and would not be shaken from his convictions so easily. With a sigh, she asked, 'Can ye tell me what it is ye've learned?'

She listened in silence while he recounted the details, as he knew them, of the raid on the MacRae bothy and McBeath's brutal attempt to force himself upon Morven. He didn't look at her during his account but stared into the fire. His body quivered, a continuous shiver, and she sensed his impotent rage and the effort of will it took to suppress it enough to speak of what happened. She thought now of the signs of bruising she'd detected on Morven's face, carefully concealed but nonetheless plain to any with a perceptive eye, and her heart wept for the lass.

On that calm market day in Balintoul, she'd endured only a fraction of the violence she sensed the gauger could unleash. As he described in gloating detail what he'd done to Duncan, she'd wept and keened, and, to silence her, he'd pressed a blade to her throat and tracing a finger over her breasts had excited himself, crowing of what he'd do to her once he'd made her his wife.

'So, I know he still has yer ring,' Jamie said gruffly. 'I've seen it wi' my own eyes. Only it's nae enough to condemn the man – Lord only knows what would be.' In a grim voice, he told of Dearg's warning. 'In the face of our desperate crimes,' he said bitterly, 'even murder can go unpunished.'

'Then it's as I feared. We are but common thieves to magistrates and sheriffs. Dross to be maligned and mistrusted.' She looked hard at her nephew. 'Ye did right, Jamie. He's nae worth giving up yer freedom fer. And neither am I.'

He glanced up sharply, and she saw his dark eyes were ablaze, his face haunted, and then she understood. Morven had not spoken a word of this. She had, Rowena supposed, felt there was no-one she could confide in now that Jamie was a turncoat. Not privy to their plan, the lass doubtless believed Jamie had betrayed his kin, brought unthinkable shame upon them all, and not wishing to heap more shame upon her dearest friend, had kept all this to herself. And suffered badly for it – as did the lad.

'Ye love her, don't ye? Morven. Ye love Morven.'

He flinched as though she'd struck him, then closed his eyes in silent acknowledgement. 'Only she thinks me a snake.' He blinked slowly. 'I dinna blame her, I do despise myself. Even supposing she knew the truth of what we planned and I did bring the Black Gauger to justice, I'd expose her father as a traitor. How could I expect her to love me after that?'

Rowena sat back, her face as pale as bone. 'Then, 'twas truly Malcolm betrayed us?'

'I believe so.'

'Oh, Jamie!'

For a moment, she couldn't face her nephew's eyes and turned to stare into the fire, watching the shifting peats crumble and glow. In that glowing, she saw the bonds of kinship and affinity torn asunder, Duncan robbed of more than just his life, but of his roots in the glen, his place in the land where kinship and whisky shaped their lives. The blood and the barley. It did flow in their veins, only Duncan's had been opened by one of their own.

'I'm truly sorry, Rowena.'

'No,' she managed. 'Dinna be. Perhaps I already knew it. And yet …' She swallowed, her face taut with pain. 'Yet I feel such *grief*.'

He groped for her hand.

She squeezed it in return, losing her voice for a moment. ''Tis Grace I feel fer. And Morven. Dear Lord, *Morven!*'

Was this what lay at the root of Morven's aloofness? The sense of hopelessness the lass seemed to weave around herself as though she were somehow set apart. Had she known? Had she suspected what her father was? What he'd done? Or was it that she cared for Jamie as much as the lad cared for her? Only, finding him to be something far less than she imagined the knowledge had brought her bitter torment. A torment she couldn't reveal, nae wi'out shaming those she held most dear.

'What've I done?' she breathed. 'We must tell Morven the truth. Make her see ye as ye really are.' A thought struck. 'Ye'll nae ken o' the bairn, then? Grace's bairn?'

Jamie focused blankly on her.

'Grace brought a wee lass into the world, sadly afore her time. Four days ago. The wee soul died in Morven's arms. I feared the worst fer Grace, but I believe now she'll live, though 'tis nothing short of a miracle. Father Ranald couldna wait fer Malcolm's return, we buried the wee soul yesterday.'

When Jamie said nothing, gave no outward reaction to what she'd said, Rowena leant to shake him gently from his dark abstraction.

'Ye see!' he cried, rounding on her. 'More affliction! Is there to be no end to the suffering I bring?'

CHAPTER SIXTEEN

SARAH STUMBLED AWAY from the cot-house. Glancing over her shoulder, she scrambled into the hollow she'd occupied earlier among the gorse. Her head reeled. Her breath came in quick spurts, unfamiliar sensations churning her belly. She dropped to her knees in the flattened grass and gasped, 'Da! Oh God, Da!'

Her plan had worked better than she imagined, for Morven couldna abide Jamie and how well he knew it. He'd not linger over-long on her now. But she hadn't considered for a moment he might fail to have McBeath hanged. She'd expected her father's murderer to swing, had dreamt night after night of his drop from the roof of Elgin's tollbooth. That wouldna happen now. She staggered under the knowledge. The gauger would go free, *was* free to carry on as before.

Her face reddened, the soft lines of her mouth hardened, and she trembled as a blast of hatred coursed through her body. 'Twas her mother's fault. Because of her, the Black Gauger had killed her da. And they'd be put out of Tomachcraggen now, she knew it. With a sob, she pulled herself up and raked her gaze over the meagre strips of land her da had cleared from the encroaching forests. Within a few years, 'twould all be forest again.

Not prone to bouts of sentimentality, Sarah doubted she'd really miss it. It mattered little where she lived, for she'd have Jamie. Wherever they went, she and her kin, he'd go with them. There was no reason for him to stay here now; Morven didna want him. But with a shiver of longing, Sarah knew she most certainly did.

She blinked away the tears that clung to her lashes, feeling the familiar sensations thoughts of her cousin lately stirred within her. The sensations grew, quickly migrating to her loins where they made her breathe hard and squirm with excitement. After a moment, she began to feel better, less powerless and overlooked and more in control.

She liked to scheme. If the truth were told, she liked it more than anything. There was satisfaction to be had from observing a well-laid scheme bear fruit, and she'd been doing it, with varying degrees of subtlety, since ever she could mind. Of course, things didn't always go her way. Guile was a quality her mam almost always recognised, and as a lass she'd been scolded for it. But Sarah was circumspect with her mother now and knew when to be wary. Yet she'd always managed to manipulate her da. She grimaced as a pang of grief struck her. It aye caught her like that. Just when she was savouring some triumph, the thought of him, the lancing pain as she minded he was gone, would come back to her and spoil it all.

Her da had loved her. Not with the paltry measure of love her mother doled out after Morven and all those wretched sick folk had taken their share. Nae wi' a shrewd glint in the eye the way her mam looked when taking stock of the manner of woman her daughter was becoming. But with an unquestioning, unshakeable sort of love. There'd been no need to compete for her father's attention. He'd aye had time fer his daughter. Nor a need to feign interest in collecting bities of weed and learning how to identify them. He'd not cared if she could do that or not. Her da never worried that she lacked the gifts of healing and second sight her mam possessed; he'd not had them either. His love had been blind and altogether unstoppable. She scowled at the blank cottage door. Except it had stopped, and while she knew she'd never get it back, Sarah was aware her great need for it endured.

At the sound of voices, she dropped onto her belly and watched Jamie leave the cot-house and make across the rigs toward the river. There was a grace to the way her cousin moved, a mesmeric quality about the sway of kilts about his lean legs, and she sensed, as she always did when she secretly watched him, that strange alchemy he possessed, that odd mix of both danger and dependability he seemed to meld about him. After a moment, she rose and followed him.

Jamie paid little heed to the flitter of thistledown carried on the warm air. Nor did he care much for the scent of wild thyme among the heather or the drone of bees. He thought only of escaping Rowena's dreadful acceptance of his failure and washing away the grime of his journey. He'd taken the flask of whisky she'd silently pushed into his hand and took several mouthfuls of it now. 'Twas fierce liquor and warmed a passage through his innards but brought him no comfort. He doubted an entire keg could do that. He tried to find a word to adequately describe how he felt but could find nothing to encapsulate his utter despondency and, weary of thinking, gave it up.

At the riverbank, he stripped off his clothes and slipped naked into the icy water. The current was stronger than he expected, and he near lost his footing before bracing himself against the pull of the undertow. The shock of icy water made him gasp, but it sloughed away some of his lethargy, and he felt some spark of his former self return. Tilting his head back, he let the stinging cold seep up his scalp, invading every follicle until his hair was all submerged and streamed away from his body, dark on the surface of the water. With handfuls of sand from the riverbed, he scrubbed at his skin until it stung and glowed pink, then, satisfied with his efforts, he stood and waded to the bank.

He sat on a rock, shivering, and let the breeze raise the gooseflesh upon his chilled skin. Slowly, the air's warmth pervaded and the tiny hairs on his body, strangely golden against the dark tumble upon his shoulders, lay flat again. Had he been wrong to come to Stratha'an? In such a place, he sensed the teachings and opinions of lettered gentlemen, the so-called enlightened of the day, were as so many leaves fallen upon the ground; they made no impression, were soon blown away. 'Twas the land that endured, the hills and stones and forests, and clinging to them, the enchantments of the past, their secrets well kept. In his mind, he heard a snatch from an old rhyme his mother used to repeat and shivered at its words.

> *He wha tills the faeries' green*
> *Nae luck again shall hae.*
> *An' he wha spills the faeries' ring*
> *Betide him want an' wae.*

He'd always thought it idle superstition, but in the dark mood of the moment wasn't so sure. He took another mouthful of whisky, the taste and scent bringing back a fleeting memory of Morven and her father's bothy, then thrust the flask away and began the painstaking business of pleating his plaid ready to belt about his waist.

It was the muffled giggle that made him freeze. There was no-one obvious among the rocks and bushes of the riverbank, but conscious of his vulnerability, he snatched up his sark and *sgian dhu*.

'There's nae need to blush on my account.' Sarah emerged from behind an aspen tree. 'And I liked ye far better wi'out that,' she added, as he pulled the sark over his head and hastily tucked the tail between his legs.

'Sarah! I'm nae decent. Ye shouldna go creeping up on a man like that!'

'Ye look decent enough to me. But if it makes ye feel better, I'm more than willing to join ye.' With a slow smile, she began to unfasten the front of her gown.

'Faith, cousin! Whatever are ye thinking on?' Jamie had to squint into the sun to see Sarah clearly, and she seemed like some fey sprite, newly sprung from the trees and peeling away the mantle of her other life. The rattle of her feet on the shingle heralded her even closer approach.

'I imagine I'm thinking much the same as you.' She eyed him with unashamed appreciation. Even without the splendid plaid he was accustomed to wearing and with his hair soaked and dripping down his back, he was still quite magnificent. Only partly clothed, he appeared startlingly vulnerable, and the urge to make him hers was so intense her head swam with it. She stood directly in front of him, looking into his startled eyes, and with a deep breath laid open the front of her gown.

Scandalised, Jamie leapt to his feet and attempted to draw together the pieces of her bodice. 'Have ye taken leave o' yer senses, cousin?' But Sarah merely caught a hold of his hand and pressed it against the thin stuff of her undergarment.

His hand met the swell of her breast for the briefest of seconds before he snatched it away, but Sarah's breath caught in her throat. 'No,' she said with a spreading smile. 'I believe I'm acquainted wi' *all* my senses.'

He gaped at her, but she merely bent and took up the flask of whisky at his feet, took a small sip for courage, and then, her eyes never leaving his face, replaced it by his side. That was it, he suddenly realised.

'You've nae been at yer mother's whisky? Strong liquor takes some lasses like that, but it's nae fer bairns, it –'

'Do I look like a bairn? Do I *feel* like one?'

Looking at her now, full-lipped and seductive and with that translucent skin and ripe body, he could scarcely imagine anyone less child-like. She looked more like some fiendish siren sent to vex him. Yet she could be sixteen at the most; little more than a bairn.

'Ye look as lovely as ever,' he said stiffly. 'But beggin' yer pardon cousin, if ye've had yer prank wi' me, is it nae time ye were minding yer reputation?'

Stung by his words, she realised he still thought her little more than a badly-behaved child. A tease at best. Her cheeks flamed. Did he nae understand how much she needed him to love her?

'D'ye think I care fer childish games?' she countered. 'I'd have thought ye'd be able to see plainly enough that I'm full-grown. Far from the bairn ye seem to imagine me.' She wet her lips. 'Or is it ye believe I've nae been touched afore? That I ken nothing o' the art o' love, is that it?'

She doubted the fumble in Donald Gordon's byre with young Angus would, in all honesty, count here, when he'd lifted her skirts, she'd taken fright and clouted him about the ears, but this was a matter of pride.

A muscle flexed along the sweep of his jaw, and he turned away to belt on his plaid. 'If ye have, then I wish to know the lad's name, and he'll answer to me.'

'How verra gallant o' ye!' She laughed delightedly. 'But there's been many lads wanted me.' The sun caught the glint in her eye. 'Will I tell ye what I've let some do? Or do ye want me to show ye?'

What he wanted was to give her a swift icy dunk in the river, that would cool her down, but with some effort, he mastered his vexation. In a way, he admired her boldness, but without a father the lass clearly lacked instruction in the ways o' the world. 'Twas his duty to guide her, not condemn her.

'I've no wish to know more, I wish only …' Frowning, he picked up his sporran. 'I can see ye've become a beautiful young woman, Sarah. Astonishingly lovely. But I'd not like to think ye'd hold yer reputation in such little regard. Many lads will want ye, I dinna doubt that, only ye should have more self-respect, cousin.'

'And you?' She held her breath. 'Do you want me?'

He hesitated before answering, but took her hand and regarded her as tenderly as his bleak humour would permit. 'I want ye as my kinswoman and my friend, I hope, but I'd not wish ye to dishonour yourself in this way.' In a deliberate gesture, he released her hand and began to retie her bodice. 'If ye wish to ruin yerself, cousin, dinna look to me to help ye with that, for I'll not do it.'

Her eyes stung, her cheeks flamed. She'd thought a display of maturity, of willing womanliness, would be difficult for him to resist. To no other man would she offer herself in this way, yet Sarah was aware that almost without exception every other man in the glen would take her without a moment's hesitation. Jamie, however, had chosen to humiliate her.

He tied the last lace and looked up into her hot face. 'I'd only wish ye to be yer mother's daughter.' He squeezed her shoulder a little apologetically, hoping he'd shown as much compassion as his dark mood would allow.

She recoiled as though he'd slapped her. 'My mother's daughter!

Does she even mind she has one? Does she care? Or is she too busy worrying ower her precious Morven and plotting wi' you?' With a stab of triumph, she saw him rear back in astonishment.

'Aye,' she said viciously. 'I saw ye. I heard it all.' She gestured skyward. 'From the tree. The one wi' all the rags tied to it.'

'What? What did ye hear?'

'Yer wee plan wi' my mother. Verra useful it was too.'

'Useful? What d'ye mean?' Jamie's heart stalled. Did the minx nae realise what was at stake here?

'Useful fer misleading Morven. Ye see, I told her ye'd gone back to Inverness on account of being too feart to stay here in the glen. She didna believe it at first, but I can be persuasive. It didna take much to make her believe ye'd abandoned us all, and she was fair riled at that.'

Jamie exhaled in disbelief. 'Why, Sarah? Fer God's sake, why would ye do such a thing?'

She had his attention now. The dark eyes were stricken, the sensitive mouth drawn in dismay. In her moment of fury, she'd thought only of striking out at him. He didna want her either, he wished her to be more like her mother! But his obvious pain brought Sarah little satisfaction. She faltered.

'Morven didna need ye.'

'Whereas ... you did?'

She nodded, her gaze sliding to her feet.

'And ye heard everything? Everything your mother said about yer da's death?'

'Aye, I heard it.'

'Have ye told anyone about this, Sarah? Spoken of what ye learned to yer mother or ... or, anyone?'

She shook her head, jaws clamped together.

He looked at her in bewilderment. A breath of wind stirred her hair, and it floated momentarily about her, then settled again as fluid and silken as a child's. Even in the face of her spitefulness, he couldn't bring himself to be angry with her, she looked so very young. And to listen to the details of her father's killing like that, with no-one to comfort her. He should've questioned her strange behaviour before, Rowena mentioned it often enough. He should've seen it stemmed from loneliness and confusion, a lass lost wi'out her da.

'Yer mam loves ye,' he said gruffly.

'She prefers Morven – you do too.'

'Ye're wrong.' How to make her see that though? He stared at her for a moment, and she lifted her chin and stubbornly returned the look. 'If only ye knew how hard yer mam works to give ye all yer father did. She's lost wi'out him too. Her only wish is to keep ye safe.'

Sarah's brows puckered. 'She chose Morven over me – she always has.'

'Only to pass on her learning to. Did ye wish to learn the healing properties o' plants, cousin, and to tend the sick?'

She shrugged without enthusiasm.

'I didna think so. But why would ye wish to hurt Morven? Or me?'

Her face was burning again, a curse of her pale skin. She clenched her teeth, willing away the tears of shame she felt gathering.

'I thought … I thought if Morven didna want ye, couldna abide ye, then mebbe … mebbe ye'd come to noticing me.'

She daren't look at him, could scarcely breathe while she waited for his reaction to this. He loved Morven. What would he be thinking now, knowing she'd made Morven despise him? Would he hate her? Rage at her? Never had she been more conscious of another person's silence, never more aware of their assessment of her. Every fibre cried out to him to see past her foolishness and understand, but when he did nothing but stare at her in dismay, Sarah blurted, 'Damn it, I love ye! I wanted to make ye love me back. But ye dinna care fer me at all. 'Tis only *her* ye want!'

He made a bewildered sound as her words struck home, stepping back, his expression stricken. What had he done to make her think that? To believe herself in love wi' him? A child. Or was this part of the bane that followed him? Wi'out meaning to, had he encouraged her to think that way? He didn't know. But if so, it did end here.

'Ye mightna be so keen to love me, cousin, when ye learn I've let ye down. Ye dinna ken yet, but I've failed ye. Failed all o' ye.'

'It doesna matter.'

'Ye dinna understand. I swore to yer mother I'd see yer da's killer hanged. I put my faith in the law, in the justice o' the land. I thought 'twas there to protect us but …' he faltered. 'I was mistaken. He's still free to … to do whatever it is he plans to do. I've done nothing but bring a scourge to all who put their faith in me.'

Sarah blinked at the undertone of desolation in his voice. He was only spouting this haiver about a scourge so it wouldna hurt so much when he told her he didna want her. So, he *did* despise her. Only, why did he look so maimed?

'Are ye not riled at me, then?'

Jamie struggled to regard his cousin dispassionately. Tears filled her eyes, bitter, childish tears he knew she was too proud to let fall and her mouth trembled as she fought to keep herself together. He shook his head.

'I'm only sorry I canna give ye what ye so plainly need, cousin – the love of a father. But I'd have ye know ye're precious to me. You are my blood, my kin, and I'd protect ye wi' my life, dinna doubt it. Only I'll not misuse ye. 'Twould be wrong of me, and I'll not do it, no matter how ye tempt me. Anyhow,' his face darkened, 'ye're better wi'out me. I'd bring ye only misery.'

'I'd take that chance.'

'But I would not. D'ye take me fer a scoundrel, cousin?' He glanced away and slipped his *sgian dhu* into his hose. Frowning, he turned back to her. 'I pray yer pardon if I've been blunt with ye.' He inhaled strongly through his nose. 'But I'm thinking 'twould be better fer you and the folk o' this glen if I took myself someplace else.'

Aghast, she stared at him, but he only bent and brushed his lips respectfully against her brow, then, with a tiny bow to her, hoist the loose end of his plaid up over his shoulder and turned away to cross the shingle.

'Only I'll see justice done first.'

***

It was peaceful and quiet in Strathavon chapelyard. The grass was knee-high and lush, sheltered from cruel north winds by a circle of dark and stately pines and the shoulder of *An Sgòran*, into which the oldest grave tablets were set. The gravestones rose silent and weathered from this swaddling, and Morven's footfalls were absorbed by the lushness in the same way she imagined the little soul they'd laid here only four days ago would be.

She found her father easily enough; he was where she'd hoped he'd be, standing before the small mound of newly turned earth. But it was what he held in his hand that surprised her. She'd never seen him gather wild flowers, but it was a crude posy of daisies and willow-herb he clutched in his hand, and when he turned to look at her, she saw that his eyes, though dry, were reddened and raw-looking.

He nodded curtly to her and knelt to place his posy by the simple wooden cross.

'I'll hew her a right gravestone,' he said gruffly. 'Wi' her name on, have it set here. And fer the others too.' He nodded toward the twin little crosses nearby.

'Aye, Mam would like that.'

He squinted up at her, and she reflected that even in grief, her father's face seemed unable to soften in any way and he looked every bit the stern stranger he'd become to her.

'The lads said ye called her Faith.' He turned a little toward her. 'A fitting-enough name, I would say.'

She said nothing but offered her hand, and he rose, grunting, to his feet. Shoulder to shoulder they stood in the thick grass, gazing upon the letters Rory had painstakingly cut into the wooden cross. Under the keen eye of Father Ranald, Rory had faithfully copied the marks the old priest had written out for him in the dust of Delnabreck's yard. Knowing her father could no more read than she could, Morven recited the words to him from memory.

> *'Faith MacRae. Born 29ᵗʰ Aug. 1780,*
> *Died also 29ᵗʰ Aug. 1780.*
> *Unto thee, Lord, we entrust her.'*

Malcolm made a choked sound, then cleared his throat and turned to look at her.

'Ye blame me fer this, don't ye?'

'Does it matter now?'

'To me it does.'

'Then aye, if ye must know, aye, I do.'

Nodding, he exhaled fiercely. 'You and me both.'

She looked quizzically at him, but beneath the mask of weather-toughened skin, his face was as unfathomable as ever. If he was looking for pity, he'd get none from her. It seemed her mother would live, but 'twas little thanks to him. He couldn't even have spent much time with Grace, for on her return from the shieling, Morven had found Rory and Donald unloading the trail of ponies, but only Alec wept at her mother's bedside. Her father, she supposed, no sooner returned had felt his customary need to get away. With an effort, she suppressed her resentment; she'd still to do what she'd come here for, and her stomach churned at the thought.

'There's something I must tell ye,' she said.

'And what's that?'

'I must tell ye what happened whilst ye were away.'

She'd carefully planned what she would say, had rehearsed over and over how she'd tell him of the bothy's discovery and McBeath's attack, but when the moment came, she found herself struggling to find the right words. A habitual desire to keep from him anything of an intensely private nature saw her searching for ways to somehow lessen the horror, found her using less explicit words regarding McBeath's intentions. At the core of it, was the insinuating belief she was to blame, a deep discomfort that it was her own misguided trust in Jamie that led to the raid in the first place.

She struggled through her account, her face flaming, then ended abruptly and cast around for something to sit down on before her trembling legs gave way. Her father stared hard at her, his breath whistling fiercely through his nose. The colour drained from his face, and his jaw hardened, seemed set in stone, the sinews standing like cords upon his neck.

'Are ye violated?' His voice shook with fury. 'By God, I'll kill the bastard!'

'No.' She swallowed. 'He was stopped before he could …'

He breathed in again and blinked as though only now seeing his daughter's distress. 'Here,' he took her by the elbow and steered her toward a raised tombstone. 'Sit yerself down here.'

She sat on the cold stone and, to escape the look on her father's face, hid her own in her hands.

'There now, dinna weep.'

To her amazement, he put his arms around her and held her against his bulk with an awkward tenderness. 'Were ye harmed? I mean … beaten badly?'

'Nothing that hasna healed. The bothy though … we'll never be able to use it again.'

'Dinna fash yerself ower that. We'll find another place fer that.'

'I have this though.' Without looking up, she fumbled in her arisaid revealing a strange shape knotted in its depths. She unwrapped the copper cooling worm and offered it to him. 'And I have the malt. After they fled, I managed to take away all six sacks and I hid them under a rock at the foot o' the falls.'

'Ye did well.' There was a note of what sounded like respect in his voice. He took the copper coil almost reverently from her. 'We'll get back the malt, dinna worry yerself ower that.'

Incredibly, he seemed not to care about the bothy. She lifted her head a fraction and found the courage to look him in the eye. His colour had returned, deepened if anything to a mottled purple, and his features seemed stiff and unnatural.

'Ye're nae angry, then?'

'Angry?' He looked a mite incredulously at her, then drew her head in toward him again. 'Child, I'm most mightily riled.' He lifted a hand to smooth down her hair, and she saw that it shook. 'But nae at you Morven, never at you.' His grip on her tightened, and he drew a shuddering breath. 'Only at that scum!'

'But I thought … what I mean is … had I nae taken Jamie to the bothy, shown him what we do there, none of this would've happened.'

'If I mind it right, 'twas Rowena asked ye to show the Innes lad the whisky-making.'

'Well, aye, but Rowena wasna to know he'd –'

'I ken that, but you werena to know it either.' He shifted position, easing her away from his chest where his heart had thumped loud in her ears and looked her squarely in the eyes. 'I'm nae concerned ower who's to blame, I ken well who that is. I'm only concerned that ye're safe.' He blinked and cleared his throat. 'All I've ever wanted is to keep ye safe – only ye've aye fought me.'

She gaped at him. Fought him? He'd aye thwarted her!

'I'd have liked it well had ye chosen to stay home more wi' yer mother. Ye're nae made that way though, I know, ye've told me often enough. And I ken ye think me unjust to treat ye so different than Alec.' He frowned, and his expression hardened again. 'But ye see, I know what's in men's hearts, Morven. What it is that drives them – the needs, the urges. I ken it all too well, fer I'm driven by them too. And kenning that, I've aye wished to keep ye away from such harm.' He glanced away as though the feel of her gaze upon him pained him and followed the line of *An Sgòran*. ''Tis all I've ever wanted, though I ken I've been a fool.'

She let her breath out with a little hiccupping sound. 'What are ye saying, Da? That ye're no better than McBeath?'

'Little better, no.'

'So ye're saying yer resistance to me learning the whisky-making. And the healing, anything I've ever wanted to do has been ower yer knowledge o' what's in men's hearts?' She drew back a little, the better to assess the candour of his words. 'Yer anger at Rowena fer sharing her skills with me, all that bad feeling, has been about keeping me from harm?'

He squeezed his eyes shut, and a muscle twitched at his jaw. 'Partly, aye.'

'And the other part?'

'Guilt! Guilt ower what I've caused!'

'But, what've ye caused?' She slipped down from the tombstone, and when he turned away, she followed him, peering up at his louring face. 'What've ye caused, Da? I dinna understand.'

'Duncan's death!' he said savagely. 'Duncan's death, that's what! Ye see, yer guilt ower the gauger finding our bothy is as naught when compared wi' my guilt.' He gave a choked little laugh. 'Mine is more damning, I think!'

She stared at him, a cold shadow crossing her soul. What had Jamie said? That Rowena believed her da was in league wi' McBeath, party to Duncan's death. But she couldna believe that. 'What d'ye mean?' she whispered.

'I couldna bear to see ye learning from Rowena. Couldna abide having to see the woman, or speak wi' her or be anywhere near her – nae when I kent I'd played a part in making her a widow!' He brought a fist crashing down on the tombstone. 'And was too guilt-ridden to even tell her.'

The cold settled in Morven's heart. 'Tell me then,' she said in a voice she barely recognised. 'Tell me how ye made her a widow.'

He nodded, his face so rigid with loathing he'd to force his words through stiffened lips. 'I was the worse for drink. Blind stinking fou, my mind fuddled wi' it. We were sat by the fire at the Craggan Inn, Duncan and me, but I left him to go gab to Craigduthel, the McHardys, anyone that would gie me the time o' day. I was loud-spoken and coarse, swollen with myself. I didna see Ghillie sat in the shadows watching wi' that weaselly way he has, and I ken now Duncan didna see him either.'

He swallowed. 'When I saw Duncan rise to go I was peeved at him, I thought him tired of waiting fer me to come sit wi' him again, and my blood flared up. He could be hard going at times, Duncan, he was that quiet. No muckle use to me when I wanted to drouth the night away, he was never one fer that.' His eyes flicked briefly to her face, his throat convulsing.

'So, I shouted out to him: "That you awa' already is it, Tomachcraggen? Ye'll be needing yer rest, right enough, afore the morn's work." He gave me a look, I mind, a quick feart look but I just laughed. "Ye'll be leaving Inverlochy at dawn, then? Wi' yer load." Fer that's where his bothy was hid. And he gave me a wee nod and was gone.' He clutched his head in his hands, and his shoulders shook violently. Morven gave him a moment before saying,

'And then what?'

''Twas the last time I did see him alive. The next night we all heard he'd been killed – caught and killed trying to save his whisky. But I could see in my mind, Christ, I see it yet, thon weasel Ghillie – Charles Stuart o' Wester Lynatoul, that's his right name – I see him rising from that dark corner and creeping away, a right pleased look on his face, and I kent he was away to tell his master.'

'Did ye not go after Duncan and warn him?'

He looked up at her, and she saw his eyes were bitter and haunted, his harsh look gone and his face all atremble.

'I meant to. In my mind, I do yet sometimes see myself doing it, I do dream 'tis what I did. But that's wishful thinking, fer there was ower-much ale and whisky in me fer that. Fer such quick-thinking, fer any measure o' judgment.' His face twisted. 'There's nae a day goes by I dinna curse myself, but I was well fou and gave little thought to Duncan. I think I supposed he'd seen Ghillie, Duncan hadna supped the ale and whisky I had after all, and what thought I had, if I had any, was that he'd take more care now and change his plans.'

Morven let her breath out with a sob. She'd been holding her breath, holding it so long she felt giddy and sick. She scarce knew what to make of her father, never mind what to say to him, but when she looked on his bowed head, grizzled and wretched, and the silence stretched grimly between them, she felt an overwhelming urge to reach out to him.

He spoke up again. 'But he never did change his plans. Likely he kent nothing o' what awaited him, poor bugger, and what happened next morning only the Black Gauger and his hirelings ken about, only 'tis nae what they said at the hearing, that much I'm sure o'.'

She looked down at her father's hands. They were calloused and scarred, clasped together as if in prayer and she felt her heart fill for him. He should've told Rowena this, but she could understand why he hadn't. His churlishness toward Rowena had mystified her, even shamed her, but now she saw it was hatred that begat it. A burning hatred, but nae fer Rowena, no, rather fer himself. She'd felt little for her da this last year, nothing above the respect she considered him due as her sire. Now she wished him to hold her again as he'd done a moment ago, hoped he might gain from her the comfort she'd drawn from him. But he was too remote from her now for that.

She touched him gingerly on the shoulder, and he flinched. 'Come hame with me, Da. Mam'll be needing ye.'

'And tell her?'

'That's fer you to decide. But ye didna cause Duncan's death. 'Twas others did that. Ye spoke foolishly – ye did make a mistake – but there were others there that night as well as you, others that might've warned Duncan and chose nae to. Dinna punish yerself ower it; it pains me to see it.'

He looked strangely at her, his grey eyes wide now and

incredulous, and she gave him a little nod and reached out her hand. After a moment, he took her hand and gripped it fiercely.

'Bless ye.' He pressed her cold fingers to his lips.

There was no edge of bitterness to his voice now. She slipped her hand under his arm and led him, stumbling, through the damp grass and away from the stillness of the chapelyard.

CHAPTER SEVENTEEN

AS THEY EMERGED FROM the thicket of alder and gean that screened Delnabreck from the south, the crofthouse came in sight, and her father nudged her. Following his gaze, Morven could see Alec sat on the doorstep, hunched almost, his back turned to them. The sight was a sad one, stirring her heart. He'd not expected to find his mother so weak, so silent and crushed in spirit, nor the wee soul dead and lain to rest already and him nae even there to lessen the pain of it. She could well imagine the look on his face and was glad she wasn't witness to it.

But when he turned toward them, she saw that Sarah was sat beside him, her face stark and pale. The girl made an agitated movement with her hand, and Morven's pity turned to irritation. From Alec's strained expression it was clear Sarah hadn't come to console him in any way but had rather brought him fresh anguish. Could she nae give him time to learn of the dead infant? Time wi' his mother afore laying her own troubles at his feet? And anyway, what right had Sarah to seek flattery from a lad she kept so carefully at arm's length? But it wasn't her concern, and with a twinge of guilt, Morven set her irritation aside.

Malcolm grunted to his son, then stopped to rummage among the packs and belongings the boys had piled by the cot-house door. From one of the bags, he withdrew a thick bundle wrapped in sacking, and Morven was curious to see him finger it a little self-consciously. With the package clutched in his hand, and showing more than a little reluctance, he went in to his wife.

She couldn't be sure whether he'd find the courage to tell Grace what had lain festering in his heart all this time, but Morven hoped her da had gained at least some measure of release. A lessening of the pressure he'd kept himself under might even allow him to reach out to Grace and draw her back to them. When he'd gone inside, she turned to her brother and their visitor.

Sarah was staring a mite fearfully at her, then flicked her gaze to

Alec, who rose to his feet. 'Sarah has something she would tell ye.'

'Aye?'

'Nae here.' Sarah darted another glance at Alec. 'Is there somewhere we could go? Somewhere more … private?'

Morven nodded, indicating Sarah should follow her; perhaps she'd misjudged the girl, something plainly troubled her.

Alec stepped aside to let them pass and looked on after them a little wistfully. 'I'll be here if ye need me,' he said, but which of them he meant, she couldn't tell.

Sarah followed her through the tussock grass of Delnabreck's pastures, past the ponies that paid them no heed and up a wooded slope behind the crofthouse. Rarely did anyone climb Seely's Hillock, it was said to be a faery *sithean*, a place spoken of in hushed tones – a place unbaptised babes were rumoured to be buried. The ancient stones rooted in its summit were whispered to hold dark secrets from the past. Morven liked to sit among the stones and sensed nothing forbidding there. She thought Sarah might speak more freely in such a place, a place she knew others preferred to shun.

Sarah made no sound during their climb. Her movements were dogged, almost reluctant, and her breathing seemed fitful, as though she stifled it to keep so quiet. Morven glanced sidelong at her several times, but the girl refused to meet her gaze. When the ground levelled at last to a flat stretch of heath near the ruined watchtower, Morven led her to the ring of upright stones, de'il stanes folk called them, where she knew they'd not be disturbed.

'Is this private enough?'

'Aye. Thank ye.' Sarah sat down in the heath and plucked a stalk of moor-grass. She frowned at the rough spike and ran her thumbnail up its edge. A scatter of tiny seeds danced into her lap. Evidently, despite her ashen appearance and marked agitation, whatever it was she wished to say required a deal of forethought, maybe even courage.

'What was it ye wanted to tell me?'

The girl glanced up, then flicked her gaze away, yet that brief exchange revealed how enlarged her pupils were, how dark, and that she seemed on edge, almost to the point of desperation.

'Yer mam's a'right, Sarah?'

'She's well, aye. 'Tis Jamie, though. He means to leave the glen, and 'tis only you can stop him.'

Morven blinked. 'Leave? But he left ye all weeks ago.'

Sarah scowled furiously into her lap. 'I lied … that is … they lied. There's none o' us told ye the truth, Morven, but I lied more than any.'

Morven leant back against a stone. There was a breeze blowing on the hillock, a rawness to the air there'd not been in the glen, and she shivered, watching the moor-grass flurry in the breeze.

'If ye mean to tell me he only ever went as far as Balintoul,' she said in a voice she struggled to keep steady. 'Then ye can save yerself the bother, fer I ken that already – I've seen him. I ken what he is, there's nae need to be delicate. He's a gauger. And a filthy betraying one at that!'

She'd not meant to be so sharp in her reply, but Sarah's persistent desire to protect her cousin rankled. Had she known what Jamie planned to do? Had she known and lied to defend his honour? She shifted her gaze from the surrounding braes and moorland to contemplate her companion more deeply.

Sarah nodded. She appeared unsurprised at Morven's knowledge of this, only breathing a little harder now.

'He only did that fer the plan. The scheme he hatched wi' Mam. 'Twas the deception he played. It's what I've come to tell ye about, fer I need ye to understand it, understand *him*, so ye can stop him from going.'

Morven blinked. Inside she felt a swirl of emotion, a longing well from within, then ebb away. What plan? What deception had he played? Frowning, she studied Sarah more closely.

The girl had been glaring into her lap all this time, plucking at the nodding heads of grass by her hand. Now, at last, she looked up and met Morven's scrutiny. Her nose was running, and she swiped it along her sleeve. Her bodice had not been laced correctly, and a scrap of pale underlinen was visible through a bulge in her gown. Her expression was a little fearful, her eyes rimmed with red.

'Tell me o' this plan.'

Sarah swallowed. 'I think 'twas the day the gauger's wife died it began. The exciseman was maddened and believed Mam used witchery to bring about her death. You'll mind it, I think?'

Morven nodded. That day was forever etched in her memory.

'He said something terrible to her, to Mam, he told her he did kill my da.' Sarah's expression hardened, and she began to tremble, an emotion Morven recognised as hatred rippling through her. 'He told her how 'twas done … the … the killing. Said they took turns to beat him, and the Black Gauger did shoot him through the chest. They stayed to watch … to taunt, till he died. 'Twas rare entertainment he said, to do something that deliberate.' She sniffed savagely and swiped her nose along her sleeve. 'I think he said this when ye werena there, Morven, when 'twas just the two o' them.'

Morven groped for the solid touch of stone beneath her fingers. The blood had fled her face, and a coldness stole over her. She'd always known something took place in that room. She'd sensed it in Rowena's strange behaviour, though her friend had tried to hide it. And she knew whatever happened had left Rowena shaken and physically sick. Yet this, this had never entered her head. Why would it? Rowena had said nothing.

Sarah went on. 'He threatened to have her arrested fer murdering his wife and bairn, fer using witchery to bring their end. He told her she must wed him else he'd have her examined, likely by the witch-prickers, and the scandal o' that …' She stopped to catch a hiccupping breath. She was breathing hard now, forcing her words out as though they might scorch her tongue should she let them linger. 'Folk have whispered against Mam afore, ye'll ken that, but a scandal like this would be enough to see us evicted. Ye see that, aye? Whether he managed to get her sentenced as a murderess or not.'

Morven was too shocked to even nod, but aye, she could see that. This was what Rowena had long feared; an accusation of this kind would play right into the factor's hands. She tried to make some sound to communicate her understanding, but none would come. One thought kept expanding in her head. Rowena wed to that brute! Dear God, 'twas unthinkable.

Receiving no outward reaction to this from Morven, Sarah swallowed hard and pressed ahead. 'He gave Mam three months to make her choice, but I'm thinking her time must be near up, and Jamie's plan has come to nothing.'

Morven shook her head. 'But what plan?'

Sarah nodded, her eyes darting from her lap where she fretfully plucked at loose threads in her gown, to Morven's face.

'Jamie swore he'd bring the Black Gauger to justice. Said he'd see the bastard hang, but first he must get close to him, must gain his trust, must uncover evidence to use against the devil. 'Tis why he joined the gaugers. Only no-one was to ken o' their plan – most especially nae you.'

Morven stared at Sarah, her face half-frozen in disbelief. Her mind whirred furiously as she fought to keep up, for none of this could be true. But already that part of her she'd hardened, the part Jamie had once melted and stirred to life, was softening, bursting with the hope *it was true*. Her breath caught in her throat. Only there was still much she didn't understand. Far too much to be grasping at the first sliver of hope offered. She needed time to think, time to decide how to feel. But Sarah was waiting, watching, fidgeting in the grass with an air of quivering impatience, anxious to tell all and there was still much she needed to know.

'Why was I nae to ken o' this plan?' she croaked.

Sarah's mouth twisted, and she bared a tooth. 'Mam was worried fer ye. Ye're precious to her, surely ye ken that? She thought the gauger had ye marked out as a mischief-maker – as her apprentice. She didna wish to put ye in danger, ye being her favourite. But there was another reason too.' Her expression hardened. 'Mam believes there's a traitor in the glen. McBeath knew my da was smuggling his whisky out that day. He kent every detail. Someone had informed him. Mam suspected 'twas yer da, Jamie did too. Only they daren't tell ye fer fear they were mistaken.' She swallowed. 'That would hurt ye. But mostly 'twas because they didna wish to test yer loyalty, fearing 'twould tear ye apart and ye might warn yer da.'

A strangled sound escaped from Morven's lips and she rose to her feet and staggered away, the ring of standing stones tilting dizzily around her. Dear God! But her da wasna a traitor – only a drunken fool.

'Are ye a'right, Morven?' Sarah was on her feet now too, peering uncertainly at her.

In an instant, Morven whirled back to the girl and gripped her by the wrists. 'They told *you* though.' Her voice was sharp with suspicion. 'Why would they do that? And how do I ken ye're telling me the truth? Ye've lied to me afore – ye've just said as much.'

'They didna tell me anything!' Sarah twisted to free her wrists. 'They never do. I was listening, spying on them. 'Tis ... 'tis what I like to do.'

Morven released the girl, and Sarah stood tensed and gripped before her, breathing hard and rubbing at her wrists. Her face was flushed, and her eyes burned with something earnest at their core. She wasn't lying, that much was plain. Sarah had held her father above all others. The bond between them was one she'd never make a lie of, Morven was confident of at least that much.

'Forgive me.' She stepped back from Sarah as though the girl might ignite if touched again. 'I should be thanking ye fer telling me all this, 'tis just ...' She swallowed. 'So hard to believe. I thought Jamie a turncoat when all along –'

'He was trying to save us. To see justice done. But there's no time to go ower all that now. He means to leave this time, he's likely doing it as we speak and we're still standing here wasting time!'

'But ...' Morven could feel Sarah's anxiety rising around her, infecting her. Her stomach began to churn, her limbs to quiver. 'How can *I* stop him? I mean, I didna even believe him when he ...' She choked back a sob as she remembered what he'd said in the bothy after McBeath's attack. *Things are nae as they appear.* And weeks before, he'd asked her to trust him, to have faith, but she'd only branded him spineless and accused him of betraying her.

'He'll nae want to see me now,' she said in a tight voice.

'He will. He'll want to see ye, ye can depend on it.'

The girl's tone held some meaning; Morven shot her a look.

Sarah curled her lip, a spark of anger lighting her eyes. 'Surely ye ken? Surely ye're nae going to make me ...? Christ!' She spun furiously around, cracking her knuckles and wringing her hands. Almost as abruptly, she whirled back again, her eyes flashing. 'He loves ye, damn it! Are ye so blind? He'll stay if ye ask him. Jesus God, I believe he'd do *anything* if you asked him!'

'What?' Morven's knees gave way, and she sank down among the moor-grass. 'But how do ye ...?'

'Holy God! I've heard him say so! I heard him tell my mam. Damn it all, do I have to hand him to ye on a platter?'

'No ... that is ... I dinna ken what ye mean.' Sarah's anger was bewildering, the energy of it crackled the air between them. Morven fought the joy now coursing through her heart and limbs, not knowing if she should believe it.

'Ye've lied to me afore, Sarah. What was it ye said? *You'd* lied more than any. How do I ken ye're nae lying now? How do I ...?' She shook her head. 'I dinna ken what to think.'

Sarah's face twitched and worked. 'Aye,' she hissed, 'I've lied.' Only, must she explain herself to Morven like some badly-behaved bairn up before the dominie? She squeezed her eyes shut and breathed out wearily. Aye, she must. Frowning, she pressed her quivering fingers against her eyelids.

'If ye mind it, Morven, 'twas me made ye think Jamie had abandoned us all at Tomachcraggen. Me made ye distrust him so.' She gave a snorting laugh. 'And I had ye fair riled at him too. Had ye believing all sorts of him.'

Morven blinked as she remembered that dreadful day. It had been a day of rain, a gentle smurr that turned to an icy downpour by the time she left Tomachcraggen, the mounting wind whipping the rain away only to bring it blattering back against her. But on that day, it was more than her body took a pelting, for her faith in Jamie had been dashed to pieces and she'd believed he'd left his kin without a word. Her eyes moved slowly to Sarah's face. Sarah had known he'd

It was almost dark by the time Jamie reached Balintoul. Ten minutes of shouting and hammering on the heavy oak of McBeath's front door eventually flushed the same frightened maid he'd seen on his last visit to the house. In some agitation and clearly afraid to open the door to the bellowing demon she saw below, the girl leant from an upstairs window, a hand clutched to her chest, and in a quavering voice asked Jamie his business.

'MCBEATH!' he shouted. 'WHERE IS HE?'

She shook her head. 'Nae at hame, sir. Doon at the inn most like, the Balintoul.'

Jamie twitched his plaid respectfully to her, turned on his heel and stalked down the earthen road, a grim figure in the gloaming, his dark mood blackening by the moment. By the time he came to stand outside the grubby little inn, the night had gathered around him, and he was breathing hard, his mood almost as black as the night. The sour reek of tobacco mingled with pot-ale and raw whisky wafted out to him on the road, he could taste it upon his tongue, as bitter as his soul.

A bloodlust was upon him. He could feel the heat and itch of it in his heart and lungs and fought to master his breathing. It had come upon him as he left his young cousin, pale and fatherless by the banks of the Avon. It had mounted further with each mile he'd covered since, his mind returning again and again to the memory of Morven's bruised and bleeding face. Recoiling from that image and unable to control his fury at it, he'd thought instead of his own parents and their enforced exile, of Duncan's savage death, of the plight of his aunt, and then, with more deadly focus, on the man responsible for it all and a pulse had begun to pound in his head.

He touched his fingers to the hilt of his dirk and felt the reassuring coolness of the blade. Another smaller blade, his *sgian dhu*, was tucked into his hose. He clenched and unclenched his fists, forcing his muscles to loosen, his mind to clear, and the blood to cease its infernal thrumming in his ears. He'd no wish to kill the man after all … nae yet at least, nae in front o' so many witnesses.

He caught a fold of his plaid and pulled it forward to cover the dirk, to prevent his hand reaching it too easily, and pushed the door open. It was stifling inside the inn. A fire roared in one corner despite the lingering warmth of the day, and the air was thick with peat-smoke and tobacco, foul with the rank odour of many drunken males herded together. After the silence of the last few hours when he'd had little more than the sound of his angry blood for company, the noise seemed unbearable and he felt prickles of sweat break out on his body.

He pushed his way further into the room. Many of the faces around him he recognised – cattle drovers and cottars mainly, men he remembered from visits they'd made to McBeath's home, occasions when he'd been obliged, as McBeath's assistant, to look on as these poor folk paid McBeath their passage. Many now eyed him warily from behind raised flagons and quaichs.

McBeath was sat at his customary table, Dougal Riach one of his hirelings sat at his side. Jamie raised his hand and steadied himself on a dusty crossbeam, then made his way over. He felt single-minded and centred now, his heart beating slower, his breathing under more rigid control.

McBeath looked up and gave a little start, then scowled sourly.

'Well, well, Lang! Ye're back with yer tail between yer legs, are ye?' He turned to Dougal and favoured him with a knowing wink. 'I told ye, did I no? Did I no say he'd be back, once he got over his *delicate* sensitivities?' He stressed the word with a scornful sneer and reached for his whisky.

'And you're quite yerself again too, I can see, after yer own wee turn.'

The unhealthy sheen to McBeath's face and his slightly exaggerated movements betrayed the extent of his drunkenness, although whether it was accumulative, or the result of this one session Jamie couldn't judge. He wondered if the gauger thought himself safer now, now that the summoning Morven had threatened him with had failed to materialise, or if the man's sins still tormented him. He shifted his gaze to Dougal.

'Find yerself somewhere else to sit.'

Dougal's grin faded, and he glanced questioningly at his master.

'Aye,' McBeath grunted. 'Young Lang here has some explaining to do.' He snorted. 'I for one just cannae wait to hear it.' He dismissed Dougal with a twitch of his head.

Dougal rose, grumbling, to his feet and with a sharp glance at his employer, lifted his whisky and left McBeath to Jamie. As Jamie took Dougal's place beside the focus of his hatred, his hand strayed unconsciously to the *sgian dhu* tucked inside his hose.

'Well?' McBeath lifted his drink. 'What've ye to say for yourself?'

'A fair bit, none o' which ye're going to like, but it'll make me feel a damn sight better – though nae as good as sending ye to hell.'

The gauger choked on his whisky, sputtering and wheezing, and stared at Jamie out of watering eyes. 'Ye insolent whelp!' He groped for his pistol, but Jamie was quicker. One swift movement saw him bring his *sgian dhu* up to McBeath's groin and press the blade against the bulge in his breeches.

'I dinna think so. Move again and I'll mak' ye a eunuch.' He leaned back in his seat and patted McBeath affably on the thigh. Hidden by the table, his other hand pressed a little harder. 'Now sit bonny and drink yer whisky and I'll try nae to let my hand slip. I've something to say – sit back and listen.'

The gauger's face was flushed purple, he looked fair fit to burst. He lifted his drink and gulped wildly, slopping whisky into his lap and wetting Jamie's hand.

'You've lost your wits, Lang.'

'It's nae Lang. My right name's James Innes. Ye'll ken the name, I think? I've the same name my father had, the man ye had put out o' Druimbeag. And of course, ye know my aunt as well. She used to be an Innes too, afore she wed and became a Forbes. But then, ye'll ken all that. Ye're well acquainted wi' my aunt I believe, since 'twas you made her a widow.'

There was a rasping sound as the exciseman's breath caught in his throat and he made a desperate attempt to shrink back, his eyes bulging.

'Be still!' Jamie gave him a sharp prod with the blade. 'If ye value yer manhood, ye'll be still, I'm nae finished with ye yet.'

McBeath's countenance had paled, now a pasty grey, and it was a moment before he was able to suck in enough breath to croak, 'What is it ye want?'

'Satisfaction.'

'What kind o' satisfaction?'

'The usual kind.'

Jamie saw the penny drop, and McBeath blinked, his whiskered jaw relaxing a fraction.

'You? Ye werenae much of a gauger, no stomach for the work. I doubt ye'll make much of an adversary, no to me.' The gauger shook his head, feeling suddenly giddy with the realisation the fiend beside him didn't plan to slit his belly there and then, he intended to settle things the honourable way. He almost laughed.

'Ye're naught but a clerk! A soft scribbler wi' pens.' Or was he? He wet his lips with a quick flick of tongue. The witch's nephew, by God. The same fine dark features, the same poise, he should've seen it before, but on a man, the features appeared more … more commonplace somehow. He swallowed, realising he'd no idea what the cold-blooded fiend beside him was, and for the first time felt the stirrings of a nameless rage. A rage at the way he'd been so thoroughly duped.

'One week,' Jamie hissed. 'Dawn seven days from now in the clearing in Mèilich Wood behind Tomachcraggen crofthouse. I'll be waiting.'

'Oh, I'll be there. Depend on it.' McBeath's lips quirked in a mocking grin. 'But lad, remember this: I was born with a sword in my hand, a pistol at my girdle. What chance dae ye think ye'll have against the likes o' me?'

'Chance enough wi' justice and the Lord on my side.'

'The Lord?' McBeath snorted, shifting back in his seat, the better to ease the pressure on his tender loins. 'With a witch in the family? I doubt ye can expect much help from that direction.'

'A sight more than you, I think.' Jamie's blood was rising again, it pounded in his head, clouding his judgment, and the urge to finish it now came powerfully upon him. He swallowed and took a deeper breath. 'What weapon do you choose?'

McBeath eyed him for a moment. 'Swords,' he said with a spreading smile. 'Swords, I think, will suit me fine. And come to that, the day will suit me even better, for I was planning a wee visit to Tomachcraggen anyhow. Ye see, that'll be three months been and gone, and I've dealings with your aunt.' He gave Jamie a pitying look. 'Shame ye'll no be there to see us wed.'

Jamie's face paled, and he stood abruptly, knocking his chair over with a clatter and quivering with rage.

'I'll see ye in hell first!'

He turned on his heel, then as suddenly whirled back and struck at the exciseman with the blade. He caught him across the cheek, a mere nick, but a gasp went up from the neighbouring table, every head now turned in their direction.

McBeath hissed, his hand flying to his face as dark blood welled from the gash beneath his fingers. 'You're a dead man, Lang.'

'Nae Lang. Know it ye all.' Jamie's voice rose, and he turned to glare about him. 'My real name's Jamie Innes – Innes of Druimbeag. Aye,' he said, seeing the widening of eyes. 'Son of the man put out of Druimbeag on account o' this maggot, this … this murdering scum. The gauger I've duped all this time. The devil 'twill be my pleasure to send on his way – straight to hell!'

There was not a sound in the inn now, save for the crackle of the fire burning in the far corner. A muscle flexed along Jamie's jawline, and he slid the blade back into its place.

'Seven days,' he hissed, then ruthlessly shoved his way out of the inn.

CHAPTER EIGHTEEN

ROWENA SAT ON BY the fire long after she would typically have gone to bed. The fire was in full blaze, and combined with the lingering warmth of the day should have kept her more than comfortable, yet still she shivered. The chill was not in her bones or flesh but in her very soul. She closed her eyes and tried to quiet her mind, tried to send her consciousness out from the calm place within her, out of worldly perception into other realms searching for answers and guidance.

Every day since that dreadful one in Balintoul, she'd made this journey. She'd quietened her mind to a deep state, then in her mind's eye had drawn a healing white light around herself. Cocooned in this way, she'd made her inner journeys, searching always for wisdom, for some connection with the Creator, for council from Him or from the guidfolk o' the *sìtheans*, the faeryfolk, for were they nae His children too?

Her route led her through a mountain pass and dense woods, past waterfalls, but always ended at a faery knoll. There she would see herself standing before a dark pool and would cast her troubles into the water, watching the ripples close over Hugh McBeath's head as he sank from sight with a resounding splash.

Now, following Jamie's revelation that the man was beyond the reach of the law, she knew in her heart deeper magic was demanded, and the knowledge made her tremble. There was only one course left to her, and thus far she'd shied away from it, so fearful was it to think on. She rose and paced the room, then took her cairngorm from its box and rubbed the gemstone between her palms. It must be done though, and inside she agonised. 'Twas a terrible thing ... aye, even fer him, and so she tormented herself.

Sitting down again, she tried to chase all hatred from her heart. No hatred must she harbour, no bitterness allow, for only humility and absolute faith would render her pure enough. Else what she evoked would be visited back upon her a hundred times over.

A draught scattered the flames in the grate, and she looked up to find her nephew standing in the doorway.

'Jamie!' She started guiltily. 'I've been worried about ye.' She looked at him again, seeing a strange light in his eyes, a grim look of melancholy and despair, and a rush of tenderness flooded her heart. 'Will ye join me?'

He nodded to her, his dark mood reflected in his eyes, and sat down by her side. 'Forgive me. It wasna my intention to stay away so long, but there was … was something I needed to do.' He turned toward her with a grave expression, and she saw the strain etched in his face and sensed he was keeping something from her. Frowning, he turned back to the fire.

'There's nothing to forgive. I might've given ye a home these last months Jamie, but you've given me far more. I've no wish to be yer keeper.'

Watching the firelight play upon her nephew's face, Rowena sensed the anger that still smouldered in him. Many hours had passed since he returned from Elgin with the news of his failure, yet where had he been? It wasna like him to linger in the Craggan Inn, yet she caught the whiff of pot-ale and tobacco on him. She shifted her gaze from his face, a little shamed at her prying. On this one night with his failure heavy upon him, she could hardly grudge him that. And if he'd no wish to speak of it, then she could understand that too, for neither one of them had need of words, the comfort was in each other's presence.

Jamie was glad of his aunt's lack of questions. The long walk back from Balintoul had done nothing to cool his hot blood, and the heat trapped within the cottage made his head swim. He'd need to tell her what he'd done, but not yet. Not while his hands still itched to choke the life from the devil-gauger and the man's mocking face still danced before his eyes. The morn would be time enough fer that, and by then he'd have found the right words.

'Will I smoor the fire, aunt?'

'Aye, thank ye.' She slipped the cairngorm into a fold of her plaid. 'I'll lie down in a moment. And dinna worry yerself, Jamie, if I'm nae here when ye awaken, fer I've a notion I'll be called away.' A ghost of a smile touched her lips. 'Something's amiss the night, I can feel it. Nothing unchancy, mind.' She kept her gaze on the flames. 'Just, ofttimes I ken when I'll be needed.'

If Jamie sensed anything was afoot, he gave no indication of it. He rose and smothered the fire, then murmured, 'Guid night to ye, then.' And feeling the press of his hand on her shoulder, she nodded up at him.

In the darkness, she sat on alone and listened to the sounds of his restlessness. Time seemed to creep by on leaden feet, but at length, all went still, and she could hear nothing above the crumble of peat in the grate and the soft scurry of mice among the thatch, and she knew that he slept.

Rising, she stirred life back into the fire and put fresh water on to warm. In the dimness, she undressed and bathed, then put on a clean white shift. Her movements were quick and sure now. She poured juniper oil into a small bowl and heated it until it gave off a smoky vapour and a sharp, clean scent. Using a dove's feather, she fanned the smoke all around herself, including the souls of her feet, until she was satisfied she'd cleansed herself of all possible taints. Only then did she push aside the loose stone in the cot-house wall and draw out the bundle she kept hidden there.

Here she kept the objects she'd been given as a child, the talismans she planned in the fullness of time to pass on to Morven. Her hands were steady now. She shook off the layer of dust the years had gathered and laid out the objects upon the firestone. Before her lay a curious collection: a sizeable ochre-streaked stone marked with many coiled grooves that she knew was called a fossil, a clutch of *glaine nathrach*, serpent stones; these she fancied to be ancient stone spindle whorls from a distant time when the making of iron had still been a mystery. And there were three small faery-bolts. She turned the flint arrowheads in her hand, marvelling at their finely-honed edges and at the faery magic that had made them so. But the last item she left wrapped in its cloth.

She could feel its malevolence reaching out to her, could taste it on her tongue, and knew she must wait until the last possible moment before uncovering it, lest its unwholesomeness infect her. Quickly she peeled three onions and placed one each upon the firestone, the windowsill, and upon the flagstone at the door along with a sprig of rowan. 'To draw away evil,' she murmured. That done, she placed her talismans in a heather creel along with a pot of salt, an iron trowel, and her cairngorm stone and covered them with a blanket. She took a last quick look around the room, then slipped out into the night.

The darkness was dense and heavy, and her heart seemed to bound in her chest, struggling against her purpose, while her breath clotted thickly in her throat. She ought to feel chilled in her thin shift, but rather a swarm of hot blood surged around her heart, and a sheen of sweat broke out on her skin.

'Nae far now,' she gasped as branch and briar clawed at her. The call of Dun Sithean was strong upon her, and she knew she'd reach the faery glade that night supposing she were bound and blindfolded. But at length her way became easier, lit by the gleam of moonlight streaming through chinks in the thinning cloud, and the tangle of Sithean Wood gave way to the glade she'd brought Jamie to almost three months before. A desperate sob broke from her lips, and she sank to her knees in the wet moss.

But there was scarce time to catch her breath, for dawn was drawing close, and in the grainy light, she could see the outline of the old oak tree hung with its burden of cloots. She worked swiftly, knowing dawn was near upon her and the magic of the rite would be at its most potent upon the very moment of dawning.

Facing toward the point in the east from whence the sun would rise, she drew a circle of salt around her on the ground. Inside it, she placed her talismans, then dropped to her knees, the wet moss staining her shift, and pressed her eyes shut. It was more than twenty-five years since she'd committed the words to memory, but they were still there, still as clear to her as they'd been the day she solemnly accepted their charge. Her voice came low and husky, but into the words, she breathed as much of her will as she could summon.

'Glaistig, sluaigh, loireag an gruagach,
duine o' loorach even uaine.
Syne skreich o' bluid quat gien
hallowit an thyne rioghachd
elfin lown an hearken.
Ilka sae lang trobhad te mise.'

The ancient words would invoke the spirits and faeryfolk of the dun, and as she felt the earth begin to tremble beneath her knees, and the sudden rush of air about her head, she repeated them over and over. The charm came sure upon her tongue now, and she heard the deep ripple of water at her feet, and at once a vigour came to her through the earth, a vibrancy to her and a fittingly darker resonance to McBeath, the cursed affliction she wished removed from her life. With the enchantment strong upon her, she dug into the damp earth with her trowel.

Dawn broke with a stain of red-gold streaming up over Dun Sithean, gilding the sacred objects before her. Quickly she withdrew the final object from its wrapping. The gnarled curve of bone gleamed wickedly in her hands, and she dropped it into the hole she'd dug for it. A horned hare's skull, she shuddered at the sight, then quickly flung earth down over it until it was completely covered.

Rowena had no notion how the spirits of the *sìthean* would help her, how she would finally be freed from McBeath's grasp, she knew only the secrets of the rite were the most elemental, the very highest magic open to her, and provided her heart was pure enough, she'd not be forsaken.

'I ask that this ill-will be taken from me, that I and my kin might endure in peace.' She patted the earth down hard on top of the object she'd buried, the symbol of her torment. 'So mote it be.'

What would be the fate of Hugh McBeath should she prevail, she tried not to think on. His soul, she deemed, was already forfeit for what he'd done to Duncan, and so it hardly seemed to matter. She took up her cairngorm and placed it atop the mound of freshly turned earth. A rite of this magnitude required an appropriate gift to be offered, a crystal was best, and she willingly gave up the dark gem. 'To whence it came,' she murmured.

Then she gathered her remaining talismans into the creel, her heart hammering in her throat, and quickly broke the enchanted circle by brushing the salt away widdershins from the west. Rising to her feet, she stumbled away. As she left the glade behind, the boom and pulse of energy left her, and her limbs were struck with a terrible weakness, but she knew better than to look back.

By the time she crawled, scratched and muddied, from Sìthean Wood the vigour had been sapped from her body, and she was giddy and shivering. Rocked by waves of nausea, she lay curled in the bracken for a time until her sickness receded. Then she slept. When she awoke the sun had already climbed high in the sky, and she felt a little restored.

'I'd nae choice,' she whispered to herself, and she knew that had been the truth of it, but there was still something she needed to do.

Half a mile to the south of Dun Sìthean, by a fork in the river, stood the stone that would serve her purpose. Badly weathered and canted at a drunken angle, the symbol stone still carried upon it the marks of an ancient Christian faith. There she would pray for forgiveness. There, among the intricate knotwork and the symbols of boar and eagle was inscribed the cross of Our Lord. There she would make her peace with the Creator, and she hoped He would be able to forgive her.

***

Sarah woke later than her usual hour and lay still, listening, unsure what had woken her. Something felt wrong. From outside came the familiar sounds of forest birds calling, the soft 'hooeet' of warblers above the twitter of siskins and redpolls, sounds that were so much a part of the fabric of her life, she rarely noticed them. But today there was nothing to overlay those sounds, and they seemed overly loud and insistent. She sat up and cocked her head, frowning. She could hear none of the sounds she usually woke to: the scrape of porridge spurtle against heavy pot, the thump of dough, or her mother's familiar tread crossing and re-crossing the hardened floor. And no aroma of fresh bannocks either.

Faintly alarmed and remembering with a tightening in her belly the events of the day before, she struggled out from beneath a pile of blankets. She pushed open the door to the main room of the crofthouse. It was empty. She crossed to the hearth. Nothing bubbled at the crook, nothing hung there at all but a pot of cold water, and the fire was all but out, stale and choked with ashes. She moved quickly to the door and threw it open. An onion sat on the flagstone, peeled and naked as an eyeball, a sprig of rowan placed beside it. Her heart gave a queer lurch, and she turned back to examine the rest of the room. Another onion sat on the firestone and a third squatted upon the window ledge.

She ran out to the yard, the byre, the steadings. Nothing. Her chest felt tight now, and her breath came ragged in her throat as she tried hard to think. What did it mean? And where was her mam? She took a deep breath to concentrate her thoughts. 'Twas only yesterday Jamie told her he did mean to leave Stratha'an, and damned if he didna tell her that after she all but threw herself at him. Offered herself like a common strumpet. A bitter taste came to her mouth. And she'd begged Morven to stop him, had told her everything and then been forced to repeat it all to Alec and his kin.

She shrank into herself now, remembering the horror of that, the burning of her cheeks, the thumping of her heart, and worst of all, the look on Alec's face. Fair broken he'd been, fair crushed wi' disappointment. And Jamie. She leaned heavily against the grained oak door. But she couldn't think on Jamie, not without the shame of her humiliation rising to choke her.

She swallowed and broke into a sweat. Where was her mam? Had she gone to stop Jamie too? Or gone to console Morven, more like? She grimaced. But instinctively she knew her mother wouldn't leave like that, not without a word, not unless she had to. She cracked her knuckles and massaged her brow. Could she be at the shieling then, wi' William? She pulled her gown on over her shift and made off through the tattie dreels barefoot with her hair loose and tousled about her shoulders.

At the shieling, William looked blankly at her, and a trace of alarm flickered in his eyes.

'Och well,' she reassured him. 'She'll be oot at a birthing most like. Or seeing to a bairn wi' the croup, that's all it'll be.' But she wasn't so easily convinced. A queer panic overtook her. The onions and the rowan, that had been her mother's doing, but what did it mean? 'Twas something to do with McBeath she sensed, but what?

It was as she stumbled, half-dazed, back to Tomachcraggen that she came upon her cousin. Recognising the towering figure, she pulled up with a start, her breath catching in her throat. He was swinging a pick with murderous effect on a great outcrop of rock. She ducked back behind a clump of broom. She should speak with him, see if he knew where her mother was. But even as those thoughts were forming, something held her back. Her humiliation was a shameful thing that coiled and gripped in her belly, and as it reaffirmed its hold upon her, she knew she couldn't possibly face him. Nae after the things she'd said to him at the riverside, the feelings she'd admitted to, and especially nae after the way he'd rejected her. She could barely look him in the eye. Yet at least he was still here, still in the glen and showing no signs of leaving, and for that she was thankful. Morven had plainly found him, thank God, and convinced him to stay.

Only … she frowned, if she was to rise from the broom now Jamie would see her, and there'd be awkwardness. Awkwardness for them both. Trapped in the bushes, she plucked at the tiny broom leaves and flicked them to the ground. 'Twas out looking fer her mam she should be, not crouched here like a frighted rabbit. Yet despite herself, her panic slowly abated, and her breathing slowed to a more comfortable rate. Watching him did that to her, though she sensed there was something changed about her cousin, he appeared … incensed almost. Certainly his blood was up, he seemed to be working out his ire upon that great mountain of rock.

'Twas the outcrop her da had long wanted rid of. Wi' that gone, he'd said, they could grow near half as much oats again, though he'd aye said 'twould take canon-fire to shift it. She snorted. Canon-fire! It looked as though Jamie would manage it wi' little more than his own hands.

The sound of his low rhythmic grunts carried clearly to her in her hiding place, and she watched as he tore off his sark and hurled it to the ground. He attacked the rock again, ruthlessly hacking and hewing, tearing boulders out with his bare hands and piling them into colossal cairns. His back was slick with sweat, the muscles at his shoulders glistening, and watching, she could do nothing but stare at him, entranced.

It was an impressive display, a glimpse at the powder-keg Jamie truly was, and, watching him, she recognised it was not so much the edge of danger he possessed that drew her, but more a sense of the deep passion that fired it. She shivered. Damn him fer nae wanting her! Damn him fer being so utterly out o' her reach.

Yet despite the longings that raged in Sarah's heart, and the injured pride that chafed her still further, she found his actions and appearance, uncommonly savage, left her more than a little unnerved. With an angry cry, he hurled the pick into the ground, and she watched him snatch up his sark and then turn toward the clump of broom she was hidden behind. With a muffled gasp, she flattened herself to the ground. His expression was fiercer than she'd expected, and she held her breath as his eyes skimmed over her hiding place. Then he turned, and with long driving strides made toward the river. She sat up and took a grateful gulp of air. Trembling now, she knelt and watched the retreating figure until he was but a dark smudge and her eyes began to water, then she crept away and returned to the crofthouse.

She was cold now, and felt small and lost and very much alone. 'Where are ye, Mam?' she whispered. She picked up the feather and the bowl of oil that lay on the hob and examined them, sniffing at the pungent preparation. It nipped her eyes and stung her nostrils, but it told her nothing. She laid them down again and looked around at the bundles of dried herbs, the powders and potions that cluttered every surface. They'd never interested her; to her they were but a means for her mam to earn wee gifts of hide and cloth, ale and maybe a leg of mutton along wi' a reputation fer dabbling in the black arts. She pulled down a bundle of some herb that hung from a crossbeam. She didna even know what it was, she reflected, never heed what it could do.

But Morven would know, a voice in her head jibed. 'Aye, and mebbe I'd ken myself,' she said aloud, 'if I'd paid more heed.' She sat down and stared at the remains of the fire. If she'd paid more heed, she might know where her mam was. She picked up the poker and stirred the cold ashes. Beneath the smoorach of ash, she found a feeble glow still lived. Leaning forward, she blew upon it, pleased with the little blaze that burst forth. If her mam were here, there'd be a roaring fire in the grate. She cracked her knuckles. 'Twas ill luck to let it go out. She rose and stalked to the window, staring out at the ripe oats and barley, the dreels of tatties, then made a disgusted sound in her throat and turned back to rummage for tinder and kindling.

It took longer than she expected, but with perseverance, she managed to coax a flame from the pile of ashes. Quickly, she slipped a peat beneath the fledgeling flame and sat back, pleased with her efforts. It wasna right but 'twas better than nothing.

She was hungry now and with a sigh realised she'd have to bake the bannocks herself. A mite put out but thankful for anything that took her mind off her mother's disappearance and the turmoil within her, she rolled her sleeves and set to work.

It was more than an hour later, when the oatcakes were cooling on the stone hob and a pot of broth bubbled at the crook, that she heard the creak of the door and turned to find her mother swaying in the doorway. She was dressed in nothing but her underlinen, torn and muddied, and clutched a heather creel in her hands. She looked so utterly unlike herself, so weak and shaken and wild about the eyes, Sarah's heart stalled in her chest before a surge of relief rolled over her.

'Thank God,' she gasped. 'But … wherever have ye been?' Her gaze dropped to her mother's scratched and muddied shins, rose to take in her hair, uncovered and snagged with bits of twig and leaf. 'And whatever's happened to ye?'

Rowena sank into a chair. Her face was drawn and clammy and her hands, grimed with the dark earth of Sithean Wood, trembled and jerked. She closed her eyes. ''Tis naught ye need worry yersel' ower.'

Sarah frowned at this rebuff, but her relief at having her mother back was too great to feel any real injury. Never had she been so thankful to see her. Biting her lip, she came to kneel before her, wishing to be held by her mother yet aware of the inherent distance between them.

'But I *was* worried,' she said, confused by the emotions that assaulted her. 'I was damn near witless wi' worry. Wherever have ye been?' She looked at the creel still clutched in her mother's hands and moved to lift its covering.

Rowena caught her hand, her fingers closing tight around Sarah's wrist.

'Ye dinna want to be doing that,' she warned. 'I've had to do what must be done, but there's no need fer you to be drawn in. 'Tis best nae to ask, my heart, 'tis better to know nothing and stay safe.'

Sarah felt a sting of resentment and wrenched her hand away. 'I'm nae a bairn! I mightna have the gifts you and Morven have, but I still ken things. I ken more than you know.'

Rowena sighed, and a half-smile touched her lips. 'Oft-times those gifts can be a curse, and I'm powerful glad ye dinna have them.'

She lifted a grimy hand and smoothed away the crease between her daughter's brows. It was the same crease she'd often seen on Duncan's brow, and she trembled, feeling his presence. 'They bring with them dangers and dark accusations, and I wouldna want that fer you, my heart.' She cupped Sarah's cheek, feeling the bloom of her young skin, remembering the blithe bairn that had become this sad girl. 'Anyhow, what is it ye ken?'

'I ken about *him*, thon bastard McBeath. I ken he killed my da, and I ken he'll have ye fer his wife or have us put out o' the croft.'

Rowena's hand froze on Sarah's cheek. 'How do ye know this?'

Sarah shrugged. 'I heard ye. Heard ye plotting wi' Jamie. And I ken the plot failed, so ...' She gave another little shrug. Yet demonstrating her hard-won knowledge didn't feel as good as she'd hoped. She scowled. 'If ye'd only thought to tell me, though, I'd nae have needed to go prowling and prying, would I?'

Rowena's hand dropped to her lap, and she sat back, blinking at her daughter.

'Ye're right,' she said at last. 'I should've told ye what happened to yer da – ye had a right to know. And ... and I should've said what that man intended.' She looked up and appeared to watch her words flounder in the air. 'But I didna wish anything to ever hurt ye. You and William are ... are *m'anam,* are part of my soul, and I love ye both that much.' She met Sarah's eyes, her own heavy with regret. 'Please forgive me, Sarah. 'Twas wrong of me.'

Somewhere in Sarah's innards came a strange tightening, a giddy spasm that clenched and made her shudder and hug down into herself. Never had she felt so full, so brimming with emotions. She blinked, then the feeling passed, leaving her with a strange glow. She thought of all the nights she'd lain in her dark box-bed atremble at the howl of wind and crack of thunder. And each time, with her soft voice and hands, 'twas always her mam who came and chased away her demons.

She cleared her throat. ''Tis alright, I dinna need to ken everything ye do. I was afraid fer ye, was all.' She blinked and swallowed. 'I know I dinna often say it, but I'm right glad to see ye.'

Rowena's throat tightened, and she drew the pale girl into her arms, a wave of tenderness rolling over her. 'Ye've nae need to say it, my heart, I know. I've always known.'

CHAPTER NINTEEN

'YE'LL BE RETURNING LATER, will ye?' The boatman held out a grubby hand to Morven and helped her from the boat, then eyed her pale countenance a little darkly.

'Aye, soon enough.' She turned away. The ruin of Druimbeag crofthouse was only a half-mile away now, hidden by the forested ridge that formed part of its land. Her eagerness to reach it was tempered only by dread that she would find it empty.

The hopelessness of her search for Jamie lay in her chest like ballast. When she'd left Sarah at the foot of Seely's Hillock, she'd thought he might return to the bothy where they'd spent so many hours together, and without considering her actions had hurried there. But even as she climbed down the rock-face, she knew she'd not find him.

The bothy was untouched. The newly replenished tinderbox sat by the fire-cairn, and beside it, she found the remains of the meal she'd shared with Donald. With a twinge of shame, she saw the crushed harebells Jamie had left as a gift for her. She knelt to gather what was left of them when something caught her eye. She reached for it, then jerked back. An axe. Lying discarded by a stack of barrels. She knew at once Jamie had thrown it there before going after the exciseman. Unwilling to touch the vile object, she rose and kicked it savagely into the falls.

As she made the climb back up the gorge, her heart beat heavily. His loss touched her deeply, the more deeply knowing she'd had no faith in him, hadna trusted his word. And it was only later, wrapped in the close darkness of the night that she thought of Druimbeag. Turning and fretting in her narrow bed, it came to her that Jamie might feel the need to go there one last time and she clung to that hope.

Anxious to find him, she was inadvertently hindered by her mother. Her father's return had done much to draw Grace from her grief, and some semblance of her former spirit had returned, but she'd been horrified at how ghastly she looked. Aged by the rigours of her labour and the pain of loss, the flesh had shrunk from her bones, and her eyes now stared from a face grown stark and pinched.

She'd wished to be bathed in wild rose water, to have her skin rubbed with sweet gale milk for its sharp, fresh scent, and her hair bound up and dressed. Morven wondered what her father had said, how much he'd revealed of his part in Duncan's death, but whatever had been said there was a welcome spark about Grace now and she followed Malcolm continually with her eyes. Pleased at this rise in her mother's spirits and keen to nurture and share in it, Morven felt compelled to comply with her wishes. She'd bathed the emaciated body and made a sweet-smelling preparation, then rubbed it into her feeble limbs. But the lines of her own body were set with tension, knowing there was still much to do – all the dairying work – before she could slip away.

It was Alec that came to her rescue.

'I could do the work at the shieling fer ye.' He'd given her a tentative smile. 'If there was mebbe someplace else ye needed to be. I ken if 'twere me had the chance to … to put things right.' He swallowed and looked away. 'I ken ye'd do the same fer me.'

She scarcely knew what to say. Sarah had plainly done what was asked, and Alec now knew the truth. Alec, her da, and likely the others as well. But knowing the truth about Jamie meant Alec must now know of Sarah's lies and schemes and that it had always been Jamie she'd truly wanted. She sensed her brother was more hurt than he wished her to know, and, not wishing to heighten his suffering, she made no mention of Sarah but gripped his hands, and he nodded and urged her to go.

Druimbeag land was beautiful – she'd forgotten how beautiful. The newly unfurling bracken fronds she remembered from her visit in early May were now grown to giant proportions, tinged over with the gold of fading summer, and beneath the dappling trees her footfalls were cushioned by a thick layer of pine needles, the scent of resin filling the air. Yet the flourishing of the land only revealed more poignantly the crumbling of the ruined crofthouse. All that remained were the bare bones of a home, bleached and picked over by the scavenging passage of time.

The rickety door she remembered from that visit was gone altogether now, and the gap it left yawned wide. But as she drew closer, she saw that the door did still hang there all askew, only it had been forced wide open. Her hands began to tremble, and she clenched them together and stooped to pass beneath the rotting doorframe.

Inside it was dark, the air thick with the pungency of decay. It caught in her throat, and she swallowed, tasting it. A faint sound came from her left. The nerves at her temples began to fire and her breath dried on her tongue. Very slowly, she turned her head. He was kneeling before the rooftree, his head bent in prayer. He'd not heard her, for although his face was thrown into shadow, she saw the earnest movement of his lips and his eyes were closed, a tremor running through his body. Struck by the gravity of the stooped figure, she could do nothing to prevent the sob that slipped from her lips.

Jamie's reaction was explosive. He sprang to his feet with a low growl, and before she could draw another breath, the sharp glint of a blade flashed in his hand. His eyes widened and he took a startled step back.

'Morven!' Still uncomprehending, his eyes flicked past her to the gaping doorway as if he expected others to follow her into the ruined crofthouse.

'I'm alone, Jamie.'

His eyes flicked back to her and he blinked, drinking her in as though she were perhaps some form of apparition likely to vanish again at any moment. He took a step toward her, then seemed to remember himself and sheathed the dirk.

'Forgive me. Ye did startle me. I feared ye were …' He thought better of divulging who he'd imagined her to be and shook his head, still not quite believing his eyes.

'How did ye ken I was here? Is it … has something happened? Has Rowena –?'

'I didna ken ye were here. I only hoped ye'd be. But I …' She faltered, letting her gaze drop, unable to bear the intensity of his. 'Was afraid I'd be too late.'

He looked uncomprehendingly at her.

'That you'd be gone and I'd nae get the chance to … to say what I came here to say. To put things right atween us.'

He shivered, and she noticed his sark was soaked through and he looked almost ill, his dark eyes feverish and fierce. The urge to touch him overwhelmed her, and she quashed it with difficulty.

'I've long wished to speak with you too. I've wished to explain my behaviour … my part in that vile business at yer father's bothy.'

Her heart began to beat in the back of her throat, making it hard to speak, and he was staring, his gaze fixed intently on her face, and that wasna helping. She took a ragged breath. 'There's no need for explanations. I do know the truth now. I ken it all, and I'm heart-sorry for the sore words I've spoken.' The sting of tears began behind her eyes, and her throat tightened as she struggled to keep them at bay. 'I'm sorry I didna have the faith in ye that ye so well deserved.'

He frowned and seemed to wrestle with himself, the silence stretching between them for so long she thought the sound of her heart hammering against her breastbone must have somehow smothered her words, when he made a dismissive gesture and looked down at his hands.

'Rowena has spoken with ye, then?'

'No, 'twas Sarah told me the truth.' Seeing his stricken expression, she added, 'And I believe it took a deal of courage fer her to do so. Can ye ever forgive me, Jamie?' She waited, her heart lodged high in her throat.

His frown deepened. 'There's naught to forgive. You thought me a scoundrel and told me as much; I expected nothing less. And anyway, ye weren't so far from the truth. I swore to protect my kinfolk, and in that I failed, as I failed in protecting you.' A muscle in his jaw flexed. 'I believe it's me should be beggin' your forgiveness, d'ye not think?'

'How can ye say that?' She gawped at him for a moment, floundering for words. 'What you did took nerve and daring. To sign up wi' the Black Gauger knowing full well what the man did, what he *is* – the verra divil himself. How many here would choose to keep company wi' the likes o' him? Aye, and risk the man's wrath should he find them out, and the blackening of their name among the glen smugglers. And all fer what? Fer kinfolk they'd known but a season?' Her voice had risen and now thickened with emotion. 'None in this glen. D'ye nae see, Jamie? It hardly matters that ye failed – ye did at least try.' But it did matter, she knew it mattered a great deal.

'And what happened at the bothy was no more your doing than 'twas mine. I see that now. Ye would never lead the gauger there, 'twas …' She shook her head, searching for some explanation.

'Yer wee brother. Though he didna know it. We watched Donald from the ridge, saw him climb up ower the lip of the gorge wi' a bundle slung upon his back. I knew at once ye must be there, I knew it in my heart, and yet when the devil went to take a closer look, I did nothing. I dithered while he beat ye, I …' He turned and slammed his fist into the rough timber of the rooftree. 'I faltered while he tried to force himself upon ye!'

He raised his hands, one torn and bloody about the knuckles, and gripped the trunk of the tree before letting his head fall onto his forearms. 'If that's nae failing ye, then I dinna ken what is.'

She stared at him. His lungs were heaving, she saw the swift rise and fall along the length of his back. She'd not thought on him blaming himself for that. She'd been too shocked to think much beyond the shame of the attack, but he quivered with the force of his anger. Tentatively, she reached out and touched his shoulder.

'Jamie.' The word came strangled and guttural. 'Jamie,' she tried again, and then the tears came along with a lump the size of a cairn in her throat. She slipped her arms around his waist and pressed her cheek against the wet linen of his sark, feeling the warmth of his skin, salty and damp.

'Jamie, Jamie,' she mourned. She was crying now and trembling as much as he. He turned, and lifting her chin with his fingers, brushed the tears from her cheeks with his thumbs, cupping her face within the earthy warmth of his hands. Their eyes met, his still dark and intense, but softening as he looked at her, his touch gentle.

'Dinna weep. Nae fer me.'

She smiled apologetically as a helpless sob escaped, breaking the tension between them. Then his arms were around her, strong and protective, and she was immersed in everything that was him. His breath was warm against her neck with a metallic tang to it, of blood perhaps, or hard toil, and she breathed again the scent of him; earthy and male. His hands were on her back, soothing and stroking, gentle yet she sensed the power in them. He groaned and pressed her closer, and she clung fiercely to him, moulding herself to his body as though she'd never release him, for she never wished to. Her tension left her, her sobs dying on her tongue.

'God, ye're beautiful,' he murmured into her neck.

'Lord, Jamie.' Still holding him, and with the rapid thump of his heart against her cheek, she whispered, '*Gaol de mo chridhe*.' Love of my heart.

With a strangled groan, he crushed her to him. 'And mine. Ye are my heart.' Loosening his hold, he searched for her mouth, his lips cold but his mouth eager and hot. His kiss was a raw release of long-pent emotion, his hands cradling her head, and she returned it with an ardour equal to his, the joy of it coursing through her veins. Shivers of delight rippled through her body, spawning melting sensations and a growing heat. Then he released her and tenderly drew up her hands to plant more kisses in the palms of her hands.

'*Tha gaol agam ort*,' she said softly. She hadn't known it until the words were said, but she knew in her heart now she spoke the truth. 'I dinna care what ye say, Jamie Innes. I do love ye.'

He tensed at her words, the wrestling of his emotions reflected in his eyes. 'Ye mustna say that.' His mouth hardened. 'Ye dinna ken how long I've yearned to hear ye say those words, but ye must never say them. Mustna think them.' His throat convulsed. 'Ye must forget me, Morven, fer I'll only bring ye misery.'

There was a note in his voice she'd not heard before, a bereft tone that stirred unease in the pit of her stomach. She drew back. 'Sarah said ye meant to leave the glen?'

He nodded. Very gently he folded her fingers and pushed them back at her. 'One way or another I'll be gone from here in a week.'

She stared at him.

'Dinna look at me that way! Ye can scarce hate me more than I do hate myself.'

'I dinna hate ye.'

'No, ye'd not do that, I know it, but I must make ye understand. Last night I gave McBeath my challenge. We are to settle the matter of my aunt's eviction or her *marriage*,' he spat the word out angrily. 'Wi' swords in six days' time. It's nae so much a matter of honour to me, but one of justice. I canna let this happen, and I've no other earthly way to stop it. Maybe ye'll mind the day I swore I'd allow no more of my kin to be forced from this glen?'

She nodded, her heart in her throat.

'I intend to honour that vow. Should I win the day, and pray God I do, I'll be a wanted man. Ye see that, aye? I'll have to flee from here, or, as a murderer, be hanged fer my crime.'

Stricken, she reared back, groping for support from the rotting doorframe.

*****

'Lord protect ye!' cried Grace, her hands flying to her face. She'd whitened as Jamie told of his forthcoming duel, and now, with Alec's assistance, groped her way to a chair at the fireside. She sat down beside him, blinking and wringing her hands.

Morven watched her with a sense of hopeless recognition. She knew well that stricken look – likely she wore it herself. And well she might, fer what notion had McBeath of justice or honour? A dirk atween the shoulder blades was the true price of the man, and that's what he'd understand. She shivered as a chill stole over her. Only, what chance did that give Jamie for a fair fight?

Her gaze returned to him. He fidgeted, stiff and upright beside her father, a dram pushed into his hands, plainly aware of the consternation he was causing yet weathering it with quiet resolve. He was set firm on this reckoning, he'd been quite clear on that, and nothing she'd said had shaken him from that course, though she'd tried her damnedest.

She could remember nothing of the trek back to the ferryboat but only become aware of her surroundings again once she was sat on the damp plank opposite Jamie, hunched and reeling from his words. He'd gripped her hands and gently forced her chin up, so he could look into her face, then winced at what he saw.

'Forgive me. Hurting you was never my intention.' He shook his head. 'You of all folk. I thought it wouldna matter to ye, that ye did think me a traitorous louse and … and this was the only way I could think of striking back at him, I wished him dead that badly.' He looked away with a shudder. 'I still do.'

'But surely there's still time.' She swallowed at what she was about to suggest. 'Time to stop this, to cry it off. I mean, ye must see the man's nae worth it? Nae worth dying ower, in the same way Tomachcraggen's nae worth it, nor …' But the words died on her tongue at the look in his eyes.

''Twas McBeath had my family put from Druimbeag. He paid reivers to drive away my father's cattle. Paupered him.' He clenched his jaw, his grip tightening on her hand. 'He admitted it to me after ye put the fear o' God into him at yer father's bothy. And d'ye know why? What reason he had to have us exiled? To break my father's heart?'

She shook her head, not trusting her voice.

He fixed his gaze on the land they were leaving behind. Turning on the narrow plank, she followed his gaze. Overshadowed by the dark mass of mountain, the familiar pattern of rig and dreel was still faintly discernible, imprinted on a land long since fallen fallow. He leaned forward, fixing her with his eyes.

'Fer spite.' He clenched her hand a little harder, droplets of blood welling from his torn knuckle. 'He suspected 'twas my father poisoned Rowena against him. Eaten with her wanting he was, and when she turned him down fer Duncan, he saw my father as the cause and engineered his revenge. Took pleasure in it.'

'God, Jamie.' She swallowed, her mouth dry as cinders. 'And now ye want yours. Justice fer yer family. Fer Duncan and –'

'Fer you.'

She drew back, her breath catching in her throat. 'But it doesna matter to me. It's only you that matters.'

'It matters to me.'

'Fer pity's sake. I dinna care about McBeath. 'Tis madness. He'll kill ye, I ken he will.' She gripped the edge of the boat, staring up at him, then let go to snatch up his hand again, trying to urge reason on him through the press of her fingers.

He blinked, a slow rolling movement immeasurably calm. 'I must.'

The finality in his voice brought a racking sob to her lips. Rowena wouldna be wanting this; likely she'd rather wed the scum. Yet his expression was set and unyielding, and at the sight of it, her heart sank without a trace. He was lost to her. She knew it as surely as she knew he was hell-bent on this course.

'Is there nothing then, nothing I can say to stop ye?'

He sighed, and his dark eyes were infinitely sad. '*Tha mi duilich,*' he said softly. I'm sorry. 'Ye see why I say ye must forget me? I can give ye nothing now, nae even myself, and I dinna wish to hurt ye further, I …' He sat back, mastering himself. 'I've naught to offer but misery, and it seems I bring that to all who come close.'

'Ye've nae brought me misery, only …' She shook her head, her throat too swollen to go on.

'Heartache, then?'

She nodded.

'Then I pray it heals quick, that when I'm gone from here, ye'll nae think so badly of me.'

She'd been unable to answer, and they sat in silence, save for the slapping of the water against the flank of the boat and the tuneless whistling of the boatman, who watched them with interest. On reaching the east bank, Jamie paid the man, and they walked on to Delnabreck in silence, Morven conscious of little but Jamie's supporting hand beneath her elbow.

At Delnabreck, her father greeted Jamie with warmth.

'Ye'll take a dram wi' me?' He stirred Rory and Donald from their prime fireside position with a swipe of his hand.

Jamie gave her a fleeting half-smile and squeezed her arm, then while a seat was swiftly found for him, Morven retreated into the shadows and listened to him recount the details of his challenge to her family.

Grace made another distressed sound and Alec hastened to fetch her some water. He lowered the cup, catching Morven's eye, and in that look said far more than he could ever say in words. She nodded back bleakly, acknowledging her brother's innate understanding. It felt as though her heart lay open, swollen and raw for all to see, and she strove to somehow defend it, tighten and compress it into some small confine within herself, some guarded chamber where she could hide away her hurt. Where she'd not distract Jamie with the sight of it. Nor fall to pieces herself at the pain of it, fer what good would that do anyone?

Her mother was still staring at Jamie with frightened eyes. She crossed herself and began a frantic prayer. Malcolm silenced her with a curt,

'Wheesht, woman! I need to think.' He turned back to Jamie. 'Ye'll have a decent-enough weapon then, lad?'

'I've the sword I bought with my exciseman's allowance. A blade of poor craftsmanship I fear, untried and likely brittle.'

Malcolm nodded thoughtfully. 'I've a sword I believe would suit ye right fine. A broadsword mair fitting fer yer size and make-up, I'm thinking.' He ran an appraising eye over Jamie's powerful frame. 'It's nae every man could wield it, but you …. It's nae been drawn since my ane father drew it upon Culloden field, but I've kept it well – kept it wi' the respect it deserves, fer 'twas drawn in anger upon those who strove to keep the rightful king from these shores. And was the last earthly thing my father touched afore he was sent to meet his maker.'

Jamie choked on his whisky. 'But I couldna –'

'Ye could,' Malcolm said gruffly. 'What I mean is, I'd count it an honour, lad, if ye'd think to trying it.' He turned toward Rory and Donald, who were now perched on the meal kist with rapt expressions, and looked pointedly at the great chest standing against the far wall.

His meaning instantly apparent, the boys almost tripped over each other in their eagerness to comply and draw their granda's broadsword from the secret place where it had lain for the last thirty-five years. Carrying the weapon between them, the boys offered it to Jamie with shy reverence.

He stood to accept it a little reluctantly, but it was plain he immediately recognised the calibre of the weapon he held. Sliding the sword from its ornate scabbard, he tested its feel, its balance, and made a series of deftly controlled strokes. A basket-hilted broadsword of immense weight, in Jamie's hands the weapon appeared little more than a natural extension of his own body.

Malcolm's quivering intake of breath was audible. ''Twas made fer ye! Show me the man 'twould stand unflinching afore such a blade,' he muttered to himself, 'and I'll show ye a fool.' He hesitated, more uncertain. 'I'm wondering if ye've had time to think much on yer preparation?'

Jamie sheathed the sword and sat down again. 'I had thought wi' prayer –'

'Yer instruction, I mean. Would I be right in thinking ye're little accustomed to the handling of such a weapon?'

'Ye would,' Jamie admitted.

'But ye see,' Malcolm rubbed the back of his neck, clearly unpractised at choosing his words with any particular care. 'The Black Gauger, God rot his soul, is well acquainted wi' the wielding of a sword, fer he is wi'out question a first-rate swordsman. Dinna let his appearance deceive ye.' He cocked one eye in a crude imitation of the exciseman's squint. 'Fer all he looks like a drunken weasel, he's the eye of a hawk, and he's as ruthless as they come.'

'I take yer meaning. I've witnessed wi' my own eyes how base the man is, how he seems to lack any human feeling.' Jamie swallowed. 'Yet my mind's made up, and I'll not be dissuaded. I mean to send the devil to hell. Should it be God's will that I must join him there, then so be it.' He glanced over at Morven and held her gaze, unblinking. 'And if I must die,' his voice now held an unmistakable edge, 'then, by God, I dinna mean to sell my life cheap!'

Morven's constricted heart strained against its confines. She glanced at her mother. Grace sat ashen and swaying, Alec grim-faced at her side. She shifted her gaze back to her father. *Do something*, she silently willed at him. *Fer pity's sake Da, make him stop this.* But Malcolm only nodded.

'I thought as much. It wasna my intention to dissuade ye, I can see how futile that would be. I meant only to be certain ye kent the nature of the man ye've pitted yerself against.' He inhaled strongly. 'And to mak' sure ye're acquainted wi' the penalty should ye succeed in running through an officer o' His Majesty's Excise.'

Jamie glanced at Morven again. 'The penalty's hanging, I know it well. Only, fer the sake of my kinfolk, who've no-one else, I'll take my chances wi' the hangman's rope. And anyhow,' the corners of his mouth quirked with grim humour, 'they'd need to catch me first, aye?'

'That they would.'

Only the barest twitch below Malcolm's right eye betrayed his emotion now. 'That being so, I'd count it an honour, lad, if ye'd permit me to instruct ye in the use o' the broadsword, fer there's an art to the weapon.'

Jamie's strained expression relaxed a fraction, and he inclined his head. 'I believe the honour would be mine.'

***

Rowena accompanied Jamie to Delnabreck the next morning for his first practice session with the sword. The day was grey and louring with layers of dark cloud gathered low atop the hills and a damp chill hung in the air. The mountains had been swallowed by the dark sky, and Morven wished the rain would come and chase away the heavy air that made her head ache. Standing in the doorway beside Rowena, she shivered.

'Ye're chilled, lass.' Rowena took her icy hands and drew them into the folds of her arisaid but there was little warmth to be found there; both women were stiff and cold with their own tensions. At length, Rowena squeezed Morven's hands a little apologetically and let them go.

Morven glanced sidelong at her. 'I know ye'd yer reasons fer keeping the plan ye made with Jamie from me,' she said. 'And I understand that, truly I do. But I wish ye to know 'twas never my father's intention to betray Duncan. He's told me what happened and it wasna an easy thing to tell. An error of judgement it was, a drunken one. He did let slip the details. If he could go back and change things, take back the liquor he did fuddle his brain with, he'd give all he has to find a way. The guilt and the sorrow … it has eaten away at him. Changed him. In so many ways. Made him surly, made him avoid ye.'

Rowena looked earnestly at her, then massaged her brow, her expression softening. 'I think I knew that. He's a good man … the best. It's just, I let grief cloud my thinking. Along wi' the conniving o' the Black Gauger. But in my heart, I've always known it.'

'He's nae the easiest to get along wi', mind.'

Rowena chuckled, then took Morven's hands, regarding her soberly. 'I know that too.' She sighed and pressed her eyes shut for a moment. 'I should've told ye what Jamie was about, Morven, I see that now. I've hurt ye. We both have. But 'twas my doing more than his, I made him swear to me.' She looked up with a haunted expression. 'Never did I wish to hurt ye, Morven. Never. Please believe that.'

'I know. 'Tis forgotten. Ye've enough to worry ye – we both do.'

Rowena lifted Morven's hands and kissed them, giving her a tight smile, a smile that thanked her for understanding, and Morven hugged her back. They parted then, with a little more peace in their hearts.

What Rowena thought of her young kinsman's decision to challenge the Black Gauger in such a desperate fashion, Morven hardly knew, for Rowena was skilled at keeping her innermost thoughts to herself. But looking at the widow's strained expression, Morven could imagine only too well.

'I dinna think I can watch this.' Morven averted her gaze from her younger brothers, who were clearing stones from the ground in front of the byre. The boys were in high spirits, evidently relishing the reckoning to come, and had plainly been set the task of clearing the practice ground of anything liable to cause a deadly slip or stumble. They worked with the blithe excitement of the very young, their high-pitched voices grating on Morven's frayed nerves.

Rowena turned back into the cot-house to attend to a draught she was preparing for Grace. With a shiver, Morven followed her inside. After a moment, she heard her father's voice rise harshly above the clamour of the boys.

'Can ye nae hold yer wheesht? How's the lad to think straight wi' that great squalloch going on? If ye've finished clearing stones, ye can go fill sacks wi' straw, and I'll hang them from the lintel here.'

The sacks of straw were to represent bodies – chests and bellies and innards – feeling sick, she turned back to her mother.

'The lad must have a great heart.' Grace glanced over at the now empty chest where the great sword had been hidden for so long. 'But what's to become o' him? I mean, even should he carry the day ...'

'We can only pray,' replied Rowena. 'And mind our prayers are nae always answered in the manner we expect.'

'What d'ye mean?' said Morven.

'Nothing ill. What's done's done, and canna be undone. We must put our faith in Jamie now and in the power of good to overthrow evil. 'Tis all we can do.'

Despite her fears, Rowena poured Grace's draught with a steady hand. 'Twould do no good to voice those fears now, but even so, she reeled at Jamie's actions, at the boldness of his deed. She'd not expected that. Even knowing the keen sense of duty the lad possessed, she'd not thought of him demanding satisfaction in quite such a manner, though she admired his gall. Yet it unnerved her all the same. The ancient rite enacted in Sithean Wood was done and final, and couldna be undone, but the question was, what sacrifice would be needed to sanction it? And would that sacrifice now be Jamie's? She prayed not but couldn't dispel the unease that churned her belly. If only he'd given her some hint of what he intended.

Yet she must keep faith, else all would be lost. Lost for Jamie and herself. She passed the fortifying draught to Morven and watched the lass carry it carefully to her mother. If anyone had any inkling of her foreboding, of her unease at the way her invocation might play out, 'twould be Morven, for the lass could sense such things. And Morven had worries enough without lending her more. There was nothing to be done now, nothing but wait and pray and keep her fears to herself.

Morven straightened, watching her mother sip at the tonic of feverwort Rowena had prepared. As always Rowena spoke sense. Faith was needed now, for Jamie didna need her fears and grief, what use had he for those? They'd only distract his focus. They were things to be hidden away, buried so deep they'd only be known about by herself.

'Aye,' she said abruptly, making Grace jump. 'We must show we support Jamie, nae cower in here like mice.' She moved to the door and pushed it open.

'Where are ye going?' Grace cried.

'To see if there's anything I can do.'

Rowena drew her arisaid about her. 'I'll come with ye.'

Out in the yard, Jamie was stripped to his sark, the linen fluttering in the breeze, while her father stood behind him moving his arms into the correct positions, placing the blade in a defensive position to ward off the fierce attacks McBeath would let loose.

'Ye parry like this,' Malcolm was saying. 'Wi' yer legs wide and firm, see, so ye canna be wrong-footed, even should the blows be fierce, and ye can dodge to either side should ye need to. Afore ye learn the cuts and thrusts, ye must learn to defend yerself, else ye might never get a chance at the other strokes. See?' He demonstrated a neat deflecting move with his own weapon.

Jamie found the correct positions easily, he was light on his feet for such a powerful man, graceful. Morven could see her father was pleased. He'd that twitchiness to his face that always gave away his excitement, for all his expression was grave.

The boys were playing nearby, aping the men's actions, capering with sticks instead of swords and she frowned at them. They were still bairns, they'd nae be thinking, but had they nothing better to do?

Seeing Morven, Jamie dropped his guard a fraction and consternation crossed his face.

'I'd have run ye through there! Ye must keep yer wits about ye, else he'll finish ye as soon as ...' Malcolm's eyes flicked to Morven and more briefly to Rowena, standing quietly at her side, and he faltered, his face reddening. ''Tis yerselves,' he murmured. 'Can ye nae see we've work to do?'

'Forgive me, Da.' For a moment, Morven felt like a child again and nodded awkwardly to Jamie. 'Only, we were wondering was there anything we could do? Any way we could help at all?'

'Was ye now?' His face reddened still further.

He would think this no place fer a woman, would likely tell her as much – she waited.

''Tis a help just knowing ye're thinking of us,' Jamie said shyly. 'Is it not, sir?' He looked her father squarely in the eye.

'Well aye, it is, aye.'

Morven had never seen her father squirm before, though he quite plainly did so now, discomfited, she knew, by Rowena's presence.

'There is something,' he said at last. He stared down at the ground, scuffing dust with his homemade boots. 'I was thinking how there's nae much sense in leaving a whole year's harvest in Rowena's fields fer the factor's men to pick ower. I mean, pray God the fight goes our way, but should it …. What I mean is, we wouldna be wanting to swell his Grace's coffers wi' the fruits of the young lad's labours, now would we?'

It was Jamie who came to his deliverance.

'That we'd not.' His face grew pensive. 'And should my aunt have to leave the glen, then the move would be made a deal easier for her wi' full meal kists.' He turned his dark gaze on his aunt. 'I think I should leave this now.' He propped the ornate broadsword against the byre wall. 'And get on wi' the reaping and threshing. Ye can see the sense in that, Rowena?'

Rowena opened her mouth to object, but Malcolm got in first.

'No, lad, that's nae what I meant.' He offered the weapon back to him. 'I thought if I sent Alec and the lads ower, the bairns are fair getting my canker up anyhow, and if Morven was willing too, then so much the better.' He glanced at the louring sky. 'They could mebbe have most o' the harvest in afore the weather turns.'

'But it's me should be doing that,' Jamie protested.

'And five days hence it's you that's to fight the finest swordsman in Stratha'an!' Malcolm drew breath with a quiver. 'Be reasonable, lad. Ye canna do everything.'

Her father then turned to Rowena, and with some trepidation gentled his voice. 'If ye've a moment, Rowena, I would speak wi' ye on a private matter.' Lifting his gaze, he found the courage to look her in the eye.

Rowena's strained expression soften to a shy smile. 'I see no need, Malcolm. Your heart is true, I know that. I'm only sorry I didna see it afore, but grief did cloud my thinking. Forgive me, but it made me distrust ye.' She frowned. 'I did suspect my own shadow.'

''Tis I seek your forgiveness,' he said gruffly. 'I was a drunken, half-witted –'

'Ye made a mistake,' she said firmly. ''Tis human to do so. There's no profit in re-examining it, that route does lead to naught but pain. But I thank ye fer what ye're doing now fer me and my kin.' She nodded to signify she considered the matter closed and turned to go.

Malcolm caught her by the sleeve, his face pitifully grateful.

'Bless ye, Rowena.'

She nodded with an awkward smile.

CHAPTER TWENTY

MORVEN STRAIGHTENED, grimacing at the numbing crick in the base of her spine as it realigned itself to the vertical. She massaged the spot through the wool of her gown and watched as Sarah made her way through the cleared rigs and oat stacks, a creel slung over her shoulders.

'Belly-timber!' whooped Rory from the neighbouring tattie dreels. He dropped his fork and vaulted the stone dyke, William and Donald trailing behind him.

Alec straightened and dried his brow, then laid aside his scythe to relieve Sarah of the creel.

'They'll nae be as good as my mam's.' Sarah stood awkwardly by as Alec set the heaped basket on the newly scythed stubble. 'But I was thinking they'd maybe go doon easier wi' a sup o' this.' She pulled a flask of heather ale from the creel and handed it a little shyly to him.

'They smell bonny enough.' Rory reached for the biggest bannock. 'And my belly's been thinking my throat was cut.'

'They'll be fine,' Rowena assured her. 'Easily as good as any I could make.'

'Nae worse, anyroads,' Rory grunted, and Donald took a fit of the giggles, snorting into his hand. William shot him a look, and he swiftly sobered and sat down beside the older boy, his wee face upturned and contrite.

Sarah smiled feebly at him, her gaze moving on to Alec. He was watching her just as closely, and she swallowed and glanced away.

'Look what's in here!'

Beneath the layer of bannocks, Rory discovered a mound of hot tatties baked in their skins and rubbed in salt. He whistled appreciatively. They looked a mite singed about the edges but that would make no difference to the boys, and after the backbreaking demands of a forenoon in the dreels, Morven knew they'd not last long.

Alec passed the ale to her, but once her thirst was slaked, Morven found she had little appetite. She picked at her food, conscious of the trouble Sarah had gone to, and of an odd change in the girl that saw her strangely eager to please yet more comfortable labouring with the boys among the tatties than with Alec, Rowena, and herself. She shrugged. Somehow it seemed a deal easier that way, easier to get through the despair of it all without Sarah's company, though that was likely unfair.

That first day the three of them had worked in silence, Alec cutting, Rowena laying the oats in bundles and twisting the oat-stalks into bands, while she bound the sheaves and stacked them. No-one had shown any desire to speak, and they'd each slipped silently into the rhythm of the harvest, drawing a numbing comfort from the toil yet enclosed in the gloom that overhung them all.

Sensitive to that gloom, today Alec had chosen to sing, old Gaelic reaping songs full of the rhythm of the harvest. And alongside her brother's deeper voice, and Rowena's softer tone, Morven had allowed her own voice to rise. She set down her bannock now, her stomach too leaden to accept it, and looked over the growing ranks of oat stacks, the rigs of close-cropped stubble. In the stoop and rise of body and melody, she'd been able to find a brief escape, a means of forgetting, for a time, everything but the deep ache of wrist and spine. She looked down at her hands, chafed and sore, and squeezed them together.

'How's the tattie lifting going?' Alec aimed his question at Sarah, attempting to draw her from her uneasy position at the edge of the group.

'Aye, grand. Anither day should do it.' Rory nodded back cheerfully, juggling a hot potato in his hands. 'And the reaping?'

Alec waggled his head. 'Might get through it by the morn's night if the rain stays away. Then there'll be the threshing and the winnowing.'

Rory grinned back, mouth full, but Sarah kept her eyes on the hills, her expression meticulously distant, and only in the flick of a tiny muscle at the base of her jawline did she give away her agitation.

She knew, of course, by now it seemed the whole glen knew of Jamie's stand against the Black Gauger, and Morven marvelled at the speed and ease at which some folk could change their opinions. She swallowed uncomfortably, but then, had she not done the same herself?

When she returned each evening, it was to the clash of metal, to the sight of Jamie and her father locked in deadly combat, turning in an endless circle of weave and counter-weave, strike and parry. And to a great gathering of onlookers, drawn to the croft to watch the extraordinary spectacle.

Word of Jamie's deed at the Balintoul Inn had spread quickly through the glen, and many now came to see if the rumours rife among its patrons were true. Finding that they were, and that Jamie had duped McBeath good and proper, these folks seemed unwilling to leave, wishing to slap him on the back or wring his hands or simply to stand and stare and wonder at his courage. Her da chased away the more ghoulish among their number, but he judged the support most now extended, 'to be good fer the lad's frame o' mind,' and allowed the rest to stay a while.

Donald Gordon of Craigduthel was among the first to come. Standing half hidden by the sheepcote, the wind whipping the dull remnants of his hair, his bonnet clutched in his hands, the old crofter watched Jamie's intrinsic skill with the sword. The lad had a sure hand and nerves of steel and he couthily observed, ''Tis a gey auld dog ye've got there teaching ye, lad.' He ducked as Malcolm aimed a good-natured swipe at him. 'But ye ken, it's said that every dog must hae his day, and I'm thinking … well, I'm thinking … ach!' He twisted his bonnet a little harder. 'Well, that your day, Jamie, must be well overdue.' He shook his head, his whiskery brows shielding the expression in his eyes, and without another word took himself back to Craigduthel.

'Will ye join us fer the threshing, Sarah?' The lines of strain ingrained in Rowena's face softened a little as she turned to look at her daughter. 'We'd be glad of the help.'

'That we would,' Alec agreed, his eyes resting hopefully on Sarah's face.

Sarah glanced at Morven and her throat contracted. 'I dinna ken.'

Aware that in some way her approval seemed required, Morven cleared her throat. 'Aye, Sarah, we'd be grateful fer yer help.'

The girl nodded, her gaze sliding off to find her mother, and Morven watched Rowena give her a little nod and a half-smile of encouragement and felt a twinge of guilt. Lowering her head, she watched the girl from beneath her lashes.

Sarah sat slightly removed from the others, diligently picking dirt from beneath her fingernails. She glanced up at Morven's scrutiny, and then quickly dropped her gaze to her lap again, where her bannock still lay untouched. In a sudden burst of activity, she tossed her uneaten bannock into the creel and set about gathering up what remained of the food. Morven watched her. Her face had grown thin, and she wore a certain crushing sense of loneliness.

'Can I help ye with that?' She rose and offered Sarah her hand.

Sarah's eyes widened, but she grasped Morven by the hand and got to her feet. Once they'd left the others behind, Morven said, 'None of this is your doing Sarah, ye ken that, don't ye? Jamie's decision, it's nae ower anything you said, his choice to –'

'To get himsel' killed?'

Morven swallowed. 'To challenge the Black Gauger. You're nae to blame, I hope ye ken that. He has his honour ye see, and sees wrongs to be righted, wrongs from years back – from the time of his father. He's set on seeing justice done, nae matter what. There's nae blame fer it. *I* dinna blame ye, nor Alec. I hope ye didna think that.'

Sarah's face seemed to crumple, but she mastered herself and nodded curtly. Wrestling the creel from Morven's hands, she turned and fled toward the crofthouse.

***

It was the following evening before the rain came, no more than a spitter at first, raising tiny puffs in the dust of the yard. Jamie breathed in deeply, tasting the fresh loamy tang on the air and glanced at the dark sky, then at the McHardy clan perched on the infield dyke doing likewise. Over the course of the afternoon, every one of the McHardys had added their tuppence-worth to the melting pot of well-meaning advice now on offer, even young Dugald, and added to the counsel offered to him earlier that day by Lachlan Doull the poacher, the Frasers of Ballantrim, the Chisholms of Clachfuar, and a parcel of cottars from Glenlivet, his head was fair buzzing with it all. Morven would soon be home, and within him, he felt the quickening the thought of her always brought. Likely she'd be spent after the backbreaking toil that was, by rights, his duty, nae hers, but she'd make no complaint, as indeed Alec and the boys made none. He lowered his sword-arm, massaging the swollen wrist she'd bound for him that morning, and shivered at the touch. 'Ye must forget me,' he'd told her, and so she must. But Lord, did it have to hurt so much?

'Aye,' Malcolm grunted, sensing the dwindling of the lad's concentration. 'The heavens are fair full o' something. We'll cry it a day, will we, and let these folk home afore they take a drenching.'

With the day's sport apparently over, the McHardy clan clambered off the dyke, the low murmur of their voices falling away, replaced by a sheepish shuffling of feet. Hal McHardy pulled his bonnet from his head, the others bowing theirs, and mumbled, 'Guid even, Father.'

Father Ranald had rounded the cottage in a brusque abstracted manner, certain imminent matters weighing heavy with him, and now stopped short, eyebrows raised at the ragtag assemblage lined before him.

'Hal.' He nodded stiffly to the man. 'And Eilidh.' He nodded again to McHardy's wife. 'I hadn't thought to finding you here.' He smiled round at the younger members of the family, a warm crinkling of the lines weathered into his face, but the glint in his eye when he looked back at Hal was altogether cooler. 'I'd have thought, man, if ye'd that much time on yer hands, ye'd be over at Tomachcraggen lending a hand with the harvest.'

'Oh that ... aye, Father.' Hal nodded, and then a mite red about the face turned and led his folk away through the gathering rain. 'Guid luck to ye, Jamie,' he called over his shoulder.

'Ye'll eh ... take a drop o' barley-bree, Father?' Malcolm enquired of the priest, pointing toward the cottage with his head. 'Just to be civil-like, aye?'

'To be civil, then.' The priest waited patiently, rain pattering on his head and shoulders, while the two men sheathed and unbuckled their swords.

At the fireside, the Father removed the thick woollen mantle he wore over his vestments, shaking the rain from it, and then used the garment to dry his head. He hung the cloak over the back of a chair and sat down, waiting for the men to follow suit. Jamie glanced at Malcolm, reading in the pallor of his face and the darkness of his eyes the apprehension within him.

'An unexpected pleasure,' Malcolm mumbled, sitting himself down beside the priest.

'Hardly that, I think.'

'Well, no,' Malcolm admitted with a wry smile. 'I've been half expecting ye these last days Father, what wi' the eh ... wi' all that's afoot.'

The priest nodded, then sat back as Grace brought whisky and drinking cups and lit a fir-candle in the iron receptacle above his head. With a quick glance into the Father's face, she withdrew to feigned business with her spindle in the far corner of the room. Malcolm poured out the drams, then, raising his drink first to Jamie and then to the priest, cried,

'Here's to the heath, the hill, and the heather,

the bonnet, the plaidie, the kilt, and the feather!'

He downed his whisky in one long gulp, wheezing as the fire of the spirit seared the back of his throat, and Jamie observed an immediate restoration of the colour to his cheeks.

'*Slàinte,*' Jamie replied, knocking back his own drink.

'Aye,' the Father murmured, sipping at his whisky. 'A good health to ye both.' He stared at his whisky for a moment, then leaned forward in his seat, his eyes moving back and forth between the two men.

Jamie swallowed. The room had darkened around them, and he gave a little start as a blast of hail hammered with sudden violence against the window and the door. It drummed more mutely on the thatch, sending a torrent of hailstones down the chimney to sizzle and hiss in the fire. The priest studiously ignored the din, and as sizeable bullets of ice ricocheted about their feet, Jamie became aware the priest was carefully considering what he'd come to say.

'I see no purpose in being but plain-spoken,' he said at last. 'Am I to take it, then, that the tidings whispered of in every crofthouse and bothy the length of this glen are true?' His gaze moved to the swords now propped against the wall by Malcolm's chair.

'They are,' Jamie confirmed.

'And the deed?'

'To go ahead the day after next. At dawn.'

Jamie felt his jaw lift a fraction and he knew a veil had slipped into place across his features, a fixed, wholly undaunted expression that revealed only the hatred he nurtured within him but would give no hint of his pain. What he would lose, regardless of the outcome of the duel, he felt as a barb buried deep in his flesh, but the wound was a private pain, and he wished to keep it that way.

The Father's nostrils flared momentarily, and he reached for the silver crucifix he wore around his neck. 'I've no wish to acquaint myself with the details of the offence caused; I've bid in this glen long enough to know the true way of McBeath's heart.' He rose and moved across to the window, peering through the rivulets of water and melting ice sliding down the pane. 'But what ye intend,' he turned and fixed Jamie with a look that made him wince. 'Is a mortal sin – one that'll damn ye forever. To take another man's life …' He exhaled, his nostrils flaring again. 'And you've thought, have ye, that ye might well lose your own?'

'Forsooth he has!' Malcolm could keep silent no longer. 'Ye dinna ken the full truth o' it Father, if the lad hadna such just cause, then

… then damned if I'd nae run the scum through myself!'

Grace let out a shocked little gasp, then quickly lowered her head to the distaff again.

The Father flinched and moved away from the window where the pelting downpour had strengthened in its ferocity. 'Then you'd damn yerself too!'

'Aye, mebbe I would. Or mebbe I'm damned already. But my conscience would be better served, I'm thinking, than it's been in many a long month.'

Father Ranald made an odd strangled sound and stepped back from Malcolm as though smote by his words. Jamie rose to intervene.

'I ken well the risks, Father.'

'To your soul as well as your body?'

'To both. But I'm driven to bring the man to justice, and this is the only route left me.'

The Father stared hard at him, and in the shadows of the priest's eyes, Jamie was unsure if he read respect or revulsion.

'Lad, the Lord is the true judge of men.' Turning, the Father began to pace the room, his expression reflecting some deep inner conflict.

Jamie watched the priest, mesmerised by the undulating motion of his robes which hid his feet and made his gliding movements appear mysterious and unearthly. He felt wearier now than at any point in his life. Tired of the long hours of combat and instruction, of the physical punishment and the nagging worry of causing an injury to Morven's father, but most of all weary of the damnable waiting.

At length, heedless of the puddles of sooty water pooled at his feet, the priest sat down again, and the lines of his face relaxed a fraction. 'I knew yer father,' he said absently. His eyes seemed to focus on something more distant than the drawn face before him. Jamie sat forward, weariness forgotten. 'An honourable man, great was the loss to the glen when he left us. But to lose another such as him …' He fell silent, jaws clamped together, and stared hard at the sodden floor.

Jamie was still searching for something to say in return when the Father lifted his head and regarded him with troubled eyes. 'God forgive me,' he sighed. 'Give me yer hands, lad.'

Puzzled, Jamie extended his hands, wincing as the Father gripped them fiercely. Then, lowering his head, the father closed his eyes and began to pray:

'Almighty Father, whose power no creature is able to resist. It belongeth to thee to justly punish sinners and to be merciful to those who truly repent.' He moved his right hand to the top of Jamie's head and gently bent down the dark head. 'Lord, I humbly beseech thee to protect and deliver thy servant James Innes from the hands of his enemies and thine. Confound their devices, Lord, that armed with thy blessing thy servant James may prevail. Bless him, Lord, to do this and to glorify thee, who art the true giver of all victory, through thy own son, Jesus Christ our Lord. Amen.'

Letting Jamie's head up, the Father cleared his throat. 'And fer what it's worth lad, I give ye my own benediction too.' He drew the silver crucifix up over his head and slipped it quickly over Jamie's. Sitting back, he drew trembling fingers across the now empty space at his throat. 'May the Lord have mercy on both our souls.'

There was silence in the room now, even the thunderous deluge outside had ceased abruptly, and Jamie looked up to find Morven standing stock-still in the doorway. She peeled back the layer of sodden plaid that covered her head and shoulders and, staggering slightly, fell back against the wall. Her face was pale as bone, and she made a small sound in her throat, then hid her face in her hands.

'Thank ye, Father,' Jamie croaked.

***

There was little respite in the rain, it fell most of that night and the next day with remorseless monotony, interrupted only by the occasional burst of more savage hail. A period of quieter rain would follow each such volley, but by evening there'd been no let-up in the deluge. Morven pulled down the kerchief that covered her mouth and nose. The air in the threshing barn was foul, dense with dust and chaff and moisture; thick as soup.

'Are ye a'right, Morven?' Alec lowered his flail, peering anxiously at her through the haze. The skin of his face, what she could see of it beyond his own protective covering, was streaked with dust and sweat, and flecks of chaff were lodged in his brows and clothing. She imagined her own appearance would look something similar.

'I thought I heard something, was all.'

The whicker of a pony came again, and Alec gestured to Rowena and the others to cease threshing and peered from the barn. Two men were approaching.

'In here,' he called, and a moment later Ghillie and Dougal Riach shook themselves in the shelter of the barn.

Rowena's apprehension was immediately palpable, and the two men glanced warily at her, then scanned the other dusty faces with scorn.

'He's nae among ye, then.' Dougal grinned. 'Thon fool, Innes? It's hard to tell, ye all look the same.'

'Aye, like rats in a millhoose.' Ghillie sniggered at his own wit. 'Where is he then, cowering in some hole?'

Alec lowered the covering from his mouth. 'What business is it of yours? Some bidding o' yer master?' He eyed the two men with contempt. Neither had made any attempt to comply with the customs of Highland civility, and each man's bonnet remained plastered to his head, feathers hanging limply.

'A message,' Ghillie replied.

'I'll see he gets it.'

'To be given to him alone.'

Ghillie glanced at Dougal, dripping by his side, and shot a look back out of the barn. The rain had turned to hail again and hissed sharply in the yard; he shivered. 'Ach, suppose 'twould do nae harm.'

Dougal shrugged doubtfully.

Plainly dredging the words of the message from some stagnant region of his brain he rarely employed, Ghillie frowned in concentration. 'Mister Hugh McBeath will await the pleasure o' his satisfaction at the appointed place, dawn the morn wi' his seconds.' At that, he beamed and glanced at Dougal, who was also beaming. 'Who will be in attendance to mak' sure the rules o' combat are ad … adhered to. Mister Innes may select twa attendants who are to be unarmed and are nae to interfere wi' the course o' the contest unless their man be mortally wounded, in which case they may carry him awa' and minister to his wounds. Naeone else to be present, nae pistols, dirks, nor *sgian dubhs* to be carried, the opponent to be searched aforehand.'

'*Both* opponents, ye mean,' said Alec.

Ghillie blinked. 'Are ye questioning the integrity o' an officer o' His Majesty's Excise?'

'I am. And his twa seconds.'

Ghillie's eyes narrowed, and he advanced on Alec, his hand closing tight around his throat. 'A young whelp that canna yet bite,' he hissed, 'would do well to mind and nae show his teeth.'

'And an ill-natured dog that's aye snarling would do well to put awa' his teeth,' said a voice from the doorway.

It was Alastair MacPherson who'd spoken, his wife Elspeth and four grown sons standing beside him.

'What business is it o' yours?' scowled Dougal. He nudged Ghillie, who reluctantly released his hold on Alec.

'None but that of a guid neighbour. My business is with Mistress Forbes, so I'll thank ye, if ye're done, to let me on wi' it.'

'Aye, well,' Ghillie thrust out his chin but backed off all the same. 'See thon brazen-heid gets the message.'

They were gone a moment later, Ghillie turning at the door to level a malignant stare in Alec's direction. Morven let her breath out. Beneath the dust, Alec's face had paled, but he gave her a faltering smile, and she attempted one in return.

'An unwholesome pair,' observed the miller. 'But rhymeless wi'out their master, 'twould seem.'

It soon transpired the miller had brought an empty cart to take away Rowena's grain for grinding.

''Tis the least we could do,' Elspeth told Rowena. 'After thon wee outbreak o' the smallpox ye treated me fer back in the spring.'

Rowena let out a choked little laugh, and Sarah moved to support her mother, laying a steadying arm around her waist. 'But I canna pay ye,' Rowena replied.

'Ye already have.' Alastair signalled for his sons to begin shovelling the grain into sacks.

Rowena seemed quite overcome, and it was Sarah who came to grasp the miller's hand. 'We're indebted to ye.' Her eyes strayed over the man's shoulder to where Alec stood watching her.

'Och, away,' Elspeth tutted.

***

Hugh McBeath dined alone that night, as he'd done every night since the death of his wife. The venison was tough and the claret, acquired from McGillivray's cellar by the factor's own manservant, Joseph Gunn, was corked and sour. It was only last March, in a blizzard, that Dougal had caught Gunn's youngest getling attempting to cross the ladder trail with a half-dozen kegs of illicit whisky. Since then, of course, the supply of claret and brandy-wine to McBeath's own home had been assured. He pushed away the glass with a grimace of distaste. It might've been as well to hand the boy over after all.

Reaching instead for whisky, his hand shook, and he gulped at the liquor, greedy for the numbing sensation he knew it would bring. He checked his pocket watch – still early. It was cold in the dining-room, but he loosened his waistcoat, aware of a disturbing quickening of his pulse and a shortness of breath.

'WHAT?' he barked, as the little maid rapped on the door and then immediately entered. 'Have I no told you to wait till you're called?'

'Oh, aye … beggin' yer pardon, Mister McBeath.'

'What is it?'

'I was wondering, sir,' she said, nervously lifted his barely touched plate, 'if ye've done wi' me fer the night, should I mebbe be getting away hame now?'

'Aye,' he said, waving his hand irritably at her. 'Go. *Go*!'

Once the girl had fled, he sat back, snorting to himself. It seemed the Balintoul gossips had done their work and there was scarce a household in the township hadn't heard of the morn's work. The girl was afraid of him, he'd long seen it in her eyes and been entertained by it. Let her run then and be damned with her.

Lifting the whisky, he climbed the stairs to his bedchamber, glad of the warmer air in the upstairs rooms and set about preparing certain items for the business ahead of him. From his wardrobe, he chose a pair of loose-fitting breeches and a linen shirt, and to wear beneath the shirt a semmit of a closely woven material packed with wadding. It wouldnae stop a stabbing sword but would at least deflect a slashing one.

These he set out on the chair at the foot of his bed. Boots and a top-coat followed, and he topped the tidy pile with a black lum hat. Bending, he unlocked the top drawer of the cabinet beside the bed and removed a silver inlaid pistol, powder and shot, and a pair of short stabbing daggers. The daggers he would conceal in special folds made into his breeches together with the primed pistol, which he would strap within his top-coat. Lastly, he looked out his sword, well-oiled and reputably unbreakable.

'Send me to hell, will ye?' He smiled slowly. 'I dinnae think it.'

He returned to the wardrobe and with trembling fingers, unlocked the door at the far side, leaning forward to run his hands over the luxurious silks and brocades hanging there. Some he'd bought from a merchant in Aberdeen, but most of the garments he'd ordered from a seamstress in Edinburgh's Canongate. Bought twenty years ago for his young bride-to-be, Rowena Innes.

Stroking the sumptuous fabrics, faded and dusty now, he groaned softly and bent to rummage among the items at the bottom of the cupboard, finding, at last, the lacy whalebone corset he'd bought one breezy Lammas Day in Perth. Flimsy, indeed almost transparent, it had long been a yearning of his to dress her in it and have her wait upon him until he could stand it no longer and would have to jerk and wrench it from her.

He lay down on the bed, a growing restlessness in his flesh, and fingered the delicate undergarment. His religion, indeed his superstition, told him to have no part of her, to take no indulgence with her, but 'twas far too late for that. Bedevilled and bewitched he was, cursed with her fixation, and after so long the wait was near over. Lang – he cursed, still calling the man that – would stand no chance armed with the second-rate blade he'd seen him carry, and with the last obstacle removed from his way …

He sat up, reaching for the whisky. She'd see sense, wouldnae let herself be dispossessed, there were the getlings to consider, though he'd no use for them here. But he'd find places for them … somewhere. And keeping his bed warm would allow her no room for witchery and the like, he'd see to that. He shuddered and bent to pour more whisky, conscious that beneath his excitement lay an unwanted sense of dread, a panic almost. Whisky would quell it, and he waited for the spirit's restorative powers to take effect, for the familiar stirrings that were a feature of his life to return to him.

When his hands had steadied, he lay back down again feeling his heart bound against the stuffing of the bed. There would be no sleep tonight, the restlessness was too great, the craving too deep in his flesh. He rechecked his pocket watch, then, groaning, reached to rub at himself.

***

That night Sarah was obliged to share her bed with Rory and wee Donald. Crammed head to toe in the narrow box-bed with them, hemmed in by a tangle of blankets and limbs, she waited out the night until in the pressing darkness she could wait no longer.

The room's tiny window admitted a pale, unearthly kind of light, and, watching it through the long hours, she'd felt the tension build in her muscles, the clamminess grow in her palms, though her mind had reasoned the dawn must still be some way off and she shouldna be hasty.

It took a further twenty minutes of painstaking inching to at last extricate herself and, heart pounding, she waited for signs that she'd disturbed the sleeping boys. Neither moved. Rory remained face down on the bed, limbs asprawl, while Donald's face was upturned, flushed and untroubled and cooried into his brother.

She took a quick measure of the room, of the shapes just visible in the darkness. At the far side where William slept there were now three forms: Alec sleeping nose to tail with William while Jamie lay on the floor, too restless to seek the company of others. His breathing was even now, and she sensed that he slept at last, although it had taken an immeasurable length of time and she'd begun to fret he'd not sleep at all but would sit up the entire night praying and staring into the darkness.

She pulled her gown and arisaid from beneath her bed where she'd stowed them and, feeling in the darkness, found the fir-candles and flint she'd wrapped in the woven wool. Her fingers trembled, but she quickly slipped into her clothes, reassuring herself that the hoard of pignuts she'd gathered while the others discussed the final details of the duel was still safely stored in the pocket of her gown. There was little hope the dun would come to her without a bittie enticement.

Tiptoeing to the door, she stooped to peer at Jamie's prone figure curled on the earthen floor. He wouldna understand, would try to stop her, maybe even curse her, but then she supposed he did that anyhow and a bittie more would make nae difference. Her scheming seemed that petty now, that contemptible.

The door latch creaked, the hinges too, but she'd thought on that and earlier greased them into silence. What was less certain was how deeply those in the other room slept – if at all. She pressed her ear to the grained oak but could detect nothing above the wee settling noises the old cot-house made in the night. It had been her mother's suggestion that the MacRaes sleep the night at Tomachcraggen, all of them, nae just Malcolm and Alec, Jamie's seconds, and they'd agreed readily enough. It complicated matters though, made it a deal more trouble to slip away unseen and unheard.

The door opened soundlessly, and she stood in the shadow of it, breath aquiver, surveying the scene in the feeble glow from the fire. Malcolm and Grace slept in her mother's bed and wee grunts and snores came from there, though she could see little of Malcolm beyond a dark heap and nothing at all of Grace. Morven lay on Jamie's makeshift bed. He'd offered it to her, had wished to make her comfortable, Sarah supposed, or to in some way make up for what he'd do come morning, or just, perhaps, to feel her close to him somehow, and she felt a twinge of old jealousy at that thought, though no more than a twinge. Morven suffered as she did – maybe even more.

Morven lay still though, doubtless aching with weariness after a day in the threshing barn, and she sifted the darkness for her mother, realising with a pang of alarm there was no sign of her, no dark shape bedded down on the floor. She closed the door and crept into the room, clutching the back of a chair to steady herself. Something brushed her hand, something curling and alive. She snatched her hand away, choking off the cry in her throat. Her mam sat upright in the chair, her hair let down in a dark mass of curls. She made no movement though, and Sarah bent her ear to the back of the chair, breath held, and listened to the rhythm of her breathing. Even it was, deep and regular. She swayed a little in relief. Her mam was apt to do that at times, to sit the night through worrying ower some sick bairn or some auld bodach breathing his last, and she'd find her in the morning slumped and stiff with cold. The wonder was she'd found sleep the night at all, but Sarah's relief was too great to ponder over it for long. Time was a-wasting.

She moved to the door and felt for her boots in the darkness. Tucking them under her arm, she lifted the latch and cast a last lingering look at her mother sat in the shadows. The night's mission would bring no remedy to her mother's plight, that was beyond her engineering, but it might at least save her cousin's life, and that alone made it worth the doing. Might right some of her wrongs. Duelling was illegal after all, and McGillivray would have none o' it … she hoped.

She closed the door behind her, soft as butter to the knife, and sniffed at the night air. The rain was past, and the air smelled earthy now with a whiff of something queer upon it, something that made her shiver. Away to the east where the dawn would come, the sky was inky black, but in the west, from some source near Sithean Wood, a puzzling light came, a queer pale lustre. Pulling her boots on, she shivered and hastened away.

CHAPTER TWENTY-ONE

ON A SPIT OF SHINGLE at the edge of Inchfindy ford, Sarah brought the garron she'd taken to an uneasy halt. She cocked her head, straining her ears in the darkness, and at what she heard the breath rattled fearfully in her throat. The pony snorted and whickered nervously, its hooves slipping and clopping on the wet pebbles.

'Steady, ye great brute.' She leant to stroke the rough hair of its neck. Yet the pony's fear was strangely reassuring; it meant the distant clanging was no figment of her imagination, though this was surely a night fer trickeries of the mind. The sound was an earthly one carried on the still night air, a calling from the chapel, a warning perhaps.

Shivering, she held aloft the last of the fir-candles, its feeble flicker throwing a tiny pool of light on the stretch of river before her. From the shadow of trees beyond the river the dark outline of Inchfindy Hall arose; with a fearful little cry, she pressed the garron on into the surging water.

***

Dulled by distance yet pressing in its tone, the ringing bell drew many a godly crofter from his bed that night to fret over what the calling, at that hour and on a day other than a Sunday, might possibly mean. But for Morven, crushed by despair and crippled by an aching weariness, the darkness had brought only welcome oblivion. And it was only later, once a faint greyness had pushed the shadows back to the corners of the room and roused the warblers in the birk-woods outside, that she stirred into consciousness; woken by the flare of peat on the firestone and the murmur of strained voices.

Dread had threaded through her sleep like some parasitic worm, and she sat bolt upright now, her stomach churning. *She had slept.* While the hours slipped away, she'd meant to pray for him, to try and bind Jamie to her with her will, yet her bone-weary body had rebelled, had failed her. And with a sick dawning, she recognised the appointed hour was near upon them.

The twinkle of fir-candles proliferated around the room and Rowena's face, dark-eyed and ghostly, appeared through the gloom. "Tis time,' she said softly. 'Jamie'll be needing a bite to eat, and I've a tonic a-brewing fer him, a drop vervain fer a clear head.' She nodded to the doorway where Jamie stood, already dressed in sark and russet plaid, a striking figure in the flicker of the firelight.

His eyes were upon her, searching, a poignancy in them, a rawness he'd kept from her these last days that spoke of his sorrow and regret, and she'd to turn from the sight of it lest the tenuous grip she had on herself should desert her. Every nerve skirled at her of his closeness and mourned the transience of it, every fibre pressed her to go on bended knee and plead for a change of heart, yet, stiffening herself, she knew better than to shame him so.

'Naething heavy fer the lad, mind.' Her father's voice seemed overly loud in the tense greyness. 'Just enough fare to keep heart and limb strong and nothing fer myself, I've no stomach fer meal.'

Morven's own stomach curdled at the thought of food, and she imagined only the boys would manage anything, their unbridled excitement bringing its own appetite. She'd slept in her clothes and wound on her arisaid now, the room still cold, or was it, perhaps, just her blood that ran cold? She crossed the room and stared out of the tiny window. Somewhere out there in the darkness, like loitering wolves, the gauger and his men would be waiting. *Lord*, she silently prayed. Protect him, *let him come back to me.*

Jamie sat stiffly at the table, Grace fretting over him, and when she turned to look at him again, he no longer exposed his grief so rawly but shielded it, guarded his pain at what the day's deed would lose him in a grim unflinching expression, one hatred and injustice had roused within him. Her father patted him roughly on the shoulder and sat down at his side.

'A sup o' something will help chase awa' the trembles and the shakes, lad.' His face was tense and drawn. Jamie nodded, but there was no trace of tremor in the hands he rested on the table, he was focused on what lay ahead.

Rowena set down the steaming infusion, the swirling green liquor a stimulant that she doubtless hoped would relieve any lingering nerves. Known as the witch's herb, vervain was a potent elixir capable of empowering any charm or invocation, and of bestowing both protection and a blessing.

'She's gone!' Rory stood in the doorway in his sarktails. 'Sarah.

Gone and never as much as stirred the bedclaes nor gave rouse to wee Donald or myself.' He shook his head incredulously. 'Spirited herself away in the night and us trussed in thon box-bed like tappit-hens in a coop.'

Alec and William appeared at his shoulder, both bleary-eyed and bewildered. 'It's true,' said Alec. He pushed past Rory and hurried out into the dark, returning a moment later. 'The dun gelding's gone too. My father's pony.' He turned to Rowena. 'Did ye know about this? Did ye send Sarah off someplace?'

White-faced, Rowena shook her head. 'I know nothing of this, I swear it. Yet … she's been stretched ower-tight inside, Alec. I felt it in her.'

'She'd nae do anything daft?' There was a catch in Alec's voice.

'No. Och no, lad.'

Yet despite her denials, Rowena stiffened perceptibly at Alec's words, and Morven had the feeling her friend would've fretted far more had morning's break, in all its significance, not been so close at hand. Rather, the widow forced a note of calm to her voice.

'She's aye been dark, I'm sure ye ken that, Alec. And though she's taken real ill ower all this, the girl's no fool, wouldna do harm to herself if that's what ye're thinking. Likely she just couldna abide waiting here on nettle-stalks wi' all of us. She'll have taken herself off someplace quiet-like, till the day's dealings are ower and done wi'.'

Rowena's answer was half bluff Morven recognised, designed to ease her own concerns as much as those of Alec or anyone else. And perhaps to smooth the water for Jamie, to ensure her kinsman remained clear in thought without Sarah's bizarre disappearance rippling his focus. Yet the thoughts of those in the room were all with Jamie and the fate that awaited him, and there was scarce thought to spare for Sarah and her games. Even from Alec, who nodded at Rowena in concession.

Jamie made no comment on Sarah's disappearance, but at the haunted look in his eyes, Morven silently cursed the girl. What was she up to now? She'd seemed that shamed these last days, that embittered with herself, and yet she *was* a dark one, and there was nae mistake there.

Her father snorted contemptuously and without looking up, continued to buff flecks of mutton fat into the broadsword's murderous blade. 'Is there to be naething fer the lad to eat, then?' he growled.

***

The air was cold enough to mist their breath, the sky clear with a growing radiance beneath the bands of cloud in the east, although the light was still grainy with the lingering texture of night. Added to the saturated ground there had been a heavy dew, the first frosts not far away, it being September already, and the two women could've followed the dark trail of sodden and crushed undergrowth easily enough, even had they not known exactly which route to take.

'Are ye certain this is the way?' Rory hissed.

'Aye, but keep yer voice down,' Morven warned. 'There's nae telling what McBeath might do should he find us.'

Those had been her father's parting words, and they rang ominously in her head. Faced with his daughter's stupefying yet iron-fast resolve to attend the duel, her father had blustered and near blown steam from his ears at the outrageous notion.

'Say what ye will. I'm coming wi' ye.'

'Aye,' Rowena added. 'I wish to be there too.'

'God's blood!' Malcolm got to his feet. ''Tis no place fer women. I've never heard the like, 'tis … 'tis scandalous!'

'Maybe, but that's how it is.'

Malcolm's face reddened, and he drank in a deep draught of air to calm himself. 'It's nae right, but even leaving the rights and wrongs aside, I could scarce stand by and let ye witness what's done here today – to either man.' He turned to Grace for support, although she gave him none. 'I'd not wish that on any woman, least of all my ane daughter. No,' he shook his head emphatically. 'I canna countenance such a thing.'

'Ye dinna understand,' Morven returned. '*I* canna countenance waiting here, helpless and blind and kenning nothing of what's happening.' She looked at Jamie. 'Bearing the fact of what's to happen is torment enough.'

Jamie's nod was infinitesimal, but she knew he understood. Malcolm turned to stare at him.

'Let her come, Malcolm, for my sake, them both, forbye. Hidden well, mind.'

Malcolm stared at him for what seemed an age, Jamie returning his look, until at last the crofter raised his eyes to the heavens with an exasperated sigh.

'Follow on, then! Only hang well back from harm's way and make ne'er a sound, no matter what ye see.'

Morven nodded grimly.

Jamie checked the fastening of his sword belt; his breathing was quick, a quiver to it, and when he met her eyes he swallowed, the lines of his face taut with strain.

'Jamie.' But he stilled her with a finger to her lips.

''Tis a need of no words, we have,' he said softly. 'Once I told ye to forget me, yet,' his throat contracted, 'yet weakness bids me ask that ye keep me in yer prayers, fer a while at least, though I've no right to ask it.' He touched his hand to the hilt of the great sword. 'I mean to spit the gauger, but whether I do or not we'll nae meet beyond this day, I think, save in my dreams.'

'I've the pony loaded.' Rory stood in the doorway, cold air steaming his breath. Through the half-open door, Morven could see her father's bay mare, saddled and packed with Jamie's meagre belongings, ready for the road.

'Lord,' she gasped over the lump in her throat. The urge to clutch at his shirtsleeves overwhelmed her, but the flicker that crossed her mother's face stilled her hand, and instead she whispered fiercely, 'Lord protect ye, Jamie Innes. Till we meet again, in your dreams or mine.'

His face betrayed a fleeting moment of desolation before he gained mastery over it and, tightening his jaw, nodded almost curtly to her. Afraid to trust his voice, he turned away to find his kinswoman standing dark-eyed and stoic, something in her expression disturbingly familiar. A glimpse at the fibre of the Highland folk he'd found here, reflected in her eyes, a window on the woman's steadfast acceptance of all that others' ignorance and suspicion had brought down on her. Or was it rather an insight into his own soul and all that pride and honour had brought him to? He swallowed, feeling the weight of misery his actions had inflicted, and, sensing that despair, he could summon no fine words for his aunt either, only murmurs of regret that he pressed gruffly upon her.

'Ye'll see my aunt safe, sir?' He turned almost with relief to the waiting crofter.

'Ye have my word on it.' Malcolm cleared his throat of its customary harshness. 'Where is it ye'll head, then, lad?'

'North, I'm thinking, to the land of Ross.'

'A fine land, so it's told.' Malcolm firmed his jaw, and half turned from the upright young man to rummage in his sporran.

Morven heard the clink of silver and could have kissed her father's grizzled cheek for assuming Jamie would have the chance to head anywhere. She watched him offer Jamie a fistful of coins.

'Take it, lad, little though it is, 'twill pay a night or twa's lodgings till ye've yerself settled in work.'

Jamie faltered. He thought much of the grim-faced crofter, considered him a kinsman almost, although there was no shared blood between them, only a shared hatred for McBeath. But looking into the older man's face, earnest and stern, he found he couldn't shame him by turning aside his charitable goodwill. His own pride was not so intractable, and he understood the gesture, sensed the crofter's admiration, maybe even the man's envy at his opportunity, and the money would be welcome, ill though Malcolm could afford it.

He nodded. 'I'd count it an honour, sir.'

Malcolm turned away and spoke roughly, more to himself than to his thrawn daughter. 'Mind now, there's nae telling what McBeath might do should ye be discovered – keep yerselves well hidden.' With that, he clapped a hand on Jamie's shoulder and, nodding to a whey-faced Alec, led the way out.

***

How Rory had contrived to accompany them, Morven still couldn't quite fathom, but in the end, it had been easier, not to mention quicker, to relent and allow it. And she had to admit she felt a little easier for his company, his solid maleness, even at thirteen years, was oddly comforting. He crashed ower-much through the briars and brambles for her liking though, next to Rowena's almost silent progress, and she checked him at last with a hand on his forearm and breathed, 'Can ye nae heed where ye're putting thon muckle great feet of yours, Rory? Ye've snapped more stems than a hart put to the chase.'

'Sorry, Morven,' he pulled a woeful face.

She nodded, and they crept forward again.

The appointed place lay over the brow of a squat little hill, a stretch of bare weedy ground gnawed by sheep, scratched by hens, and swept clear of treacherous debris by William only the day before. A thick forest of birch-wood, pine, and juniper scrub hemmed the place, and it was to within this covering that the three cautiously made their way.

Morven shivered and glanced at Rowena, the fine hairs on her nape beginning to rise. Rowena nodded back tensely and roved with her eyes, indicating her own awareness of a watchfulness in the trees, a rustling and snapping of twigs that owed nothing to Rory. The air was damp and oppressive, and it seemed the forest birds had taken flight, leaving behind the silence of bated breath and a whispering suspense that raised the gooseflesh beneath her gown.

It was Rowena that saw them first, and at her sudden stillness Morven and Rory froze by her side. Through a break in the trees, Morven could see Ghillie's head and shoulders and almost all of Dougal, lounging against a tree at the far side of the clearing, his head cocked to his companion. She drew back behind an old birch tree. With the barest of movement, Rowena reached out and guided Rory further into the tangle of scrub. The women exchanged a fearful look. Unlike her da and brother, these men carried muskets, long hunting muskets that each held up to their shoulder, an upper corner of plaid looped over the lock of the weapon to protect it from the damp air and drip of trees. Wide shoulder belts testified that both carried swords.

Worming around the tree and peering from behind a great gall sprouting from its trunk, Morven risked a better look. Close by the men, she could see two garrons tethered and browsing contentedly. Alongside stood a far larger animal that she took to be McBeath's mount. She drew back again to watch with one eye, her cheek pressed hard against the tree's cankerous growth. The hirelings had plainly been set there to keep watch, and while they displayed a degree of swaggering importance, she saw that beneath cock-feathered bonnets their faces were wary and alert.

Dougal scratched absently at himself, then glanced about, hastily returning the pleats of his kilt to within the realms of decency. As his plaid fell back into place, she noted the swing of dirk at his girdle.

'Christ!' whispered Rory. 'They're both armed to the teeth.'

'Shh.' Rowena sank into the bracken. 'I hear Jamie.'

Morven could hear him too and, holding her breath, lowered herself into the sodden undergrowth. Hitching her skirts, she crawled on hands and knees to a fallen bracken-sprouting log, flattening herself behind it. Most of the duelling ground was now in her field of vision. She gestured to Rory to follow her lead, and he joined her a moment later, face sparked green, a dark trail heralding his furtive slither through the moss and the cowberry.

'There they are,' he whispered needlessly.

From her position in the wet bracken, Morven could see the back of her father's head, and Alec now too, waiting at the near edge of the clearing only a matter of feet away, their backs to the trees. Her stomach lurched; Jamie already stood in the centre of the ground, facing the squat figure of the exciseman, his face set and fists clenched at his side. McBeath was dressed – indeed to Morven's mind seemed a deal over-dressed for what they intended – in breeks and polished boots, a black lum-hat, and thick black coat. But it was the expression he wore that chilled her most. Suffused with blood, his whiskered face trembled and jerked in what could only be a mighty rage.

'How in God's name did a common muck-the-byre come by a sword like that?' His harsh words carried clearly on the still air, and he pointed an accusing finger at the great scabbard hanging at Jamie's side. ''Tis hardly the blade of a landless byre-lad, a mere heather-lowper!' Deliberately he used the hated Lowland term. 'Aye, and a lying cheating one at that. Was it witchery? Is that how ye came by such a sword?'

Jamie didn't raise his voice, yet the three hidden in the bracken heard every word.

''Twas given me.'

'Given you? By whom?'

'By me, ye black divil!' Malcolm made no movement toward the pair measuring each other in the centre of the ground but shrugged away Alec's restraining hand. 'And 'twas given to me by my father, and to him by his father afore that.' Pulling himself straight, he squared his shoulders and levelled a black stare at the exciseman. 'Heather-lowpers all.'

'By you? Delnabreck? Another muck-the-byre!' McBeath's voice rose in an incredulous little laugh. 'It'll be as old as the hills then, 'tis a wonder it's no long since rusted away.' He shook his head scornfully, but it was plain he was shaken by this turn of events, that he'd not expected his opponent to come so well armed, and was now realising that armed with such a blade, Jamie's reach would exceed his own by a good few inches.

''Twas given fer the contest,' Jamie said with painstaking patience. 'And auld as the hills it may be, yet it'll nae have escaped yer notice the hills are still here while, as God is my witness, I intend to make sure you're nae fer much longer!' He inhaled forcibly and said on a calmer note, ''Tis an equal measure to your own blade, McBeath. Or do ye question what's undeniably true?'

The exciseman's colour had deepened, and a jagged little scar stood out purple above the growth of beard on his cheek. Turning to his two gaping assistants, he snapped, 'I'll have that insolent cow herder searched. *Now*, by God!'

Dougal started into hasty activity, Ghillie grinning and drawing a pistol from beneath his jerkin. 'A pleasure 'twill be.' He winked cockily at Jamie.

A twitch of muscle at Jamie's temple was all that betrayed his irritation, but he raised his hands obligingly, revealing the folds of his sark hanging slackly. 'I carry only the sword. The weapon of yer choice, McBeath, if ye mind.'

'We'll see soon enough how true that is!'

Jamie shrugged, his eyes glittering dangerously. 'Search me then, and have done with it.'

Ghillie's search was a deal more thorough than was needed, Dougal holding his musket, and when finally he slid his hands up beneath Jamie's kilts, Jamie growled at him,

'That'll do ye. Ye dinna suppose I'd stoop so low as to conceal arms about myself?' His eyes moved to the hireling's master, and he cocked a scornful eyebrow. 'But now, to keep things on an even keel, I'll be having your man searched, eh?'

McBeath laughed uproariously at that, even the twitching Dougal breaking into a nervous grin. He jerked his head in the direction of Malcolm and Alec, standing silent and rigid beneath the trees. 'Ye dinnae expect me to consent to a like treatment from old Delnabreck there and the whelp?'

'I do.'

'Then you're a bigger fool than I thought. 'Tis me'll have them searched.'

'Damned if ye will!' snarled Malcolm, taking a step toward the livid-faced exciseman.

'Enough of this.' Jamie warned Malcolm off with a flick of his head. He fixed the exciseman with a cold stare. 'This is betwixt you and me McBeath. I'm tired o' yer games. Ye've made it plain enough how little meaning ye place upon yer honour, yet …' he drew breath, loath to reveal the hurt he carried within him. 'To me, honour means all. Ye've wronged my kinfolk and fer that I intend to make ye pay.'

There was a snort from McBeath, and Jamie stared hard at him, his patience whistling away down his nose along with his breath.

''Tis satisfaction I've come fer. By God, I'll have it from ye in blood!' He drew his sword with a sound like a scythe cutting through hay. 'Stand and face me if ye're man enough!'

The exciseman drew the length of his own sword, the rising sun lighting it with a wicked gleam. 'Man enough and more!' He wet his lips with a flick of tongue. 'Man enough to deal with the likes of you, Innes, and still have sap left for more pleasurable business like the servicing of your kinswoman. 'Twill be three months since I spoke with her of that, but once we're wed, I'll be expecting her on the flat of her back a sight more often than that.' He sneered with more than a hint of relish. 'How think you she'll fare as my bed-mate? A willing mare, I'll wager.'

Jamie's face darkened, blotches breaking out on his neck. He made a half-strangled sound in his throat as he struggled to give vent to his fury, then, with a feral howl, lunged at the exciseman.

Through the roar of blood in his head, Jamie heard the feral sound but didn't recognise it as his own. A bloodlust overtook him, filling his lungs, swarming up his throat and rendering him senseless to anything but the urge to strike down the foul creature. At the look of startled terror that flashed across the exciseman's face, he experienced a stab of satisfaction, then the gauger leapt back wildly, dropping a hand to the ground to balance himself and brought his sword up in a desperate attempt to slew away the lunging blade.

Their swords clashed with a rasping metallic ring, and the force of his attack brought Jamie thundering down on his opponent, off-balance and breathing hard. McBeath had his sword up again and took a slicing swing at Jamie's midriff, the blade slashing the empty air, the draught it created pulling Jamie up sharply.

He grunted in shock. The gauger was quicker than his squatness suggested and a deal deadlier. He'd need better judgment than that, would need to take more cunning stock of his opponent. They circled each other, Jamie striving to clear his head of the murderous rage that fogged his judgment. He could hear Malcolm's voice urging him on, though whether the crofter did so in reality or whether he summoned the words himself, unwittingly from memory, he could no longer tell.

Keep yer guard up, lad. Watch fer yer chance! Should the bastard go doon, be after him to finish it. Straight after him. He'd be after you – depend on it!

He parried a cutting blow with the flat of his sword, his wrist and finger bones dirling at the impact. *Dinna take the full force, twill brak' yer wrist – parry it awa'! Watch fer him reaching ower-far. 'Tis you'll hae the edge there!*

The savagery of his own attack surprised him. His chest ached with the pounding of his heart, his wrist and forearm screamed at him, but he embraced the pain, absorbed it into his hatred, the physical reality of it preventing his slide into reckless folly. More than once he hurled the creature away with a great grunting heave, panting with the effort, the stink of the man's breath foul in his nostrils. Then they circled each other again, the tip of his sword searching for a way in, weaving and striking in relentless pursuit, grating in protest against that of the exciseman.

Steadily the thrum of blood in his ears quietened, and he heard the guiding voice, clear now and insistent. *Hold yer legs wide and firm so ye canna be wrong-footed. Mind and breathe! Watch fer signs o' him tiring, but dinna lose sight o' that blade!*

As the heat of rage receded, so his grace and agility returned, and he was able to sidestep McBeath's thrusts, darting away, then engaging with lightening ferocity, slitting the black stuff of the gauger's coat and opening a bloody gash in the flesh beneath his earlobe. All else shrank from his consciousness but the sinuous silver streak the exciseman wielded and the expanse of buttoned topcoat, flayed and tattered, that danced tantalisingly before his eyes. McBeath was stumbling and panting now, his hat gone and the hated face stark with fear.

Now's yer chance, lad. The divil's flagging. Move in to finish it!

It was true, he saw it in the gauger's desperate grimace and slashed at the hated features, thinking only to wipe the scorn from the loathsome face. An image of his own father arose before him, bent under the strain of hauling a cart laden with his wife and worldly possessions together with his young son far from the land of their kin. The poignancy of the image drove a storm of seething blood around his heart, and he bayed with fury and struck at the exciseman, opening a great rent in the man's topcoat and on into the flesh beneath, blood quickly leaching out.

The exciseman shrieked, swiping wildly at his opponent, then lurched away, shouting for his henchmen.

CHAPTER TWENTY-TWO

'Morven!' Rowena grasped her by the shoulder and gave her a little shake. 'Morven. Look, lass.'

She was trembling, her chin pressed hard against the peeling log, her fingers stiff and nerveless. She daren't risk taking her eyes from the clashing figures for fear it was nothing more than the force of her will that kept them from killing each other. 'What? What is it?'

'I dinna rightly ken. See fer yerself.'

'Thundering great flames o' hell!' swore Rory, starting in fright at her elbow. And then Morven turned herself and could do nothing but stare and stare.

They were crowding through the trees, stooping under low boughs, tramping over sodden bracken and branch. Crofters and herdsmen. Cot-wives and their bairns, babes happed at their breasts. Young and old, and, stalking before them like some staffed and be-robed vision from the Holy Bible, the diminutive figure of Father Ranald Stewart.

Rory was on his feet now, still spouting a stream of profane oaths, a look of incredulity on his face. Every way she turned, Morven could see folk pressing forward in great hordes, flocking to the edge of the clearing, their faces set grimly.

Craigduthel tipped his bonnet to her as she lay in the wet bracken, then elbowed his way past, an iron-shod pitchfork held upright in his grip. She blinked. She turned to Rowena, but her companion was staring with equal disbelief as the entire McHardy clan streamed past armed with sickles and flails.

'My dears.' The Father hauled them both easily to their feet and clasped their icy hands. 'I pray we're not too late.'

'But ... but what –'

'Now's not the time for explanations,' he said hastily. ''Twas your mother here and the boys kindly showed us to this place.'

Morven twisted around and there she was, blundering through the bracken, wee Donald pulling at her hand. William was tight-faced at her side.

'Morven! Thank God, Morven, but is he …?'

'Still living,' Rowena assured Grace. 'And seemed to have the measure of the exciseman, though I fear it's nae ower yet.'

For a moment the women clung to each other, hungry for the comfort of familiar face and touch, then Morven twisted away. 'But how?' She turned to stare around her.

'Father Ranald,' answered Grace. 'He called together those o' the parish as would come, those that heard the calling, and bid them raise as many of the others as could stomach no more injustice in Stratha'an.' She shook her head with a wide-eyed little shrug. ''Tis what he said. They came by Tomachcraggen asking to be shown here.'

'Is it a battle, it'll be?' Donald turned to hug William excitedly.

'No, dear, I dinna rightly ken what 'twill be.'

From the direction of the duelling ground, angry shouts were ringing out, and the women exchanged a fearful look, then shouldered their way through the crowd.

Morven could hear the Father's voice behind her, but his words were lost in the commotion. What was he doing here, a man of the cloth interfering in a duel? Had he taken leave of his senses? His principles? But more pressing still was the question of the crofting-folk he'd brought with him. When it came down to it, where would they cast their hand in a choice between the exciseman all knew held the factor in his pocket, and the stranger once judged the undoing of them all? But there was no time to dwell on any of that. The crowd was gathering along the tree-fringe, and the women were obliged to join them, squeezing their way through a crush of woollen-clad bodies, jostling for a glimpse of the duelling ground beyond.

'Here,' offered old Jessie MacBride, making a space for them, 'we've a grand view from here.' She was with her even older sister Eliza, their watery eyes sharpened in anticipation. Eliza had brought along her spindle, a thing of great beauty carved from horn, though it was now tucked long forgotten beneath her oxter.

'Whit's that he's saying?' She stretched her scrawny neck, dishevelled hair straggling from beneath a grubby kertch. 'Damned if I can hear the black divil.'

Morven doubted the spinster sisters had come through any genuine desire to uphold the equity of the combat, as the Father had likely done, but suspected their real reasons lay more in an elemental relish of the spectacle.

'I canna be hearing right myself,' she muttered.

274 THE BLOOD AND THE BARLEY

Eliza grunted in disappointment.

McBeath was backed against a small drumlin in the ground, wheezing and bleeding profusely. Around him whirled Dougal and Ghillie, eyeballs near popping from their heads, muskets held ready on bend of elbow.

'What trick is this?' The exciseman turned on Jamie in furious indignation. 'Betwixt you and me, eh?' He swung his sword in a wild gesture at the watching crowds. 'What's all this, then? What of the honour ye made so much of? What o' that, eh?'

The blood pulsed hotly through Jamie's veins and his chest heaved, every fibre of him throbbing with the energy of the fight, yet despite the thrill of the clash, McBeath's barb found its mark. 'I know naught of this!' he growled.

'No?' The gauger narrowed his eyes. 'I think different. If I mind how it went, ye said ye'd have the Lord on yer side. Only, I didnae see then just what ye meant.' He jerked his head at the Father, now standing at the edge of the duelling ground, a spare little man when set against the breadth and girth of the exciseman. 'I didnae realise ye meant *literally*.'

Jamie's nostrils flared. 'This is ….' He cast his eyes over the Father, and the waiting crowd congregated among the trees, then shook his head in confusion. 'I've no notion what this is but it changes nothing, I mean to send ye to hell regardless.'

The exciseman shifted his gaze from Jamie's baffled face to the silent gathering, then back to his opponent. He swallowed, his anger losing some of its substance at the sight of so many crofting-folk ranked grimly along the tree-line. What in God's name did it mean?

'And you told me ye'd have *justice* on your side. Is this it, then? This is *your* notion of justice? A rabble of hill-folk arrayed against me, whipped up by yon false minister and likely the witch-woman as well? This is Innes justice, is it?'

'None o' this is my doing.' Jamie turned in frustration to the priest.

'But,' pressed the gauger, 'ye can hardly deny the outcome's now weighted in your favour. That this is a far cry from the honourable contest you spoke so high-handedly of.'

'It never was that, and well ye ken it!'

The voice was her father's, although he was lost to Morven in the press of people.

'Nae when ye'd yonder sleekit pair kitted out wi' blade and barrel and held ready on yer word.' His voice rose in anger. 'I say let them fight fair, Father, wi' nae paid man to swing the balance!'

A cheer went up from the crowd.

'Aye,' cried another. 'Call off the hirelings, tether them like the dogs they are, and let's hae this settled fair and square!'

Morven turned to Rowena; it was Grant of Achnareave who'd shouted out, the old herdsman who damned Jamie so callously after the Beltane fire. Taken aback by the man's complete change of stance, she moved to voice her astonishment when Rory bellowed in her ear.

'Let's hae the gauger searched as well, Father! He'd oor man raked like a common brigand – let's see what he's got alow that weel-stuffed coat!'

There were shouts of support from the crowd, the mood shifting from one of uncertainty to unmistakeable defiance. Slowly folk began to press forward, muttering and calling out.

'Get back!' shouted Ghillie, raising his musket to his shoulder. 'Get awa', all o' ye, or so help me I'll mak' sun and moon shine through ye!'

'Fer the love of God, man!' Jamie raised his sword in a futile attempt to protect the crowd behind him. With a swing of kilt, he ran the length of the clearing, gesturing wildly, his sword glinting in the risen sun. 'Stand back! I beg ye all, stand clear. I'll have no innocent blood spilt. Christ, man!' He turned on Ghillie. 'Can ye nae see there're women and bairns among this crowd!'

'A damned lynch mob's what I see.'

'Call him off, McBeath! Afore the fool shoots someone.'

The exciseman's face was colourless now, the bones of his features unpleasantly severe beneath a corpse-like complexion. His face twitched, and he stared at Achnareave and the enraged crowd, his mouth gaping. Damn it all, had the world gone mad? The confounded muck-the-byres owed their living to him, yet they were turning on him in droves and with an unwarranted savagery. Did he no allow the smuggling of barley-bree to go on unmolested? At a price maybe, but unmolested all the same. Damn them, their ingratitude was beyond belief!

He drew his gaze along the ragged front line, then swiftly backtracked, his attention centring on one face with a jolt of understanding. She stared back openly, dark-eyed and bold and infinitely fascinating. The woman who possessed his every waking hour. A shiver rippled through his flesh, excitement rising through his innards; what she did to him during the hours of darkness he'd confess to no man. *She* was the reason for the hill-rabble's mutinous mood. Indeed, she was the reason for the hill-rabble. Rowena

Forbes. Witch-woman and tormentor of his soul. The witless fools were but tinder to her spark and the witch had fired them like a swathe of dry heather.

His tongue felt thicker than he'd known it, out of place in his mouth and rougher than any bout of drinking had ever made it, but he swallowed hard, his heart pounding. A show of authority was needed here. Hill-folk, he'd long judged, were of little more value than the cattle they herded and no shrewder than a hirsel o' sheep. Show weakness, and they'd flock to the witch and her kinsman, yet show steel, and they'd soon remember who held the real power. And she could yet be his. Filling his lungs, he tamped down his unease and contrived to raise his voice above the clamour.

'Keep things on an even keel, is it? With a lawless pack baying for my blood? Why, if I'd no the presence o' mind to bring along my seconds here, I might well be swinging from a tree already.' He shook his head. 'I'll no be calling them off.'

The clamour heightened until the Father, half forgotten in the stramash, hailed the crowd in a strident voice. 'I'll have calm! Calm, d'ye hear? We're civil folk and let's nae forget it.'

Father Ranald was in no mood to mince words with the exciseman. He jabbed a finger at Ghillie. 'Should that man kill, Mister McBeath, in front of all these witnesses, God help me but I'll see him hanged and you along wi' him, fer 'tis well known the man does naught that's not the bidding of his paymaster.'

'So ye'd hand me to the pack?'

'I would not. I give ye my word, as a servant o' the Lord, no man here will interfere. Stand yer men down, show ye've no dirk nor blade hidden about yourself, and ye're free to take satisfaction for whatever offence has been caused ye.'

The exciseman's whiskers twitched once more, his face set in a look of perfect incredulity. Was he expected to take the word of an idol-kissing priest? Damn her, but the witch even had the Popish cloth dancing to her jig. Ghillie would stand firm though, and he'd take orders from no saint-loving Father. He shifted his gaze from the balding priest to his rattled attendants.

Ghillie looked back darkly, noted his employer's pallor, the patch of blood spreading through a rent in his coat, the tic beneath his left eye, then glanced at the wrathful priest and lastly turned to survey the waiting crowd.

'Nay,' he muttered, lowering his musket. 'Ye dinna pay me near enough to swing fer ye.'

In an instant, Alec relieved him of his musket, and Morven

observed a flash of satisfaction cross her brother's face. Swiftly he searched the man, then piled the hireling's weaponry upon the pile her father was removing from a more compliant Dougal.

'Well, McBeath?' Jamie's voice rose in challenge. 'Are ye prepared to show ye've no like arsenal stowed about yerself?'

Loosening the laces on his sark, he threw the linen wide and in a bold gesture jerked the garment free and hurled it to the ground. Gasps rang out as all now looked on Jamie's naked flesh, smooth and vulnerable and finely etched with muscle. At his throat hung Father Ranald's silver crucifix.

'Well?'

Swallowing, the exciseman glanced down at his own costume, his hands jerking defensively to the fastenings. The Forbes woman had done this. The cunning temptress had set a trap for him.

''Twas the witch brought me to this. The Forbes woman. She's cursed me that one. Cast a beguilement on me, a fixation that makes me burn with the wanting of her.'

''Tis yer own flesh does that,' Jamie snapped.

'No, I tell ye, this burning's no natural. There's no deliverance from it but to take her to wife.'

'Never!' shouted Rowena. 'I'd sooner be served wi' removal papers and dispossessed than wed to the likes of you.'

At Rowena's outburst, Jamie glanced up, locating her in the crowd and nodded grimly to her. His gaze shifted and lingered a moment on Morven's face, relief at seeing her shining in his eyes.

'And removed you'll be,' McBeath hit back. 'Once the factor hears of your murdering ways – yer witchery. Every one o' my bairns stillborn, every pregnancy blighted by your hand.'

The crowd made a shocked sound like the north wind rushing through the trees.

''Twas God's will, nae mine. I did my best to save them.'

The exciseman shook his head, his face working feverishly. He scanned the crowd, sensing a subtle shift in the sympathies of the rabble stirred by mention of the factor, and perhaps reference to his dead children. He stifled the triumphant twitching of his lips. Could it be that what he'd always considered to be the mindless vagaries of Highland fealty, swayed by distrust of the law and those set to uphold it, might yet come to his aid? Lord, were they no' a flock o' witless sheep? If he could just keep a grip on his nerve, and with a show of bluff, he might yet slip from the witch's snare.

He pulled himself straight, his eyes riveted on Rowena, his voice sharply commanding. 'You'd do well to mind, devil's temptress, I've the factor in my pocket. One word from me and he'll have your removal writ signed and served. You'll scarce have time to stir yer next potion, but there'll be fresh tenants a-turning Tomachcraggen soil.'

The rabble raised its voice in a threatening manner, a disturbing sound close to a snarl, a sound the exciseman cared very little for when from the pinewood at the far side of the clearing a loud crack rang out. The boom reverberated, followed by a bellowing roar. McBeath squawked with fright, tripping over the incline behind him, and landed sprawled on his back.

'In your pocket, am I? By God sir, but it's you would do well to mind your place!'

William McGillivray's pistol was still smoking, the reek from its muzzle as dark as his countenance. But it was only when he stepped fully from the trees that Morven appreciated just what she'd been looking at all this time. That what she'd taken as the pattern of light and shadow cast in slanted shafts by the newly risen sun, was in fact, a body of men stood among the trees, armed and still as standing-stones. How long they'd been there, how much they'd seen and heard, she could only guess at.

'God's truth!' the factor roared. 'It's a rum tale I've heard this day! And a foul mood it's put me in. Roused in the wee hours with tales of murder and forced marriage and imminent dealings to the death. Highly illegal dealings, forbye. And now I'm to be cried puppet, clay in the hands of this loose-livered scoundrel. A cat's paw, by God!' He turned and crooked a finger. 'Come hither, girl!'

Morven's eyes widened, and she was conscious of Rowena drawing breath sharply through her teeth. Stumbling from the pinewood, Sarah's face was stony, and she cracked furiously at her knuckles. Plainly aware of her cousin's incredulous stare, along with those she drew from the crowd, a furrowing of her brow was all that marked it. She neither looked at him nor acknowledged his presence, although it was plain Sarah was acutely aware of her cousin and the dismayed expression he wore and had no wish to witness it.

 No tinker-girl could have looked more bedraggled and begrimed. Her pale hair was uncovered, wildly tousled, her face as pale, yet in the carriage of her head, the set of her shoulders, it was evident Sarah retained the essence of her arrogance. She glared at the exciseman, still half-sprawled at her feet, and curled her lip.

'Well? Is it nae as I told ye, sire? Is he nae the most loathsome creature?'

Morven turned to Rowena, seeing her companion's eyes fill at the latest twist of her emotions. So, Sarah's flight in the dead of night had been little to do with collecting her thoughts and a great deal to do with summoning the factor in his role as Justice of the Peace. Jamie wouldn't thank her for her interference, but Morven could've kissed Sarah's haughty cheek.

Six strides took McGillivray to the prone exciseman, who stared up open-mouthed. Bending, the factor seized McBeath by the collar and dragged him to his feet. 'Loathsome, sir, doesn't even come close!'

It was in mounting disbelief that the factor had watched the antics of the exciseman he'd considered, not friend exactly, but certainly close acquaintance, and had been appalled. Of a mind to allow the young Highland lad to take his satisfaction, for he was plainly the finer swordsman and had put on a grand show, he'd thought to cry a halt to the proceedings upon the drawing of first blood or upon the eventual disarming of one or other. The arrival of hordes of onlookers, however, had somewhat confused the issue, although he felt no confusion now. None at all. Public humiliation at the hands of the exciseman had focused him sharply. Indeed, had outraged him. William McGillivray played puppet to no man. He drew a ragged breath, his jowls quivering, and addressed the exciseman with barely-concealed rage.

'I was brought here, only half-believing mind, to put a stop to this utterly lawless settling of scores.' Drawing another ruthless breath, he levelled the transfixed exciseman with a black stare. 'Now I've a notion to let it continue – on a more level footing, mind.'

Blinking, and momentarily robbed of his faculties, McBeath let his sword drop to the ground. He stared down in horror as the factor, with grim-faced deliberation, withdrew a small clasp-knife from his doublet pocket. Opening the blade with a flick of thumb, he proceeded to slit the fastenings of the exciseman's top-coat with a ruthless little flourish. The garment, amply padded from within, burst open with a series of little pops, revealing the incriminating leather strapping and glint of pistol beneath.

'Confound it, man!'

McGillivray made a disgusted sound in his throat. To blazes with the exciseman, but the young rustic had a higher regard for the principles of fairness and honour than the so-called servant of the Crown. He shook his head at Jamie. 'I'd have the scoundrel searched to the skin, lad, as is your right in the circumstance.'

Jamie stared at the factor in astonishment.

Malcolm and Alec needed no second telling, complying with zeal and taking but seconds to discover the daggers concealed among the exciseman's breeches, his pistol, and that he wore some manner of protection, some cowardly contraption about his person packed with wadding.

'Damned if he's nae stuffed like a cock-turkey!' Malcolm declared.

'Weel, let's hae him plucked!' shouted Achnareave. 'Oor lad's in naething but his kilt and bare hide. Let's hae them fight as equals!'

'Aye,' hollered Rory. 'Aff wi' his claes!'

A great roar went up, and in the bedlam that followed, Morven was borne forward, pressed from behind by an onrush of people, elbowed and shoved, her feet knocked from under her. Twisting, she caught sight of Rowena, also carried along, and cried out to her. The cry was swallowed by the din, twenty years of hardship and repression wrought by one man erupting in a spasm of anger the likes of which she'd never seen. She found her feet in time to see the hated black coat, symbol of McBeath's tyranny, flung from hand to clutching hand above the heads of the crowd; a prized trophy of his downfall. Then she was grasped by the shoulder and swiftly hauled from the furore.

'Stay by me, and ye'll be safe.' She looked up into Jamie's face. Taking her hand, he quirked her a grim smile.

As suddenly as it erupted, the uproar died away, and she could see that it was now Father Ranald who stood atop the drumlin, his staff raised, pleading for calm with his congregation. McGillivray's men had emerged from the pinewood but stood by uncertainly, flanked by the factor who watched with decided indifference. Evidently, he'd washed his hands of the exciseman and intended to let glen justice take its course, whatever that might be.

Clutching at Father Ranald's vestments, McBeath now quailed behind the priest, the shreds of his clothing hanging from him in tatters. All pretence of authority had been stripped from him, and he shrank from the crowd like a cornered animal.

'You'll no let them at me, Father?' His face was stiff with fear. 'I mean, you're still a man o' the church, even be it the Roman one.' Locating Jamie in the crowd, he released the Father's robes and raised a quivering finger. 'He's the witch's kinsman … her instrument … as are all these!' He threw his arms wide, taking in the entire gathering, now congregated about their priest. 'This is *her* doing.' Swiftly he shifted the finger of accusation to Rowena, who was sat on the ground a little apart from the others, rubbing at her bruised limbs. 'Can you no see? That woman's mistress o' the dark arts, and these … why these are naught but her disciples!'

'You'll watch yer tongue!' snapped the Father. 'These are my parishioners, every one decent, honest, and God-fearing.'

'Then she's taken you in too!'

The Father's exasperation showed plainly on his face. He drew an enraged breath. 'I first met Rowena when she was but five years of age, on the day she lost her mother. Every day since I've been blessed to call her friend. Even as a child she had a gentle nature but in womanhood, the Lord has seen fit to bless her with wisdom and insight along wi' a gift fer healing. Make no mistake, the woman hasna an ill-hearted bone in her body, still less any ill-will.'

Deliberately he raised his own finger of accusation. 'If there's any here possessed wi' dark thoughts and urges, I believe 'tis you, sir, fer Rowena Forbes is no more a witch than auld Jessie MacBride there.'

At mention of her name, Jessie beamed with pleasure, revealing the blackened stumps of her teeth nestling in a pink mouth.

McBeath recoiled. 'Then you're one of her disciples too!'

'I'm no such thing!'

But the crowd had heard enough.

'Son o' Belial!' Achnareave's eyes widened in shock. 'To show such disrespect, such profanity to a man o' the cloth! Ye're nae even fit to stand upon the same ground as the Father there.' His voice took on the weight of judgement. 'I ken what it is ye are – ye're an obscenity, an affront to decent God-fearing folk!'

'Blasphemer!' Hal McHardy swiped the air with his sickle. 'Foul-tongued skite!'

McBeath let out a skelloch of fright as a clump of sodden peat struck him on the chest, splattering him with mud. Morven turned in time to see Sarah, screaming her hatred, wrench another dripping sod bare-handed from the ground and take aim again, her face contorted with rage.

Her fury took hold among the crowd, spread like a contagion to hate-fired cries of, 'Blasphemer! Devil's get! The fiend's fit only fer the rope!'

Malcolm pounded him with his bare fists. 'Devil take ye, ye murdering scum!'

'I've his tree picked oot!' whooped Rory.

Others spat on him. Women and old men. Even bairns took turn to fling fistfuls of sod at him and flail him with whatever came to hand.

Skirling with fright, arms wrapped around his head, shoulders hunched against the blows, the gauger lurched through the trees. The McHardys gave chase, howling like wolves. Others joined them until a great horde pursued the exciseman and his hirelings through a dense tangle of brambles and away through the forest, the sound of their anger shrill on the morning air.

'I'll have no lynch-mob!' bellowed McGillivray. 'Not while I'm Justice here.' He gestured with his head to his waiting band of men. 'I'll have the three of them before me and tried justly for their crimes.' Grimly, his men fanned out like huntsmen through the trees.

The commotion receded at last, and Morven looked up at Jamie. 'What'll happen? What'll they do to them? I mean … will he be back?'

Jamie had no answer for her. He sat down abruptly and thrust his sword into the weedy ground. Dazed, he shook his head then pulled her down beside him. As if to verify his understanding of the facts, he took her hand and pressed it to his lips. He lived! Was untouched, and the gauger gone. There'd be no desperate flight up into Ross-shire or beyond. Shoulders shaking, he let out a choked little laugh and pressed her hand to his cheek, the coldness of her fingers sweet against his own hot flesh. She leaned into him, let him shelter her from the violence that rode the air.

It was a dry clearing of the throat that broke the spell between them.

'A fitting outcome in the circumstance.'

Bemused, they looked up to find the factor regarding them both with cocked head.

'I adjudge who is unfit to be tenant to his Grace and therefore in need of removal, not the Board of Excise nor any of their officers.' He inclined his head to Jamie, who struggled to his feet. 'Your aunt will have her rental renewed at Martinmas, sir, upon the payment of the customary tack duty. You have my word on it.'

Jamie's delight took a moment to register. 'I … I dinna ken how to thank ye, sire.'

'No need. Nothing need be done or changed, and I congratulate you on a fine piece of swordsmanship.' Lips pursed, McGillivray nodded once to emphasise his decision. 'A very good day to you both.'

Lifting his bonnet to Rowena, who stared back open-mouthed, the factor turned on his heel and affected a stiff bow to a be-muddied Sarah. 'Your servant, ma'am.' Then cried curtly for his horse.

***

The month of October was a sight drier than its predecessor, though a bitter wind skirled through the Cromdales, shaking the birks of their bright foliage and driving dark storms across the glen. The wind, however, had died away during the night and the day had dawned mellow and soft, a mantle of mist lying in the hollows of the land. Morven had picked a posy of wild rosehips and haws, all that could be found now, and added a handful of bracken fronds, gilded bronze and curled by the hand of frost. They'd mark the wee soul's grave until the next squall scattered them.

She'd come to the chapelyard with Rowena and waited while her companion prepared her own posy. A shelter of pines screened them from the site of the new chapel, although looking through the lower branches, Morven could see the new stone structure with its exposed timber roof, an open ribcage, awaiting its covering of slate. The slate, local Cnoc Fergan schist, had been gifted to the parish by the Duke himself and lay in stacked pallets by the side wall. It would be no humble heather thatch for the glen's newest place of worship.

Yet Morven knew it was not a glimpse of the chapel that had brought her here, nor even a desire to honour the little soul's grave, though she'd aye do that, but a more straightforward reason. A reason that quickened her pulse and hung now from the framework of the chapel roof, a leather apron wound about his waist. Hal McHardy was Jamie's companion, and their voices came to her through the mist, though not their words, only the occasional snatch of song while they worked and Hal's tuneless whistle.

Hal had crowed of chasing the Black Gauger near ten miles down the glen.

'He'll nae bother ye again,' he'd told Rowena. 'Nae in my lifetime. Nae if he kens what's good fer him.'

And it was said Grant of Achnareave had washed the foulness from the gauger's mouth with a hipflask of raw whisky. Near drowned the wretch 'twas told. Remembering the foulness of the man's breath upon her, Morven shuddered.

But in the end, fearing he'd be lynched, the gauger had blubbered and prostrated himself at the feet of the factor's men, near naked, bloodied and spent, and had pleaded for a fair trial. He and his hirelings now languished in Elgin's tollbooth awaiting that trial.

Yet if he was truly gone it did not feel so to Morven. Though a new Officer of Excise bid in a humbler home in Balintoul and extended a more flexible grip upon the smugglers of the land, it seemed something of the Black Gauger's sway remained. And with it a remoteness between Jamie and herself. An unexplained restraint he maintained, a will o' the wisp feeling she could neither catch nor fully identify that distanced them in some perplexing way.

Maybe she'd expected too much of him, imagined he carried her in his heart as tenderly as she held him. But then she'd find his eyes upon her, wistful and intense, and she'd not think it imagined at all but would puzzle over the regretful flicker of his eyes as he shifted his gaze away and the frustrated pulse that beat at his throat.

'He's the best worker the Father has.' Rowena followed her gaze. 'Jamie. Has fair put his back into the work. His way of thanking the Father fer what he did fer us that day.'

Morven gave no answer, although she felt Rowena's gaze, concerned and assessing, turned toward her. The new chapel would soon be completed, weather-tight at least, and once consecrated would make a fitting place for Alec and Sarah to exchange their vows. Stooping, she laid her posy on her infant sister's grave.

'Jamie's agreed to give Sarah away.' Rowena laid her own posy. 'Wi' my heartfelt blessing.'

Morven nodded. She knew that, but since the day of the duel Rowena had found it well-nigh impossible to contain her sheer thankfulness, and at times it did burst from her.

'I couldna ask fer a better man fer my Sarah than young Alec. Nor a finer man to take her father's role than young Jamie. Supposing I scoured the whole kingdom, I swear I'd never find such able kinsmen.'

'Aye. I know that.'

Rowena fell silent. Over the last few weeks, she'd watched these two drift tortuously apart and had puzzled over it, although she sensed pride lay at its root. 'His heart is yours,' she said softly. 'Ye ken that, aye?'

Morven made a slight shrugging movement. She'd thought she knew it … once.

'Only, he's a proud man, mebbe a mite ower-proud.' Rowena's voice lowered, took on the note of astuteness Morven knew so well. 'He'll nae wish to come to ye empty-handed is what I think. He'll wish to give ye what he doesna have to give. Land. He'll wish to give ye land.'

Morven looked blankly at her, and Rowena nodded and smiled a little shyly.

'I've seen it afore. 'Twas in his father and I ken it's in me. That hunger fer a scrape o' land. Stratha'an land, oor native land. 'Tis what he'll wish to give ye, and I'll wager he'll ask nothing of ye till he's got it to give.'

Morven opened her mouth to counter the notion, then let it close. Land? A rental from his Grace? She'd not thought on that, but Rowena could well be right. She felt her gloom lift a fraction. And to think her da cried *her* stubborn! Jamie must surely own the condition. Yet he was all she wanted; could it be he was too proud to see that?

Jamie looked up from the length of timber he was cutting. The distant drum of hooves carried clearly in the still air of the day; he'd not have heard it yesterday he judged, nae above thon wild and buffeting wind. But he picked the rider out at once, a dark shape moving swiftly across the bronze patchwork of rig and heath.

A journeyman from Elgin was expected, a roofer to demonstrate the craft of slate-laying, a skill little called for among the humble cot-house and bothy dwellers of the glen. Jamie thought it likely he'd take the bulk of the labour upon himself, with maybe Hal McHardy, for of all those who'd given their time to the chapel's construction, Hal had shown the greatest willing and the most dogged endurance. He'd grown fond of the wiry crofter with his thick brows lifted in a permanently questioning expression and his droll sense of humour. He cried out to him now.

'A rider, Hal! Think ye 'twill be our slate-layer?'

But as they watched the dark figure's approach, Hal ceased his whistling, and both men fell silent. The journeyman would ride a sturdy pony, and would likely bring a cart filled with the implements of his trade, and maybe a few lads, underlings or apprentices. This was a lone rider moving fast, and the beast was large, clean of limb, finely bred and, by the sound of it, iron-shod.

'It couldna be …?' Hal turned to Jamie.

But no, as the rider neared it became clear this was not the Black Gauger returned from disgrace but the factor himself out giving stiff exercise to his fine black hunter. McGillivray reined in the beast and dismounted, then waited patiently for one of them to take it from him and tether it nearby. Obligingly, Jamie did so.

'A fine day we're having, sire,' said Jamie, for want of anything better to say.

'Mild fer the time o' year,' added Hal.

'Indeed, indeed.' The factor strolled over to the pallets of uncut slate. He stooped to peer at them, then straightened and stepped back to view the simple sandstone frontage with its twin buttresses and short bell tower.

'*You* built this?' he said in astonishment.

'No, sire. Every able man in the glen turned his hand, and there were drawings, diagrams to follow drawn by a man o' letters.'

'Jamie did much o' it, though,' Hal chipped in.

A man of many talents, McGillivray mused, too valuable to be allowed to idle his days away building Popish kirks. He hadn't seen it before, indeed until the last few weeks he'd gleaned his information almost entirely from the treacherous exciseman, but James Innes he could see quite plainly for himself possessed many of the qualities his Grace would look for in a tenant.

'And you intend to reside here? In Strathavon. Put down roots, so to speak?'

'My roots are here already, sire. All that I am is here. But aye,' Jamie added, seeing the factor's bemusement. 'I plan to bide in the glen now, wi' my aunt.'

'Your aunt? Mistress Forbes, then, who holds the tenure of Tomachcraggen?'

'Aye, sire.'

The woman was a widow, McGillivray knew, with a willful daughter, an *arrogant* and willful daughter, he thought with an inward chuckle. The girl had put up a forceful argument the morning of the duel. Indeed an impassioned plea it had been to drag him from his bed at that hour, though she'd been damned winsome with it, and he admired that in a woman. Her mother was reckoned to be a witch, that could account for the girl's nature, but still, winsome was winsome wrapped in any religion.

'And there will be no difficulty, I assume, in the paying of her tack duty come Martinmas?' McGillivray said.

'None, sire. I have the siller counted out already from the sale of her grain.'

'Commendable, commendable.'

Hal shuffled his feet, uncomfortable with the direction the factor's questions were taking. Surely, he didna mean to evict Rowena after all? 'Was there something ye was wanting, sire?' he asked a mite bluntly.

The factor cleared his throat; he had to be sure of his ground before making any offer. 'Since you mention it. As you may be aware, his Grace the Duke has a number of vacant possessions throughout the glen. Land requiring improvement – clearing and draining and so forth. Such rentals are only offered to those deemed to be of sound character by myself. I, as it were, put forth the applicant's cause to his Grace if, and only if, I'm convinced of the calibre of the applicant's character. None but decent, upstanding tenants will I abide.'

He pursed his lips, hands clasped behind his back, and paced for a moment. Jamie turned to Hal, who shrugged his shoulders, mystified by much the factor said.

'In that context, I wish to offer such a rental to yourself, sir, an assignation of say, nineteen years to begin at Martinmas in the year of our Lord seventeen hundred and eighty. What say you to that, James Innes of Tomachcraggen?'

Jamie gawped at McGillivray, momentarily robbed of his tongue. 'Do … do ye speak in earnest, sire?' he finally managed.

'Come now, I'd not jest on such a matter.'

Jamie let his breath out. The strangest, giddiest sensation had begun in his innards, and he felt it rush up hotly to his face, bursting upon his features in a face-splitting grin.

'Then I'd say thank ye, sire. Thank ye and God bless ye!'

He turned and caught Hal by the hands. Beaming, Hal pumped his hands up and down, then linked arms with Jamie, and, whooping with delight, spun him around, kicking his legs out in a gay little jig.

'That's settled, then.' The factor's jowls wobbled in satisfaction. 'I'll have the papers drawn up. I was thinking, perhaps, of Lynavoulin up by Clachfuar croft, not too much felling would be required as I recall it and –'

'Sire,' Jamie cut in. 'If ye dinna mind, I'd much prefer the lease on Druimbeag on the far side o' the A'an.' Looking over the factor's shoulder, he caught sight of Morven and Rowena, bending under the sweep of low pine that sheltered the chapelyard, then straightening and making toward him. They'd been attending the graves he knew, and were now looking at him, and each other, in astonishment. It wasna every day ye danced a wee jig in front o' the factor, he realised. He turned back to McGillivray, the thread of his thought gone, and stared a little stupidly at him.

'The crofthouse at Druimbeag is no more than a ruin.' McGillivray grimaced in distaste. 'And the land has run to seed, is rank with elder and thorn, so I'm told. I think I can find you something a little better than that.'

'Nothing that canna be cleared, though,' Jamie persisted. 'And rebuilt. It's just … just Druimbeag is the place o' my birth, sire, and I hold it dear to me.'

McGillivray pulled a face, a gesture that indicated quite plainly his opinion of Jamie's choice. 'Have it your way,' he said with a stiff bow to the two approaching women. 'Then the lease of Druimbeag is yours, sir. May you never have cause to regret it.'

Jamie's breath quivered. 'Oh, that I'll nae.' He took Morven's hands, then pulled her to him and kissed her fiercely. Releasing her, he laughed at her incredulous expression.

'I'm come home!'

She slipped her arms around his waist and pressed her cheek to his heart. It beat strongly, strong enough for them both.

''Tis where ye belong,' Rowena said firmly.

Morven would have echoed Rowena's words had she been able. The drum of her heart beat so loud, it seemed to fill and tightened her throat.

'If ye want me,' Jamie added shyly.

A hotness welled behind her eyes, matching the swelling in her throat, but she blinked and smiled through it.

'God, Jamie,' she blurted. 'I do want ye that badly.'

A Note from Angela MacRae Shanks

Thank you for reading The Blood And The Barley. If you enjoyed it, I would be grateful if you'd take a moment to leave a frank review at your favourite online retailer such as Amazon UK or Amazon USA. Reviews are very important to me and help other readers like you find my work.

This is my first novel, I am currently working on my second, also in The Strathavon Saga. This is a prequel to The Blood & The Barley and is Rowena's story, seen from her eyes, unfolding the circumstances that led to her brother's eviction, her marriage to Duncan, and revealing the events that spawned the love/hate relationship between Rowena and the exciseman, Hugh McBeath. On completion of this, I will continue Morven and Jamie's tale. If you would like to be notified when the next book is available and to receive exclusive material from it prior to its release, please sign up at **www.subscribepage.com/angelamacraeshanks**

I particularly welcome contact from readers. If you have any questions, comments, suggestions or criticisms, I'd be delighted to hear from you. You can email me at:
angela@angelamacraeshanks.com or contact me on my website: **www.angelamshanks.com** or on Facebook at **www.facebook.com/angelamacraeshanksauthor**

Please see over for a glossary of Scots words used throughout the novel.

The Scots Tongue

The Scots language is wonderfully expressive, and I have used it freely throughout this work, both to add authenticity and a sense of time and place. It is my hope the meaning is generally inferred, but for readers unfamiliar with the Scots tongue a glossary is provided below.

anker – a liquid measure of spirit and the barrel containing it: approx. 10 gallons.
bide – dwell or reside
canker – bad temper, ill-humour.
cooried – nestled or snuggled.
crabbit – out of humour.
crowdie – a soft curd cheese.
cuddie – a donkey or obstinate horse.
dram – a small measure of whisky.
drouth – a drunkard.
fash – to fret or fuss.
fou – drunk, intoxicated.
garron – a small sturdy horse or Highland pony.
gauger – an exciseman; one who collects excise taxes.
haiver – to speak nonsense or foolishly.
hirsel – a group of sheep of the same kind.
kebbock – a whole cheese, especially home-made.
kertch – a traditional head covering of linen worn by married women.
lum – a chimney.
muckle – large or great.
quine – a young woman.
reiver – a cattle raider.
semmit – an undershirt or vest.
skelloch – a shriek or shrill cry.
smoorach – fine dust or crumbled peat.
spaewife – a woman who can prophesy or foretell.
squalloch – a loud shrill cry.
stramash – an uproar or commotion.
tinker – an itinerant trader dealing in small goods.
thrawn – contrary, obstinate or stubborn.
whin – common gorse.

Lightning Source UK Ltd.
Milton Keynes UK
UKHW041423060519
342182UK00001B/101/P